Martha B. Wilbur

1.00

THE DOCTORS

ANDRÉ SOUBIRAN

The Doctors

TRANSLATED BY OLIVER COBURN

G. P. PUTNAM'S SONS   NEW YORK

First published in France as *Les Hommes en Blanc*

To
GEORGES DUHAMEL

Part 1

BEGINNING OF THE WINTER TERM

Chapter 1

THE LONG, DESERTED CORRIDOR rather depressed me. It smelled of floor polish, cold tobacco smoke and the night's sweat—that faint sour smell from unmade beds. I was standing outside the door of my room, looking at the visiting card I had just put up. I was sorry there was nobody else there I could have proudly shown it to, nobody to read what the card said:

JEAN NÉRAC
Medical Student
Cité Universitaire

Well, here I was at last, with my own room in Paris. I had been in the great city a whole hour, full of energy and optimism, ready to conquer the world and confident I was going about it the right way. Even my train-weariness had left me, despite the fact that in the excitement of leaving home I had not slept all night. But together with a certain stiffness in the joints those hours without sleep, on the hard wooden seat of a third-class compartment, were a small price to pay for the sense of joyous freedom I felt. I was no longer the same person who had stood on the platform at Toulouse yesterday evening. That phantom of my former self had been slowly fading all through the night, and had finally vanished at the end of the journey—like some tired old passenger on the same train that you say good-by to and forget about on reaching your destination. I said good-by to this ghost in the early morning when the outskirts of Paris

3

appeared in the distance: factories, black houses, gray gardens with wash hanging out to dry, and the lights of the suburbs flashing past. We arrived at the Gare d'Austerlitz, and once on the platform I almost began running, as if afraid of being pulled backwards, as if my whole future were in jeopardy. I was nineteen years old.

Through the door opposite came the noise of a typewriter rattling away furiously. In other rooms I could hear people talking, and somewhere in the heart of the hostel a violinist was practicing. Behind all the doors I could imagine rooms very like mine, with students inside them idling away this dull October morning, making the most of the last few days of their vacation. I went on to the next door, and found on it the name of Mahmoud Ben Raïs, student of chemistry. The door after that belonged to one D'Andriamaro-Razafintzara, student of dental surgery. Further on I read *Do-Dong-Kien, law student.* All these names seemed to beckon me, showing me the whole world in vivid kaleidoscopic pictures; I imagined brown faces and yellow ones, black skins like those I had known in my childhood, the scents and savors of vanilla and tea. I moved on from door to door, and each one opened up vistas in all directions. A Breton name hit me in the face like a cloud of spray; and immediately, with the taste of salt on my lips, I was off to distant lands, sailing before the mast for three years, like the heroes in the adventure stories of my boyhood.

Bursting with the spirit of universal brotherhood, I eventually found myself back at the door directly opposite mine. My head was still in the clouds, but the inscription on this last door brought me down to earth with a bump, back to the bleak and gloomy corridor. This card said *Victor Petitjean,* with *Diploma of Philosophy* printed below. Underneath this the word *Author* had been added in pencil, perhaps ironically.

Without having any idea why, I felt an irresistible desire to meet this neighbor of mine at once. He might label himself a little pretentiously, but his name at least had a resolutely European flavor. Yes, this Petitjean should be my first college friend.

4

Immediately my brain started racing wildly ahead in this direction, and in a few seconds I was already anticipating all the joys of friendship.

I was just going to knock, when the door opened abruptly and I saw the literary philosopher silhouetted in the doorway. He was completely nude, and held a towel in his hand. He looked at me, noticed the open door of my room, and said, "Well, my lad, you're my new neighbor, are you?" As he spoke, he moved out into the corridor, and I had a chance to see him more clearly. I guessed he must be about twenty-five. He looked rather feeble, with a big flabby belly, sagging cheeks and a sallow complexion. His hair fell over his eyes, and as he thrust his hand up to push back the offending locks, he addressed me again:

"Well, I hope you can put up with the noise of the typewriter. I bang on it all the time."

His tone was far from cordial, and this remark sounded more like a warning than an apology. Still, Petitjean was the first student I had spoken to since my arrival, and I felt quite pleased at meeting him. I answered politely, "I'm sure you won't disturb me, M. Petitjean"—I did not dare address him yet as one student to another.

"Why not? Have you come to Paris for a holiday?"

Choking, I retorted quickly, as if it were a profession of faith: "I've come to study, of course."

Petitjean passed in front of me, but before going for his shower he turned back to remark sarcastically, "Yes, I can see that. You'll probably be first in the tango class."

Following this polite remark, I saw his big white buttocks disappear behind the door of the shower room, which he closed after him. Then I heard a cascade of water, and Petitjean emitting little gurgling sighs of pleasure while under the spray.

I had been at a loss for an answer. His sarcasm was backed by such an air of experience and self-assurance that I felt at a disadvantage. And now I was left standing in the corridor, my joyful mood shattered. Nothing more for me to do there.

I went back into my room, and went over to the mirror to

5

hold an immediate close-up inspection of my face. In the line of the eyebrows, in the wrinkles of my brow, in the contractions of my jaw, I looked for evidences of energy and enterprise. But despite all these efforts my face remained just the same, and I suddenly became infuriated with the effeminate wretch the mirror showed me. A budding gigolo, my neighbor had thought. But after all, his unattractive appearance would make it necessary for him to live by work alone.

I began to feel cold, so I turned on the radiator and then took a closer look at the unfamiliar room. It was a bit gloomy, with a rather tasteless wallpaper consisting of yellow nasturtiums climbing on blue-gray latticework.

From the prospectus I knew that Empire House, where I was to live, had been built four years earlier, one of the first hostels in the Cité Universitaire. In four years, a succession of careless students had made the two chairs distinctly shaky, besides staining the surface of the table, splashing brown marks all round the washbasin, and greasing up the wall at the head of the narrow divan-bed.

In the first joy of arrival I had found the room magnificent. I saw it now as very ordinary, an impersonal room, already faded and featureless. And this was the room to which I must carry all the heavy burdens the future might lay upon me. Instinctively I did what anyone does who feels alone and lost between four unfamiliar walls: I moved toward the window.

The room was on the ground floor, and the window looked onto a lawn with a little tree which I thought was probably a flowering cherry, its branches already reduced by the autumn to a thin skeleton. Farther on, you could see the buildings of a neighboring hostel, a bit of the boulevard and of the Parc Montsouris, a small patch of sky. It was a quiet peaceful scene; I found it somewhat melancholy.

I had seen enough. Suddenly feeling almost sick with weariness and lack of sleep, I went over to the divan. I hesitated a moment about leaning my head against the halo of grease my predecessors had left on the wallpaper; and then decided it was silly to be so particular. Of course I must be just like all the other students who had reclined on this divan. For this room told clearly enough of long hours spent at the same table, with the window as narrow horizon, and nothing changing but the light as season followed season in endless study; it told too of youth continually sacrificed for a result always in doubt.

Apparently the room had not been aired all summer, which gave it an unsavory smell, while its gloom seemed to become more oppressive. From time to time a big lorry could be heard rumbling by on the boulevard, then silence would fall once more. A sudden acute loneliness came over me. Even my neighbor had repulsed me, and his sneer had given me clear notice of my plight. There was no one on whom I could unload even a small part of my pangs and doubts. I felt alone in the world, crushed by silence and solitude, and the room was too strange to hold out any hopes of being a straw I could cling to.

Back in Toulouse I could have taken refuge on my old divan, where I had dreamt so many dreams, making and remaking my life, conquering the world as I went along. But I had never slept on this bed in Paris, it knew nothing of me, it possessed no magic to comfort me; and even if it had, I should have missed my mother's tender presence near me, and the old familiar walls of home, laved each evening by the vast caressing breath of southern winds.

For a long while I lay stretched out on the divan, and eventually I dozed off. Suddenly the whole building seemed to wake up, and the corridors were filled with noisy life. I looked at my watch; it was twelve o'clock. I did not feel hungry, but leaped from my bed at once. To regain my confidence, I needed to be with other human beings. I was determined not to be left there alone when the silence returned.

By simply following the small groups of students, I came to the Cité restaurant, a makeshift wooden shed surrounded by wasteland, wooden fences and building yards; from the outside it looked like a workers' canteen or a Salvation Army hut.

Inside, the din was terrific. Shouts and laughter and clatter of crockery, fusing with cigarette smoke and the smell of food, drifted up to the dirty brown ceiling in an amorphous mass. Checked there, it flowed downward again, enveloping any new arrival in a bewildering complex of smells and noises.

A long line of students moved up, tray in hand, between railings, toward a counter where dishes of stew and vegetables simmered gently. They were served by girls in blue blouses and small caps suggestive of a reformatory.

Passing near the tables as I moved up in the queue, I had ample opportunity to look and listen. Odd snatches of conversation rose out of the hubbub in a babel of foreign tongues. I saw faces of every color, and decided that every nation and race on earth must be represented here. It might almost have been a DP reception center, since many of the restaurant's customers looked very poor. Their ties were mere knotted slips of wool, they wore old patched jackets, and trousers without cuffs that tumbled over their heels. Yet they carried it all off with an air of natural affluence and independence. There was a fair sprinkling of beards and many exotic hair styles.

A lot of the girls were obvious blue-stockings, with unattractive faces; they used no powder or lipstick, and seemed almost proud to be plain and unremarkable. But I did notice a few pretty ones, including one Nordic-looking girl with long fair tresses; I followed her with my eyes as she went towards the exit, admiring the easy assurance of her walk. Indeed, although in my new suit I must have looked quite smart compared with these poorly turned-out youngsters, I thought what a wealth of experience they had had in comparison with me, how full of promise was their future. I looked with envy at these ardent, restless, determined faces, and the down-at-heel shoes beating impatiently on this new land they were all set to conquer.

In the far corner of the restaurant I found a place at a table for four. Before starting to eat, I took stock of my three neighbors, all wearing shapeless black jackets, and all with big spectacles gleaming over weak myopic eyes. Their finger-nails were bitten to the quick, and there was much vigorous gesticulation to accompany the stream of clever talk and dogmatic pronouncements which poured from their lips:

8

"Take Joyce's *Finnegan's Wake* now—there's the typical Anglo-American novel for you, carried to its logical extreme— a vertical section of life which really reveals its innermost structure."

"Look, old chap, people have known for some time that you can analyze the whole sea from one drop of water."

"Remember Gide," said the third, "our actions belong to us as the flame belongs to a match. Personally I like my fictional heroes to be driven into action by one insane impulse."

In the heat of the argument the one who had just spoken looked at me. I had never even heard of Joyce, and the whole discussion was largely lost on me. But having read some Gide, I felt justified in nodding approvingly.

At the next table two Indo-Chinese were yapping away in their own language. Behind me a group of students were engaged in fierce debate.

"Whatever you say, if I see green, I'm bloody well going to paint green."

"Well, suppose I paint yellow when I see yellow, while you see green and the world sees white, who's going to judge between us?"

Two young students brushed past me with their trays, and as they went by I picked up the tag-end of what they were talking about: ". . . for me to believe in it, the major premise of any philosophy must be a rational expression of our real feelings. . . ."

I felt quite proud of having even a silent part in this feast of ideas, this headlong flow of wit.

I began to eat the contents of my tin plates. The food bore little resemblance to my mother's delicate cooking, but I was prepared to find anything delicious. My neighbors, as if surfeited with eloquence, rose simultaneously and left. Another person slouched up to my table, with books under his arm, and put down his tray opposite mine. Petitjean—I recognized him immediately. Dressed, he still looked far from impressive. Under a shabby old black mackintosh, a threadbare gray flannel suit was showing at the neck and sleeves. He also recognized me.

9

"Hullo, there's the new boy."

At the same time he threw a practiced look at my tray, and added sardonically: "Well, well—red wine, two desserts. An eight-franc meal. The younger generation seems to be made of money this year."

I said: "I get eight hundred and fifty francs a month."

"Well," said Petitjean, "here are two pieces of advice for administering this vast fortune. I present you with them free gratis and for nothing. First, never take anything till you've found out exactly what it costs; second, choose what you do buy really carefully. You've just taken wine and two desserts, for instance, when for the same price you could have had something much more substantial, like me—to wit, three portions of potatoes. In this place—and anywhere else too, for that matter —don't order any of those fancy concoctions; they look all right, but as far as calories go they're completely out. Man's finest quality is his endurance, said Goethe—but you'll find it takes a lot of it, even on eight hundred and fifty francs a month. Poor old stomach—youth's most expensive organ."

He bent down to his enormous laborer's meal, and started eating in small careful mouthfuls; he was not going to waste any of this vital nourishment. I watched him with pity, determined not to let my ardor be damped by this gloomy recluse. All the same, I did a quick mental calculation, and found that sixty meals at eight francs came to nearly five hundred francs. With two hundred for the room, plus lunch and the metro, plus all other expenses, Petitjean seemed to be right, I should very soon be broke. And I had actually thought I was quite rich!

Petitjean broke into my thoughts, saying: "Eat it up while it's hot. You'll have the whole year to look over these cretins." And before tackling his second portion of potatoes, he was off on another subject:

"I noticed you while I was in line. Even from a distance I could see you gawking at this half-baked intellegentsia. If you've got time to waste, you couldn't do better to listen to *them*, they'll talk to you all day and all night too. They'll make your head reel with a whole heap of clever-clever intellectual nonsense which has already been repeated *ad nauseam*—and doubtless you'll be quite dazzled for a while by their intellectual brilliance and erudition. It's so damned easy to substitute academic theories and systems for the realities of life, which are a damned sight more complex.

"For curiosity's sake," he went on, warming to his subject, "just take a look at the people here. They can be divided into two distinct categories. First there are the chaps with a little money of their own—or their parents'. They are dumb as they make 'em, spending four or five years in preparation for their old age. All the foundations laid for a moderately comfortable middle-class existence, backed by a few safe investments. So for four or five years they almost kill themselves working, they never seem to stop—and where does it get them? Comparative security, small savings, and eventually a pension to retire on. Then there's the other lot, the plutocratic playboys who are just having a good time here; very loud-mouthed and full of their own importance. But afterwards they turn respectable soon enough, going into father's business, putting on their carpet-slippers at home, making sure there's a nice little nest-egg at the bank. Talk about fattening up pigs for the market—and they call *that* the elite!

"Dammit all, I despair of the younger generation here in France. They may still have a small amount of brain left, but no guts or spunk—or else it goes straight down the drain. And as for the foreigners, they come here from all over the world with only one idea in their heads: to explore Montparnasse and try out the best local brothels. There aren't ten Frenchmen in this room, there may not even be five, who really want to do anything big and adventurous with their lives, anything revolutionary. No, I despair of them. At the age of twenty, they're given a heated room, cheap meals, and a small allowance—people treat them politely as an elite, and that leaves them completely satisfied. Instead of thinking how they're going to smash the world to bits and then remold it nearer to their heart's desire, the dirty little fools go off to sleep and dream about their pensions. If you've got any guts in you at all, you'll steer clear of the whole lot of them. Keep to yourself, and plough your own furrow."

He had been talking in a hollow voice punctuated by sardonic laughs. What a Job's comforter, I thought. Had he ever, I wondered, known how to enjoy life at all? I did not dare now to look round the room. I only hoped he would get up soon and go. He took a long time masticating the rest of his meal, but at last he had finished. Before leaving he looked at me and asked abruptly: "What are you going to take up here?"

I saw his passionate gray eyes, whose fire somehow redeemed that flabby face, and replied with a sudden exhilaration which I could not really explain: "I'm taking medicine."

When Petitjean had gone, I got up too. Outside it was warm and sunny, and the autumn afternoon was bathed in a soft golden light. All down the boulevard it was like a festival of youth, for which the Cité hostels had been specially built. I passed the buildings of France House, clustered picturesquely around a lawn like a village in some Ruritanian musical comedy. The clock on the tower said two o'clock. Students sauntered along the pavements and down the alleyways, while in the street an endless procession of cars flashed past. Light breezes scurried across the sky, and in the Parc Montsouris the big trees gloried in their russet foliage. The November chill would soon be upon us, and before it came I, like all the others, wanted to savor this last touch of mildness in the air, bringing back memories of the summer holiday that was now past. The Cité basked in carefree tranquillity, and I savored this too, thinking what a charming setting it made, how it would give me comfort and solitude to work there, on the very edge of the bustling town. Ten yards from the Boulevard, Paris was left behind and silence reigned.

While I had been at lunch, my room had become warmer, and I definitely liked it better. I decided to take complete personal possession at once. I hung my favorite pictures on the wall, and placed on the shelves the books I had carefully selected to take away from home with me; they included a number of novels dealing with doctors or medicine. When I had finished, the room was no longer any old room, it had become "my room."

Finally I set out on a shelf in the cabinet some bones I had bought a good while earlier for my anatomical studies; the ivory polish and the dirt which had accumulated in their hollows were indicative of the long and studious usage they had received. The triangular base of a shoulder-blade was inscribed in India ink with these lines:

> What have you done with your soul, skeleton?
> Candle, what have you done with your flame?
> Deserted cage, say what have you done
> With your beautiful bird and its song so brave?
> What have you done with your lava, Vulcan?
> What have you done with your master, slave?

The author? Victor Hugo. I had found it magnificent, and had learned it by heart a long time ago.

To these second-hand bones I added the skull I had bought two days before leaving Toulouse; it was new, pale yellow, and had a dull soapy look. Before installing it in the cupboard, I amused myself by playing with the joints of the jaw, so that I could hear the teeth chatter and the springs twang. I looked at the grinning, snub-nosed face, at all the holes and projections and indentations with which I should soon have to become familiar, and I caught myself feeling the reliefs and depressions of my own skull, conscious of a hard white individual existing inside me like a double.

I was excited by this pilgrimage among the mysteries of my own body. I felt my jaw, to find under the ball of flesh the three vertical ridges of the model; and I told myself proudly that no layman would act thus; this anatomical research already showed a doctor in the making.

I decided to keep the skull on my table next to the rubber stethoscope. Then I walked back as far as the window, to take in the general effect. "It's really something," I thought, regarding the books and pictures, my copper Buddha on the bookcase, my writing-pad ready on the table near the stethoscope and the

13

skull. I found the ensemble decidedly picturesque, with a sufficient flavor of the metaphysical: a true medical student's room. I sat down at the table; I was happy, and imagined with joy the long succession of quiet studious days I would spend here.

I looked out the window, and saw the frail little tree standing out there all by itself, its outline pointing skywards. I felt a strong fellow-feeling for this tree, as if it had long been my faithful companion. I leaned out to see a little more of the trees and sky and lawn. In this shady corner the air smelt of ivy and damp earth; occasionally a fresh breeze would flutter the dead leaves on the ground. I leaned out farther, and suddenly felt almost giddy. Another picture came to me, and all at once I saw no more the soft lawns, the beautiful russet trees gently swaying, the light clouds in the sky. Behind the curtain of the great park was Paris, fascinating, turbulent, unknown Paris, with its canopy of smoke covering the vast amphitheatre of hills, so that the very clouds were lost in a purple-gray haze. Clamorous noises rose to meet me from the promised land; I strained forward to hear them. How I had longed and hoped for Paris, and now here it was, only a few yards away, offering itself, calling me with its multitudinous sounds, beckoning me with every breeze that blew.

In an instant I had forgotten the warm room, the peaceful surroundings, the sun shining softly on the lawn. As if answering a call, I left my room abruptly. I had already waited too long. Out onto the boulevard I went, hatless and coatless, and set off towards Paris, almost running.

Chapter 2

MY MOTHER had let me play alone at a very early age. This freedom gave me the chance to dip eagerly into the delights of books and of the streets. It is true that these two sources of pleasure are within the reach of all, yet not everyone finds in them his treasure and his happiness, as I did.

Materially we were far from well-off. As far back as I could remember, we had lived, mother and I, in conditions of comparative poverty. There were only a few vague memories, already blurred and fading, of a happier time that had gone, of a blazing sun and a perpetually blue sky; of a cool spacious house and long drowsy afternoons; of black servants to play with me, and of white-clad Europeans wearing ridiculous sugarloaf caps like the heroic pioneers who had conquered Africa for the French.

This was all that remained in my memory of Dakar. The first World War had caught us at Vichy, during a visit to France, the first my parents had made since settling in the colony. My father was called into the army and my mother decided to stay at Toulouse, where she had relatives. When my father was killed on the Meuse in 1915 he left her very little but memories—and a few stacks of files full of bills and business letters. In our Toulouse garret these were the only remains of the export house founded by my father, which had not survived his death. If my mother hoped for help from her family, she was soon disappointed. Finally, she opened a small tobacco store. I was four years old.

The shop was small and dark, at the bottom of a narrow building with a peeling front, in between two fine red-brick private houses. It opened on to a square facing the Law Courts, but trams were continually passing in front of our door, and unless she could actually see me near her, mother was always thinking I might be run over. Most of the day I remained in the shop playing by myself, while mother did her embroidery, sitting near the window so as to see better.

I understood nothing of our new life. Meeting this atmosphere of gray melancholy, the light and gaiety of the outside world seemed to fall back exhausted. Besides, so many things had changed since we had been living in Toulouse. I hardly recognized my mother, who never seemed to laugh any more. As the days passed, a halo seemed to grow round her head. It was the sort of halo often worn by young widows who have left the pleasures of love behind them forever. Eventually, alas, it makes them look like old maids, even when there are children near them.

From time to time the shop door would open, and mother would get up to sell a cheap packet of tobacco to one of her regular customers—court clerks, students, policemen, or sometimes a laborer from that part of the town. Afterwards the shop would relapse into silence.

In the back room, which vaguely served as a storehouse, I discovered some old cigar boxes still smelling of powder, honey, vanilla and sandalwood. I never tired of constructing enormous buildings from these, and afterwards giving them furniture and inhabitants cut out of catalogues. Or else, in the days before I could read, I would look at the pictures in odd back numbers of the *Traveller's Magazine*, a stack of which our predecessors in the shop had left forgotten in a corner. Between these dark walls all fixed outlines seemed to merge and become lost; yet even here in the shadow of mourning, I still spent long wonderful days building my childish fantasies; and I began to learn the taste of happiness.

Here too, fifteen years early, I gradually started my apprenticeship in medicine.

16

Our neighbors in the suburb, coming to get their tobacco, got into the habit of lingering in the shop. Finding there a sympathetic ear, they would pour out their worries and troubles, and all the family gossip. Mother also kept a stock of the forms needed when applying for government aid or positions. Often when she had given out these forms, people looked so embarrassed that mother made them tell her the whole story, and helped them to fill out the form or to write the difficult begging letter. With simple people, one confidence justified breeds other confidences, and throughout the district it soon became quite normal to come and consult her.

One afternoon there appeared in the back room a worn but still solid morris chair, a table, and a new electric bulb. The back room, in fact, became a consulting room, an office for all the affairs that depended on my mother's goodwill and good sense. And for fifteen years I was there every day, watching the continual comings and goings of her "clients": first a housewife would sit stiff and uncomfortable on the edge of the armchair, so soft and different from the hard caned chair she was used to; then perhaps a working man would come in, his cigarette slipped behind his ear, clutching his cap in both hands and turning it ceaselessly as he listened to mother's simple explanations.

Since I was still so young, I was allowed to stay there playing in a corner. Later, coming home from school, I would sit at the edge of a table to do my homework. Mother let me go on doing it there unless she thought my presence would worry anyone or unless she had to discuss some delicate matter involving "loose women." This vague epithet represented for me the extremes of debauchery and shameful conduct.

I prudently hid the interest I felt, in order to watch both mother and the client. On her face I read neither vulgar curiosity nor callous indifference. She listened seriously, with just the right degree of attentiveness to keep the speaker's confidence and even encourage it. From time to time she would nod her head approvingly, as if nothing she heard could possibly shock, dishearten or disappoint her. But knowing her well, I could guess how much she was on the alert, eagerly straining to catch in flight the significant word, the involuntary admission, the revealing gesture. All the time she was listening for those dark secrets which the heart must unwittingly yield up to her.

Then she started asking questions. Up till then I did not always see what the stranger was trying to hide; and on my own I should certainly have had to give up the riddle as hopeless. But sometimes, listening to mother's questions, I saw the solution. This was when she went straight to the point, lighting up the fundamentals of the whole matter with an incisive word. After that she would only need a few sentences to show the other person where his interest or duty lay.

But sometimes her questions continued to baffle me. She seemed to be trying to delve into the deepest recesses of the soul, searching for some unconscious stirring of buried feeling, which must be brought out into the light of day, to be openly confessed or at least recognized. Just at this point she would often stop her questions. Either there were words which the other could not yet utter with true frankness, and she knew she must wait until he could; or the questions may have seemed to her too blunt or cruel, or she could see that they were no longer of any use. Whatever it was, I remained in the dark, piqued to come so near and yet be so far from understanding this mystery. Now, I felt, I shall never know the answer properly, or at best only guess it much later on.

In fact when I grew up I understood better the wide variety of verbal duels that went on between my mother and the clients, and the very different tones of voice and manner she used in each case. Among those who came to sit in the armchair were many shy or nervous people needing encouragement and an easy delivery for the secrets they felt to be shameful or absurd. There were those who lied to my mother or, almost unconsciously, to themselves; to these she had to reveal their own true natures in words by clear, direct, unambiguous questions. Others, through adversity, had become prickly and oversensitive, bearing their hard lives with a sort of angry pride; to this type she must say nothing which might seem to insult them with a pity they had not demanded. And again, from time to time, there were those who merely "acted" unhappy or poor. At first mother allowed herself to be taken in far too often; but she soon learned to protect her simple kindness with considerable insight and shrewdness.

It was a strange spectacle for a child to watch. Taking care to hide my passionate interest, I looked on at this *Comédie Humaine* with its sudden contrasts: laughter and tears so close together, happiness and suffering, nobility of character shining forth or carefully concealed, gray dreariness and black despair, acts of meanness or bad temper—and also vice. I caught a glimpse in advance of the terrifyingly large number of instincts that are conveniently summed up under this impersonal label.

This was Life—with a capital L—passing before my eyes. Life with its daily struggles between Good and Evil, in which my mother believed she was working for the coming victory of all the good people over all the bad.

For years every day was an apprenticeship to me, in which I learned to observe, understand, and sympathize. I also learned to be happy at her side, and to be happy, like her, in simplicity, and with the help of my books, in the shadow of a little provincial tobacco shop.

But at moments I felt the call of other forces rising inside me. Perhaps I had inherited from my father certain fits of temper and obstinacy which at times upset my usually calm and amiable nature. Was it from him that I developed a passion for adventure on the seas—or possibly from those finely decorated cigar boxes in light wood, with their exotic scents and their gilt labels covered with blue seas and shady palm trees? Or perhaps, once I had learned to read, it came from the back numbers of the *Traveller's Magazine*, carrying the *Story of The Indies* by Bartholomew de Las Casas, companion of Columbus. And at night I would dream of hearing Rodrigo de Triana, the lookout man, born in a Seville slum, giving his first shout of joy on sighting the New World. Then, still dreaming, I would fall to my knees on deck, weeping with emotion, as the whole crew from captain to cabin-boy had done long ago.

This *Wanderlust* grew with age. I had always been quite definite about studying medicine, and mother eventually agreed it should be at Paris. After dinner one evening she took out her pen once more and filled out a big form. As the widow of a colonial servant, she was applying on my behalf for a scholarship at Empire House in the Cité Universitaire. Meanwhile I kept walking round and round the table, wild because I myself could do nothing to speed the application.

For two months I waited in agonies for the answer. I was sure they would not take me. Every day in my room, with its shutters drawn since morning against the hot July sun, I kept turning over and over in my mind the hope which I already pictured as stillborn. Yet looking at my table, my ancient sofa, my books, I felt I should die if I had to stay there any longer.

At last, toward the end of July, I found one morning in the letter box the envelope with the Empire House heading, stamped with a postmark—happy omen—saying, "Support the Cité Universitaire. Save the Student Elite." I trembled as I took the envelope in my hands. Till I had opened it my future was in suspense. I ripped it open. The answer was affirmative.

I stood there near the letter box in the narrow passageway, with its permanent smell of greasy water left by an open drain. I looked at the old peeling wall without seeing it. Dazzled by the new life which I felt had already started, I set sail for distant shores, squaring away for a long voyage far from home and family.

Chapter 3

"GOOD FOR YOU, young medico. All set to conquer Paris, I see."
It was the day after my arrival, and Petitjean had noticed the
white coat rolled under my arm; wearing this, I should be recognized as a student and have the freedom of the hospital wards.

Besides being so sarcastic, he seemed to like asking unexpected
questions; and this time he said: "Have you had morning coffee
yet and taken the Metro?" On my saying I hadn't, he was at
once off on a new flight of fancy:

"In that case you're about to become a true Parisian this very
morning. Don't forget there are Parisians tramping the streets
of American cities, Parisians lost in darkest Africa, who shed
bitter tears each day as they recall their two lost loves, morning
coffee and the Metro. How wonderful to start the day like this!
Think of pushing up to the crowded counter to get your coffee,
dunking your bread as you take the first sips, seeing the coffee is
just the right color for your personal taste. And after that think
of the mad rush to the ticket barrier, and the newspaper which
is so passionately interesting when read over the next man's
shoulder and so completely dull when it's all yours. Think too
how without blushing you can run your hand over the legs of
the pretty little girl squeezed up next to you. Only look out for
the real whores, and don't start pinching *their* bottoms, or they'll
probably give you a slap in the face in the name of virtue."

"But I wouldn't . . ." my attempt at a protest was quickly
overridden.

"Don't interrupt, you'll do it too. Everyone does. And you'll learn the trick of slipping through onto the platform without buying a ticket. Or say you've got a second-class ticket, you'll soon be getting out of the over-crowded carriage and moving next door—keeping an eye open for the conductor while you look over the charming ladies who travel first-class. Then sometimes you'll hang about on the platform, waiting for one particular young person to turn up—she always seems to arrive just about this time in the morning.

"You think I'm trying to be funny? I assure you that although these are only simple pleasures which cost you nothing, someday they will seem too wonderful for words, just because everything was new to you at the time. You may think you have forgotten them, but forty years later you'll be missing them. And one day when you're feeling blue, amidst all your most important memories of love and success, they'll come up and hit you, reminding you of the days of your youth. And on that day you too will feel very close to tears. Ah well, don't let me keep you—go and start developing some Paris memories of your own."

With that Petitjean left me. But in fact I had risen early this first morning, intending to develop memories of quite a different kind.

Before leaving Toulouse I had asked a fifth-year student for a list of some of the medical celebrities in Paris. He gave it to me, inquiring whether I was going to try to get myself elected to the Academy. No, I was not quite as ambitious as that. But I had come to Paris before the term officially started, simply to spend all this last week getting a close-up view of the top men in the profession, whose reputation had made me choose Paris as the only place to study medicine. So here I was on this first morning, eager to see these great men. I felt proud and excited and burning with curiosity.

In all the hospital departments what happened was more or less the same. The first-year students had not arrived yet, and the head surgeon was only followed by a small troop of residents, internes, and senior students, plus a few voluntary workers. Lost amidst these last, scarcely daring to follow them, I found my way into a ward. From the hollow of each pillow the tense, expectant looks of forty patients were directed on the same face; like them I had eyes for him alone.

I had imagined that this man, a leading light in the whole medical world, would be distinguishable from other men at first glance. But I soon came to the conclusion that my conception of an illustrious practitioner such as this had been distinctly naïve. My physicians always had penetrating, kindly, intellectual faces, easy imperturbable gestures, and usually elegant little beards. My surgeons looked powerful and muscular, they spoke with absolute assurance, they had piercing eyes and strong sure hands.

I did meet some men who conformed more or less to this ingenuous mental picture, but I saw far more who contradicted it astonishingly: great physicians with harsh impassive faces and imperious voices, abrupt and even surly in manner; and great surgeons who were short and undistinguished, pale and sickly to look at, and who spoke softly and even humbly. These first mornings, however, there were plenty of imposing figures to impress me. Full of admiration I watched them move through their departments in a solemn hush. They seemed engrossed in far-reaching problems which had to be solved to save their patients' lives, yet they would barely glance at these same patients in passing, with an air of indifference and almost of disdain. The assistants and students who accompanied them wore just the same expression of unheeding superiority and strictly professional curiosity. Hidden away in the back row, I secretly envied them.

I only found out much later on that some of these men who were physically so impressive had very second-rate intellects and decidedly unstable characters. There were others who had no sense at all of their own dignity. The students were always telling funny stories about them. Some were handicapped by ungainly figures and sometimes by quite abnormal ugliness. Yet I detected in the manner and bearing of these men a wealth of kindness and patience and insight, and I immediately felt sure I was seeing the true face of charity.

So I followed the others from bed to bed, seeing what was done and listening to the doctors asking their questions. I could feel that some methodical inquiry was mysteriously proceeding. I could only guess at what it was all about, like one blind and deaf; yet I was sure there must be some universal key to reveal its hidden meaning. With a curiosity I could not have concealed if I had tried, I kept my eyes glued on the great man who held its secret.

How wonderful it was that he with his brains and fame and position should be dressed in the same ordinary white coat as the most modest of his students, that he should bend over the poor patients, touching without disgust the greasy skins sticky with sweat, absorbing serenely all the stenches given off from bodies and wounds and bad breath.

During these first days, I saw one really extraordinary thing: a doctor looking at a patient afflicted with the disease which bore the doctor's name. How passionately I peered forward to watch that strange pair, the Doctor and his Disease, joined together till the end of time. I could feel that I was seeing here the finest triumph, the fulfilment of the greatest ambition that scientific research could offer: this name would survive as long as Medicine itself. I listened to the tone of authority with which the great man spoke, and now I could scarcely be sure whether he was talking to the patient or to the disease he had discovered.

How privileged I felt to be there, listening to this doctor, who was bringing science alive to me, as it can never come alive by mere book-learning. For here I was drawing inspiration from the living source, where a new facet of ultimate truth had been delivered to the world.

I tried to imagine all that had led up to this moment of birth. The doctor had noticed certain things occurring again and again, certain ideas had flashed through his mind as he was examining a patient or during a sleepless night. Probably he had reviewed these ideas several times, and then forgotten about them again, at least on the conscious level. And then at a certain moment in history he had brought them together in a few pages of writing

24

—and there was a new entity in the world of disease. By this doctor, through this patient, I had suddenly heard a universal language. It was an exhilarating sensation, giving promise of heroic adventure, my entry into a world where nothing is impossible.

One morning I watched a great surgeon operate. A fascinated spectator, I took in the whole scene as something completely new in my experience: the glare of the spotlight over the table, the flash of chromium, the shining whiteness of walls and floor, the blood, the clicking of the instruments, the sharp words of command—"forceps, swabs, sutures"—the surgeons' methodical gestures, the silent, padded movements of the theatre sister and the nurses, the hushed attentiveness of the watching students. I kept my eyes on the chief surgeon, watching the hands especially. How swiftly and strikingly the power in those nimble, supple fingers was converted at need into an extreme delicacy of touch. Inside the red gloves the life in those fingers seemed to pass right down to the end of the steel instruments they were holding.

At the end of the morning when the head surgeon left the theatre, surrounded by his usual group of followers and pupils, he seemed happy. Once more he had acquitted himself brilliantly, and he went off through the wards with a light step, as if he had forgotten his burden of suffering and blood.

In one of the wards a patient operated on that morning had just regained consciousness, but was slowly dying. The operation had been very risky, but the surgeon had tried it all the same, like a man accepting a sporting challenge. As he passed through this ward, he noticed the patient and stopped by his bed. The dying man obviously recognized the surgeon. His work-worn hands kept opening and closing on the white drawsheet. One of them now met the surgeon's hand, gripped it and clung to it. In its final desperate agony, the poor flesh made this instinctive appeal for warmth and support, which it could only find in other flesh.

I saw the famous surgeon answer the mute appeal in that poor hand by taking it in his own hands; while the audience round him stood there in silence. That morning, in their presence, he had taken every action, used all the resources, of which skilled surgery is capable; and now they watched him perform the humblest and most elementary action known to medicine. The dying man was comforted, his face lost some of its tension, and he lay still. It seemed as though this solemn moment might last for ever; then the patient gave a final hiccoughing gasp, and it was over. Only then did the surgeon lay at rest the hand, which fell limply on the sheet. Then with his entourage he left the dead man's bed, and moved on.

Not long afterwards I had a shock. What I had seen the surgeon do that day was apparently a most uncharacteristic action on the part of a man notorious for his unscrupulous ambition and mean intrigues. When I heard this I experienced the sadness of a believer momentarily doubtful of the truth of all religion, because he has been confronted by a bad priest. Then, very gradually, I began to realize that this bad doctor should not make me doubt the truth of Medicine. I had read how, by the bedside of a dying man, a mysterious grace comes to even the worst of priests, even one who has been disgraced and defrocked. "Even Judas Iscariot," said the text, "was the Lord's chosen servant for all eternity." Now I had seen with my own eyes how this bad doctor, by the unique grace of Medicine, had been able to give consolation.

"To cure sometimes, to relieve often, to console always"— that was an old adage summing up Medicine. Even in the hands of the meanest of doctors, even when he can do nothing else, there is still one thing he can do, I now realized: he can give hope to a fellow man.

I realized this even better next morning in one of the medical wards. During the Chief's round, the whole group stopped at one bed for a longish while. The patient was a man of about forty with a fine intelligent head—rather in contrast to those we had just passed. His face was emaciated and very pale, his eyes feverishly bright. Even for one who knew as little as I did, it was obvious he was in the grip of some lingering, inexorable

26

disease; and in the tortured look he gave the surgeon you felt he knew or at least suspected this.

By the questions put to him I realized that he had been under observation for several days in this bed. The doctor addressed him with a tonic friendliness quite different from the way he spoke to other patients. With them he was more like some high official of a charitable institution, soothing the inmates on his visit with a vague bonhommie that did not sound altogether sincere; but he did not adopt this tone with a patient whose sensitiveness was as obvious as the distress he was suffering.

The doctor bent over to listen to the heart. First of all he stared into emptiness, with expressionless eyes, like someone listening at the door. Then he half closed his eyes for better concentration. I could see he was attending very closely by the way his face had somehow slightly contracted. When he straightened up again, he was once more smiling optimistically, and in quite a normal tone he asked the resident, as if the question were of little importance: "What about his blood culture? Have we had the result?"

"Here it is, just came up from the lab," said the resident man, taking a sheet of paper from his apron pocket. The Chief took it, looked at it, and said to the patient triumphantly: "You were quite wrong to give up hope. It is true you have a streptococcus, but look at this, it is the non-hemolytic type." Several times he repeated the word "non-hemolytic" jubilantly, tapping the sheet of paper to prove he was inventing nothing, that here in black and white was the good news with all it meant. "Of course it is still streptococcus, and it will take a good long time before you are completely cured—but we'll get there in the end. Very fortunate that it's non-hemolytic. You do understand what that word means, don't you? Non-hemolytic, not destroying the blood. Your streptococcus is non-hemolytic." He underlined this "non" which nullified the danger.

The man looked at him as if dazed with joy at this miraculous promise of a cure. Almost choking with emotion, he dropped back onto his pillow, his face suffused with a thick sweat. Stammeringly he repeated: "I understand, doctor, yes, I understand." I thought Lazarus rising from his tomb must have had the same expression in his eyes when he looked at the soft sunlight again.

When the round was over, the resident said to the Chief in the corridor: "What shall we do for Number 14?"

"The Oslerian endocarditis? Try what you like. It's important to look as if you're doing something, otherwise he'll understand. Poor fellow—you saw, didn't you? He's intelligent, he knows all about his case. He's looked in medical dictionaries and knows its a streptococcal endocarditis. If only medical dictionaries were banned to the public, he wouldn't have read in one that he was a hopeless case. I was lucky to be able to stress the non-hemolytic character of the streptococcus. At least that's a fairly plausible hope for him to cling to."

"How long do you give him?"

"Two months at most, he's a lovely case. . . ." And a gesture of the Chief's hand indicated a fatality against which he personally could do no more. Then he began to discuss the origin of the soft murmur which he had heard when listening to the patient's heart. You would have thought now that he was talking of observations made on some laboratory animal.

At first I was merely disconcerted, thinking I must have somehow misheard. "What is he talking about?" I asked someone next to me.

"The Oslerian endocarditis, of course, with the non-hemolytic streptococcus."

"But when he told the patient that was the redeeming factor—"

"He said that because he had to say something. It's really the non-hemolytic type which is the most serious. The fellow has no chance at all. The Osler is a disease from which you never recover. There's nothing to be done. The man's had it, he's quite definitely had it."

No chance at all, nothing to be done—these phrases of despair were all I could take in. For a moment I was completely knocked off my feet, and I stared uncomprehendingly at these men in white all round me who stayed calmly discussing this unfortunate patient as if he were suffering from no more than a light cold. Good heavens, there must surely be something that could be done, some cure to try, a vaccine or serum or ray treatment, something, anything. It must be tried very soon, it must be tried immediately. This man was dying and no one seemed to be bothering about it. I felt I was watching a man drown, while on the banks everybody else went about their own wretched businesses and refused to hear his last terrible screams. Inside me the first seeds were born of a terrible anguish which I felt would grow and grow.

The Chief was still talking. From the lips of this man in good health came technical phrases, dry, hard, cold: stories of gigantic vegetations found on the walls of the heart, of torn or thickened valves. At one stage he told the resident: "You'd better try and see his heart at the post-mortem, to verify this hypothesis."

He talked about this patient as if he were already dead, and they all listened to him, pressing round him so as to miss nothing; some even took notes. Plainly these sinister words were full of importance for them; for me they remained incomprehensible, so utterly meaningless that I felt a dull rebellion swell inside me. It was all very fine for the Chief to make his generalizations on cases of endocarditis; but I for one could not turn away so easily from the tragedy of this particular case. Surely there was nothing which could lessen its horror, certainly not mere technical curiosity.

Standing there behind the others, I had to stay silent, when I would like to have shouted out to them: "That's enough, why can't you stop? Don't you understand that it's horrible?" And what was it in fact that I found so horrible? What did I want them to stop? They should stop showing this medical indifference, using these arid scientific tones which come so easily to the healthy. It was monstrous to treat a living man as if he were already a corpse. They should stop this criminal surrender without fighting.

Criminal? This was the word which had just slipped out in my thoughts. But it opened up a dizzy abyss, before which I drew back in fear. I must be mad to think up this word, it was

29

almost blasphemous. I had a feeling of terrible impotence, I saw a vision of death in all its fatality as a hostile black mass which would never move, which could never be penetrated. To my shame I realized that I had just been reasoning like any layman, always expecting miracles from his doctor, always ready to talk of ignorance or murder whenever setbacks are encountered or mistakes made. Yes, my rebelliousness was a compound of false sensitiveness, brashness, inexperience, and romanticism.

But suddenly I saw again the white lips of the patient with the streptococcus, the distracted anguish in his eyes, and then the empty hope he had been given. Once again I felt my anger rising against the Chief and his assistants who stayed there without doing anything for him.

Nothing to be done, nothing to be tried? Well then, what was the point in being a famous doctor, with people coming to consult you from the ends of the earth, if you failed completely on a case like this, and calmly declared it beyond your resources? What on earth was the good of all these hospitals, appliances, phials of drugs, laboratories, assistants, nursing sisters—and all these medical geniuses, if they came to nothing more in the end than a few charitable lies?

How on earth in the heart of Paris, fifty years after Pasteur, could they declare themselves beaten by a microbe, without even fighting? And if they would not even attempt the struggle out of pity for their patient, they should at least have been ready to struggle for my sake. I had admired them, I needed to believe, to defend the spirit of my faith. Till then I had always thought the doctor's motto was *We must*, not a mere *Perhaps*. We must struggle on, we must persevere, we must discover, we must cure: this was the efficient cause, the categorical imperative, our duty, our destiny, our glorious cross. If in this whole edifice of science there was nothing at all which could save this patient, if all my life as a doctor was to be nothing but a sinister procession of patients abandoned to death, I might just as well abandon this sort of career right away, or else, like many fine spirits including Tolstoy and Molière, merely make fun of Medicine and its laughable pretensions.

When I left the hospital a few minutes later, I was still seething with sullen rebelliousness; the swarming world outside broke in on me like a tidal wave. People elbowed me and jostled me and nearly pushed me off the pavement. I accepted everything in a spirit of sardonic bitterness. Poor wretches, they little knew what I had just seen.

For a long while I walked on the edge of the crowd. In an endless stream they ran towards the metro or a bus, entered shops and restaurants, settled down outside the cafés, laughed, did business, ate and drank, all unaware of the hospital nearby and the ominous message it had given me. But when I too came out of a peaceful little restaurant after a meal and found myself caught up once more in the bustle of a boulevard, I felt as if heavy bonds had somehow been loosened, as if this habitual act of ordinary life were stronger than my revolt and my distress of mind. But before plunging resolutely into the city with its myriad sounds of health and happiness, I had a moment of remorse. Had I the right to forget this morning's patient so quickly? And yet, I thought to myself, I could not go on, all through my medical career, dashing my head against a wall. I could not forswear all happiness just because people kept on dying. Certainly nothing would be quite the same again after this apprenticeship in death and suffering. But outside the hospital and its patients nothing could stop life going on as it always had, any more than I myself could keep my senses closed for ever to the sights and sounds of the street.

In the evening, as soon as I got back to my room, I got out my textbook on internal pathology. I found the chapter on Endocarditis, and turned the pages till I came to the Osler variation. Since the morning, although I had not dared admit it to myself, I had been nursing a completely irrational hope that there might after all be some chance of saving Patient No. 14. Perhaps I could find some cure whose existence the Chief might have forgotten in his excess of scientific knowledge; perhaps by reading each line with care and concentration I might eventually discover a suitable formula.

Opening the book, the Oslerian endocarditis took on for me the traits of the patient I had seen, his face drawn with pain. I learned that first his strength had been slowly sapped by the fever, and that, strikingly pale as he was now, the pallor would deepen to a quite amazing whiteness—until it was replaced by the fixed and final whiteness of death.

In the middle of the text was a sketch of a heart split open to show its valves covered with gray vegetations. For me it was the heart of Patient Number 14, on the day it would appear, yellowish and dark red, on the table at the end of the postmortem. I was never to forget what I was reading. All my life it was to remain in my memory, inextricably bound up with this one patient. For the first time I came to appreciate that all through my life as a doctor the pain and distress of others would be the unique and inexhaustible source of my own advance, bringing me new resources of knowledge with each new experience of suffering. And now I realized too the true medical sense of the word "beautiful" when used of a case or a wound, like someone talking of a beautiful flower.

As I read, I began to understand that for Patient No. 14 there was really nothing to be tried, nothing to be done. He was irremediably, irrevocably condemned to death, already beyond all human help. In the Chief's attitude there was neither indifference nor criminal passiveness. My revolt had been the idiotic temper of a spoiled child—just like my tantrums as a small boy, trying to wring from my mother some miracle she could not always accomplish. That time was a long way back. Every type of cure had been tried out one by one, and throughout the world's hospitals the research and the experiments continued: till now in vain. One day, perhaps tomorrow or the next day, they would be able to save other patients like No. 14. But for him at this point in time there was certainly no hope whatever. It was as simple as that.*

The more I read, the more my indignation cooled and my distress was resolved. I began really to come to grips with reality,

Translator's Note: In 1943 the use of penicillin cured for the first time a case of Oslerian endocarditis.

to see that even the greatest doctors are only men, that we are no longer in the legendary heroic age when great love could bring a man back to life.

"Non-hemolytic—you do see what non-hemolytic means?" I caught again the echo of the Chief's cheerful friendly voice repeating his white lie, which gave the patient a transfusion of hope like the drops of new blood he could never receive. And again in my mind's eye I could see the Chief smiling to soothe the wan face looking up at him in anguished inquiry. How fine he was, this man in white, subject like all men to error or impotence, to whom another man stretched out an imploring hand. Indeed all men stretched out their hands to him, imploring protection against death, to which they must all one day come.

To heal sometimes, to relieve often, to console always. The adage gave a true definition of the powers of Medicine. But now I saw in it a deeper and more splendid meaning than I had imagined at first. This very morning the words "to console always" had sounded to me like a mockery; I had thought them a somewhat dishonest way of confessing impotence. But now, by the side of tragic defeats, they lit up Medicine with a new hope which had in it the stuff of divinity.

I still felt shattered by this test of my faith, but I was happy to have been through the ordeal and come out on the other side. I knew this moment of respite was only a truce between two battles. Already I could foresee other heavy attacks which would be launched again and again, year after year.

The next attack in fact was not long delayed.

Since coming to Paris I had often met in the corridors a long brown box, carried by two orderlies, which I guessed had a corpse inside. And I had expected to find in the wards an atmosphere heavy with funereal gloom, a devastating pallor everywhere, and the beds full of dying men, blood and pus, groans and screams.

Instead, to my astonishment, the scene had seemed comparatively normal and peaceful. In the long row of white beds, sheets and dressings hid the wounds. Suffering seemed dumb. Instead

33

of groaning, the patients talked to each other, and some laughed. Almost all of them seemed to be getting better, and I saw scarcely any on the point of death. Gradually I became reassured, but all the same I remained discreetly in the last row of students so that I should only see wounds from a distance and if necessary could turn my eyes away at once without anybody noticing. But I never had to do so.

Before long I imagined I had become inured. I congratulated myself on getting over the initial queasiness so much more easily than I had dared hope. I soon had a rude awakening.

One morning I went with the others into an isolation cubicle. The patient, supported by a pile of pillows, was sitting half upright in her bed. She was a big woman of about sixty; she was gasping, and at each gasp it seemed as though in all that huge ward she could not find a single breath of air to gulp down. At times I thought she was actually choking, and she would sit up straight with her nostrils quivering and her eyes almost out of their sockets. Her hands went to her throat, her tongue flickered like a mad thing between the slate-colored lips, which she kept vainly opening, thrusting forward as if this would help her to snap up the air, always just out of reach. The puffy bluish swellings around the lips looked as if they concealed some invisible gag. A nurse was supporting her, trying to keep her in the bed, wiping the sweat from her brow, making her inhale oxygen. For hours she had been helping this woman to struggle against the most appalling of deaths—death from asphyxia.

I saw the Chief and then the interne fix their stethoscopes at the level of her heart and then of her lungs. After that their examination of her breathing and rattles only lasted a few seconds; for them the diagnosis was clear enough, and when they passed to the next patient one of the students was already preparing the intravenous injection which had been ordered.

The horror of this slow asphyxia kept nagging at me all through my rounds, and yet, as soon as it was over, I went back to the isolation cubicle. I looked at the patient from the entrance. She was alone and had fallen back on her pillows; she seemed to be resting more peacefully under the effect of the injection, and I came nearer her bed.

From close to, she still looked extremely tense. From time to time her face still contracted crazily, and it glistened with sweat. Her breast rose and fell in short panting breaths, her eyes were closed. I stood there a moment to watch her respiration. Reassured, I thought I would try to listen to it with my brand new stethoscope. I was just about to place it gently against her breast, when she made a sudden movement, a gesture of bringing her hands to her throat as if to tear away some irresistible obstacle which was once more stopping her breathing. She opened her lips, not to cry out, but in a sudden pathetic thirst for air. I knew it was a new crisis, but the agony I now saw appearing on her face was something different from before and even more terrifying.

Her head stiffened and fell back. Frothy saliva appeared at the corner of her lips, she opened her eyes and they began to roll. On her features there was still a moment of hesitation before the mysterious act of acceptance took place. Then there was a sort of spasm, and I thought: "She's going to die, she's going to die." All at once I understood: for the first time I was going to see what a face looks like when death comes into the eyes—and I was afraid.

My horror was such that I threw my head up and almost shouted out loud, calling for help. It was all over by the time I turned again to the patient. Death had flooded over her face in a few seconds, though the eyes remained open and still held their expression of terror. The nurse came, and from my look realized at once what had happened. She bent over the patient and said simply: "Yes, she's dead." Then she closed the eyes, keeping her thumbs on the eyelids for a moment. Then she removed the pile of pillows and immediately laid the body flat, as if nobody who had died should be left sitting up. Finally, with a complete absence of emotion, she began to lay the body out.

I had never watched anyone die, and I experienced the instinctive horror which has haunted the human race since the beginning of time. All men have talked of it, and I had read about it so often in books: that dazed, uncomprehending stupefaction before death's awful power, which in one tragic second sweeps away irrevocably all that life has built up. Now I had had my introduction to the grim, implacable being that all men must learn to meet, and I left the hospital ward with sadness in my heart. I was going to be a doctor, and would have to face death almost daily. Could I ever become immunized to the sight of death—or must I feel it each time as poignantly as I had felt it now?

During the next few days I thought about the whole episode again and again. I urgently needed to find some meaning in what I had seen that morning. If this was part of my initiation as a doctor, I must find something in it to steady me. Gradually the whole of that morning faded from my mind except the symbolic picture of the nurse. I saw her again at first near the bed, capable and infinitely helpful as long as there was anything she could do for the patient's relief. Then I thought how she would have behaved had she been there instead of me at the actual moment of death. It was of no use then to try to do anything further, and she would have showed the same absence of emotion as when she had in fact found the patient dead. She had thus given to each moment its right place in the medical scale of values. The horror of these attacks of choking, the long, long hours of terrible suffering for a woman still completely lucid, who was enduring a living death—then was the "doctor's hour." The true pathos was then, not in the final second of agony, despite its tragic poignancy and the endless question it raises of what there may be in store for us outside this existence. For by this time the doctor's work is done, and the whole scene has moved on to planes deeper than consciousness, already beyond life; and the body surfeited with suffering turns to unfeeling dust, beyond all succor at last.

The finality, the disintegration, the nothingness—all this gradually lost for me the mysterious and frightening power it has over most men right from childhood. Every doctor takes on himself a burden of suffering and death which is part of the

36

human condition; but without risk of callousness or fear of indifference I could at least detach from that burden the last agonizing moment of death. So much seemed cruel, so much seemed hopeless, and in these hours of initiation I was assailed by doubts from all sides. Yet at the bedside of this dying woman I had found the clear, effective respect for life which allows the doctor to remain, right to the end, active, calm, and compassionate; leaving to others, faced by the new impersonality of the corpse, the blind and barren *timor mortis*.

Each morning after this, during my initiation as a doctor, I found the old mysteries being clarified for me one by one, in similar ways.

The day I went to the Hôtel-Dieu Hospital, at the exit to the ward where the Chief's round had just taken place, I saw a young woman stop the doctor as he was passing. She held in her hand a note of introduction from some practitioner in the town who wanted the great man's opinion. Although it was not his regular consulting day, the Chief sent her into the ward reserved for consultations. He sat at his usual desk, while the little group of students settled down in chairs or remained standing in a semi-circle.

I had already watched several consultations, and knew the usual procedure. The patients would arrive one by one, the men naked from the chest up, holding up their trousers while their suspenders hung down; the women would be in petticoats or panties, showing flabby bodies, rounded bellies, sweaty arm-pits, and shabby underwear—which was sometimes distressingly dirty when they had to undress further than they expected. It very quickly became difficult to breathe in this atmosphere, and as the morning wore on the procession of mournful humanity turned into a sort of single collective entity, impersonal and utterly depressing.

The Chief on this occasion had the patient sit in front of him under a strong light. Then he re-read the letter she had handed to him. She was a very different type from the usual procession that entered this room for diagnosis. Before she sat down, I had

37

seen that she was tall and well-built, with an easy attractive manner. When she was seated, I observed further that she was a brunette and rather pretty, in her late twenties, quite smartly dressed in a dark suit and hat. She looked round her, somewhat embarrassed to have so many people watching her. When he had finished reading the letter, the Chief asked her a few questions, and then said, "Please undress."

I had not imagined for a moment that she too would have to do this. The patients who sat on that chair were usually almost naked when they reached it, and because they were poor and ugly they seemed almost without personality or sex. But I suddenly found it shocking that this attractive young woman, still in her clothes and even wearing gloves, just as she looked walking along the street, should suddenly have to show herself naked in front of some fifteen young men, complete strangers. Simultaneously, and obviously with the same thought in her mind, she blushed. Her look went from one to the other of us, she started to slip off her coat, hesitated, then nervously took off hat and gloves. After that she got out of her coat, and appeared in a light silk blouse.

I must try to explain my feelings. I imagined seeing this woman in the street, with men continually passing her, all staring at her in a way that meant they were mentally desiring her as a woman and undressing her. This desirability she had somehow brought in here with her, through her personality, her clothes, and the swinging hips of a woman who knows she is attractive to men. Now there was her perfume in the room, too, and then, when she began to undress, something more besides: her own personal smell, the deep warm smell of a dark sensuous body.

She took off her blouse, and the top of a silky pair of panties, edged with lace, could be seen appearing over a sun-tanned skin. Now that I had seen a little of this stranger's flesh, I was no longer looking at her face. My eyes went to her body, watching intently. In an agony of suspense, as if it were something I could not possibly hope for, I waited for her to perform the simple action of taking off her skirt; she slid it down over her thighs,

38

hopped out of it, and appeared almost naked. You could see the brown points of her breasts, the elongated curves of her thighs. But just as, a minute before, I had stopped looking at her face, I now forgot about her breasts and thighs. My gaze, full of a tense anticipation, penetrated the delicate tissue of her underwear to find the stomach, and then travelled down to the dark triangle—as if I had never seen a woman till this moment.

And suddenly I was frightened that I might be caught with this tremendous surge of desire showing in my eyes, on my face, even through my breathing. With a violent effort I jerked my eyes away. The first person I saw as I turned my head was the Chief. He was looking at the young woman thoughtfully, waiting till she had finished undressing, but behind his glasses the watchful eyes were the very picture of reflection. You could guess that he had already formed his judgment. Soon the naked flesh would reveal the signs he probably felt sure of finding there; this was all he was waiting for, and it would confirm his diagnosis. Seated near him, the Resident was talking to the interne, explaining something to him. He spoke in an undertone, sometimes looking at the patient and sometimes elsewhere, according to the ideas he was expressing at the time. One of the students was finishing marking on a card the results of the interrogation.

In the semi-circle of white-coated students watching, one was surreptitiously glancing at his watch, probably thinking of an appointment he had to keep, while others were talking in a low voice. If the flash of desire had once passed through their eyes, they had certainly regained their self-possession by now, and their looks were merely indifferent. Opposite me, almost hidden in the last row, I did see one face without this neutral quality—but seeing this person in the grip of instinctive passion, I was horrified, as if I had been his accomplice. His lips were half open and quivering with excitement. In his whole face I seemed to see a reflection of my own, staring and gaping at this woman, spoiling and bruising her—a disgusting look, almost a carnal act.

Suddenly I felt ashamed of the mad lust which can be unleashed in men by the body of an unknown woman. I turned back to the Chief. While I had turned my head, the young

39

woman had finished undressing. She was completely naked. The Chief bent forward, and began his examination; all eyes were fixed on him and the woman. He himself regarded her intently, and plainly at this moment she was the only object in his mental field. But there was a side of her which he did not seem to know existed, or which he preferred to ignore. She was under his eyes in all her nakedness. Engrossed in some bitter, intimate secret, he looked at the flesh and beyond it, and she was not violated by his look. A profound reverence and compassion protected the beautiful sensuous body, clothing it in the utmost purity and innocence, even while all these men continued to look at it. This woman was no more naked, was no more a woman; for all these watching males she was simply a patient.

I watched with them, and I began to see her now with different eyes. I saw on her hips the pink mark left by her garter belt, her unsupported breasts bending over a little, on her smooth belly a slight scar from an appendectomy, and lower down, towards the fold of her groin, the skin where it became tender and dark.

From now on I knew her completely, and it all seemed to me very simple. I was close to her, the warm smell of her flesh was in my nostrils, I was almost touching her body. For a few moments she made part of my life and my thinking; and yet she had become as remote for me as if whole worlds and centuries were between us. I began to pity the poor wretch whose look I had surprised. He had remained a mere male, always ready to pounce on the first woman who crossed his path. But as for me —I had become a doctor. For me all women would be naked from now on, but that nakedness which fascinates the male would separate them from me, would isolate them, would form their best defense against any desires of mine.

One day, I thought, beautiful women will come to consult me, and I shall have to bend over them, ready to understand the secrets they will confide to me. I shall need to convince them, to console them, even to make myself attractive to them— the better to cure them. They will lift towards me their faces filled with anguish, bowed with the heavy load of passion and

40

despair and lust. I must feel a lover's devotion, intuition, and tenderness, and yet always remain merely their doctor. I must understand their desires, and yet resist all desire myself, and remain only a friend of infinite helpfulness and devotion. . . .

The examination was over, and the patient was about to get dressed again. While she was still naked, I took a last look at her, so that I could retain in my memory the splendor of that body and all it had unwittingly taught me. I did not know her name, nor anything about her; and she was almost leaving. But she was no longer merely a patient; she was all the patients I must henceforth help and respect and love with a selfless love, which can never hope for realization.

That morning I learned how a doctor must think of a woman.

Chapter 4

ABOUT ONE O'CLOCK in the afternoon hordes of visiting relatives were all set to invade the wards each day. It was high time then for me to leave the hospital, though I left it regretfully. As I went out, I passed all the families waiting patiently for the opening of the front door at the regulation hour. I carried my white coat ostentatiously under my arm, proud to be recognized as a medical student, a privileged being for whom there were no forbidden doors—not just a poor scared hospital patient.

Later on, I should be working far too hard to have much time for distractions. Realizing this, I allowed myself these eight afternoons of complete freedom before the official beginning of term, hoping to rediscover the Paris I had read about, the face of its past and all its ghosts. I was nineteen years old, saturated with literature, and I imagined that books had already taught me most of what I needed to know about life. I took a romantic scholar's-eye view of Paris, and dashed at the city with a passionate enthusiasm. Enthralled by all I had dreamed of and read about, I scarcely noticed the people I bumped into on the sidewalks. I thought little, in fact, about the Paris which lives and breathes day by day in myriad forms. Nor did I quite appreciate that it might need a good deal longer than a week to absorb the subtle charm of the city's gray and black stone—which, after the old red brick of Toulouse, I found rather disappointing.

I only saw Paris through the fiction heroes who had poured into the city their life-blood, their joy, and their sadness. And often in the twilight, when the autumn haze robbed objects of

substance, I would visit certain parts of Paris with a special sense
of exaltation, for they seemed to me full of unseen presences and
subtle auras, to which the ordinary passer-by could never hope
to penetrate. I felt some hidden power had drawn me to them
irresistibly, as the only person who could receive their mysterious
message, could understand their deep and secret meaning.

The last evening of the vacation arrived all too quickly. In
the morning I had been to Dr. Charcot's Salpêtrière, following
one of his successors through the neurosis wards. I left by quiet
convent-like passages, in which old men were enjoying the last
bit of late autumnal sun, and passed the fountain immortalized
in *Manon Lescaut*. Coming out, I crossed the boulevard, and
walked through a succession of quiet streets, without cars and
almost without people; I even noticed one lane where grass grew
in the middle of the pavement. Here too, as I strolled aimlessly
on, ghosts were all round me. By the street-names, rue l'Arbalète
and rue Mouffetard, I realized I must be just next door to the
Pension Vasquer, famous in Balzac's *Père Goriot*.

I had lunch near the Pantheon. Afterwards I rushed off to the
Medical School. I found it at the end of a short street full of
exotic restaurants, stuffed animals, and shops full of surgical
instruments. I had to stand in line for two hours outside the
secretary's office, but when I came out I held in my hand a brand
new booklet on which was inscribed, *Paris University, Faculty
of Medicine*. For the umpteenth time I repeated to myself the
counsel which Mephistopheles gave to Faust: "Choose yourself
a Faculty." I had chosen mine a long time ago.

Before I could consider myself definitely a student, however,
I still had to pay my matriculation dues in the rue Gît-le-Coeur.
As I came out of the office where these were collected, I noticed
that the little street emerged onto the Seine. Daylight was beginning to fade. The sellers of second-hand books on the river
banks were shutting up their cardboard cases full of illustrated
tomes, yellowing paperback novels and brown-and-gold fine
bindings. Evening shadows were lengthening between the
houses, but overhead the clouds were ablaze in the setting sun,
and the river seemed to be flowing in a haze of red dust. Over

43

the top of a bridge Notre Dame glowed in the distance. I watched it turn from pink to purple, from purple to gray, until it faded altogether from sight. The night was upon us; everywhere the shops had lighted up.

I felt too happy to be stifled in the Metro, and decided to walk back to my room. I followed the rue Saint-Jacques, and came to other streets stretching on and on, picketed by yellow-lit lamp-posts, with low little houses on either side. A breeze had risen, touching with chill the mildness of the night. I walked on briskly to get warm, and as I walked I looked at the sky, which retained the sunset's red afterglow. The twinkling stars could be seen only very faintly between the blaze of city lights and the fiery red sky. But towards the south, over the farther suburbs, on the outskirts of the city and towards the open country, blue night with all its stars took over again.

I thought of the summer nights when I had gazed up at the stars with my boyhood friends and we had scanned the heavens for the Northern constellations, while I had secretly longed to see the Southern Cross, and carry out my dream of one day sailing southwards. Strolling along this evening, I laughed at this boyish wish. It was a different and far grander wish I was going to fulfill tomorrow—when I began my Medical Career. I was flooded with a magnificent feeling of joy, echoing the rejoicing in the sky's red glow; and I was sure that the great city, with its festive lights, was opening up to me, was welcoming me, was favorable to my sanguine youth. My sense of well-being grew so rapidly that by the time I reached the Cité Universitaire, I found my overflowing happiness almost too much to bear.

In the corridor, about to open the door of my room, I was halted by the noise of Petitjean's typewriter. I had not seen him again since the day I had taken on his recommendation my first morning coffee and my first Metro; but I had followed his advice beyond this. For a whole week I had scarcely spoken to a soul, and I had taken no notice of my neighbors. For one thing I did not trust my own character; I felt I belonged too closely to a southern race which prefers talk to action, which enjoys playing the *dilettante*, and changing its mind between morning and evening. Moreover, ever since my arrival, I had been full of the extreme touchiness of any provincial in a great city. I wanted to give nothing away to any new friend who might prove after all to be an enemy. But tonight this harsh solitude weighed heavily on me, I needed to sit down and talk to somebody. I would have confided in anyone, a stranger, even an enemy. Petitjean, after the morning he had talked about morning coffee and the Metro, had ceased to frighten me, and in the urgency of my need for friendship I was ready to put up even with a heavily sarcastic Petitjean. Standing facing his door, I still hesitated for a moment, and then knocked: "Come in," shouted Petitjean.

The light from his table-lamp did not extend beyond the type-writer; the rest of the room was in deep shadow. Petitjean turned, but asked, "What do you want?" so crossly that I did not dare admit I had no real reason for coming in. I quickly asked if I could borrow some matches, but I could not help looking at the incredible litter of papers, books and files piled up on the floor and against the walls; and at the photographs and sketches covering the walls, which in the darkness I could not properly see. Petitjean understood my curiosity, and directed the beam of the lamp on to the wall, revealing photographs of film stars, models of cars and yachts from glossy magazines, travel pictures taken from tourist agency brochures. To see Petitjean's pear-shaped face and the tattered old jacket he used for an indoor coat, next to the glamorous photographs of opulent luxury exhibited on the walls, made a brutal and somewhat pathetic contrast. Petitjean evidently realized this, and he gave a bitter little laugh:

"Seems quite mad, doesn't it? But I depend on my photos of pretty girls. They're my private harem—as a friend of mine says, they're the only women allowed by the directors of this establishment. Cars, yachts, superb views, these are my luxuries, my ticket and passport to the beauties of the world. I have them constantly under my eye, and that gives me the courage to wait for them. And then, you know, they're useful in another way too, these pictures. They keep me thinking all the time of material wealth on a rather higher level, the sort which will one day be given to genuine idealists in that juster society they themselves will have built."

His eyes roved fiercely round, as he stopped for a moment, to take stock perhaps of that future society which was seething in his brain. I could find nothing to say, but this did not seem to matter, since Petitjean clearly enjoyed talking for his own benefit, and his pauses, presumably, only marked the time for a little self-applause. He started again, more gently:

"I was a bit unkind to you the first morning you got here. That's because of the bloody character who was in your room last year. He looked a little like you, good-looking boy, law student, but the most affected, precious, pretentious little pansy you ever saw; one of those so-called intellectuals, without a clue about real life. He talked to me sometimes at first; but then he gave me up completely the day he saw I earned my living by doing typing; and he even complained about the noise of the typewriter. Of course he didn't need to do typing or anything else like that, he'd gotten all sorts of scholarships and grants and prizes for himself."

I made a gesture to show I was not like that, and he went on: "Yes, I know. You're broke. That's one point in your favor. And then you're going to be a doctor, that's even better. Later, I dare say, you'll be just another poor bugger who's got where he wanted, and merely indulges his instincts and vices and any virtue he may have left. But at least at nineteen you have ideals and are willing to take risks. You refuse to stay in a smug society which cheerfully ignores the existence of poverty and want, so as not to have to think about it. You are still willing to see that men are hungry and naked and wretched. If that's the way you are now, I hope you'll always keep a trace of that idealism, and at least remember that injustice and inequality exist."

With growing joy I had caught a note of warmth and sympathy in his voice. I was about to thank him and humbly offer him my friendship, but he had evidently decided he had said enough for one evening. Abruptly he brought his monologue to an end:

"Well, here's to a better society. But meanwhile I received

my third rent reminder from the bursar this morning. To pay that up I've got to finish off an idiotic translation before dinner. Here are your matches. Enjoy your dinner."

On coming back from the restaurant, as a preparation for the official beginning of term next day, I set out on the table a clean hospital jacket, new notebooks, and my university catalogue.

This last I opened once more, stopping at the page provided for stages in a medical career. I imagined them passing already in quick succession: student in the Paris hospitals, interne. I even went as far as resident, but I would not let imagination carry me further than that. I did think about it again, though, when I recognized Petitjean's slouching step in the corridor. I opened the door at once, and he came in, wearing his old black raincoat. He came up to the table, looked at my preparations for the morning, then at the stethoscope and skull placed somewhat dramatically side by side, and finally asked:

"Well, young Nérac, what made you choose medicine?"

The question was so direct and unexpected that I hesitated for a moment, before answering in a vaguer way than I should have wished:

"I don't exactly know. It's always been understood that I was going to be a doctor. From the fifteenth century to the Revolution there were doctors in my mother's family. I've always thought it was a fine profession."

"Yes," said Petitjean; "any profession's a fine one if you're drawn to it by a real vocation, and not just as a means of earning your bread and butter. I'm a writer. That's the only thing I can be and the only thing I want to be. I don't remember ever having wanted to be anything else, and I shall remain a writer all my life, even if no one reads my books and no one believes anything I write. Eventually I'll damn well force people to believe it."

He sat down on the divan. For a long time he went on talking about himself as if for months he had not had the chance to unburden himself in this way. He explained to me his special brand of communism. His use of this word made me feel curious and slightly scared. Petitjean's communism proved to be a lonely and intellectual kind. With spiritual weapons, using all the resources he had, he strove by his writing to set men free.

Cut off by his family, he was living from badly paid private tutoring and translations, until such time as he could get his own books published. To satisfy his conscience, he disciplined himself to live with as little contradiction as possible between his life and his ideals, making as few concessions as possible to a society he despised.

Suddenly he cried: "Aren't you a rebel too?" Without leaving me time to answer, he went on passionately: "For my part I'm a big enough rebel for thousands of people, I'll shout from the housetops what the rest of them daren't even say out loud. The world's leaven, that's what I'd like to be—the hidden force that will make it explode. . . ." He got up abruptly and left.

I went to bed, but could not go to sleep. My eyes open in the darkness, I could still almost see Petitjean's strange mournful face. If his eyes were a fanatic's, they were also the eyes of a true missionary, working whole-heartedly for a cause he believed in, and not merely to satisfy some selfish ambition. When he had asked me the reasons for my choice of profession, why hadn't I dared talk to him frankly? I might at least have pronounced the word "vocation" once, echoing his own use of it. My decision *had* been partly dictated by a boyish desire to restore the long line of country doctors, which had lapsed since 1803 and which my mother had continually talked about in front of me with a good deal of pride. But my decision, though it had remained firm, did not really imply a vocation; the vocation came later.

I had my mind so firmly made up that my mother, although delighted by my choice of profession, felt she must try to give me a clear idea of just what it meant. When I was about fifteen, she had questioned some doctor friends in the back room, in my presence.

She had asked one of them: "Will your son be a doctor too?" and he replied: "No, although I must say I should have liked him to follow me as I followed my father. But he doesn't want to.

48

He tells me he wouldn't want his wife and him to have the sort of life his mother and I have had. No private life, you can't even be sure of a whole night's sleep with your wife. You hardly dare kiss your children for fear of contagious disease. No Sundays or holidays, and your profession always standing between you and your family. Worries and problems over patients, who never really appreciate all you're doing for them. Constant pinpricks from people jealous of your position. And in return for all these cares and burdens, you don't earn as much as a moderately successful tradesman. Ah, life has changed so completely since my young days—perhaps my son is right. Medicine is too fine a profession for the present age."

But I had friends who were burning to become missionaries and even martyrs if need be; others who were going to be great soldiers, or submarine captains, or intrepid airmen. They did not want to be protected against the perils of land and sea and air; and I, like them, felt inside me marvellous powers of noble endeavor for something bigger than myself.

My mother started worrying as to what I should specialize in when the time came. Someone quoted to her with a smile the well-known aphorism: "If you have three sons going in for medicine, make the least gifted an obstetrician, the strongest athlete a surgeon, the cleverest a general practitioner." At once, with magnificent presumption, I chose to become a doctor. Then someone said in front of me: "If your son is clever, let him take the full seven years getting qualified. It's a long hard struggle, but it opens up a career that's really worth working for." Hearing this, my mother told me she would very gladly sacrifice herself to help me take such a long and expensive course. "A very small sacrifice," she said, "compared with your own. You'll have to pay for that decision with your whole youth, and see all your friends living independently, earning their livings, starting families—while you'll still be only an ill-paid overgrown student."

But I had begun to imagine what life would be like at a hospital: the research, the students, the wealthy patients I would make pay through the nose for the benefit of the poor patients, whom I would treat free. Certainly a man could have no finer profession in the world. True goodness must be so wonderful, and so easy.

For months after this I lived in an aura of lofty idealism, keeping haughtily aloof from my schoolfellows, revelling in the brave and lonely path I must tread. At sixteen or seventeen, thinking about leaving school, they all discussed their future careers. You could guess already which ones would turn out mean or lazy or greedy. Most would soon sink into a dreary little middle-class rut—shades of that prison house were closing fast. But there was a little group among them, not all of them the best or most regular pupils, who could all be recognized, whether their parents were rich or poor, by an urge for conquest and domination. They wanted to assert themselves, to impose on others their ideas and intelligence and force of character. You could somehow pick out from this class the probable future leaders of the community, for they were endowed with two gifts which are worth their weight in gold: willpower and imagination. Despising the mediocrity of the others, I started going about with this group, and gradually, in the flush of my pride, I too had dreamed of making my mark, of domination and conquest.

Around me the hostel was in silence. Then the noise of typing began again. The picture of Petitjean came to me very vividly, with his flabby cheeks, the hair falling over his forehead and the mechanical gesture with which he pushed it back, his look of enduring poverty with sardonic courage—and the fervor in his eyes. Strange messenger to be sent to remind me this evening of the vital spark without which intelligence means nothing: unselfishness and a love of your fellow men. "Watch and pray"— Petitjean's question had in effect made me do just this, on the eve of my first day as a student.

Solid achievement, ambition, success: I began to realize how I had confused them all and mixed them all up. Just as I was leaving Toulouse, an old doctor friend of ours had given me some notes he had written. He was one of those old doctors from a bygone age who still wore a frock-coat and white tie. "Here, son," he had said: "I'd like you to have these notes of mine;

50

they may help you plan your career." I slipped the sheets of paper into my wallet without looking at them, and there they still were. I lit the lamp and read them.

> *People with talent,* they began, *commonly confuse success in medicine with true achievement. This confusion is to be deplored. I don't say the two things are contradictory, for they often go very well together. But the second does not necessarily follow from the first. The elements of success in a lad of eighteen are easy to discover: good opinion of himself, not too sensitive, keen on winning prizes and distinctions, unromantic, settles down easily to a regular routine, knows which side his bread is buttered. With all these qualities his colleagues are sure to think very highly of him, he will be sought after at medical conferences, the world will praise him. But none of this means that he will necessarily be a good doctor. He would do just as well in metallurgy or politics.*
>
> *If, on the other hand, our eighteen-year-old aspires to true achievement, then it is not so easy to say what qualities are needed. It may sound priggish, but frankly, here is the sort of boy I should like to see go in for medicine. He should be simple and affectionate, ready to fight for what he believes in and quick to answer a challenge. He must be able to give without calculation what he'll get back, to learn steadily without becoming a pedant, to watch patiently without envy. After this, to become a good doctor, all he'll need is a good teacher.*

I repeated to myself: "They often go very well together." Words and phrases took on a new meaning. To study, to work for exams, to qualify, this remained the first duty, but it was not the supreme ambition. However fine it would be to have your name known, with subordinates running round you, hanging on your lightest word, the real triumph, more splendid than any professional kudos or prestige, was to be able to fight against suffering with better weapons. There could be no greater glory than to save a patient, to see death and anguish slowly pass from a face, making way for a new hope and the first uncertain smiles of the convalescent.

I felt I was stifling. I went to open the window, and leaned out into the cold night. The reddish glow had not yet faded from the sky, still gay with the festive lights of the city. But behind this brightness I could now see something else: the fiery furnace of grief and distress and inequality, through which humanity gasps for life and calls frantically for help in an agony that never ends. I thought of all the harrowing things, all the tragic things, I had seen in the hospitals each morning, all I had been able to discern in people's faces, even in the streets. "All this terrible suffering"—this had been the cry of my fifteenth year. And now, starting my studies, I added: "It must be possible to do good, to alleviate so much pain."

I felt a sense then of somehow being renewed and made whole. Yes, I had always known the battlefield on which I would fight. I had chosen it well. "To thine own self be true." I felt I could believe in myself once more, having just rediscovered my true self.

Part 2

THE MODEL STUDENT AND HIS DAY

Chapter 1

SUDDENLY, in the darkness, the alarm goes off. I open my eyes for a moment; it is still pitch black outside with raindrops pattering against the window panes. But the sound of the rain is drowned by the pitiless noise of the alarm, ringing and ringing. Here am I snuggling down in warm sheets, with all these arrears of sleep to make up, a long weary day behind me, and another just starting: hospital, dissection, library, seminar, and then back drowsily to the hostel by the last bus. Four months now of this dreary grind, interspersed with journeys in fetid tubes and along dull gray streets where the sun never seems to shine. But the alarm cares for none of these things, and merely goes on calling me to wake up, wake up.

I won't wake up, I can't. I am too deeply rooted in the bliss of bed, safe and cosy and warm, obliterated, powerless, with no will of my own. Only this terrible noise must be stopped, I must find strength for that. So an uncertain hand goes out, still half asleep, a finger just enough awake to grope for the button which stops the alarm, and then to turn on the bedside lamp.

Seven-twenty-five. Still five minutes grace. Time to spew up all the accumulation of self-pitying bitterness inside me. And then my morning shower. Praise be for the showers; they finish the job of draining all the poisons of the night out of my system.

At the door of the building, a storm hits me. A terrific cloudburst, and the whole hostel and boulevard and park are swimming in rain. The clumps of trees in the park are buffeted by great gusts of wind, swirling back their bare branches. People

55

scurry by, huddled under umbrellas, and I myself set off at a run, trying to avoid the wide puddles rippling in the gale.

The morning starts like any other. I have breakfast at a brightly lit cafeteria near the Metro. A horde of other soaking mortals comes in with me, also breakfast-bound. They shake themselves, wipe off some of the rain, absorbing for a moment the warm damp atmosphere, the bright lights, and the noise. Then they start pushing forward to get to the trays of bread and butter and the baskets of rolls.

I like this contact every morning with all these strangers under the pink neon lights. I like the smell of roasting coffee, and the hubbub of talk and laughter, starting all their days with the cheerful light-hearted clamor of ordinary life. But they all keep their eyes on the clock, and the revolving doors have a continual two-way traffic. They open onto the warmth and light of the milk-bar, but they open too onto the driving rain outside, the backwash of icy wind, and the entrance to the Metro, in which the soaked crowds are constantly being swallowed up.

In the Metro itself there is the same all-pervasive damp, which will last all through the day. Everything is sticky or slimy; the hand-rail, the cement staircase, the greasy floor with old tickets floating in the puddles, and the sweating walls along the passages to the platforms.

The train comes by at 8.40. Surging onto the platform with the rest, I jump on the train as the whistle blows. It starts moving out of the station, and then I sit down. My journey takes thirty-five minutes, and everybody who has any distance to travel settles down comfortably and opens a paper. Or else they start yawning, wishing they were back in bed. Sometimes they actually go off to sleep, their heads fallen backwards and mouths half open. This looks so ugly that I feel it would stop me from ever going to sleep in public.

After four or five stations the car is full, and the air is almost suffocating. Even now that I've had months to get used to it, this remains an ordeal for me, and when I'm early I take the noisy old tram, even though it's slower and more expensive as well.

Today, thanks to the rain, the smell is even stronger. The reek of wet clothes is now added to the customary odors of dust, cheap scent, stale sweat and huddled-together humanity.

Well, I'm on my way to the hospital, and I must admit that this is the right sort of preparation for it. These people have carried it about on them so long and so unthinkingly, this smell of labor and poverty, that by now they have completely ceased to notice it. When in the crush a coarse breath hits you in the face, you catch a powerful whiff of garlic and alcohol. But beyond that, the atmosphere is redolent of squalor and disease, and the blend of odors recalls very strongly the peculiar "hospital smell" which I shall be breathing in the next few hours.

Yes, the hospital smell is easily recognizable, whether it is diluted by the size of the ward or concentrated round one bed, choking nose and throat, turning the stomach and sickening the heart. There are many variations, but each tells its own tale of gangrene, intestinal disease, abscesses, putrefying flesh. Your clothes are impregnated with this smell, it goes right under your skin and becomes part of your own breath. It stays with you from one morning to the next, as if you had never left the wards, as if it would stay with you and on you for ever. . . .

A man carrying large market baskets pushes past me to get out at Les Halles. Had I taken the surface car, I should now be in the middle of the Boulevard Sévastopol among all the trucks transporting produce. They are piled high with vegetables, which despite the gasoline fumes still give out an aroma of damp soil and pure country air. But all in vain would I try to substitute this remembered country smell for the stench that surrounds me. It is too strong, too thick, almost as substantial as something you taste. "You could cut it with a knife," I think to myself.

With a squeak of brakes the train comes into a station. It is Gare de l'Est, my station. When I get out onto the platform, the rain has stopped. By the station clock it is 9.20; I shall be just in time at the Saint-Louis Hospital.

I enjoy walking these last few hundred yards. Even more than the shower when I get up in the morning, it gives me a sort of healthy mental appetite before I tackle the laborious day ahead

57

of me. I reach the hospital calm and alert, with cold cheeks, wet nose, icy ears—having given my lungs a good airing before plunging them for three hours into the stuffiness and stink of the wards. But above all, this city scene helps to put me in the right frame of mind before I begin the morning's work.

Every morning I come up a street lined with some very old tenements. Because the ancient hospital has given me my only acquaintance with this part of Paris, it always seems to me sunk in a sort of despondent gloom. Just at this time bleary-eyed landladies are emerging for a few minutes from dark basements, sweeping the pavements in front of the house; as I pass, I see gloomy passages and the bottoms of squalid staircases. In unsanitary rooms, behind the closed windows, I can imagine thousands of beings condemned to incurable poverty. I look at the many bars and drink shops and their clientele, a flux of workmen, truckdrivers and bargemen, standing there with their glasses of cheap liquor. And when I pass a couple coming out of some near hotel, I think of the sordid love-scenes which have been taking place inside.

But nonetheless I look at them all with the same tenderness I feel for the people on the Metro. Poverty has given them all a very strong family likeness, and if they are not exactly the same, they are very little different from the people I have seen passing through our back room in Toulouse, or the people I shall meet again in the hospital.

At the end of the road the Saint-Martin canal makes a wide bend, and sprawls out in a calm expanse of dark greasy water. I often stop at the entrance to the iron gangway running over the lock, which looks like a Japanese bridge. You can see sturdy barges moored all down the stone wharves, and warehouses and sheds. On fine mornings there are always people standing by and watching as the locks open. The bargemen exchange jokes with the lock-keepers and an extra spice is added to the scene when a foreign barge comes along, marked with an outlandish name.

Just as I pass over this foot-bridge, the rain starts falling again, tracing thousands of small rings of gray water, which

58

ripple mournfully against the wharves. Immediately beyond the canal, at the bottom of the rue Richat, you can see the first buildings of the Saint-Louis Hospital. From all the great streets in Paris, from all over Paris and all over France—indeed, if you think of the lepers, from all corners of the world—patients are flocking to the narrow lodge gate. The main gate opens to admit an ambulance, and I sneak in behind it.

The clock has just struck the half-hour. For a few seconds its vibrations go on echoing plaintively over the old slate roofs, till they die away at last in the din of the street. This clock always seems to me to be striking two quite different sorts of hours: one sort is animated and happy, for the healthy who come and go outside these walls; but for sick people the hours it strikes are heavy and uncertain and deformed—featureless hours which, besides the sick, only doctors can understand.

Other students are hurrying, like me, to the men's surgical ward. The students' locker room is at the end of the ward on the ground floor, and you can get there directly from the courtyard; but I much prefer going through the ward. It always reminds me of a church. Ten big supporting pillars expand into intersecting arches when they reach a low ceiling. Thick walls and narrow windows insure that the light of day penetrates only fitfully.

It must have looked much the same in the days of Henry IV —the walls, the long rows of beds and patients, the weight of hot air bearing down on you as soon as you get inside the door. The very first gulp of it makes breathing an effort after the fresh air outside.

All sense of place and time is wiped out for these men by sickness and isolation, and as I come in each morning to see them lying round the ward, I soon stop thinking about the picturesque old walls and the medieval setting.

From a distance I look towards my two beds, Number 25 and Number 26. I am anxious to know if I shall find there the same two patients as the evening before, or whether there has been a new admission during the night. Each of the first-year students is given two beds to look after, as his special charge. If he is conscientious, he feels that the new admission is his big chance. He will be the first to examine the patient and make notes of his observations, which he will later read out eagerly in front of the Chief. He can make a good impression by showing off his brand-new knowledge, and it may lead to his helping one of the senior students give an anaesthetic or change the dressings. But before I come up to my beds I can see there is no new admission for me this morning.

In Number 25 I can still see the old man with the strangulated hernia, who had an emergency operation yesterday. When I reach his bed, I say "Morning, grampa," to him, forgetting that he is stone deaf. They took out his dentures for the operation, and have not yet given them back; he goes on silently chewing his gums. With bewildered eyes he watches me pass.

The patient in Bed 26 lies flat on his back. He raises his head a little to see me go by. As on so many other mornings, he greets me first: "Morning, M. Nérac." "Morning, Armand," I reply, pressing my hand lightly on his feet through the sheets; I am imitating the interne, who often uses this way of saying a friendly hullo to the patients as he passes through the ward in a hurry. Armand knows quite well, however, that I shall be back in a minute and that he, alas, will still be there. You don't leave your bed so suddenly when you have Pott's disease and are lying immured beneath loads of plaster.

In the students' room, some of the others have already arrived, and are getting into their white coats in a leisurely way. Thomassin is holding the floor, and seems very excited, as he always does when talking about jazz.

"These Negro musicians, they're marvellous, they're simply staggering."

"But do you mean," asks Merlet, who believes in getting things straight, "that it's a marvellous film or merely a marvellous jazz in the film?"

"The film," says Thomassin, "oh, I couldn't care less about it as a film. What's so superb is seeing these musicians. They've re-discovered what music really is, which means playing just what

60

comes into their heads. As we were coming out, some stupid idiot near me said: 'Negro music—you can have it.' I could have strangled him. They are the pure musicians—they don't separate creation from performance—and we are the degenerates. The only thing we seem to be able to do is put down our ideas on paper and get them played by others."

Merlet looks slightly worried. "Would you like scores abolished altogether?"

"Ah, if only that were possible. After all, the essential thing is just what is *not* written down, it's the vital spark added by the performer. All these big concerts, with the orchestra sticking to unchangeable scientific regulations—that's not live music. It's sterilized, without any vitamins. But the Negroes really have got vitamins. Think of Ellington when he starts improvising."

I have got my coat on by now, and I return to the ward. I shall never know the name of the film, nor the end of this debate on jazz. What would be the use? I have no time in the evenings for films or concerts, anyway. If I stayed in the cloakroom, I might begin missing these things. I know I should not have the will-power to leave, and I would go on listening till the roll-call started. I pick up the case-notes hanging at the foot of Number 25's bed, and he watches me with his air of bewilderment as I examine his temperature chart, feel his pulse, palpate his stomach and inspect his little bottle of urine. Everything is all right; I am pleased with this conclusion, or more precisely, I am pleased with knowing the way to arrive at it. Among the innumerable signs and symptoms to be looked for, I have at least in four months absorbed into my repertoire a few guiding principles.

I move on now to the Pott's disease. Armand is twenty, and he came into the ward soon after the beginning of term. Since then he has been on his back, encased in a plaster corset. The arch on the ward ceiling and the top of a window are all he has to look at.

"Still no news for me, M. Nérac?" Before I have even reached him, he challenges me with this question. It is the same question every morning. Will I ask Sister? Or the interne? For the Chief has promised to have him sent for convalescence to the sanitarium at Berck. Since that promise was made, he feels that every day spent in this hospital ward is one day wasted for his cure. He is desperate.

"Oh, it can't go on like this. I don't get any sleep. And I'm in such pain. People aren't made to lie on their backs so long. Please tell me, M. Nérac—how much longer shall I be here?"

"You know what Sister promised, my friend. The first free place will be for you, and down there with the sea air you'll be fit again in no time. The Chief said so himself."

I wish I could believe my own words. I am always afraid I shall lie unskillfully, and Armand will guess I am lying. It is much harder to tell this sort of lie than I imagined, especially under the steady gaze of two hollow eyes with dark lines under them.

"Let me get out of this bed, or I'll give up. I can't stand it, I can't stand it." He is ready to cry like a child.

I do not have to reply, for Bougeard, the interne, has just come into the ward, and I can leave Armand without looking as if I'm running away.

Bougeard holds in his hand the list of students, and the Sister is off fetching the late arrivals from the locker room. We are all here now, and the roll begins. "Adenot?"—"Here." "Alliaume?" —"Here." "Bellienaz?"—"Here." "Chavasse?"—"Here." Yes, even "the great Chavasse" is here for a change, for yesterday the Chief warned us he would come down heavily on any absentees. "Thomassin?"—"Here." "Verschave?"—"Here." "Zwegurzovitch?"—"Bless you," answers Chavasse in place of the student concerned, as if greeting a sneeze. Whenever he is there, Chavasse never passes unnoticed. Very tall and powerful, he has a big, merry, bearded face, and has never quite grown up. The eternal student, and more especially, the eternal medical student. He failed his entrance exams first go, and he seems quite ready to flunk out again at the end of this year. At this rate he'll need ten years to qualify.

There are forty on the roll, but only about twenty of us stay to follow Bougeard on his round, forming a closely packed row of attentive heads at each bed. This serves as a screen, behind which Chavasse and the remaining students of my year will be chatting in undertones, sitting on the edge of neighboring beds, reading the patients' magazines, or even disappearing to other parts of the hospital. Out of each group spending a term in the surgical wards, about half develops a strong taste for dermatology. They listen to the consultations in the outpatients' department, or else visit the hospital museum. In either case they come back with horrifying descriptions of squamous or gangrenous chancres and ulcers, of faces, limbs and sexual organs eroded or discharging pustules.

The mornings when he does follow the round, Chavasse gets in the first row, pushing himself between the five or six foreigners he calls "the tribe." According to him, they are lost to any sense of decency, they're always sneaking in to see and do more than anybody else. They want to examine each patient, even though it is extremely tiring and painful to be constantly examined by unskillful students. There are several of the French students who do exactly the same, but Chavasse is such a ferocious nationalist that he only notices the "dagoes" doing it. All through the round he keeps digging his elbow in the chest of Poubs, standing on Nescu's toes, tripping up Kowski. He keeps a stern eye on their behavior with the patients, and great is his wrath when he hears one of them addressing a patient as "old fellow."

"Oold fel-loo," he pouts, in savage imitation of their accent, "Old fellow, indeed. You'd think the little runts owned the place. Only the Chief and Bougeard have the right to call a patient 'old fellow'; when they say it, it really means something. You dirty bastards, can't you even wait five years? You'll be sitting very pretty then, you'll be finding plenty of dopes to open their doors to you, *and* their purses; who'll invite you to have a go with their wives, who'll be quite ready to be taken in by any outlandish mumbo-jumbo you care to use."

Chavasse in a real temper is a frightening sight. One morning he accused some olive-skinned foreigner of attempting to examine a young woman's vagina. She was crying bitterly in protest, said Chavasse, and he had his hands on the offender's throat. We had to pull him off by main force.

Even when not venting his spleen against the foreigners, Chavasse is still kept very busy. The patients call him from all sides, and he goes blithely from bed to bed. Remarking that if he's going in for surgery he'll have to learn to "cut hearts" where necessary, he plays cards with them, and gives them useful tips on the game. He calls them all by their Christian names, pulls their legs, and gives a humorous twist to their complaints. "How's your new wing getting on?" he asks the fracture case in Bed 5, and to the haemorrhoids in Bed 14, "What about the ancestral piles to-day?" The fistula in Bed 20, despite the stitches in his anus, joins in the general laughter when Chavasse inquires about his "Crater in the Moon."

Sister is more willing to let Chavasse do dressings than the rest of us. Chavasse takes advantage of this to pinch the nurses, with the excuse that it's all part of their day's work to be pinched. "And so we put the finishing touches to this fine piece of needlework," he solemnly announces, when taking out the stitches on the sixth day after an appendectomy. There's an old man in Bed 11, who has to have a lighted catheter put up his urethra; he lets Chavasse do it without protesting, merely to receive this encouragement: "Cheer up, Grandpa, I'm going to get your bladder all lit up." Even the orchitis in Bed 29 forgets to groan when it is Chavasse who is going to change his pad of cotton wool: "I promise you," says Chavasse, "I'll get your two Adam's apples straight back into the shopping bag afterwards."

Though he is an ordinary student like the rest of us, he receives special treatment; he has become one of the personalities of the surgical block, one of the few students, indeed, whom the Chief seems to know as a person. He usually calls us "Gentlemen" or uses a plain surname; but Chavasse, owing to his beard and frequent absences, has caught his attention. The Chief always refers to him as "the great M. Chavasse." Bougeard has a soft spot for him too, and can usually be disarmed by a flash of Chavasse's wit. The patients, of course, adore him.

64

I feel jealous. I am there every morning, scrupulously attending all through the surgeons' rounds, and listening to all the clinical instruction they give. I am trying my hardest, in fact, to be a model student; and yet nobody has noticed my existence. The Chief and the interne, whom I admire with all my heart, seem unaware of my application, and except for Armand none of the patients guesses how much I share their sufferings—which is just about all I can do for them at this stage. Whereas Chavasse, with a few jokes and some heavy clowning, makes them his friends for life.

The first patient on this day is in the special glass-walled cubicle at the entrance to the ward, where the most serious cases are always put. He is a very bad burns case who was admitted three days ago. Head and hands and the whole of his body are enveloped in cotton wool. He looks as if he had already been placed in a shroud, completely untouchable. Only a small part of his face can be seen, and it is so swollen that even the nose and eyelids are only just recognizable. From the lips emerges a faint spasmodic death-rattle, a breath so slight it would not cloud a mirror. But before going into this coma the poor wretch filled the ward with his screams of pain. Sometimes they were the loudest and most piercing shrieks that suffering can ever have brought forth; and sometimes they were long hollow moans rising from the very bowels, the sort everyone feels he can hear in his own flesh.

During my four months in this surgical ward I have heard plenty of the different types of cry wrested from men in great pain. A fractured cranium died here of traumatic meningitis, bringing me my first acquaintance with the meningitic cry, shrill, brutish, like an animal with its throat being cut. It comes at such regular intervals that you find yourself waiting for the exact moment; its stridency, once heard, is unforgettable. But that animal cry, lost to rational consciousness, was less shocking than the screams of the man with burns: a man who was sane and conscious in the grip of the most frightful suffering imaginable.

As soon as all hope was given up, Bougeard had him kept filled with morphia, so that now the patient's only sign of life is this unconscious mechanical rattle; he can feel pain no more. The rattle gradually swells, fades away like a dying dirge, then breaks out anew, indescribably feeble and sad. But those who for days have had their ears pierced by his cries find a merciful silence in this light breathing they hear. It means the end of pain and vain entreaties and despair, the utter surrender of earthly hopes; it means resignation and peace.

We go back into the main ward. Bougeard comes up to the first bed. I follow him closely. This takes the best part of the morning, for he brings himself down to our level of beginners' knowledge, explaining, commenting, guiding our replies as we come to each patient in turn. Dr. Bougeard is "our" interne. He is experienced—and this gives him tremendous prestige in our eyes.

In the first weeks it was only in his company that I dared to venture beyond my own two beds and a few near them. The rest of the ward seemed to me like some unknown land, only partly explored, which even the boldest adventurer would enter with caution.

The Chief told us on our first day: "Take an interest in the patients, talk to them gently, examine them carefully. It's an important part of your early training—learning the bedside manner."

Take an interest? This was all very well, but the rest of the advice presented more difficulty. It would be all right if you could start off by studying lesions and their signs on a dummy —like a newly qualified surgeon practicing on a corpse. But a ward can never be a laboratory where any student can carry out elementary practical experiments. It is full of living, sentient beings, forty of them in this case, for whom each illness or injury is an extremely serious business. The new student is bound to be affected by the individual feelings and reactions of the patients, and these are not easy to reckon with.

So even after four months I prefer to go from bed to bed in the wake of Bougeard. I only need to stay by him to see and understand everything. Pain is a commonplace to Bougeard, who started doing medicine eight years ago, yet he has not become callous, or insensitive to the patient's feelings. He is a good listener, and is full of encouraging words for each patient; he is not afraid of using white lies where it seems necessary. He has to attend to what each person is saying, and he knows how to conceal his impatience; but I can usually tell just when the man still holding him by the coat has lost his attention, and when he starts to think of the next patient. If someone were to talk to *me* in such distress, believing in me like that, I feel sure I could never move on to the next bed. And I admire especially the way Bougeard, as he leaves, will reassure a patient by simply placing a hand on his shoulder.

The pace of the round varies from bed to bed. Sometimes Bougeard only glances at the temperature chart, or opens a dressing to see how the wound is progressing. An anxious cheek may be patted encouragingly, or adjustments may be made to a traction apparatus, which has become slightly displaced. At other times, if the case merits it, things go much more slowly.

Bougeard stays quite a while by an old man with cancer of the stomach, who has been under observation for several days. The words he uses to the patient are very guarded, but with us he goes into the most technical medical jargon. "You see the cachectic facies, the inflammatory oedema. Moloena is present—the neo-plasm is certain."

He utters these technical terms with an apparent calm, which is reassuring to the patient, should he try to understand what is wrong with him. In hospital there are certain words the doctor must never utter; elementary consideration for the patients demands this, as Bougeard taught us our very first day in the ward. Cancer, tuberculosis, syphilis, post-mortem—these words are replaced by equivalents less charged with terror, and perhaps through using them the doctor may in the end come to forget the full horror of their real meaning.

I am still too much of a novice not to feel a shock at the use of the word which means cancer. While Dr. Bougeard is talking to us, I can picture the tumor slowly developing in the man's stomach. It appears in my imagination as a mighty mass over-running this skeleton—for the man might as well be dead already. His skin is corpse-like, a sinister straw color; and the tumor is the only part of him which is still horrifyingly active and alive.

As he looks at the next patient's temperature chart, Bougeard makes a gesture to the Sister, who is already lifting the sheets and removing the cradle which protects the leg from the weight of the blanket. With a snip of the scissors she opens the dressing to reveal an enormous white ball which was once a knee. All is now, between a thigh reduced to a bone and a withered lower leg, is a blue-purple tumor stuffed with rubber tubes dribbling pus.

"Forceps please, Sister." The interne removes one of the tubes, which comes away from the flesh with a squelching noise. The hole this leaves has the pinkness of a mouth, and inside it can be seen the pale bone itself. The interne explores the aperture, pulling its lips apart a little with the forceps, and inserts a new tube. Then he has a brief chat with the patient, and does his best to put new hope into the poor devil, with his fever-bright eyes and hollow cheeks. Meanwhile I watch Sister Juliette finish the new dressing with neat, rapid gestures, sparing the patient all unnecessary pain.

Sister Juliette is disconcerting at first, and even alarming. Her whole face looks as if it is congealed, owing to an enormous old scar which stretches one eyelid so far it is almost vertical. Her nostrils gape and her lips contract, giving her a permanent pout, which becomes a deathly grin when she talks or smiles. Near the scarred parts the skin looks hard, thick and irregular; and as she wears her cap rather low over her forehead, one always wonders whether it hides other sinister secrets. You often meet in the corridors members of the hospital staff who have similar facial disfigurements. They are former patients, I gather.

Our ward Sister has apparently been like this for a long time. It is hard to put an exact age on her corpse-like face—probably she is in her forties—but I can imagine the time when she was a young girl and had to endure countless scarifications of the flesh,

68

her tears of pain mingling with the blood from these agonizing incisions.

Sister Juliette lives in the hospital. She spends the greater part of her time on the job, and she loves this ward. Horrifying sights are so commonplace here, of course, that her scar hardly even arouses curiosity. And no groaning patient would think of staring at the withered flesh, when he sees such gentleness in her eyes: the uncurious gentleness she would like to have found twenty years earlier in the eyes of others, when she first passed them with her hideous disfigurement. But healthy and happy people can rarely attain the knowledge which comes to those who have suffered much in their own person. I learned this at home, and Sister's personality reminds me of it daily: the knowledge that with those who suffer, weak sentimental charity is useless. Instead of an artificial pity, one must truly share their suffering, and try to act effectively to relieve it.

The round is approaching my own two beds, where I know the patients better. I feel they belong to me a bit, these neighbors of "my" two patients: I find them hard to think of separately, for they are all complementary to each other, both for company and for mutual support when in pain. Chairs between the beds are used as tables on which to play those interminable games of cards you only find in hospitals, barracks, and prisons. There is almost always a residue of sticky cards among the impedimenta lying about on the tops of the lockers by their beds. Those who can't play, talk. They tell each other about their work and their families and their lives. These lives often sound alarmingly complicated to me, but they seem to consider them perfectly normal, something to be taken for granted. They also tell each other all the reasons why they've just got to get better quickly.

In Bed 22 is "the Chief's peritonitis." The whole ward knows what strides the patient has made since the day they saw him come in vomiting violently. His nostrils were pinched, his pulse was racing, he had dark circles under his eyes. The Chief did an emergency operation on him, and he is now in the early stages of convalescence. He is not yet used to the light in the ward, and it still seems to dazzle him. He is just beginning to come to life again, to feel his strength returning.

This morning, when the newsboy came round, Number 22 bought a magazine and made an effort to read, but it was too soon. His arms were still so feeble, and holding the magazine up it felt like a ton weight; while his head seemed light as a feather, so unsubstantial on that pillow it made him dizzy. But he smiles all the same. "There are people worse off than me," he seems to say. "The poor chap in the next bed, for instance, he hasn't got anyone to go back to. When he goes out, he'll have to get going again with his handcart. At least I've got a fine wife waiting for me at home."

The chap in the next bed, Number 23, is doing well and will soon be able to go out. His rupture will hold. "Sentence suspended," mutters Chavasse, almost to himself. (He has just rejoined us after finishing a hand of bedside bridge.) "Will hold," qualifies Bougeard, "as long as you take things easy for a bit." The poor fellow shakes his head, thinking that this is not so simple. He almost died, and already, before many days have passed, he will be leaving hospital and dragging his pushcart with heavy loads once more. In his eyes you can read an unutterable weariness, a longing for surrender, a dream of being finished for ever with all tomorrows.

The scars from 24's stitches have completely healed up. "Closed for repairs," remarks Chavasse out loud. "For discharge," adds Bougeard, signing a chit to that effect. The man has been waiting for this several days, and his face lights up at the hope which has become a certainty. He looks towards the end of the ward where the door will open for him to go out.

I marvel at the way all the faces, which seem so much the same when you merely pass them in a hospital ward, can from close quarters become so infinitely different. Often it is the difference between waiting anxiously for an operation and hoping eagerly for discharge.

With No. 25, as I guessed, everything is taking its normal post-operative course. The interne uses this patient to remind us of the causes and symptoms of strangulated hernias in old men. The patient, too deaf to hear what is being said, resolutely continues to recount tales of his childhood during the Franco-Prussian War, and the terrible colic he had from eating rats during the great siege. Chavasse is delighted, and works his way to right near the front, in order, in his own words, to "hear Grandpa discoursing so bowelfully on his intestinal struggles."

No. 26, the Pott's disease, lies on his back, never moving, waiting for the rounds. Every morning the interne gives him the same false hopes as I have done a little while before. Like me, Bougeard repeats the word "perhaps," which the patient, with all his instinct for self-preservation, translates as "certainly." This "perhaps" has to be repeated every morning to gain time, to allow the truth to sink in slowly, week by week, with as little shock as possible. Every day Bougeard renews his promise of a journey to Berck in the very near future and of a certain cure by the seaside. As Armand grows impatient at so many postponements, Bougeard invents new and highly logical reasons to reassure him every day. But I always wonder how long it will take before the patient puts on that look of utterly despairing resignation, of apathetic indifference to every new promise, which will show he has at last understood. I am coward enough to hope it may be after he has left us.

Disease is the great equalizer—that's what they say, and I suppose I believed it before coming to hospital. Now I become more certain of the opposite every day. It is true that the man with cancer of the stomach will die the same death whether he is a duke or a garbage collector. The same surgeon will operate; both patients will have a few months or a year to survive, the same slight improvements will be followed by relapses; they will go through, in fact, the same stages of suffering and despair. But poor Armand with his Pott's disease loses a little more of his chances daily in this hospital ward.

What he needs is a different environment, different food, a change of air, and home comforts: things the wealthy patient can obtain quite easily. While Armand is waiting for a free place at Berck, he must look forward to weeks more of melancholy hospital existence in a congested ward, near all these suppurating wounds which may add further infections to his own fistulae.

I know too now that there is one surgical law for the rich, and another for the poor. When a leg is to be amputated, the surgeon knows whether it will be replaced by an ordinary wooden leg or by a costly aluminum artificial limb—and he will amputate high or low, according to this factor. Several weeks ago we had a case admitted of tuberculosis of the bones of the foot. Without delay, so that the patient should not need a long stay in hospital, and to avoid fistulization and the risks of infection, the Chief amputated. But he told us he could have preserved the foot for a rich patient.

One of the morning's admissions is lying in the next bed. He has a grumbling appendix. After examining him, M. Bougeard tells him with a reassuring smile: "We'll be removing it; there's nothing to it, you know." "Okay, doctor," the man replies in a cheerful, common accent; "Every guy in the place has been tellin' me I'd have somethin' yanked out before I got through."

"Philosophy of non-attachment," comments Chavasse.

The patient in Bed 28, admitted yesterday morning, is a man of about fifty with the sleek, self-possessed manner of an ageing playboy. I looked at him very sympathetically yesterday and felt sorry for him because of the extraordinary and unpleasant accident which had brought him into this surgical ward. For several days, he told me, he had been suffering so acutely from haemorrhoids that during the night, desperate for relief, he tried to push back the bundle of swelling veins with a bottle—which unfortunately had slipped and gone up into his rectum.

When Chavasse came along, late as usual, I was pleased to have this curious story to tell him. He heard me out and then went up to the patient's bed and spoke to him for a minute. Then he came back to me in the corridor and said: "You'd believe anything, wouldn't you? Your man with haemorrhoids didn't have to overwork his imagination with you. Can't you see that he's just a pansy? Why, it's obvious. When he can't find

72

anyone to sleep with, he tries tickling himself with a medicine bottle. Well, he was a bit unlucky—although I don't know, by using a bottle he may have avoided galloping gonorrhoea—one of the specialities of the tribe. And with perseverance, a few years from now, he'll be able to stuff a whole beer bottle up there. Ah well, if he enjoys it, I suppose that's his cup of tea."

A little later on, Bougeard stopped at Bed 28 and listened to the patient's version of the accident. Then he made a digital examination of the rectum and found the roving bottle that had gone astray. Afterwards he went on to the next bed, as if this case was nothing out of the ordinary. I watched him in astonishment, thinking I should at least hear him say something to show disapproval; personally I felt I could not look at this middle-aged pervert again without showing my disgust. I had watched Bougeard's face closely: it showed an almost imperceptible smile at the moment when he was listening to the haemorrhoids story—a smile which said, casually enough, that he was not taken in.

Yesterday, late in the morning, the Chief operated on this patient. The sight was really pretty revolting. "You could get a soda-siphon up there," whispered Chavasse. The Chief foraged for some while with a forceps, before extracting the bottle. No more than the interne did he discuss the moral or aesthetic factors in the case.

Today Bougeard stops at this bed again and looks at the temperature chart, questions the patient as he does the others, and then moves on. Plainly this is to make us understand that we are not here to judge the wretched pervert but simply to look after a patient.

The round is almost over, and already the students start dispersing, leaving the interne at the last few beds, where the ordinary cases are put. We pass them with the same indifferent glance; they are quite uninteresting—or rather they are interesting only to themselves. Yet they are naturally quite wrapped up in their own pains or wounds, and however ordinary their cases they do not stop suffering. It merely makes others less aware of their suffering.

73

It is the Chief's hour in the clinic. I go as far as the corridor where the patients are waiting. There are about fifteen of them. A whole bench is empty; evidently the consultation has already been going on for some time.

On the other benches they are still crushed up together, waiting patiently without moving. There is the same clinging, acrid smell of poverty as in the Metro, but here the stink of decay blends oddly with the reek of ether and antiseptics. Black clothes have become green, green clothes have gone gray, while cuffs and white collars and underwear have turned a bilious yellow. Amidst this medley of unappetizing colors a few snow-white dressings here and there stand out in glaring contrast.

As I am about to push open the door, it opens of its own accord. Out walks a strapping youth with an apelike mug framed between a big turtle-neck sweater and a cloth cap, which he has just put on again. His head droops, and he has the dejected pout of a child who has just received paternal chastisement. Crossing the corridor, he notices we are observing him, so he straightens up and tries to recover what is probably his normal expression of cocky self-assurance; then he shuffles casually away. But it is fairly obvious that his heart is not in it, and when he has passed someone murmurs: "Doesn't look quite so tough now, does he?" For a moment faces relax in general laughter.

I go in, closing the door softly behind me. My fellow-students are all standing round the Chief and the patient he is examining. Then the circle breaks up. The Chief keeps his eyes fixed on the patient, as if to make sure of understanding him completely; and the patient, a thin man in a vest, holding up his trousers with both hands looks anxiously at the oracle.

Standing, the Chief carries his fifty years athletically enough. Seated, he looks perhaps a little too bulky. A white skullcap is thrust down firmly on his head, and this hides his hair, but does not hide a vein on his forehead which always swells up when he is operating or thinking hard. He is not handsome, but he has a strong cleancut face, which is almost austere; and there is the same quality about his eyes, nearly buried between high cheekbones and bushy eyebrows. I always feel slightly terrified in his presence, and patients seeing him for the first time are far more so. Yet those on whom he is to operate entrust themselves to his care with no expression of anguish; you can see that they are at the same time resigned and yet completely confident of his skill.

The Chief looks at this patient for a long while, mechanically snapping the joints of his fingers—a common gesture of his. When I first saw his big rough hands with their short fingers, I was disappointed, for I had pictured a surgeon's hands as fine and nervous, almost elegant—an artist's hands. But the Chief's hands, in spite of their apparent heaviness, soon revealed themselves even to my inexperienced eyes as capable of the most delicate task they might be called on to perform. They could be strong, supple, exact, sensitive, as the case required. They seemed to me almost intuitive hands, and I realized why in old books the emblem of surgery is an open hand with an eye in the middle of the palm, signifying skill and insight.

Each time the Chief reflects in this way before giving an opinion, I hold my breath. I feel nearly as keyed up and tense as the patient I see in front of him. There is always intense drama in these people coming to consult the Chief, feeling the sword of Damocles over their heads. The patients lying in the wards have already been examined and, as it were, labelled; most of them are mentally submissive to their lot. It is not often that they wear the expressions you see here, or use the pathetic phrases you sometimes hear in the consulting room: "Oh doctor, is it serious? Must I have an operation? What about all my family? I have young children, and they've no one else to look after them but me . . ." "Doctor, I'm in the Civil Service, and I have to do two more years before I can retire. If anything happens to me, what on earth will become of my family? . . ." And one morning the naïve poignancy of this cry: "Please, doctor, you'll save my leg, won't you? I'm twenty years old." This from a lad with sarcoma of the femur, one of the most terrible forms of cancer.

The patient is still standing. The Chief puts a few more questions to him, then says to him in a cheerful voice admitting of no shadow of doubt in the patient's mind: "There's nothing

75

much wrong with you, my friend." I watch the man's reactions. For a moment or two he does not seem to take it in properly; and then all of a sudden the tense look vanishes from his face. It is as if the storm-clouds of suspense have been scattered, and the sun has begun to shine for him once more. Just at first its rays are so powerful he seems dazzled.

But already the Chief has another patient seated in front of him. As for me, I must go back to the ward; for I do not consider myself free till they have come to my Bed 26, and done poor Armand's dressing.

"That patient's bound to get fistulae. The abscesses have spread a good way already." That is what the Chief said three months ago, commenting on Armand's case for our benefit. "A lovely case, it's sure to develop pretty fast." The hopeless gesture which finished the phrase helped to mitigate the impression of scientific brutality left by the words. That same evening I opened my textbook at the chapter on T.B. of the bone.

I read how the tuberculosis slowly eats away and destroys the bone. I pictured the chronic abscesses descending from the vertebrae, following the muscular sheathes down to the pelvis and hips, while the vertebrae themselves disintegrate. I pictured the abscesses compressing the nerves, paralyzing the limbs and stabbing them with agonizing pain. Sooner death any day than this.

The morning after that I saw the young man again. During the morning they were going to put him in plaster, and he was sitting up for the last time for months and months, perhaps forever. He did not seem to be worrying; it was just a nuisance to have to wear this plaster casing for a few weeks at most. He imagined he had a particularly painful and persistent form of lumbago, and he was quite confident he would be cured of it rapidly.

One day, as the Chief had prophesied, an abscess opened and formed a fistula; several others followed after that, and the dressings had to be changed almost every day. The session became increasingly painful for the patient, since to reach his back comfortably he had to be rolled on his side and left like that for a long time. I happened to be there when they did the first dressing. Wanting to make myself useful, I helped to turn the patient on his side, and afterwards held his hands. Standing there in front of him, I could see nothing of what was being done to his back; but every time the dresser hurt him worse than usual, I could feel it myself through a sudden increase in the grip and trembling of his fingers.

The next time it was he who shyly asked me to hold his hands. Since then I have always done it of my own accord, because apparently by my presence I can almost casually save him some suffering. Each time the dressing is changed, I am profoundly stirred by the feel of his thin fingers and moist palms. When the dressing is finished he lets me go free; but before he does so—I don't think I am imagining it—he gives my hand a furtive squeeze of gratitude.

Nobody, of course, allows us first-year men (except Chavasse) to do much on the wards: at most a few intravenous injections and small dressings. But helping Armand in this modest way has changed the whole meaning of my mornings. For the first time I feel sure I can be useful to a patient. Ignorant little squirt of a "first-year foetus" (to use the scornful parlance of the senior students), incapable of doing anything of any medical importance, I can still help. By simply taking a patient's hands in mine, I can relieve his pain. It is a wonderful sensation and gives me an unexpected feeling of power.

Since then I have stopped following the other students when they stroll through the hospital or waste time gossiping together in odd corners of the wards. I prefer to spend any free minutes I have with Armand. I draw confidences from him, I get him to tell me of his life as a newsboy, streaking through Paris bent over the narrow handlebars of his bicycle. I don't stop with Armand, of course; I go to other patients as well. First of all I started talking to those in the next beds, and listened to their life stories. I was startled to find them very like those I had overheard when my mother talked to her clients.

I am quite content with this role every morning. Whatever complaints the patients have, whatever confidences they bring me, I listen and try to understand; and to have a listener seems

77

to give them some relief. Sometimes I think I am almost the only student to do this, and that all the others are only interested in the wound or abscess or fracture. But then I have also noticed that I am shy of talking too familiarly to the patients in the presence of others. So perhaps they are much the same. Through a stupid sort of childish bashfulness or false modesty, they too may be hiding a secret desire to be genuinely kind and good.

This morning it takes a good while before the student dresser and the nurse arrive at Armand's bed, trundling the dressing cart. I am waiting, I sit on the edge of the bed, listening to him talk. "I say, M. Nérac, when I do get to Berck, how soon do you think I'll be really cured? Six months? A year? I shall be much more patient there—but you'll see the difference when I come back. You don't know the Forest of Fontainebleau, do you? I'll get a bike for you, and we'll all go off together some Saturday, you and I and Henriette and two or three of the lads, and boy, you'll see what fun tent life can be. I'll lend you my sleeping bag. Saturday night we can play the harmonica by moonlight, and on Sunday we'll do some rock climbing. You'll be my best man at my wedding, won't you? Promise? That's fine. One of these days you must meet Henriette. They're keeping her busy at the factory just now; and then on Sunday she has to look after her young brothers, so it's two whole weeks now she hasn't been able to come. It's too long."

Every time he feels a little better, as he does now, Armand rediscovers the optimism of his twenty years, and tries to build a bridge between a sport-loving, open-air past, full of week-end cycling and camping, and a future of the same sort plus something extra: his fiancée, whom he met a few months before coming into hospital. I know he has no other "family" but this Henriette, who is obviously spacing her visits more and more, and soon, I expect, will not come at all. She must have guessed the truth and is frightened. Can she really be blamed? Armand always keeps a little suitcase by him, containing all her letters and photos. When I see him taking them out of the case and looking at them one by one, I get the feeling he is trying to

78

deceive himself. He pretends he is no longer in the hospital, but in the middle of a solicitous family, all fussing over him and ministering tenderly to his needs. It must be terrible when he finds himself alone again with heartbreaking reality. To postpone this moment as long as possible, I ask him to tell me again about the time he was a handler at a six-day bicycle race.

From bed to bed the dressing cart comes slowly up. From my vantage point I can see it arriving in front of each patient, and can watch on their faces the intricate reactions provoked by the morning's most painful minutes. I feel that the way a man behaves when his dressing is being changed often shows up his real character. Sometimes, for instance, in flabby jowls or thick lips or a brutish face this test reveals a trace of real nobility which you would never have suspected before. The soul is momentarily stripped bare.

With its jingling bottles the trolley arrives at last at Bed 26. The nurse uncovers Armand's emaciated thighs and wasted calves. He has been having much pain in his heels, and Sister has used one of those very effective little dodges which are as much part of her knowledge as the deeper secrets of nursing. Every morning she puts the peel from half an orange under each of his heels. Consequently when the sheets are removed, the smell is a queer mixture of fruit and antiseptics.

Every day the dressing takes a little longer. Today the dresser seems to be a quite unconscionable time cleaning up the unhealed scabs which chafe the flesh, and changing the tents of gauze and wool which are full of pus from the never-ending fistulae. Armand squeezes my hands. "M. Nérac, please tell me a bit about what's going on. It's not too good, is it?"

"Of course it is. Don't start getting excited. Not being able to move about has set you back a bit. But a breath of sea air in your lungs and all that will soon be gone."

He is silent for a few seconds and then starts groaning softly. "It's no good. I can't stand the smell of that ether. It's turning my stomach. I feel I'm going to pass out." Several times I have to wipe the thick beads of sweat which keep forming on his cheeks and brow.

79

At last it is over. He is once more stretched out on his back. He lies there inert, his eyes closed, with all his strength for the day exhausted. As I try to talk to him, he half opens his eyes with one of those pitiful smiles a patient gives, which say more clearly than words: "Thanks, pal, but please leave me alone now."

It is at moments like these that I feel conscious again of how terribly little I can do. Seeing the nurse and the dresser move away quite serenely to the next bed, I long to acquire as quickly as possible the precious gift of relative insensitivity—since being sensitive seems no help at all.

The corridor is empty, and the clinic hours are almost over. The last patient is stretched out on the table in the "gynae" position. She is a working-class woman in her fifties, and the interne, following the Chief, has been making a vaginal examination. There is blood on his finger-stall when he withdraws it. While he is doing this, the Chief, at a distance from the table, uses the occasion to comment on the case in an undertone: "A probable cancer of the uterus. And it may have gone too far for us to operate. You see the difficult problem this case sets up by developing so insidiously. With so many other infections the organism is amazingly sensitive, whereas with cancer it often remains quiescent right to the last moment. This woman has no pain, she only complains of her general condition. If it hadn't been for a few drops of blood, she wouldn't have come to consult us."

"What a cancer—she's had it," says Chavasse behind me—but very much *sotto voce*, for even he is slightly in awe of the Chief.

Released from the uncomfortable position she has been occupying, the patient gets off the table and comes up to the Chief. He turns and tells her: "I'm afraid you'll have to come into the hospital for a few days." First of all the woman looks as if she did not grasp what has been said. Then a look of horror comes into her eyes, and she almost shouts: "But Doctor, I've nothing wrong with me." She gives a little gasp, and looks round the group, seeking some encouraging look to support her in making this statement. Then she goes on, with an uncertain quaver in her voice: "I only came here as a precaution. Since my change of life I've been losing a little blood, but I don't feel any pain. It can't be serious . . . it can't be serious—can it?" Now she is almost pleading, imploring for reassurance.

"No, Madam, it is not serious at present, but it might become serious. You must come in straight away." Addressing Bougeard, the Chief goes on: "Give her an admission slip for tomorrow"; and finally, turning to the patient again: "Yes, it had better be tomorrow."

His words are spoken with a sternness which at first used to surprise and even shock me. But I have gradually come to realize that this bluntness is really the kindest way of persuading hesitating patients to accept his advice. By adopting an abrupt manner he tries to shake them out of their easy-going attitude and convince them their case is serious, worth coming back for—yet not desperate.

"But I don't feel anything, I don't feel any pain." In her distress the woman repeats this evidence like an affirmation in court. She clings to it as if she were drowning. She feels submerged in a sudden void where nothing comes to the surface but these words, whose meaning none of those round her seems willing to grasp. The Sister urges her gently; she is used to all this and will gradually bring the woman round to the idea of coming into the hospital. In a day or so she will be occupying a bed in one of the women's wards, this poor wretch who unsuspectingly carries her death in her belly like the stone in a fruit.

"All right, gentlemen," says the Chief, "you are dismissed." Almost all the students scatter immediately, running off towards the cloakroom, chasing each other down the corridors in a mood of hilarity and relaxation. It is twelve o'clock.

Sometimes at the end of the morning there is an interesting operation on, and I go to watch it. The Chief is not too keen on the aseptic effect of a crowd of students in the theatre; but at this late hour the few zealous souls remaining are tacitly admitted to the room, providing they keep away from the table, with their hands behind their backs, and only try to follow the instruments working, under the glare of the spotlight, on the little rectangle of scarlet flesh left exposed in the arena of white towels. Spectators as ignorant as we are, and at such a distance from the scene of activity, have practically no chance of seeing or understanding properly what is going on. But what appeals to me is the dazzlingly bare, severe atmosphere, the smell of ether and steam from the sterilizer, the surgeon's cryptic movements, the few abrupt words spoken, and all the mysterious ritual by which new miracles are daily performed here.

My taste for the operating theatre did not, however, prevent me from almost passing out one day when I stayed on alone at the end of the morning to watch the surgeon and Bougeard operating. They were amputating a leg with senile gangrene half way up the thigh. A nurse was holding the leg, which was enveloped in an immense pile of cotton wool as far as the knee. I was standing near her, interested but slightly repelled, watching a huge round incision being made up to the top of the femur. The surgeon then inserted a slab of metal in this gap in the flesh, which enabled him to collect the mass of muscles towards the root of the limb and expose the bone. I felt that the heat of the theatre, always intense, was becoming intolerable, and my ears began buzzing; but I made myself go on watching the butchery in progress.

A moment came when the surgeon needed some instrument which was not to be found on the tray, asked the nurse to get it, and said to me: "Here, you, take the leg for a minute." I seized it, and for a few seconds I stood holding the heavy limb quite rigid as if it might run away from me. My fingers dug deep into the cotton wool on the dressing. The surgeon took up a little saw, and began to manipulate it like a skilled carpenter. You could see the saw going to and fro, biting small splinters off the bone; then the steel came to a thick pulpy mess of powdered bone and blood and marrow, where it could not grind any further. Suddenly there was a dry snapping noise. I was holding the leg with such force that it came away sharply in my hands, soft and unsubstantial, light as a feather. The man now had only a stump.

I remained like this for a few seconds, still grasping the pile of cotton wool; and I realized then that, right from the beginning, instead of holding the leg I had been clinging to the cotton. My head began spinning, I felt I was going to faint, and I wanted to clutch at something before I fell. Once again it was the amputated leg I was clasping convulsively to my breast when the nurse came to my rescue, took it away from me and led me into the corridor for air.

Today, however, when I push the door of the theatre ajar, it is silent and deserted. From the glass ceiling the bluish light falls soothingly on the white room; in the middle of the room stretches the long outline of the operating table, bare and shining. It seems to be waiting, in perfect order, for the next time it will be used.

When I cross the hospital courtyard making for the entrance gate, it is half past twelve. The porter has closed the gates and only opens them if anybody is going out. Outside there is a crowd waiting on the pavement, pressed against the hospital walls. Two steps above the crowd, I look over serried ranks of outspread umbrellas glistening in the rain. From minute to minute the crowd grows, people hurrying towards the hospital. The porter never lets them come in till it is exactly one o'clock, and then you can see them rush through the courts and corridors, eager to reach the beds of their relatives. To be among the first to get in, thus gaining a few minutes extra for their visit, these people often wait patiently in the rain for nearly an hour.

Against the pavements opposite, little carts are drawn up, selling flowers and oranges, sweets and toys. The air all round smells of wet violets; and a toy windmill with red and blue wings turns frantically in the biting wind. Will it turn at all in the stuffy air of a ward for sick children?

Yes, at this crossroads, everything still speaks of the hospital. I feel a familiar superiority to the hushed crowd of patients' rela-

83

tives. I slowly push through the exit and go on my way; yet how much I prefer these wretched little carts to the shining shop windows beyond, with their gay displays for happier folk.

I return by the same way as I came this morning, till I come to the Gare de l'Est, where the crescendo of noise from street and crowd finally pulls me away from my memories of the morning. At last I am out of the narrow circle in which I have been revolving for two or three hours, with its unique horizon of dark walls and endless rows of patients lying in white beds.

A quarter to one. A tram is just leaving for the Latin Quarter. I jump on and remain standing near the door. This is the best position if you want to see everything in the long succession of boulevards that take you to the Seine. They are all varied, animated, full of color, like a huge country fair—even under this grim rainy sky. I love this spectacle; after a heavy morning at the hospital, it brings a wonderful feeling of relaxation; my pleasure in it is constantly renewed.

But I find that medicine has already changed and enriched the world around me, giving new significance to ordinary sights. Everywhere in the streets my eye now discovers new values. First they were anatomical; but then I had only the skeleton to go by and my new discoveries were not very striking, for the only visible bones on the human body are the teeth. But now I have learned where the muscles are. I can begin to watch them moving and living on the bodies of each passer-by. When I see a pretty girl's legs now, I look out for the double heart-shaped muscle of her calf which contracts as she walks; and this evokes the appropriate word: *Gastrocnemius*. Gradually, through the knowledge which comes my way in the consulting room or during the hospital rounds, I have picked up a few ideas on human pathology.

At the entrance to the Gare de l'Est there is an old woman who roams tirelessly among the crowds there, selling pencils. Her eyes are misty and the red lining of their lids turns outwards. When she looks at me, offering me her wares, I think: "A fine ectropion." Of course this is only giving an ordinary name to a phenomenon which anyone can observe, but in this

84

crowd there are other less obvious signs of illness to be caught. I can already recognize the general sallowness and slightly red cheeks of a cardiac case, the prominent temporal vein of an arteriosclerosis, the characteristic bone-structure of acromegalia, and the rolling stare of goiter. I can never see those little brown moles on an old man's face, without thinking now: "Possible cancer: should be removed."

These discoveries increase in number every day, and each new one exhilarates me. I feel like a young savage finding some new weapon. But one morning when I had just learned the significance of different-sized pupils both for diagnosis and for prognosis, a man of about fifty got into the tram just opposite me. I happened to look at his eyes, and noticed that one of the pupils was reduced to a pin-point, while the other was considerably dilated. I was very excited, and would like to have spoken to him. Here was a chance meeting, yet he carried in his eyes the signs of his imminent death; I wanted to warn him but did not know how to—and he got out at the next stop. For several minutes I felt quite upset, then I quieted down. Of course the man must have known for a long time the secret enemy he carried in the marrow of his bones. All the same, I often thought of this encounter as evidence of the fearful insight which medicine would gradually give me.

Chapter 2

HALF PAST ONE. I have bolted some lunch at my usual scruffy little restaurant in the Latin Quarter. A good many people are waiting for an empty place, and mine is immediately taken. I gladly yield to my successor the little bit of space I occupy in front of the paper tablecloth, covered with red circles left from all the wine served since noon. You can usually tell too, as you sit down, what is on the menu here, by the traces of food left on the forks.

After this I have some coffee at a nearby counter, and this marks the end of the midday truce. Next I have to return to the battle. I find the clinging blackish stain at the bottom of my coffee cup somehow symbolic—of the new strength and stamina which this beverage gives me every day. Here I regain my appetite for the long afternoon's work ahead. I would sooner do without my food than miss this coffee.

I reach the main gates of the medical school at a run. There are usually a few people sitting on the old steps at the entrance. But today the courtyard is empty, apart from a few latecomers like myself hurrying towards the Anatomy Wing.

The vast central corridor has already sucked in its hundreds of students, scattering them to right and left; in the dissecting rooms the anatomy classes are about to start—or, in the case of our class, has already started.

The white-coated lecturer, standing on a kind of raised dais, is vigorously sketching on a blackboard the region to be dissected. He rubs out, starts again, rubs out again—and surrounds

86

himself with a rainbow of chalk dust: red for the arteries, brown for the muscles, blue for the veins, and white for the nerves. On his left is a skeleton hanging on a gallows, christened by Chavasse "Captain Carcass." Our cadavers are lying on a long row of tables, and at the side of each an attendant sets out a pan to collect the discarded remains. The scene suggests a table laid for a macabre funeral feast—where the dead are the main dish.

It is very dark today. The rain has started again, and you can hear it pattering down on the frosted glass ceiling, which admits only a very niggardly light. On the side opposite the windows it is almost like night, and the whole row of students begins chanting in rhythmic chorus: "We want lights, we want lights." Eventually four strong bulbs are lit above each table. Near the windows the cadavers have a deep pallor, and the lights make them look all yellow, producing queer effects quite different from their normal appearance. Lit up in this way, the bodies are all that can be seen, and we ourselves fade into the shadows like supers in a play.

They are just about finished, these twenty-five cadavers, which were delivered to us in one piece two months earlier. They are old friends now. They have given us good service and let us take all manner of liberties with them.

We work in small groups. One group has cut off the legs of their subject (to give the cadaver his most respectable title) between the top of the tibias and the bottom of the femur, which are now mere stumps; the odd sections of leg and half-carved-up joints remain abandoned on the corners of the table from one session to the next. Meanwhile those dissecting the upper limbs keep the arms stretched out from the thorax in the shape of a cross, slipping a board under them and then nailing the fingers down to it, one by one. Curiously enough, the thought has not struck me till today, but each of the cadavers, in its small circle of light, looks like a poor wretch who has been crucified. There the victim lies with outstretched arms while we, the executioners, pierce his hands and break his feet and are now proceeding to count his bones, one by one.

After two months I have quite stopped seeing in these bodies any resemblance to the human beings they once were. It did not need two months, of course; a single hour did the trick. You had only to make your first incision in the skin, reach the yellowish fat, and cut off a few muscle ends; and before many minutes had passed, any sensitiveness you might have felt as to the technique employed in the noble art of dissection had pretty well vanished.

Four months ago when we arrived at the Anatomy Wing for the beginning of term, we rushed to this tall dark hall, hoping to find bodies. Instead, all we saw under the light from the frosted glass ceilings were collections of bones hanging from brackets by little steel chains. At the entrance to the hall an attendant was giving out a humerus, which had been painted red; this seemed odd to us, but he explained that the coloring was to prevent theft. Near the lecturer's chair "Captain Carcass" was swinging gently round, and Chavasse gave voice to the general disillusionment by crying mournfully: "Only bones, dry old bones!"

Until Christmas we amused ourselves with these bones. We played the drum on the tables with the tibias, we played knucklebones with the vertebrae, we fenced with the femurs, and we used the brain-pans as ashtrays. The scalpels meanwhile, all oiled and sharpened, remained in their cases. It seemed like a mere continuation of the zoology classes of our Intermediate year. A great effort of the imagination was needed to see these red bones as having once formed part of a living human body. They had as much polish from continual use as a collection of ivories. We were eager to get going on real cadavers.

The more impatient spirits attempted, though without success, to bribe the attendant who looked after the embalming room where the cadavers were stored. And Chavasse naturally found a way of accompanying one of the anatomy demonstrators to that room. We were all rather intrigued by this mysterious word "embalming." When Chavasse came back, he looked a little pale, but he savored his advantage for a while, and we had to plead with him before he would talk.

"Hush now, my children. You want to know how the pick-

88

ling is done? Well, I wouldn't mind telling you, only I'd rather not offend your sensitive stomachs."

"Go on, don't be a fool. You're dying to tell us."

"All right then, I'll tell you. Here goes. In civilian life, when a man's dead, he should be able to say to himself: 'Alone at last, three cheers for my return to the soil.' Here it's exactly the opposite; he joins a community in a tank. In a room as cheerful as this one, only smaller, I saw some very wide marble tables. On them laid out two by two, to keep each other company, are the cadavers, very pale and well-behaved and parallel. They talk about the dignity of death—well, these stiffs are dead all right, but they certainly aren't dignified. Men and women, naked, all mixed up together, absolutely unimportant, nobody worrying about them at all. Above each corpse hangs a huge glass funnel with a rubber tube at the end. This tube goes down into the thigh or the neck or even straight into the chest through a crack kept open by a wooden wedge. Through this tube they swallow about five pints of the best phenol from the vat. Finally, at the end of a few days, they're whisked behind a glass partition, and there they are set out on exhibition. My friends, what a sight is there! Fifty stiffs on a huge bar, all a ghastly chalky white. It's a bit of a cliché to say 'deathly white,' but it really has some meaning for me now.

"The exhibition is to find out if the pickling process has been successful. If it has, the attendant told me, you go on to the entankment. And he showed me some big iron tanks with stocks of corpses floating on their backs in filthy brown water—quite revolting. But that's not the most disgusting thing. The worst is what I saw on the ground in a corner of the room. A great bloody heap of feet and hands and heads and arms, only you can't really recognize any of them in that incredible pile. It's more like a heap of rotting meat, all gray and shrivelled and mouldy. It's awful—even some big fat juicy worms making a meal in the pile would add a little gaiety. But no, nothing moves at all. You've only got this awful nameless Thing, like the leftovers from a cannibal feast. And guess how the Thing is used —oh no, none of it is wasted. The attendant told me how he salvages the bones, scrapes and polishes them, and then they are sold to students, not quite a complete set but presentable enough, as the bones of skeletons. And the unusable scrapings he heaps up in the coffins, and off they go to the dump, with the sawdust and cigarette ends, old papers, orange peel, and so on from the floor. A fine system combining garbage and eternal rest. My God, these poor bloody stiffs, they deserve a bit of peace at the end of all that, a chance to return to the dust like anyone else."

My neighbor, Souléry, a fair-haired and somewhat affected youth with a taste for poetry, felt obliged, in sympathy, to provide a doleful echo in verse:

The dead who in their tombs must bleed
Will find their vengeance sweet indeed.
And when it comes, ah pity those
Who fall beneath their awful blows.

"Oh, do you think so?" said Chavasse, momentarily impressed. "I don't know, though. The attendant didn't seem worried. He was wielding a mean shovel, and filled a whole coffin in front of me. After all, what chance would you have on judgment day if you were a cadaver sawn up into such small pieces? It looks like they're all boxed up and no chance of a come-back."

"But are they real coffins?" asked someone.

"They are regulation model real deal coffins, in the shape of an elongated hexagon, respectfully based on the shape of the human body, but chock full of shapeless carrion, a hash made up of four or five corpses in portions handy for shovelling. It certainly makes a queer impression. You feel a coffin is the wrong receptacle; a refuse bin would be more appropriate. And that's what is officially called the 'Embalming Room.'"

"How perfectly horrible!" said Souléry in a shocked voice. "Up till today, when anyone talked to me about embalming, I imagined millionaires or kings who wanted to die as grandly and expensively as possible. Or else I thought of pyramids and mummies and myrrh and aloes—the sort of thing you get in Théophile Gautier, or Cocteau for that matter:

90

Your dream is ancient Egypt, and yourself
Are now the Mummy with its golden mask . . .

With these tales of garbage-pail coffins, you're destroying all my fine illusions."

"And to think," said someone else, "how for a single corpse in a black hearse, trams stop, the police give a military salute, passers-by raise their hats carefully, and everybody with any sort of physical complaint immediately feels quite ill."

"Oh well," admitted Chavasse, "I must give the old school its due. I saw a good mummy, if you'll forgive my Freudian language, floating about in the tank, and they treated her very sympathetically. If you feel like having fun and games with her, Souléry, just slip the attendant ten francs from me, and he'll show her to you. For that sum he took me round the whole of his waxworks. He led me into a vaulted cavern which looked like an old dungeon. He turned on a light, which shone rather dimly, and then plunged his whole arms into a huge tank and started foraging; he couldn't really see anything in it, the water was too filthy. Then he said: 'Hooray, I've got her,' and after separating the limbs he brought a cadaver up to the surface, saying: 'Isn't she beautiful?' He held the body above the water and went on repeating: 'Isn't she beautiful?' as if he were offering me his daughter in marriage. And the funny thing is, she *was* rather beautiful. She had a pretty little blond head, and a shapely girlish body. But so incredibly white, a real snow maiden, almost a milkmaid if you see what I mean."

Souléry, still somewhat stunned by these macabre details, groaned.

"Well frankly, it was a pretty awful sight, the black dungeon, the white girl and the filthy water," Chavasse went on. "The attendant wouldn't let me go, he showed me the whole chamber of horrors: the head of a guillotined Arab, with jaw and skullbone sliced off by the blade; the skeleton family, with Pa and Ma upright against a wall and Sonny Boy squatting at their feet; mere brown bones with a tiny piece of withered flesh round them. They have been there at least a hundred years. And then there are the foetuses and new-born babes in a tub. One is a hydrocephalus, with a huge head like a pumpkin and a body like a spider; blind too, with a hare's nose and web-feet. I'd had just about all I could take. I tipped him again and then scrammed."

"Sure you're not exaggerating a tiny bit?"

"Go and ask the Dean for a visiting permit, and if I've not been telling the naked, unvarnished truth, I'll stand the whole room a pint. But it really doesn't need any embellishment, it's quite enough as it is."

During the next few days several of the boys went on the prowl to the Embalming Wing. They found the door locked, but by standing on the window sills they managed to see the long rows of marble tables on which side by side, in pairs, the cadavers were getting their dose of phenol. The attendant saw them, came out laughing, and brought them inside. He was used to this. Through bashfulness, feigning indifference, I had not dared follow them; but one evening after the lecture had ended, when it was already getting dark, I went up to the windows, climbed onto the ledge, and over the top of the frosted glass saw the extraordinary spectacle Chavasse had described.

In the midst of his corpses the attendant was sluicing the floors and marble slabs, keeping an eye on the tanks, checking the embalming. I could not tear myself away from that window. Motionless, my eyes glued to the glass, I stayed there a long time, watching the man in overalls working away among his subjects with the patient calm of the surgeons I saw operating in the mornings. This double row of cadavers certainly had something terrible about it, but the horror of the spectacle was perhaps less overpowering than the thought of having one day to get used to it, just as the attendant had done . . .

When I left the window, night had fallen; the courts and corridors were dark and silent. As I passed in front of the big amphitheatre with its lecture halls, the doors were pushed open abruptly, and onto the circular balcony poured a crowd of students, jostling each other, laughing, shouting. They were talking physiology, and were evidently in their second year;

their care-free light-heartedness was so obvious that I felt a sudden desire to be like them without delay.

I left the school. Outside its gates people went by with no inkling of the horrible things going on behind these walls, not fifty yards away. Further on, near the Boulevard Saint-Michel, I passed groups of noisy students of my own age, who were probably just starting law or science or some arts course. Here in the Latin Quarter was the center of the intellectual life of France. The university students were mixed with the senior *alumni* of the best Paris schools in their gay colored caps, smoking pipes to mark their emancipation, and chanting their dirty songs defiantly with guileless cynicism. Like me, their sensitiveness had not yet been too much blunted, and they felt powerfully the call of happiness. They too were at that uncertain, confusing age at the end of adolescence when the world is full of marvellous new experiences. But it also brings out things in yourself and the world that are difficult to understand.

For all their bravado these boys would gain their experience of life very slowly, and much of it from books at that. Like their elders, I thought watching them, they would only learn bit by bit and by experience that man was a low creature, terrifyingly low. Whereas I, each morning at hospital, was being given brutal training in life's bitter realities.

Soon I should know intimately this body poets sing of, this body men wear out without understanding. Heart and brain, eyes and lips, do not always mean love and thoughts, looks and kisses, when you have once held in your hand the brown musclebound heart, the white cake of the brain, the shell of a shrivelled eye, a corpse's snub-nosed grin. Among all these youngsters of my own age, soon I alone should have had my baptism in knowledge of all a man is in body as well as soul. I felt an immense pride to be walking near them with all my newly discovered secrets. There was a savage exultant joy in my heart, which I savored the more because I knew it was deeply tinged with despair.

For a long time I walked on in the crowd. I was just starting

93

out on my way of life to which I was already deeply committed, which would separate me from most other men. It was in a way depressing to realize that I should never again be free from care, as these my contemporaries were now. Yet on this dismal November evening, smelling of soot and fog, I felt in my heart a mixture of anguish and glorious exhilaration, which I would not for worlds have been without.

The presence of Chavasse makes our corner of the room a center of attraction. When he is not strolling round himself, people come to visit him from other tables, to hear new stories and hospital gossip, or perhaps some definitions out of a humorous Dictionary of Medicine which he knows much more intimately than our textbooks. For him the occiput is "the Head's Behind," the socket of the eye is always "Eyeball Inn," the pubis is "Mount Venereal" and the penis is "Piddlewell Point."

He is in high good humor today, having invented a scheme— we have heard this five times already—for making a useful profit out of failing one's exams. "Two months before the exam, I choose a hotel, as noisy as possible, and move there. In due course I present myself for the papers, and as there is no justice in the world I shall probably flunk out, whereupon I shall immediately sue the manager for damages plus interest. Charge: the disorderly conduct at his hotel stopped me working for my exam."

"How will you prove it?" someone asks.

"Oh, I'll have the clerk of the court go there first, of course, to certify that the noise is intolerable."

By general agreement it is deemed a good idea.

As long as his patriotic prejudices aren't aroused, Chavasse's humor is good-natured, and it certainly adds little touches of brightness to dreary and monotonous days. Each time he does or says something to make us laugh, it gives us the momentary illusion of being happy. And this may seem simple enough when we are all together; but when we are once more on our own, beset by all manner of weaknesses and worries, then weariness and despondency begin to work on each of us singly. To escape

94

their onslaught, we have all invented some sort of special antidote.

There are antidotes even for the sharpest crises. My friend Manenc, for instance, left the hospital one morning even more sickened than I was after my first post-mortem. He had just watched the P.M. of an eighteen-year-old girl with a terrible hereditary syphilis, who had died after a fortnight's illness in one of Manenc's two beds. Her death agony had lasted forty-eight hours, during which she had groaned and shrieked, struggling between the bars of a cradle bed. Her liver, with a trace of treponema, could have been interesting, so the doctor asked for a post-mortem. Manenc went along with the interne. Having experienced the same thing myself, I can well understand his horror before the thin body with its abdomen hideously swollen. His dead girl was only eighteen years old, and he had followed each dreadful phase of her last agonies.

But when he told me of the scene he admitted that the most grisly thing of all was having to undress her. Trying to remove her underclothes, he could not get off a pair of knickers which had a dark stain spreading over them. Eventually they came away, tearing in the process and revealing the source of the brown matter discharging, which was like decayed blood. Manenc came out of this session overcome with revulsion, but his distress of mind was so much greater than his physical disgust that he went straight to the nearest wine-merchant and bought a bottle of champagne. Returning to his room, he removed the cork and solemnly drank down the whole bottle, after which he lay on his bed, completely out. At least he was sure of thinking of nothing at all for several hours, which would allow time for him to forget a bit and recover his composure. He had chosen a good dry champagne so as to have no hangover. This kind of moral anaesthetic must be rather exceptional, and I can't say I have ever used it myself.

A far commoner antidote is to hurl yourself frenziedly into your work. Some from ambition, and others merely to forget everything else, will resolutely avoid thinking of anything but future examinations and degrees. At Chavasse's table there are two rather overgrown youngsters, shy, pimply and self-effacing. They are dissecting the lower limbs and show no concern at all for anything happening in the rest of the room. In the first weeks everything bewildered them. They were scared of Chavasse's exuberance, and upset by the coarse songs; the first dissections left them utterly nonplussed. What saved them from this nightmare, as it has saved me too at times, was to be nothing but a brain buzzing with medical and anatomical problems; and also to be obliged to work with their hands. By concentrating on their work they stopped seeing it as an abnormal and revolting chore and found it a game of skill, capable of bringing as much satisfaction as an experiment in chemistry or the solution of an abstruse geometrical problem. Work is now their impenetrable protective shell, and all through the session I hear them reciting at each other whole pages of anatomy—in an undertone, so as not to annoy Chavasse.

In view of this discretion on their part, Chavasse is content to ignore them. Though when he does happen to speak to such nonentities he affects to forget their names. He never calls them Claveau or Laroche but attracts their attention with a contemptuous, indiscriminate "Hey!"

Some of the other youths came here with special outside interests and hobbies which are still very effective in taking their minds off too much medicine. Thomassin, for instance, lives in a long syncopated jazz dream. Daviel has a nice tenor voice and hums away softly all day like a painter on a ladder. Souléry of course soaks himself in poetry. He is doing his medicine reluctantly and only to succeed his father in some provincial practice. While awaiting his unhappy fate he drinks expensive *apéritifs* in Montmartre cafés and rubs shoulders with the contemporary intelligentsia, and he tells us daily of all the celebrities he has recognized. Often he will recite for our benefit some of their poetry, with which he incorporates a good deal of his own work.

In four months Souléry's poetry has taken on a distinctly specialized quality. First of all it was osteological, at the time when we were dealing with the skeleton:

96

> . . . *Vertebral column, O rosary of bone*
> *Whose beads can ne'er be told . . .*

or else

> *O tree of bones made to the body's measure . . .*
> *O tree of bones that walks and jumps and dances . . .*

He tries to imbue his work with original poetic value, but its greatest merit is doubtless in allaying the depression he feels at our incursions into dead bodies. Perhaps, in fact, he has escaped from the cruel realities of the sensory world, and no longer sees the white-bearded old man he is dissecting. Among the intricacies of the flesh, he is too deeply absorbed in chasing metaphysical metaphors and similes. Whereas at first he almost swooned at the sight of all these cadavers, dissection—and the whole mortuary scene—has now become almost a staple diet for his muse.

Chavasse made a few attempts to have this esoteric surrealism explained to him, but soon gave it up. Today, while he was punning away on the heart, that "left-wing organ," he scarcely uttered a protest on hearing Souléry's joyful anticipation of the forthcoming opening of their common cadaver's thorax:

> *Let me decipher with this scalpel's art*
> *A dead name on the pillars of the heart.*

A somewhat peculiar hope, but we have heard much worse from our poet, and Chavasse went on with his puns. Souléry continued to declaim, while passing a slightly greasy hand through his fair hair with an elegant and quite undisgusted gesture.

Then there are the three Indo-Chinese students. I have long since given up all attempts to fathom what goes on in their minds. I suppose there may be daemonic forces hidden behind their smooth façades, but I cannot imagine what, unless as Chavasse affirms it is the dream of national independence. With Nerovici, on the other hand, I find it simple enough. He has the stubborn, invincible optimism of his race, and as he can work night and day himself without warmth or affection or cheerfulness, perhaps his tired eyes scarcely see the depressing scene all round. To keep up his courage, to heal every wound to his pride, all he need do is think of his mother and behind her the centuries of tortures and insults and humiliations. And then he can imagine the brilliant revenge which a little Rumanian Jewish student, by sheer hard work, will one day take on all the world's Chavasses.

Our five neighbors, the "Boys from Burgundy," are temperamentally allergic to such deep spiritual considerations, and they would laugh heartily if you talked about their "vocation for medicine." In fact they are doing medicine because their parents, rich Burgundian winegrowers, have advised them to choose a career which pays, and which in five years time will bring them back to the paternal vineyards. In any case, if their patients don't bring in enough income, the vineyards will, and so, doctor-winegrowers to be, they carry on their medical studies with a happy complacency natural to the scions of a prosperous countryside. They are close friends, with most of their tastes in common; both at hospital and in the medical school you hardly ever see them apart. They each have their own specialties. Robertot has a wonderful head for alcohol, Lecourt is fond of puns, Jeannel is *the* bridge expert, and Bourgeot, by blowing against his thumb, can give superb imitations of a hunting horn, a weeping calf, or a pig having its throat cut.

As to Barrière, he is the Great Lover; that is practically all he thinks of. He seems to suffer from a perpetual erection, and to secrete semen as copiously as saliva. I have never met anyone of his age with such potency in this field or who applies himself to its exploitation with such methodical concentration. By his own account he is constantly on the watch for an opportunity, any chance encounter; exploring the pavements, the Metro, the buses, with the persistence of a beggar, going from one girl to another, and engagingly suggesting to each—like a vacuum cleaner salesman knocking at every door: "How about a little loving? I'm sure you'd like a roll in the hay." He sets great store by his personal theory of speedy love: "It's in, it's out, you clean up." For he has no time to waste on any one girl when there are dozens of others ready and waiting. Obviously he is not interested in virtuous women, but his seduction figures are certainly impressive. He can never get rid of one woman quickly enough before dashing off to the next. His compulsive impatience in this respect is almost pathological. Each pretty girl he passes in the street must momentarily symbolize for him the whole species. The whole female sex is beckoning him, has got him by the short hairs, as he declares. How can he possibly resist them?

His conversation has a cheerful bawdy vitality, quite lacking in self-consciousness or affectation; he disdains euphemisms. Yet I do not feel embarrassed to hear him announce: "I'm going to pick one up this evening. I need to have a clear out." All the words and phrases he uses convey admirably his ingenuous and functional conception of love; and this unsophisticated attitude is somehow rather disarming. It did not prevent him, however, from having his second dose of gonorrhoea while three of the other Burgundy boys were having it for the first time. Jeannel had the inexplicable good luck to escape this epidemic, which occurred about two months ago.

Chavasse smelled out almost immediately where the trouble lay, but Lecourt hesitated a long while before admitting very dolefully: "I really think I've got it." Chavasse was consoling: "I'm not surprised. You always had a flair for that sort of thing."

The next day Bourgeot, Robertot, and Barrière also looked very pale when they arrived, and Jeannel spent that afternoon and the next few days in frequent visits to the lavatory to make sure he too was not developing something. He really seemed more worried than the others, and he found this uncertainty extremely wearing. Chavasse, of course, tormented them ceaselessly.

"How touching it is, this genito-urinary fraternity! I wonder what developments there will be in your grand game of gono-poker. Perhaps one of you will have a straight venereal flush, or even a full house with syph as well. In a few years' time you'll be taking your prostates to special massage parties. What a happy souvenir for your old age. Of course it's very important for a doctor to get as much personal experience as possible."

During this time the Boys from Burgundy tried to find out the source of the epidemic afflicting them all. But as they were very communistic and very changeable in love, they never reached complete certainty on this point. Morning and night they would gather in Barrière's room, he being the expert, for the mutual strengthening of morale, and there they would sit round a basin, administering permanganate washes to one another.

For us as their neighbors this epidemic was quite useful. Through talking about it for four weeks, we now have very definite ideas on gonorrhoea, on the merits of arsenic, bismuth, or permanganate as preventive treatments. Chavasse quotes with authority the works of Professor Janet who predicts that there may soon be a vaccination or cure for it, a consummation devoutly to be wished.

A little learning of pathology can in one respect be a dangerous thing: in four months we have all become confirmed hypochrondriacs. Any slight ulceration of the lips is bound to turn into a chancre. That pain in the knee is obviously a symptom of a tubercular white swelling, that stitch in the side also means tuberculosis in its early stages—we shall soon be in a sanitarium. After a boil we have all watched for the first signs of a perinephritic phlegmon. This hypochondria is apparently a well-known characteristic of the early days of medical studies; but for poor Bellienaz it reaches a positive frenzy of fear, and for four months his life has been one long torment—carefully fostered by Chavasse and the Burgundy boys.

All day long Bellienaz feels himself, palpates himself, gives himself a thorough examination, with rigid eyes and contorted features. I have already known him to suffer from, in order of their appearance, tuberculosis of the kidneys, cancer of the kidneys, sarcoma of the femur, dolichocolon, glaucoma, dry pleurisy and a tumor of the brain. He has already had done on himself all possible tests of blood and urine; they have X-rayed his lungs, his thigh, his intestines; they have examined his eyes; he has not dared to ask for a trephining, and as a second best he contents himself with keeping a close watch on his pulse. Last week he had feverish aches; he is sure he has made a miraculous escape from infantile paralysis (it is his third miraculous escape from this illness alone).

At the hospital Bellienaz protects himself with gloves and an apron even when he turns a doorknob. As soon as he has touched a patient, he dashes for a bottle of strong disinfectant. He is panicstricken by the idea of contagion. Chavasse collects for his benefit the most terrifying stories of epidemics traveling from Berlin to Paris in twenty-four hours; of the imperceptible scales of scarlet-fever which are enough to spread the illness to any distance even through a letter; and of microbes lurking for years inside carpets and floorboards.

Making the best of a bad job, Bellienaz has all his handkerchiefs saturated with eucalyptus. Every now and then he brings out of his pocket a little brandy flask, rolls a mouthful of it round his mouth, gargles with it and then swallows it. Chavasse, who calls this gargle "the leper's kiss," promises him an alcoholic cirrhosis before he has taken his finals. But Bellienaz has never been quite so worried as he was during the Burgundy boys' gonorrhoea. Chavasse began preparing the ground by referring to the extreme contagiousness of the gonococcus; your eye need only be touched by some contaminated object, by fingers, for instance, or a towel—and in a flash you could be doomed to purulent ophthalmia, or worse. The blind you see begging at church doors have very often, according to Chavasse, done no more than that.

Following these preliminaries, the Burgundians approach Bellienaz about twenty times during each dissecting session. Sometimes they discover dust on his eyelashes, and reach out a finger to remove this, amiably insisting despite his frightened protests. At other times they borrow a book from him, read a few pages while blandly fiddling with their fly-buttons, and then return it to him at the very moment when he has just taken off his gloves. He looks then as if they are offering him a snake, and I believe he might really fall ill had they not finally decided they are cured.

Bellienaz has never been able to explain to me why he chose medicine in the first place. I suppose he may have yielded to some morbid fascination; and if this is right, the more terrifying the prospects, the more irresistible would be the fatal attraction. In the same way someone learning to bicycle will dash towards the very obstacle he wishes to avoid. Or it may be that Bellienaz regards the world as one vast realm of dealers in death, divided into the noble caste of doctors and the "untouchable" patients. In this case he has perhaps chosen to be a doctor in the hope of participating in some special immunity, or at least of learning very rapidly how to acquire it.

The only place in the world where he is at ease is the operating theatre. To live as much as possible in this comforting little aseptic universe, Bellienaz has made up his mind to become, eventually, a surgeon. Chavasse says he can imagine him as one very easily, living on the job, continually wiping himself clean with antiseptic swabs, subsisting on thoroughly boiled eggs as his main diet, drinking nothing but pure alcohol, and dressed in completely sterile white linen.

Philippon, who dissects near Bellienaz, somewhat dismays me, though he has quite an attractive face and personality. He is usually smiling and is plainly the type who does not take himself or life too seriously. He claims to know many doctors in good practices, men with plenty of experience, who have provided him with much relevant information as to the requirements for a successful medical career. Here are his figures for the qualities needed: living quarters and staff, 25%; sartorial elegance, 25%; car 20%; natural presence 14%; discretion 10%; bedside manner 4.5%; medical degrees etc., 1%; medical knowledge 0.5%.

Fortified by his knowledge of these prime factors, Philippon treats anatomy, histology, and even the hospital with an amiably off-hand air (0.5%); nor evidently is he much concerned with higher medical degrees (1%). On the more basic qualities of personal presence, discretion, bedside manner, he has nothing to learn. He already gives careful attention to his sartorial standards; his trousers always look freshly pressed, and his suits are impeccable. Already too he has a fine sports car, which is often standing waiting outside the scenes of his practical labors; in it is his girl friend, an elegant young lady, elaborately made up, who poses for fashion advertisements and magazines.

Where he gets his money from is rather more mysterious. According to malicious gossip he is a bit of a pimp, while some even assert that he is not afraid of practicing abortion; but Chavasse, who knows him fairly well, declares that he is a genius at bridge, a very competent backer of horses, and does a bit of business in the second-hand car racket. Last week, under the seal of secrecy, Chavasse told me about one of his transactions.

Philippon, it seems, bought a splendid American car fairly cheap, drove it around for a few days, and then decided to resell it. Evidently he had for once been cheated; a cylinder head was cracked, and the garages wouldn't even look at the car. Philippon reflected; he found such a dead loss intolerable. So he took a heroic decision—an accident covered by the insurance. To arrange his collision he went out with the car one day fairly early in the morning, and parked it in a small road coming out onto a busy street at the corner of which a friend was posted. This friend suddenly lifted his hat, the agreed signal. Philippon stepped on the gas and came out into the street at full speed, just in time to see a huge truck loaded with paving stones hurtling down on him. This was more than he had bargained for, and he braked, swerving as much as he could; the truck did the same, but carried by sheer weight, could not avoid ramming the car. Philippon was extracted suffering from shock but otherwise unhurt; and as the truck appeared to be on the wrong side of the road the insurance paid up. Telling me of this exploit, Chavasse was at first highly enthusiastic: "Pretty good luck, eh? His pal might have chosen something better to collide with; he might have been killed. He's certainly got guts, has Philippon." But after a moment's reflection he qualified his admiration, saying: "Just the same, I think that was going too far. He's a bit of a crook, don't you think?"

I certainly did.

The last at that table is Villecroze, and I do not care for him either. I far prefer the blunt obscenities of the five Burgundians to Villecroze's Don Juanesque tales. He is dark and handsome, and thinks himself a regular Adonis, quite irresistible in love. His specialty is schoolgirls, we gather; none of them can resist him. Between two cigarettes he will describe his methods with coarse satisfaction to anyone willing to listen.

But the most disturbing personality of all is that of Jules Bellot, commonly known as Julot. He is supposed to do his dissection at the other end of the room, and he chose a table near the door, so as to be able to get away quickly. As soon as it is near three o'clock, he takes off his overalls and is ready to go; it only needs his derby hat to complete the long black silhouette. But without it you can see better his faunlike goatee, his jutting cheekbones, green eyes and long pointed ears. His clothes are quite unsuitable to his age, and he makes no concessions to style: wing-collar, black tie with a gold tiepin, tightly cut jacket with no padding, trousers narrow and very short. In this, his customary get-up, he looks like a cross between a process server and an undertaker.

I did not need to go to his table to find out that this legendary figure comes from Rouen, where, ever since he was fifteen, he has been on intimate terms with every prostitute, procuress and pimp in the town. He has a room at the Cité Universitaire, but you never see him there, for he has chosen as his second residence the area round the Boulevard Barbès; partly because it is near the hospital where he is doing his clinical, but more for a special nightclub near there which his Rouen associates had recommended to him. He soon became disgusted with this house, however, which he finds far too respectable, and he prefers exploring the brothels of the rue de la Charbonnière, the shady small hotels near the Gare du Nord, certain arches under railway bridges, and some low dives where he claims to have found marvellous bargains. He has been involved in several brawls and acquitted himself in them very creditably. This is not surprising, for beneath his ill-fitting clothes he conceals some powerful

104

muscles. Indeed he has a disconcerting habit of doing alarming acrobatics with the stools on entering the dissecting rooms— with his hat still plunged firmly on his head.

Julot is very willing to tell us about his nocturnal adventures, which are well-studded with obscene details. What I most object to is his almost obsessional eroticism, far exceeding the traditional pose of student bawdiness.

Chavasse has not seen Julot come up. If he had, he would have greeted him, as usual, with a barrage of insults: "Hallo there, you walking penis, you two-legged phallus." But for the moment Chavasse is busy watching the two girls who are dissecting next to each other four tables away from ours. He is enamored of one of them, who is very pretty, but at present it is the other he is concerned with. She is an extremely plain girl with large spectacles perched on a nose which always seems pointed towards her cadaver, so that it looks as if she were wanting to sniff it. Because of her short-sightedness she gets so close to it that Chavasse has christened her "Mlle. Cannibal."

In general, except when they are really very pretty, Chavasse detests women doctors almost as much as he detests foreigners; he feels they are trying to break into a typically masculine profession and thus usurp the prerogatives of the male.

A few days ago some joker cut off the penis of the two girls' cadaver at the level of the pubis. Chavasse first of all accused Mlle. Cannibal of having nibbled it off by mistake. Since then he must have found this version too moderate, for today he asserts that he saw her cutting it off and slipping it into her handbag to take home. With the best will in the world, some of us protest, we do not find this plausible; but Chavasse claims to have had absolute corroboration from the anatomy attendants.

"Just ask Paul, the one with a curly moustache and a slight limp. He'll tell you a few things. Hardly a year goes by apparently without his finding one or two girls emasculating their stiff. They're like the voluntary nurses during the war; just can't control themselves any longer. Besides, all the girls who do medicine are more or less perverted; otherwise what would be the use of their spending five years as students merely to learn to produce children? For of course they all end up, even the dowdiest of them, by hooking some poor devil and marrying him."

"Nothing very unusual there; quite commonplace, in fact," says Julot behind me—he has passed from table to table and eventually reached ours. "Ask in the library for Epaulard's treatise, Lyon, 1901. You can read plenty of similar cases there. Mlle. Cannibal combines necro-sadism, necrophagy, and active necrophilia, alias vampirism. It's nothing like as good as the cases of Blot, Bertrand, or Ardisson, but it's not a bad beginning, all the same."

By now we have all turned to look at the alleged vampire; from our table she can be seen half buried in her corpse, her concentration making her even plainer than usual. We all burst out laughing at the idea of her committing the abominable vices suggested by Chavasse, to which Julot has added such artistic verisimilitude. It is really too hilarious. Bourgeot, still shaking with laughter, asks for further details about the said M. Blot.

"He disinterred bodies in cemeteries and then violated them. But he was a sensitive spirit: he didn't want to get his clothes dirty so he placed some sheets of white paper taken from the cemetery wreaths under his knees. You can imagine the scene, can't you? The tombs, the black cypresses, the pale moon, the whiteness of the paper on the freshly dug soil, the open coffin, the dead girl half . . ."

"For Heaven's sake, shut up," screams Souléry.

"What's the mater with *you?* You don't like vampirism in prose? You prefer it in Baudelaire.

> *Yet shall no worms' cold kisses there*
> *Devour you, till these lips of mine*
> *Have kissed your form and being divine,*
> *My decomposing fair.*

Just think of the magistrate's face if Blot had declaimed this in court. It's quite relevant, as a matter of fact, to what he did tell the magistrate: What can one do about it, your Honor? We all have our passions, and mine is corpses."

Souléry tries to concentrate on his own corpse, but Julot goes on placidly: "The trouble with you is, you have no scientific objectivity. Death is aphrodisiac, everyone knows that. Put a male pigeon in a cage with a dead female pigeon; he'll try to lie on her. After all vampirism is only a matter of opportunity and temptation."

"Temptation? You think there's a temptation?" Even Chavasse seemed somewhat shocked.

"Keep calm. You'll agree that if Mlle. Cannibal hadn't a corpse here at her disposition she wouldn't have gone out at night to disinter one in a cemetery. And if you'd read Krafft-Ebing, you fastidious fellow, you'd know too that one of the preparatory stages for necrophilia is the sexual attraction roused by physical abnormality: like people who only fall for hunchbacks or eskimos. Oh yes, and I assure you the one-legged pro who hobbles about every evening at the corner of the rue Blondel does a fair trade. Now you, I believe, have a weakness for redheads. That's a tendency along the same lines already; how do you know you may not have your bottom on the slippery slope that leads to vampirism. Don't you see, man: when you take advantage of a screen to pinch the behind of some ginger-haired nurse, a few feet away from a dying man, or when you've seen two or three chaps die in a morning, and rush after a carroty girl immediately you leave the hospital—that's the beginning of necrophilia, still platonic and almost physiological. It's Nature wanting to make up the losses of the morning, tickling your guts to make you want to have a go. That's her method of re-establishing equilibrium and balance in the farmyard. Once you find this stage agreeable, there's nothing to stop you going on. You've got all that's needed here, right under your hand."

"Why don't you try it yourself?" suggests Chavasse.

Putting on his most artless air, Julot replies: "Suppose I have already?"

But as Souléry exclaims, "You're crazy," Julot adds before

getting up: "Well, I might one day—but it's not really for me. In any case, I'm not bothered about what goes on inside me. I just follow the mood of the moment. We all have our secret vices."

Julot gets up and saunters away calmly. There is a moment's silence as we watch his long black figure disappearing, looking more like an undertaker than ever. Claveau and Laroche look dismayed.

Chavasse sums up: "Oh, he talks big, but I wouldn't put that quite past him. What a dirty pig, though. I think I can claim not to be a prude . . ."

There is a murmur of assent at this.

". . . but the amount of filth even I can take is limited. Let him spout that stuff at you for ten minutes and you're sunk. When you get home, you don't feel you can kiss your own mother. Talk about people with minds like sewers."

Nearly every session, in the course of his strolls round the room, Julot tries to provide Chavasse's sexual empiricism with rigorous scientific foundations. He has already given us a summary of Freud's theories, and explained how chastity can produce deep repressions, conflicts, phobias and psychoses. Up to this point Chavasse agrees with him, but his good sense rebels when Julot recommends unlimited sexual license to avoid these neuroses. This would mean indulging, where necessary, the most extraordinary aberrations and perversions. On any sexual subject Julot's erudition is quite inexhaustible, for pornography and books on sex psychology are his staple literary diet; he spends on these two classes of books all the money which does not pass into the hands of the local procuresses or the stockings of the local prostitutes. Through hearing Julot, we can all discuss exhibitionists and fetishists, sadists and masochists, with fair competence; and the parents of Claveau or Laroche would probably be very startled at the knowledge their offspring had gained of the more *recherché* forms of sexual perversion.

For my part I feel for Julot the sort of embarrassed curiosity one has for an invalid or a pathological case. From the beginning

108

I have felt unhappy listening to him. Nor is this through prudishness, even though his abominable stories reveal almost incredible depths to which the human soul may sink. For everything he says, unfortunately, may be a fact, and I do not think a doctor should be afraid of facts; as I learned from the pervert with the bottle, the doctor must be acquainted with all the aberrations and vices there are, since he is bound to meet them often. And besides I feel quite clearly in myself the vein of underground sensuality which we all hide from ourselves with such hypocritical complacency. No, I am unhappy, not so much at what Julot says but at the way he says it, at his quite deliberate and gratuitous obscenity. It is a kind of sterile, perverted exhibitionism, this unpleasant atmosphere he carries with him, systematically lewd and vicious.

I often wonder why with such an outlook he chose medicine as a career; and I am ashamed to think that he and Philippon and Villecroze (I put Chavasse on a different level because I often see his decent and generous side at hospital) will one day be doctors. For in France even the worst student almost always qualifies in the long run, given a little persistence. Future priests are thrown out of their training colleges, but throughout medical school there are no tests of moral standards to weed out the unsuitable. For five years Julot, Philippon, and Villecroze will be parading from hospital to hospital their indolence, sneers, and cynicism. Yet one day, almost automatically, they will become doctors, and their unworthiness will be charged against the whole of the profession.

I see some with less natural conviction trying to imitate them. This type too will go from table to table like buzzing flies, hawking scraps of gossip, seeking out the dirty joke, capable of wit but apparently incapable of fine feelings, telling stories of hospital life or of women which reveal a complete lack of respect for human suffering and for other people's personalities—a sort of sneering contempt for genuine love. With them too I used to wonder: "How dare these playboys think of becoming doctors?"

But most of them are not really playboys. I have come to

realize this eventually. They are only trying to fool themselves. This cynicism is a mask or alibi, long studied, to hide from others and stifle in themselves the distress which assails them.

We all have the same reactions and the same mental conflicts. To all of us is presented the simple alternative of running away or defending ourselves. But I feel both sorry for, and afraid of, the many young men of our day who have taken refuge in cynicism.

I too have my private antidote or exorcism. When I feel weary or depressed, to forget my surroundings I look towards the fourth table away, where the two girls are working. Among the five heads bent over this table I pick out, next to the profile of Mlle. Cannibal—poor girl—the face of her pretty colleague.

Like Chavasse I have been madly in love with her for several weeks. I have felt this devouring passion sometimes with horror and sometimes with delight, growing in me. In the rush and mental confusion of the first days I saw it as a refuge; but at other more lucid moments I would remember that I had solemnly resolved to omit love from my program. I had no time to waste, I must remain entirely free for my studies.

I had taken this decision advisedly, on what seemed to me strong grounds. Since my intermediate year I have always distrusted girl students. Doing my "Inter" at Toulouse, I had been in daily contact with girls, and for practical work in the labs I had teamed up with a Polish girl.

I wouldn't say Krysia was exactly pretty, but she had a strange sort of charm. She had a deliciously exotic voice, and she used rather strange French words and idioms. Beside her I felt clumsy and lumpish, and though she herself seemed poor enough, I felt quite desperately poor.

For several weeks I thought only of her. Despite my bashfulness I caught myself staring at her every minute with a fixed and distracted eye, so that for seconds I was quite unable to reply coherently to her incessant questions. I gradually realized that, although she perhaps liked me well enough, she was mainly interested in perfecting her French, and was only drawing me out more and more for whatever she could learn from me. I was fearfully disappointed, and tried to fade out of the picture rapidly. I relapsed into solitude, fighting shy of the other pretty girls as well, and lumping them all together in the same mistrust.

My theory of the girl student dates from this disappointment. Even the prettiest I refused henceforth to consider as women. To do this, I only needed to associate them with using the microscope, which forces anyone to make unattractive grimaces, with dissecting a frog or a rat or a slimy octopus, or with the stink of hydrogen sulphide in chemistry experiments, or with the smell of corpses or the hospital. As to woman, the species, I had wiped them out of my life for I don't know how long. I wouldn't think of them. The memory of my only actual experience of love, my terribly disappointing initiation with Krysia, still filled me with acute disgust.

It was with this firm resolve that I arrived in Paris. Yet a fortnight later I had fallen for another girl student.

I only needed to see her at the second anatomy lecture and, on the next day, at the first class in osteology. From that day on I knew her face better than the bones we were examining.

I found out about her, which was not difficult. All our class was talking about her, and I had no trouble in convincing myself that she was not an ordinary student like the others. I learned that she was about twenty-six or -seven, and was called Mme. Dupras.

Chavasse, always well informed, gave me full details at once. She was the widow of a young doctor and had decided to follow her husband's career. "As far as I can gather," he went on, "she thinks it will help her to get over his death. Oh boy, wouldn't I like to help her with that too! She's wonderful. What's more, she's not at all difficult or upstage. You can talk to her without her looking as if she thought you wanted to pinch her bottom."

I had heard enough, and in any case I did not care for this rather crude homage. Unwilling to listen to more of it, I always avoided talking about her to Chavasse after that.

A good many of the students approached Mme. Dupras and talked to her quite happily. I watched them, torn with jealousy, finding them all bolder, cleverer, with greater poise than myself.

I continued to contemplate her in silence, not even daring to rest my eyes directly upon her. I would look at something or other far behind her, but at the level of her face; and in this way I did not miss a single one of her movements. I saw at once that when talking to the others she smiled at them all with exactly the same degree of friendliness—that and no more. To have only the right to be friendly was not enough, and I said to myself that I would sooner not approach her at all than get only an ordinary casual smile. It meant so little for one who loved her as I did. What I wanted was to be allowed to love her with all the passion I felt welling up inside me. What I hoped—though I cannot imagine how I ever reached this ridiculous hope—was that I could talk to her, tell her how unhappy I was, astound her with the strength of my love, and that then she would gradually come to reciprocate it.

One evening after the last lecture I decided to follow her, and when she was alone, a long way from the medical school, to speak to her. She walked serenely on, and we both crossed the Boulevard Saint-Germain, and took the rue Dauphine in the direction of the Seine. A few more steps, and I was going to overtake her, when a young man passed me and, approaching her, began to speak to her. She went on walking as if she did not hear him; then she turned her face slightly towards him, and what he read on it obviously cut short the compliments he was framing and made them die on his lips. He walked away very quickly with a constrained smile on his face.

I followed her for a few paces more, then realized all at once that my plan was absurd, that my hopes had vanished, and that the unknown suitor had saved me a humiliation at the mere thought of which I trembled. I stopped, feeling stunned.

The idea of having escaped this humiliation naturally encouraged that small voice inside me, which from the first had been counselling prudence and reminding me of wasted hours and studies impaired. The small voice grew and gained control. Gradually my alarming early passion was allayed. At first there was still the feeling of having some unique personal claim on that face. I could not stop myself gazing at it with a kind of despairing tenderness. Then it became a diffused dull ache, always there, never coming to a head. Finally, rather than an affectionate tenderness, it remained a discreet secret friendship. Since then I have kept her image gently in my heart. Asking nothing of her and expecting nothing, I made her a part of my life. After regaining my composure I plunged feverishly into my work again; and in this environment she has been like a breath of fresh air, a pure untainted spirit from my past emotional life. When I think back to the anguish I suffered because of her, I smile with a lofty wisdom at the youthful madness I have now outgrown. And when I am tired of remaining bent so long over my old cadaver, when amidst so many depressing sights I need encouragement and reassurance for the future, then I raise my eyes towards her—just as I do today—and look for a moment at her charming profile. It is a pleasant resting place while I wait for a new love.

"At the end of my last lecture, ladies and gentlemen, some of your colleagues came up to inform me that certain anatomical descriptions, in which I employed geometrical comparisons, were too difficult for them. And yet the anatomy I teach you is so classical as to be almost commonplace, and the description of the liver which I gave you recently figures in all modern treatises. I showed in detail how the liver, taken as a whole, can be compared to the upper segment of an ovoid with a major transverse axis and a large extremity on the right which has been bisected from left to right following an inclined plane—looking at it from above, in front of it and on the right. The surface of the liver, I added, is subdivided into three faces. This, I should have imagined, must be crystal clear to the meanest intelligence; yet some of you have apparently been astonished that an ovoid could have three faces . . ."

"Go and shove it, you old bastard," shouts Chavasse, carried away by his hatred for our professor of anatomy. I had to admit that Alliaume's imitation was wonderfully true to life. Besides the strict geometrical parallels beloved of our professor, he hit off exactly the jerky walk in front of the blackboard and the way he breaks up the chalk into little bits with his thumb as he walks up and down. Everything is there, the sharp birdlike manner, the dry grating voice, the cold glare, cutting like a scalpel and indicating clearly that his branch of medicine deals with dead bodies and not with human beings.

"I have already stressed for you very often, gentlemen," continues Alliaume as imperturbably as his model, "that the study of anatomy is an intellectual exercise full of philosophical import. Anatomical description is an art, like any work of synthesis, like all intellectual reconstruction. . . ."

Under the solemn intonation Alliaume even catches the imperceptible passing tremor in the professor's voice suggesting a glacial, high-pitched, anatomical enthusiasm. The whole room applauds the imitation.

"Ah, gentlemen, anatomy is the science of sciences, and how much it is to be regretted that the student beginning his medicine has not to show certificates in mathematics, as well as in physics, chemistry and natural history. If he had, the intimate connection between anatomy and geometry would not be such a deep mystery to most of you, and in ellipsoids, conoids, sinusoids, and hyperboloids we should find a means of describing the human body in universal formulae."

"Up yours," shrieks Chavasse, echoed by the whole room in chorus, unloading on the mock professor some of the terror the real professor inspires. He was reputed to be an extremely severe examiner, and when he passed amongst us a respectful silence reigned throughout the room. Fortunately he cannot be everywhere at once, and towards the end of each session every room begins to get a bit out of hand. This is the time for "scrap battles," the legendary battles in which the students hurl the sad remnants of their cadavers at one another, often with horrifying results. Yet these combats serve to clear the air and keep the students from becoming too neurotic about their gruesome tasks. These fights occur far less frequently than we had imagined from the traditional stories, according to which they form the common pastime of dissection classes. More often someone calls out, as today: "Hey, Julot, how about a song?"

Without needing to be asked twice, Julot goes into the strains of *Ring-a-rang-a-roo*, in which everybody soon joins him.

> *"As I was walking down the street*
> *A fair young maid I chanced to meet.*
> *She said to me, if that suits you,*
> *I'll give you a game of ring-a-rang-a-roo."*

On the "Roo," Julot, the Burgundy boys, Chavasse and some of the other wilder spirits snatch up their stools and, using them as mounts, charge madly round the room, down the bays and between the cadavers, until the second verse begins. Meanwhile the rest of the class roars out the chorus:

> *"Now ring-a-rang-a-roo, now what is that?*
> *It's something soft like a pussy cat.*
> *It's covered with hairs and slit in two,*
> *That's what they call a ring-a-rang-a-roo."*

Often without any reason except the need for a break, two or three lines come from one table; and almost at once a hundred lusty voices hurl passionately through the cigarette smoke the words most of us knew before leaving school.

The tunes, true and tried from long use, many of them adapted from folksongs, somehow always seem rousing. I would never be the first to break into one of these songs, but in singing them with others I feel full of exhilaration. Whistling or singing does not hinder the hands from working; quite the reverse. As to the words, they are sometimes funny, always dirty, but the dirt is unimportant, and even in this room where nothing could very well seem indecent, with its naked cadavers and exposed sexual organs, they are about as shocking as a comic valentine.

> *"Her father's house it was so nice,*
> *We crept upstairs as quiet as mice,*
> *And got in bed, yes just us two,*
> *And started a game of ring-a-rang-a-roo."*

In the moment's silence left by the final "Roo," the taps give several preliminary splutters and then start running noisily, spurting onto the zinc of the basins.

This is the signal for Chavasse, Julot and the others to stop their hilarious gallop during the chorus. They dismount immediately and dash towards the exit with the mad haste of prisoners being released. There is a swirl of movement in the same direction, and the volume of voices is abruptly reduced by half. After one more verse the song, deprived of its choral support, fades away indifferently.

For a few minutes the corridors are still animated and noisy; then the room relapses into a hush in which you can once more hear the rain pattering on the glass skylights. About four o'clock, Nerovici and those who have been touching up their dissection while waiting for the next lecture, depart. Soon I am the only one left at my table and I begin folding up my equipment. As I cover my subject up in the oilcloth, I remember that this is really rather futile now, for my work on him is almost at an end. In the room the silence becomes oppressive; I leave behind only a few over-zealous souls, who will in due course be turned out by the attendant. Already the darkness of evening is coming on in almost imperceptible waves; soon the shadows will drown out the corpses, like flotsam on their heavy marble rafts, already floating in a twilight full of mournful wreckage.

Between half past four and five I take a rest, and I enjoy this more particularly because it is possible to do it only by cutting a lecture.

I have my little habits. Quite near the medical school there is a man who sells hot chestnuts. Every afternoon he stands there with his cheerfully steaming little cart. The first fresh air I breathe on coming out of the school is charged with the delectable aroma of roasting chestnuts, blending with the fog and soot which I now know to be the characteristic smell of a Parisian winter.

The first few days after dissection I went to lectures in anatomy and histology; but soon I gave this up. I could read it all up in textbooks at home, in my own time. As soon as a lesson goes on too long and begins to sound like some solemn address or sermon, my mind shies away and starts wandering. In that case I do not force it, but let it roam where it will.

When the day is fine, I usually go down to the Seine for half an hour in a favorite bookshop. I stop at the medical book-shops in the Boulevard Saint-Germain, to browse in the boxes of second-hand books outside. In one shop I have discovered some tomes more palpitating with medical and historical myster-ies than any detective story. I go there today to dip into some of these for half an hour, crushed between an old gentleman mastering the Constipated Man's Ten Commandments and a schoolboy with highly flushed cheeks who is devouring a treatise on sexology.

Five past five. I have had to abandon the fascinating stall to another booklover, and go back to work. Right at the bottom of the main hall of the medical school, in front of the door of the library, a few students are walking the hundred steps up to the balcony, with cigarettes in their mouths; three others, lean-ing on the wrought-iron banisters, are deeply absorbed in a little game they are having. At the bottom of the staircase, just below them, a marble statuette of Nature appears to be unveiling her-self before Science, and in this gesture she holds above her head a sort of shell. The game is to flick ends of matches or cigarettes into this shell, and even, should other projectiles be unavailable, to spit into it. This exercise seems to provide an excellent mild relaxation before returning to one's books.

As I go by, I watch sympathetically these fellow galley-slaves of mine. Mornings at the hospital and, at first, afternoons at the medical schools, this is our common initiation, the same collective pasturage for us all; giving the minimum basic knowledge, which with a little luck at the end of five years will allow us to call ourselves doctors of medicine.

In the evenings, from five o'clock onwards, we are free. For some this is the traditional hour for visiting cafés or the cinema, going to the dance-halls or seeing a girl friend. But we certainly

117

seem a rather serious younger generation, for the majority go back at once to their rooms or shut themselves up in the university library. Their private homework is just beginning, and great efforts are made outside the medical school curriculum, for beyond mere qualification there are coveted prizes and distinctions, which will put the best appointments in their way. Fellowships of the official medical or surgical societies, that is the happy prospect of which they all are dreaming, as I am myself.

In the huge main room of the library all the rows of tables are crammed at each corner with bent, attentive faces. No one speaks, but above the studious heads the vast space is full of muffled sound, the scratching of pens in a hurry, the turning of pages, the dull clap of books being closed; and as the librarians walk along the walls hung with books from the ceilings down to the floors, their steps make the iron gangways ring. You can almost hear the soft buzzing of thoughts, so eagerly are these studious youths gathering their store of mental pollen.

Chapter 3

AT NIGHT on the Boulevard Raspail I am the only person, as usual, waiting for the last bus from the Opéra to the Porte d'Orléans. The tall, snub-nosed monster comes pounding down in the pouring rain, bespattering the pavement all down the street. It stops just long enough to let me jump on the rear platform, and then continues its course along the deserted boulevard, carrying me off in its narrow jolting prison. The rain shuts us in more securely than bars.

Inside the bus it is hot and damp. In the first-class seats a few evening dresses peeping out below ladies' cloaks, and a few dress shirts showing in the gaps left by silk scarves, serve as a reminder that the bus started from the Opéra. But in the second-class seats, you recognize nightworkers, waiters and cinema attendants, for instance, who conceal their professional uniform under nondescript old gabardine coats. Many of them are already half asleep, with sagging cheeks; they start at every jerk of the bus, and I find my arm suddenly numb from a wet shoulder leaning on mine.

Through the rain and the soft blur of the glass the gloom of the night outside is abruptly diminished; the dim halos of strong lights try hard to reach us. I wipe a corner of the glass. I know we are coming to Montparnasse.

The bus stops at the corner of the Rotonde. A few passengers get on; the conductor, in a hurry to get to bed, rings the bell straight away, and the bus moves complainingly off again.

I do not like traversing Montparnasse in this way; and perhaps

119

this is why instead of remaining near the entrance of the bus I usually go right in and sit down up front. Even after four months' effort I realize that I have not completely attained the detachment needed for contented monasticism. Every time I cross Montparnasse at midnight, I feel weary of the excess of concentration and regularity in my life—and I feel a crude hunger for freedom. I stop going forward unresisting, unmoved, like a child toward sleep, like a prisoner making for a cell into which he locks himself. The corner of the glass which I have wiped clear is like an eye I would like to open on the living world outside; and every night that world escapes me as it does tonight.

I see the long brightly lit terraces of cafés, the entrances to noisy dance-halls. All around, on moving signs, in zig-zag flashes, in huge letters, thousands of neon lights flicker along the façades, routing the darkness and dyeing the roadways blood-red with the glittering radiance of their reflections. Even this evening, when sullen rain seems ready to drown the whole city, there is a milky glimmer, very high in the sky, like a pink glow already heralding the real dawn.

When I stand on the outside platform of the bus, I can see better the café clients at their tables on the terraces, and people lifting the heavy velvet curtains at the entrances to the night-clubs. I feel a bit like a little flower-girl, or an old beggar with a limp cap lying out on the pavement beside him—or like a mere loiterer in the streets. For here is all this passing gaiety of which I catch but a fleeting glimpse. I hear snatches of dance tunes, I cast glances at the unknown beauties who roam through the crowds with inane smiles on their faces.

But soon the bus leaves the blinding lights behind, and the long boulevard is once more deserted. We are back with vistas of empty pavements and closed doors, dark corners where street meets street, and then we pass the big cemetery with its mournful mass of tombstones. I turn back toward the lights, and for a moment more I envy all those I have left behind, ranging from bar to bar, from dance-hall to nightclub. They have the freedom of this quarter where each gleaming sign invites them to try its hospitality, where gilded pleasure and light-hearted revelry await them at every turn.

The part of the glass I wiped is now black again. But even now I gaze in the direction of those magic lights which always shine for others only. And then I turn my head and see my fellow-passengers on this bus, still dozing with drawn features and tired mouths. For them as for me, no revelry this evening—or any other evening.

It is still raining when the bus reaches the Porte d'Orléans. The wind hurls the rain into my face, as I dash down a boulevard pitted with puddles. The rain has scarcely stopped since I made the same dash sixteen hours earlier in the other direction. Other bent figures are hurrying through the rain and the night in the direction of the dormitories.

Seeing these wanderers returning late at night, I remember how we all set off for Paris this morning. We are like the New-foundland fishing boats which all day plunge through the fog alone, and in the unfriendly evening darkness seek the welcoming red and green lights of the mother ship. Perched at the top of the hill, the Cité is like some tall ship buffeted by the gale, whose lights beckon us from afar. For however early you leave, how-ever late you may come back, there will always be some obsti-nate late-nighters, some unwearying early-risers, shut up in their rooms, patiently keeping watch on the bridge between twilight and dawn.

Before entering my hostel, I look upwards. Just above the door, amidst all the drawn curtains, a light filters through a window; I knew it would be there beforehand. It is the lamp of Bouvray, now in his last year of medicine. Every night for three months I have seen this lamp burning. In front of it he is working for his finals with an unremitting grim determination, like a woodman attacking a giant oak.

The passage is silent and empty. I go past the doors of my neighbors with their exotic colonial names; I have sorted them out now, and in the early days I sometimes spoke to them. They showed very little interest in my approaches, and I was soon discouraged. Away from the sun of their own countries, they have lost all their sap; they have only one childish and obsessional desire, to Westernize themselves immediately and at all costs. I meet them in the passages, paralyzed with cold under huge padded overcoats, their heads huddled between their shoulders, seeking the warmth of their scarves. The little you can see of their dark skins looks lead-blue, while the yellow-skinned ones seem to have withered like old bananas.

Usually they exclude from their rooms and their clothes anything reminiscent of their own countries. My copper Buddha is decidedly more exotic than the hideous views of Paris, overlaid with sham mother-of-pearl, which Do-Dong-Kien has hung up in his room. Nor do I stop at the door of Petitjean's former room. He has left and it is two months now since I last heard that coughing and the continual rattle of his typewriter. I hardly know the room's new occupant. Bouvray is little more than an acquaintance, and I have no longer a real friend in the whole of the hostel.

My friendship with Petitjean—how often I turned to it in the first few weeks as a haven of refuge! In his own extraordinary way he gave me a taste of real friendship. How well my heart agreed with his, despite that strange savage humor he had. Shall I ever find another friend with more real generosity and warmheartedness?

Since my disillusion over Krysia, the Polish girl, friendship has seemed a thousand times surer than love; and when I met Petitjean, I was thrilled at this wonderful opportunity to gain a better understanding of myself and the world.

At first it was far from easy. No one else but me ever went into Petitjean's room; he must have discouraged all his fellows one by one. His difficult personality in itself was a big initial obstacle. People were always embarrassed and often exasperated by his insistence on discovering stupidity and baser motives everywhere. He certainly had little gift for enjoying life. On some evenings he would look at me temperamentally and aggressively as soon as I entered the room, and then abuse me angrily. At other times, when everything seemed to be going well, at a single word of mine, or for no reason at all, he would call me a bloody fool and complain that he had been wrong about me all the time: I was only a dirty little bourgeois like the rest of them. I hung on grimly, however, and in the end, bit by bit, he became used to my being there, until finally he came to adopt me as his confidant. From the moment he started really treating me as a friend, I felt he was influencing me deeply, giving me a new insight and understanding, drawing out of me a new personality whose existence I had never previously suspected.

Every evening I brought him the uncertainties and discoveries of my day, and I was fascinated to find that from a different viewpoint they had once been his too. I admired Petitjean a great deal, so I was proud to think our experiences ran somehow parallel; and of course, as the young always try to imitate those they admire, I tried to become like him. Looked at from closer quarters, his conception, and mine, of medicine as "one of the humanities," seemed to provide a clear introduction to life's true principles.

Often I was amazed at quite unexpected points of similarity in our views of life. He told me one day, for instance, that real communism meant not only pitying others but sharing their feelings. This almost made me feel I was listening to my mother in her back-shop—or to Sister Juliette of the scared face, as she bent over one of her patients.

Petitjean's particular brand of communism was so violent that it had made him an outcast to his family and former friends. Like him, I had found it necessary, on starting medicine, to live strictly on the level of harsh realities; I was proud to accept this necessity which set me apart from all my contemporaries. I too had obeyed a call. When he spoke to me bitterly of his family, which had rejected him as a fanatic and a failure, when he told me he had more friendship and fraternal feeling for many unhappy strangers than for his brother—it occurred to me then that I was nearer some of the patients in the ward than were their own families.

Even in the days of his most painful privations, Petitjean never became utterly discouraged. When I felt myself beaten by the sort of life I was now living, I could gain new courage by seeing how alone he was, and yet how confident of the future. Like him I would rejoice in the stark grandeur of my lot. "I find it exciting to be young in an age like this," he would exclaim. "No generation before ours has had a magic formula like communism for remaking the world." Whereupon I would think with pride how I, later on, might be among the people working to make medicine truly one of the humanities.

Sometimes when I arrived in the evening I would find him engaged on some translation or other bread-and-butter task; but more often he would be working on a book which he had begun writing during the vacation. My first curiosity on coming in was "the book." I would have liked to dash straight to the table to see how many pages he had got through; but I did not dare do this, having once been snubbed for looking. So I waited patiently till he was willing to read me some extracts. It was a kind of intimate diary, an *"apologia pro vita mea,"* into which he poured each day all his disgust and anger and passions and hopes. He had enough material there for twenty dramas, and there was something pathetic about the vast scale on which this project was planned.

You could read in his book resignation, the acceptance of suffering, patient waiting, and a courageous search for his true destiny. Far better than at the hospital I learned from it about sorrow and bitterness, I understood the torments of hunger and humiliation and greed and lies, I faced the full tragedy of man's inhumanity to man. The diary had whole pages of denunciation, defiance, and abuse, a tumultuous thundering torrent of quite extraordinary violence. But in other pages a gentle unemphatic humor surprised me and made me smile; while others again radiated a wonderful tenderness for the brave, the unassuming, the sincere. He expressed in the diary the happiness he found each day in simple things—for they were simple to him: in poverty without obsequiousness, in candor unafraid, in the joy of planning a new order of society which should one day restore harmony and justice to the world. He expressed in these pages

124

his burningly clear vision of the future and the new hope it brought to mankind.

He was writing his book on the pages of a sort of horticultural almanac (a publisher had given him a whole pile of these) printed for a nursery gardener who had meanwhile gone bankrupt. On each page his manuscript was headed by an old country saw and selections of flowers. When I came in, he would put on the accents of a Norman peasant to say:

"If it thunders in November, then a good year is in view
If it's chilly in December, then the farmer's hopeful too."

Or else I would find him speculating on the fascination of flowers' names, and the infinite variety of flowers there are. He would try to imagine all the different kinds of carnation and marigold: *Pink Queen, Child of Nice, Bonnie Lassie,* and all the rest—and sometimes he turned over several pages in advance to come to the poppies with their wealth of splendid names. Here he was in this book, talking of destroying society and redistributing its wealth, yet he wrote it on scrap paper fit for pulping. Some inverted snobbery there surely—but he would not admit it. When I expressed surprise that he could write prose of such bitterness in the midst of so much floral sweetness, he clarified his position:

"It's like this, old chap. I have appointed myself plenipotentiary of the new order, where the enjoyment of flowers and natural beauty is the birthright of all. But just at present while most men are living in muck, I am obliged to go on ranting about this deplorable fact. It's not my fault if I have to deal in fire and brimstone in order to get my voice heard at all."

One evening, just before the Christmas vacation, I found him lying down, looking ill. He welcomed me as usual with one of the countryman's saws:

"At Christmas if too late you roam,
At Easter you'll have to stay at home."

125

Then he regaled me with a news item giving statistics about the number of unclaimed bodies at hospitals, which had apparently increased continuously since the recent economic depression. "It's lucky for you," he said, "masses of corpses to dissect. But I'm surprised these poor wretches are any use to you. After all, they've never really lived." That evening his cheerfulness was obviously rather forced, and he admitted to me that he felt feverish.

"What can you do?" he asked me. "One of my pupils had a slight cough. I told him that didn't worry me. After all I had the choice between losing twenty francs or catching a spot of flu."

For three days he remained lying down in his room, and his temperature did not go down. He coughed and complained of a pain in his side. The Cité had no infirmary, and on the fourth day I began to feel worried. I suggested to Petitjean that I should bring him a fifth-year student to have a look at him; he accepted. Bouvray came, and after completing his examination told Petitjean: "You've got a touch of pleurisy. You really should be in a hospital."

Petitjean did not reply. I followed Bouvray into the corridor, and he added: "That's quite a nasty pleurisy your pal's got. I'm afraid it's probably tuberculous. If you like I can ask my Chief to take him into his ward."

When I came back into the room, Petitjean was sitting on his bed waiting for me. He started questioning me immediately:

"Your magician didn't want to tell me, but I've got water there, haven't I? My calendar was right; it said this morning, *An adverse year comes in with rain. . . .*"

I tried to protest but he interrupted me.

"Oh don't bother. It's very nice of you, but I quite understood. My mother was tubercular, and one of my sisters had a good deal of lung trouble. Although they disinherited me, I still have this little legacy from them. It's really rather a waste of time chucking everything for freedom—family weaknesses will always out. Ah well, the bacilli have got me before the revolution. Rather a pity. If I'd only had three square meals a day, I might have saved the world yet. Having too little money for too long, even if you don't die of it right away, is just as bad, really, as having too much. You never quite recover from either."

He stopped a moment, and then went on: "Luckily the gods have given me a sense of humor, and really the best part of the story is what I'm going to cost our bourgeois State. A good old syphilis, and they'd have got out of it with a few free injections twice weekly, but even the cheapest T.B. sanitarium is much more expensive. Highly logical really: while I was more or less healthy no one took any notice of me, but now they've let me get ill, they'll have to spend more money on my illness than they would have needed to keep me healthy. Crazy world, isn't it!"

Still sitting up in bed, with flushed cheeks, he was obviously becoming much too worked up. I made him lie down, then turned out the light and told him to go to sleep.

Next morning Bouvray did the necessary, and in the afternoon an ambulance came for Petitjean. I went with him to the hospital, settled him in bed, and was just going, when he asked me to do a few things for him. "And please," he said, "don't say I'm in the hospital, should my friends" (he made a grimace at the word "friends"), "come for news of me. I'd hate them to come all this way to see how thin one gets if one doesn't lick their boots and tell them what fine fellows they are."

When I got back, I cleared up his room and took the pictures off the walls. Altogether they made up only a thin pile, this riot of beautiful girls, expensive cars and yachts, and idyllic panoramas. Bouvray helped me to pack two valises full of papers, books, and old clothes, and I put the rickety typewriter away in a corner of the cupboard. The day afterwards I went to see Petitjean. They had drawn a little liquid from his pleura. He lifted his shirt and said to me, "Here, listen to my water supply and have a free lesson. They say it is typical. It seems my breathing is soft, distant, and expiratory. Before we part, I shall at least have taught you that."

I sounded his chest carefully, and for the first time heard the characteristic breathing of pleurisy. Then he introduced me to his neighbors: on the right was an old alcoholic, by now completely sottish, who was dying of cirrhosis; and on the left a cabinetmaker of about fifty with heart disease. He looked shy and kindly, and I was not surprised when Petitjean told me he had found in this man the true communist faith—a very gentle communism, looking forward to a sentimental and almost bloodless revolution, after which all men would love each other as brothers.

I went to see him every day during the Christmas break, and a little later he left for Brévannes, till there was a place for him at a students' sanitarium. The day before the Easter term started, people had come to disinfect his room; and it was now occupied by a new student.

At first, whenever I went by the door of Petitjean's former room, I couldn't help stopping. I felt something was missing when I had to go straight to my own room without knocking at that door and sitting down for a moment on the corner of that sofa. I even thought I should always miss Petitjean, but after only two months I have learned a new aspect of life's cruelty. You have a friend you admire with all the enthusiasm of youth; and for whole months you see him every day. You listen to him and confide in him, and without him life seems empty. The separation comes, and you are panicstricken at having this essential prop withdrawn. At every turn you think, If only I could show him this, could ask his opinion of that. You show no one, you ask no one, and finally you observe that life goes on still, that it has never stopped going on. The friend you thought you could not live without is gone, and you feel that lack of him no more —or so it appears, for in reality it is only much later that you realize how much you have lost.

In any case from then on I deemed it prudent to wipe friendship as well as love out of my life. Since then, when I have felt too strongly the need to talk to someone, I go to Bouvray's room with the excuse of asking him some small service. Except for the evenings, when he goes to tutorial classes, I can be sure in advance of finding him in. He always receives me kindly, lends me books and notebooks. He talks to me for a few minutes, lifting his bespectacled eyes towards me. This is enough for me.

What I have been looking for from him, far more than any instruction, is the stimulation and tonic of his example and a confidence that the same stubborn will to work can win success for me as well.

One evening, when coming home through Montparnasse at midnight had left me more than usually wistful, I went up to Bouvray's room. He was still working, of course, and I asked him: "Always thinking about your finals, shut up between hospital and your room? Don't you ever want anything else?"

He removed his glasses, taking advantage of even this second's break in his work, and rubbed them with the corner of a handkerchief as he looked at me through those rather dim myopic eyes. Then he answered: "No, one can't have everything. One must choose."

"Really, you don't regret anything? Never?"

"Oh well, at first I probably did have some regrets. But for a long time I haven't felt a prisoner any more. The prisoner is a man who wants what is outside his reach, beyond the walls of his cell. Personally, I don't feel now that anything exists, or even has ever existed, outside all this. It is not only a forbidden world, it's something not quite real, it's almost a figment of the imagination. And I live without regrets, I am content as I am."

Stretched out on my bed, turning out the bedside lamp, I savor the sweetness of those last lazy moments before sleep. I feel tired from the long day, and this tiredness will very quickly bring me to a half-dream state, before plunging me sharply into slumber. But till then I enjoy this feeling of healthy youthful fatigue, very different from the physical and mental lassitude of the old.

For a few seconds tonight, as every night, with my eyes open in the darkness, I take stock of today, which has been so like all my days of the past four months. The first few nights before going to sleep I was often appalled at my loneliness, and wondered how long I could stand it. I kept thinking back to the peaceful familiar life of Toulouse and this sapped my courage to face the difficult months and years I knew were ahead of me.

But now I am fairly pleased with myself, proud of distress and difficulties overcome; hour follows absorbing hour, and I forget my fears and anxieties and futile worries. In case of doubt work puts things back in their right perspective. Each day is full and hard as a diamond.

A gust of wind beats a tattoo of rain on the windows, bringing me out of my reverie for a moment. Then the night takes over once more, a night quiet and sad as men's saddest dreams; but the happiness I feel inside me is quite enough to soothe and lull me. Yes, all's right with the world, and I can say I am happy. I see ahead vistas of countless days full of unselfish ardor, opening on vast fields of knowledge of man's body and soul. Every day will bring its dazzling conquests. These dark and ascetic periods are the climax in the long process of my growing up; they are the essential cornerstone on which the whole building will later rest.

I feel slumber stealing over me, and welcome its approach with a smile. For a few seconds longer I linger at this unique point when the long day is over at last and a new one has just been born. Then I softly surrender to sleep, beginning already my impatient dreams of the new day.

Part 3

SPRING AND SUMMER

Chapter 1

It was my first Parisian spring. Without moving from my table I could see the flowering cherry framed against the window. All winter I had watched its slender form stretching ever upwards, the bare branches glistening with rain. It was like a Japanese print, with dark red lines delicately traced on a dripping gray sky. Halfway up the trunk the tree was supported by a stake, and altogether it looked stunted and miserable, thwarted in its growth, ill-rooted in a sickly lawn. Rich chiefly in rubble and cement from the old fortifications, the soil could provide no nourishment for the poor little tree. Yes, I pitied it on days when I was sad, just as I pitied myself: for both of us time seemed to be passing fruitlessly by. But the grass on the lawn found something to live from; and the cherry tree too, after bursting quietly into a thousand brittle buds, had by now flared into brilliant white flower.

Till last month, whenever I felt weary of sitting still and studying for too long, I used to walk across the room two or three times. But the coming of spring gave me a new habit: I would lean out of the open window and let myself feel drawn by all that I saw. The tree was now a charming sight, in no need of my pity as it reached towards a sky warm and blue and serene. I would stay at the window quite a while looking at it. Yet even two or three weeks ago the sun was little in evidence on this side of the hostel, which faced north; it stayed in a bluish shade, chilly and damp, with an earthy smell of rotting ivy. After a few minutes I would be forced to shut the window again with a shiver and go back into my room, friendly with the snug warmth of winter.

Then the sun too became stronger, and even the shade grew brighter and warmer. The cherry tree's white blossoms vanished petal by petal, to be replaced by frail new leaves swaying at each breath of April's tempestuous winds.

One afternoon, between two chapters of anatomy, I allowed myself a few minutes at the window. Spring was very much in the air today, you could feel it in the trees and the lawn; all around the Cité everything was bursting with gaiety and new life. How fresh the night seems sometimes when you come out of an airless house. In the same way my head was turned by this glorious clear blue sky, by the smiles and promise of happiness I could imagine in every joyous quivering breeze. I tried to return to work, but suddenly I felt enormously lazy. I had an irresistible desire to leave everything, go out on the lawn and bathe in the pools of sunshine.

I knew my work had been falling off in the last few days; probably a passing weakness with which I was paying for a winter of strained application. But in any case this dark room was my winter, and without more ado I left it.

Sitting on an old iron seat at the top of the hill in the park, I watched the paths curving down where children were running around between two rows of young mothers, nurses and placid old men. I expect I was the only one, among all these people, to be taking a break from pressing work. Certainly the sight of this simple carefree crowd was very restful; I justified my idleness on these grounds.

When I look at my life during those last six months, I think of an old horse turning round a mill with blinkers on his eyes to stop his getting giddy. All those long weeks I had been in blinkers, turning round and round the narrow circle: Cité, Hospital, Medical School, and tutorial classes at St. Luke's. This was the only way I had been able to carry on, letting time flow stagnantly by without a single ripple on its surface.

Alone in my room, I sometimes felt stifled under the solid

134

mass of work. I was haunted at night by the laughing faces of ghosts from happier days. Several times I felt as if I had been walled up in my room for weeks on end; but each time the storm passed, and till now I had triumphed over these crises fairly easily. So I had not felt too disturbed by the onset of this period of sluggishness; it would pass like the rest. And yet, sitting on the old seat, I started thinking gloomily of the coming exams. All at once I found the park too placid and felt I had to mix in a crowd, had to hear its talk and laughter.

At the Porte d'Orléans the crowd was pouring out of the Metro, running for suburban buses. Cars were hooting impatiently at pedestrian crossings; the cries of paper sellers announced late editions of the evening papers on which the ink was scarcely dry. Most people wore a smile, seeing the long working day at an end. Lovers met, and on the terraces of cafés customers spread out as far as the trees on the edge of the big cross-roads. This was indeed the merry month of May, all light-heartedness and indolence, and even through the fumes of petrol the air smelt fresh and warm and sweet, scattering vague promise of happiness throughout this sweet seductive city.

I was tempted to take one of the buses waiting in front of the green kiosk, to savor the brightest beauty of a Paris evening, at Concorde, the Louvre, in the Champs Elysées, still streaming with the glory of the setting sun. But the habits of seven months of careful living were not to be lost all at once, and I slowly turned back towards the Cité.

All around me, under the trees of the boulevard, in the delicate shadows thrown by the setting sun, there were carefree groups of students laughing and taking their ease. Sometimes their gaiety irritated me, but tonight I found it delightful. I recognized among them a few casual acquaintances, with whom I usually exchanged a "hullo" on passing. This time I would have liked to have stopped and chatted, or to have strolled along with them in the same cheerful unconcern. But you do not always meet friends when you are looking for them, and this evening no one called out to me.

135

The twilight came down, cool and calming. In the evening air the lawns smelled of the country, and I caught a trite little tune floating up from them, which was succeeded by a strident jazz number. Lying on the grass round a gramophone, students were listening, as they watched the glow of the evening sun disappearing imperceptibly and a pale stage moon rising in the background. The last few evenings this same gramophone had made me shut my windows, and even then the melodies still reached me, and I had to block my ears with both fists before I could really get back to work; otherwise I should have been carried away, drifting into the dreamy distance. You could still see the whiteness of a few summer frocks, as the bodies stretched out idly on the grass disappear into the shadows. How I longed to be one of them—and the strength of this longing showed me how much my will-power has been slowly sapped by the winter's work.

Very well then: having no friends, I decided to walk a while by myself before going to bed. Unsettled and weary, I felt sufficiently melancholy by now not even to want company any more. I skirted the park railings. There is a long avenue beginning at the bottom of the park, with high walls on either side belonging to a reservoir and some railway depots. In the winter I had always found it deserted.

That evening it was full of people. Some no doubt had come down from their tenement houses for a breath of fresh air; but many of them seemed to have a single objective, which became evident as I approached the Place Denfert Rochereau with its statue of the "Lion de Belfort" in the middle. Around the statue there was a fair on, and the noise gradually concentrated into a single jubilant medley of blaring bands, roaring roller coasters, dodgems banging, merry-go-rounds turning—the whole jovial tumult of cheerful crowds. Fairs have fascinated me since childhood, and here were all the ingredients, with their old intoxicating delight.

Here were the roving bands of rowdy youths, the lovers clasped tightly in each other's arms, the families who had linked arms so as not to get lost in the crush. I let myself be carried

136

along with them right to the end of the fairground, where the Metro comes above ground into a boulevard dark and deserted. Several times I walked back and forth from shooting ranges to merry-go-rounds, from photographers to games of chance. To and fro I wandered with the merry jostling crowd, regulating my progress by its own unhurried pace. Lost in its midst, I was happy once more, naïve and enraptured as the ten-year-old who had visited fairs with a few treasured coppers deep in his pocket, going from stall to stall undecided what to choose.

Toulouse had two traveling fairs a year, in November and in May. When I was about fifteen or sixteen, I gave up going to the winter fair and squelching about in the icy mud. But in the spring, having worked long hours studying for exams, I would say I had a headache and go out after dinner.

These evenings I used to go out to escape from my room, impelled by the same vague desires which send men forth onto the streets when day is done. But in the thick dust of the fairground as night was falling, in the overheated atmosphere, amidst the vulgarity and sensual excitement, with pairs of lovers hiding from the garish lights in dark corners—in this environment I felt more lost still, simultaneously numb with solitude and almost dizzy with excitement. It was the same overmastering instinct which made my blood race when I read in a book about passion and desire.

These torments and temptations had started, of course, several years earlier. The school friends of my early teens were already watching the girls coming out of school and escorting them nearly home by devious roundabout routes. I envied but did not dare imitate them; I knew I should never have the courage, and then I had no smart clothes like they had. Instead, I would develop a sudden passion for an unknown girl, follow her to her own door without daring to speak, and dream of her all night. The next day I would find some detail in her unworthy of so pure and great a love, and then I would not even want to see her again. And all the while I was living in an exalted secret world, my heart running over with nobility and devotion. But

137

even on this lofty plane I was not proof against guilty desires and fantasies. To repress them, I would try thinking of the girl I would love, whose form I would watch for, tense with hope, as I went to our imaginary lovers' meeting.

Only last year I thought I had found this miraculous creature in Krysia, and for the time being my disappointment there made me a misogynist. To forget her, I started working furiously, but I still could not stop thinking of her. Thinking a little healthy exercise might help, I joined a rowing club. There were a good many girls in it, but I kept myself prudently clear of them.

Several of us had hired a small cabin on the bank of the river where we rowed. The neighboring cabin remained vacant till the fine weather started in June, when it was taken by a married couple. The husband, a commercial traveler, was only to be seen on week-ends; the wife, on the other hand, used to come to the cabin almost very afternoon. From the heavy lines on her face you could guess that she was nearly forty, but she was still very pretty, a brunette with a good figure. Above all she had considerable sex-appeal, which she stressed in a most disturbing way.

My friends watched her settling in with obvious interest, but they were soon enough disappointed. Our neighbor came to the cabin, went out alone in a skiff, and returned discreetly to the city. On Saturdays and Sundays her husband accompanied her. The boys were just about to give up interest in her completely, when one day our pretty neighbor appeared in a boat with the club's official Don Juan.

The next day the pair were seen together again; and the days after that as well. On Saturday the supposed lover and the husband played tennis—singles. The boys watched the game with keen attention. They saw the lover, one of the best players in the club, carefully sending very easy balls which the husband could have taken almost without moving; for a whole hour, however, the latter rushed about, sweating and gasping, playing the most atrocious shots and swinging his arms about with quite unwarranted violence. He looked a perfect fool, and when after the game my friends heard his opponent congratulating him on his game, they commented, referring to the rabbit's wife, "Looks like she's playing ball all right."

By the beginning of the summer the husband had already changed his tennis opponent several times.

Just before the holidays it was the turn of one of the lads in my hut to be singled out as partner. Pujol was tall and powerful, the hope of the club eight-oar crew, and on the following Saturday we watched him play tennis with the husband.

Till then those in our cabin had been no more than good neighbors with the wife. But from the day she chose her lover from our midst, she often came in to see us. She called us by our Christian names, and insisted we should use hers, which was Mado. By the same token we went quite freely into her cabin, which she had conveniently provided with a couch, easy chairs and sherry glasses. As she was obviously broad-minded and unlikely to be shocked by our student jokes and songs, we found considerable pleasure in having a woman with us. We even believed, in an excess of team spirit, that our cabin was arousing the jealousy of the rest of the club; Mado was our envied mascot.

I had slightly modified my distrust of women. I was friendly enough with Mado, but remained somewhat reserved and polite. I should have preferred not to know how intimate Pujol was with her, but this discretion was difficult to maintain, for Pujol himself was quite uninhibited. To anyone willing to listen he would recount that Mado was "a whirlwind—but it takes a little time to get her going." Sometimes we heard them at it through the thin partition, and the rest of the boys shouted across their encouragement and rowdy chaff, which seemed to embarrass Pujol not at all. One day I heard them on the couch, frighteningly near me, when I was alone in the hut. My heart was beating fast, and I stood there listening tensely as if rooted to the spot.

Exams over, Pujol (being broke) returned to his family at Carcassonne, and the others also dispersed. The only one from Toulouse, I stayed on as the cabin's solitary occupant. Mado's husband took his holidays, and was surprised to find no more opponents at tennis—since Mado remained virtuous all through

August. Then he returned to his samples, and disappeared again for the week.

Two days after his departure I happened to meet Mado on the landing-stage. All the boats were out, and I asked her to come out in my skiff. We went up the Garonne. I concentrated on skulling my very best, a little ashamed of my thin wrists and slender forearms. It was extremely hot.

I avoided more than a few glances at Mado, who remained more or less silent all through the row, keeping her eyes closed as if she were nearly asleep. I felt she was looking at me all the time, and found this very disturbing, combined with my physical tiredness, the heat, and the dazzling reflection of the water. On our return, when she invited me into her cabin, I realized she intended to add me, for all my puny muscles, to the series of he-man lovers she had had.

The cabin was narrow, and you could feel Mado's presence everywhere. Getting something for us to drink, finding the glasses, squeezing the lemons, she was continually brushing past me. Alone near her like this, I dared not look at her. Since the day I had heard her gasps behind the partition, I felt I had been secretly desiring her body, and fearing it. I was trembling, whether from impatience or fear I did not care to analyze. But when she drew me to her and pressed her lips on my mouth, I felt this kiss should never end; and it was Mado who, to regain her breath, was obliged to push me back for a moment.

She drew back her head, breathed deeply, and looked at me with a slightly wry smile, as if she had just bitten into one of the slices of lemon lying on the table. Then in a hungry voice charged with emotion, she said to me, "Darling." I thought I was hearing the sound of her voice for the first time. Its accents no longer seemed slightly vulgar, and though I realized how horribly trite the word was, on those over-red lips I felt it was charged with magical meaning.

Anxious to make the most of the pleasures of initiation, she sent me away, saying "Come and find me tonight." My throat was dry, and I could not have answered her. I left her at a run, carrying away on my lips a taste of soft skin and perfumed flesh.

As I left the club, light-headed, I knew that nothing in the world would stop my going this very evening to my first lovers' meeting.

Two hours later I knocked at her door, and she told me to come in. But I saw nothing of the little flat; nothing existed except her and the carnal future opening up before me. The sudden onrush of pleasure had almost hypnotized me, and I let myself be led. Mado drew me into her bedroom, and when she passed in front of the open window, still bright with the rays of the setting sun, I saw beneath her dressing-gown the shadow of her naked form. Yet with all the beloved body so near me, I could only think of one thing; the rest my eyes heeded not at all. Already Mado had taken me in her arms, and my shadow blended with hers. My only impulse was to press closer to her and to fall with her as she drew me down onto the bed. What wonder and delight the body can conceal; what a sublime discovery I had made. Ah woman, women, all women, all mine, all. . . .

But when exhausted, annihilated, drained of all desire, I tried to relax at her side, Mado would not let me go. She was frantic, she groaned with a frenzied, brutish fury, as if in one paroxysm she would pour out the whole of a pain too great for her to bear. Under her pressure I was obliged to go on playing, with a dreary concentration, my masculine part.

I looked at Mado, and no longer recognized her face. I felt I was literally seeing an animal mask, aged, contorted, terrifying; the half-open lips were turned upwards in a swooning greed, and the eyes fixed upon me were completely blind, going right through me but not seeing me. I felt my very existence was forgotten, I was merely the impersonal instrument of her selfish pleasure, and certainly a clumsier instrument than all my predecessors on this bed. Suddenly the pupils of her eyes dilated, brimming with a voluptuous intensity. Horrified and uncomprehending, I looked at the ghastly gape of the mouth, at this face with all its primitive instincts exposed.

We were now lying side by side, but Mado stayed near me, gasping, caressing me with a hand still clenched, murmuring incoherent words to me in a hoarse stammering voice. Then she seemed to grow calmer and slowly come to herself; yet for me her face still looked withered and wilted. Night was coming on and it furrowed the face with deep shadows, revealing an irresistible weariness. I did not dare move, to escape from this body on fire, nor did I repulse the hand laid on me, still holding me.

At last Mado abruptly got up, went into the bathroom, and closed the door. A beam of light appeared beneath me. I heard the noise of taps and running water, while I remained alone in the dusk, desperately conscious of my aloneness. To be treated to this bestial pantomime, when I had had such high expectations. If this was love, what a disillusion, what a bleak triumph!

Coldly, almost aggressively, I looked around me. What I saw, sunk in the shadows, was the havoc of a bed, a pile of sheets, a strange room, pretentious and vulgar, a tasteless, conventional parody of luxury.

What a poor thing is the act of love without love itself! How sad a thing when even the pleasure is so horribly short-lived! Not that I knew much about it on this first occasion; but at least the mechanism had been taken to pieces for me, and I had seen the whole sexual comedy acted out in slow motion on one face. I had seen from too close how the smile changes into a deathly grin, how pleasure cloys, how bodies knit together will fall apart, how all I thought pure and beautiful can turn to decay and rottenness before one's eyes. Stripped now of all masculine pride, I had a bitter taste in my mouth, I was humiliated and resentful. Was this really the love I had dreamed so much about, or was it only a travesty? For perhaps even then I must have guessed obscurely how illusory is mere carnal desire.

In the darkness I looked for my clothes. I dressed hastily, and when Mado opened the door and put on the light, she seemed surprised to find me ready to leave. She had attended to her make-up, combed her hair and put on a silk dressing-gown. She looked the same person I saw at the club, with her soft skin and fresh complexion, frighteningly desirable once more. How hypocritical—there was nothing left on her face of the animal mask

142

I had just seen; and I hardly dared look at her. With a caressing gesture she pushed back a lock of hair which had fallen over my brow; I wanted to recoil, but could not avoid the touch of her hand, and this seemed to destroy my will-power. Already the memory of that hungry sagging face was becoming blurred. Already the caress in her smile went subtly through me, and I had to struggle hard against the ferment of sheer lust she had just released in me.

I remained silent. "Feeling a bit disgusted, darling?" said Mado. Then as I did not answer, she went on: "Men often feel like that afterwards. Come closer."

Men felt like that afterwards! In a flash I saw with frightening clarity, doubtless sharpened by jealousy, the cynical succession of lovers drawn into this room, pulled onto this bed with her. Suddenly I found enough courage to say that it was getting late and I would have to go. In this hall, before opening the door, Mado pressed me to her to kiss me. It was shaming that I should still be stirred by this kiss, yet certainly, had she clung to me then, I could never have left her. But she pushed me gently outside, whispering, "See you tomorrow."

I could not sleep that night, but by dawn my decision was made: there would be no tomorrow. At breakfast I told my mother I felt tired, that Toulouse was too hot in the summer and I wanted to go and stay in the Pyrenees with my uncle, leaving that very day.

My mother looked surprised, then regarded me more carefully. She was shocked by my pallor, by the circles under my eyes, by a dark gleam in them which she had not seen there before. I was sitting at table, and she bent over to kiss me on the forehead. She was a woman who could often read people's thoughts without the need for words; but I wonder if she guessed then the strange way Providence had chosen of answering her daily prayer. Though "delivered from evil," I was no longer the gentle, diffident, trusting boy she would have liked me to remain indefinitely. Lured into the forbidden garden, I had chosen to leave it, and now I had closed the gates safely behind me: a painful and deliberate choice, for which I could claim some credit. But how my mother would have trembled to hear of the agonizing crisis which had helped to bring her son to manhood!

Well, it was eight months now since this incident took place; and ever since August I had struggled to wipe out that memory, to forget my disillusion and disgust.

But how could Love and Woman maintain their prestige in the eyes of a budding doctor, from the moment he enters the Anatomy Wing or sets foot inside a hospital? Love deals many a cruel underhand blow, and I had seen some of its victims from all over Paris going through the gates of the St. Louis Hospital with me, every morning of my first two terms.

It was not, of course, that I did not know already the risks which are run even in a casual embrace. When I was in school, all the older boys had been taken to a moral film entitled *The Kiss That Kills*. Huge posters outside the cinema showed a young sailor bending over a lady of the port, and holding her in his arms. The next morning the whole school was talking about the goings-on of the night before. For the older boarders, accompanied by a junior master, had also been taken to see the film, and almost half of them had profited by this exceptional nocturnal excursion to run off during the interval to a specially notorious street quite near. They had returned to school in the early hours, a good deal the worse for liquor. For them curiosity had been victorious over fear; but I had left the cinema shocked and dismayed by this warning.

In the absence of opportunities for such dangerous adventures, the film's alarming message gradually faded from my mind. Thereafter, when I read the notices on public comfort stations saying *Syphilis lays low the strongest* and *Gonorrhoea is the scourge of society*, I paid them little heed. I regarded them with the same indifferent eyes as the obscenities scribbled up near them on the walls. I had had no worries on this score when I was with Mado, but since starting at St. Louis I had been attacked by the old terror of disease.

Crossing the courtyard of the ancient hospital, you read on

the panels on each side of the main door: *Venereal diseases. Consultations every morning, 9 to 11 a.m.* In the early days, seeing this notice, I used to watch the patients with curiosity, imagining them to be all syphilitic. In that crowd there were sordid elderly prostitutes, their faces plastered with powder, their lips too red, going up quite unconcernedly for their intravenous injections. I also saw young women go by with fresh and innocent smiles on their faces, and was amazed they could still smile like this. I soon learned, to my great relief, that here as in other hospitals there were many in the crowd who had bronchial or liver or heart complaints. Whereat I once more appreciated the attractive smiles I observed in the courtyards.

One of the first days of term some of us went to the out-patients department, which at St. Louis had a rather special and unsavory reputation. We saw a noisy crowd waiting in a huge hall, crammed miserably together on endless rows of benches; old hags and tattered beggars looking as if they had vermin running all over them, side by side with scared workmen and slum housewives. Children cried and pushed each other between the benches. The smell I knew already; it was common to all hospital consultations. But it became quite suffocating near the screens, behind which the patients undressed in sections of fifty each. Here it was a concentrated stench of flesh, sweat and poverty. But the most extraordinary sight was the consulting room itself.

It was the hour for women's consultations. At the entrance I felt I had to force my way through into the hot, sticky air. From the door, behind which the patients were pressing forward, four rows of half-naked women spread out in the shape of a fan. Across the huge high hall, well lighted by large windows, they came forward in broad daylight like dancers in some grotesque ballet, heading for four tables placed near the windows, where awaited the doctors surrounded by their pupils. The files progressed slowly, with the undressed, embarrassed women not knowing what to do with their hands, scratching themselves, crossing their hands over their breasts, or else trudging forward with the resignation of cattle—till the moment they arrived in front of one of the doctors, who examined each in turn, palpating them, fingering them, scratching their scabs with a wooden spatula, spreading out greasy hairs with a swab, exploring the bend of a groin or the sweat-soaked hollow of an arm-pit.

That morning, besides scabies and endless other skin cases, I saw some chancres and hideous venereal growths. It was horrible, but almost reassuring. Where was love in all this, where was the woman of my adolescent imagination? Not in these pitiable creatures with bloated flesh, drooping breasts, and lips half-open on the stumps of rotted teeth. Only here and there could you occasionally see a girl with a better figure or younger than the rest; and even then her talk was vulgar, her underwear of dubious cleanliness, and she would probably be covered with eczema. There was nothing left of love as idealized by the longings of a young man's heart. There was nothing here, even, to stir a young man's healthy flesh to desire other flesh.

Another day I went with Chav to the clinic for syphilis injections. There you really saw only hardened cases, about two hundred waiting their turn to go into the cubicle and receive, behind the white curtain, their dose of arsenic, mercury, or bismuth. I found my terrors again there. For although I recognized old hoarse-voiced prostitutes amongst the crowd, I also discovered many young faces looking fresh and innocent, concealing their defilement all too well. Seeing them pass one by one, I often said to myself, "That one there—if I saw her any other place but here, how could I think of her being diseased?" Which Chav translated as: "Start playing around with any old whore, and you'll find yourself in Julius Caesar's position: *Veni, V.D., vici.*"

Every morning we could see the bodies of women spread-eagled on the operating table. All human joy and mystery mixed with degrading and destructive diseases and with organs fulfilling the lowliest of functions. To add to the shock, there were also those who had taken steps to get rid of an unwanted child. They usually tried it over week-ends, and on Monday morning we always found several such cases in the wards, of all ages, bleeding and feverish, determined to have their wombs scraped.

146

Towards the end of the morning, if we went to the theatre, we were sure to see one of them stretched out on the table, legs held raised in the air while the intern prepared to plunge a steel curette into the lower part of her abdomen; no anaesthetic was given. Then began the screams of pain, the gasps and entreaties, while the curette went to and fro in the uterus. Because of the terrible shrieks caused by this operation, you had to bend over the gaping thighs, daubed with iodine, in order to hear under the curette the "uterine cry," the harsh raspy grating sound indicating that the bleeding muscle was at last scraped to the quick, that the woman's body had nothing more left of the importunate little living cyst. But sometimes in the days after that one of these women would die of infection, and nothing could be done to save her.

These first mornings in hospital, purged of sentimentalities and human pretensions, Love seemed to boil down to a matter of two dangers: disease or a baby. You even began to wonder if men and women do not simply try to idealize the act of love by imbuing it with all sorts of fine qualities which it patently does not possess.

Even Chav, who certainly did not as a rule go in for complicated self-analysis, admitted to me one morning that he had been decidedly shaken by these sights. We had just been watching a sample of pus being taken from a uterine cervix.

"All this is pretty horrible," he commented. "It makes me ill to look at a woman in that cold-blooded way with her legs sprawled out and the speculum in position, staring at you like a round eye with a tear right at the tip. God, it quite alters your ideas about the pretty girls you see in the street, having to examine them like this. I used to enjoy imagining what a girl had under her skirt, but only on the surface, of course. What happened in the interior was something quite separate, it didn't interest me at all. But now you can't possibly ignore it, what with their blasted speculum and vaseline and rubber gloves. No good thinking about a little crack, you've got to damn well fall into a big hole. And what a hole! It's no earthly use for these females to swing their bottoms and scent them and cover them with lace; they just can't get away with it. I'll never be able to help thinking of their slobbery innards now, probably peppered with treponema or gonorrhoea. And the saddest thing is, that once you've seen a girl with her legs in the air, they all look alike, there's no way of telling one from another. Why get worked up to block one hole more than another, why not use the hole in a gaspipe for that matter? Oh, I've stopped thinking about it, it put me off my feed. Let's hope I get used to it soon, or else the outlook's pretty bleak for me."

A week or two later, however, he said to me as we came out of the hospital one morning: "Look at that little piece over there, on the pavement in front of the baker's. I see some possibilities there." I decided that for him too the crisis had been resolved.

This might be reassuring for Chav and the Boys from Burgundy. Stripping love of useless sentimental claptrap, it might make things much easier, providing complete sexual satisfaction at a very reasonable psychological price. But as for me, I had not left Mado one August evening to allow genuine passion to be robbed thus of its mysteries and privileges; it could not be determined by a sort of erotic bio-chemistry. Yet the next minute I thought of all I had seen at hospital, and wondered if I was falling into an absurd idealism which denied biological determinisms and the most obvious laws of sexual physiology.

It was just about then that Father Mornay, at St. Luke's one evening, asked one of the lecturers to say a few words to us on the subject of sexual morality. He had a wedding ring on his finger, he was a doctor, he was older than we: good qualifications in our eyes for dealing with these problems. He must certainly know what he was talking about. "In the human species," he said, "as with animals, the voice of instinct is admittedly very strong, but with Man physiological urges are not the only thing at stake. The phenomenon of sex is radically altered by spiritual factors. Man needs the whole of love, not only the part concerned with procreation. We must accept Nature as it is, and in using emotional and sensual attractions, Nature is working towards a loftier goal. That goal is not only the transmission of life, as with animals; it is also, and simultaneously, the moral elevation, through love, of the only creatures capable of love in this sense."

Positive chastity in a young man, he explained, consisted less in doing without immoral pleasure than in the love for higher things, and having respect for the future of a woman who later might bring to a home her sweetness and strength and fertility. But this young doctor who was talking to us must have known through his own experience that such chastity is not easy. Perhaps it is even more difficult for the young medical student than for anyone else, in this very outspoken clinical environment where excessive regard for modesty is not the fashion.

"It is well known," he went on, "that sexual excess blunts intellectual activity. It has been said that to fulfil the full range of its potentialities the intellect requires well-developed sexual glands, and at the same time repression of sexual appetite. Freud is justified in speaking of the enormous part sexual impulses play in our conscious actions. Yet his observations chiefly refer to those who are mentally sick. We must not generalize his conclusions by applying them to well-balanced people who possess the normal degree of self-control. While weak neurotic characters become more abnormal through repression of their instincts, strong characters are made even stronger by this form of self-discipline—and habit here is the great healer."

For seven months, before going to sleep, books closed and lights turned out, I had been haunted by the memory of Mado; on these occasions I forced myself to think of something else, of my daily preoccupations, of my work. So as not to fall by the wayside, feeling my resolution still too frail, I had returned to the dream of a successful future, with only a vague mental picture of when or how it would come about; except that it would include the happiness of living some Great Love. And in the end I dropped off to sleep, thanks to my extreme physical weariness and the perpetual arrears of sleep I needed to make up.

Chapter 2

"B PLUS. Rather my type."

"B plus? You're going too fast, man. Face pretty enough, I agree, and nice saucy breasts. But wait till we can see her from behind. I want to see if she's got nice firm buttocks, the way I like 'em."

On one of the Cité's lawns six of us were squatting, or lying flat on our stomachs, chewing blades of grass and looking down at the boulevard near the iron gates. We were watching the procession of people taking their Sunday walks, and my companions were grading each feminine figure with any claims to prettiness. Though they could not hear our judgments, the unwitting candidates knew we were looking them over by the way our looks converged, and were secretly flattered. The older women, no doubt, thought of some dashing lover, and the girls of their future husbands. Almost all slanted inane smiles in our direction. We were students, with all the prestige attached to that word, and from such groups as ours the long-awaited male might one day come.

It was the usual Sunday crowd, families at full strength taking their constitutionals. It was traditional for them to walk as far as here, and they had done so well before the Cité was built. In those days, when the park was full, late-comers would cross the boulevard and climb on the humps left by the old fortifications. Spreading out their handkerchiefs, they would sit there for whole afternoons at a time, vacantly watching the smoke from little heaps of grass and rubbish being burnt by the local scavengers. It made no physical or mental demands on them, and they were quite content with this rather dismal use of their leisure.

And now we students were sitting in their place, watching them file listlessly by. The Sabbath atmosphere was pleasantly restful, and we savored it for some time. Then some of the boys began to get bored, and Grosrichard suggested a beauty contest. This woke the group up in no uncertain manner. Usually on Sundays the Cité had a quiet and rather deserted air; but with exams drawing near, the students who came on the lawn this Sunday might be jeopardizing their immediate future at the University. Their consciousness of this fact was also indicated by a fair number of books and notebooks strewn on the grass. Slipped under the head, these made very useful pillows, encouraging easy slumber.

I myself was fed up with fidgeting at my table, making my chair creak backwards and forwards, yawning at my window. So I had come out to join them. My sluggish phase had lasted for five days already, and when I felt the call of the outside world I did not resist very sternly. If there was only some small mechanical job to be done, like copying out a diagram or writing up my notes, I would give it up and go out onto the lawn. I never ventured outside the Cité, though; my walk to the fair near the "Lion of Belfort" had revealed too many temptations.

On that evening, remembering Toulouse fairs, I had left the fairground without stopping to think, and soon found myself alone on a long pavement picketed with street-lamps, following an endless bare wall above which you could see the tops of stone crosses and the roofs of vaults. I was skirting Montparnasse Cemetery. Then the dark road emerged abruptly into the Avenue du Maine. A cinema had just come to the end of its program, and under its cataracts of red lights the crowd was pouring out, thronging into nearby cafés and mingling with the crowds coming from the rue de la Gaité. Girls smiled purposefully on the pavements, men came up and spoke to them; lovers who had not had their fill in the cinema passed by, still kissing each other. Laughter and perfumes, coy looks and caresses, blatant lovemaking on public benches and a blur of couples locked together in dark corners, all acknowledge the power of the old urge. It was everywhere, to the end of the world; and once again it was in my own flesh, slowly returning to consciousness at last.

It was all very well to decide, in a moment of revulsion one evening eight months ago, that my body should remain a dead thing. But did I really hope that this resolve would kill for good the strongest instincts of the flesh? Of course there would come another evening when I should hear again the imperious call of love, in sky and trees, in the faces all round me, in everything that was alive.

That evening had come. My heart and body were numb with loneliness, but this evening they had been kindled to new life by the sweetness of the spring. Oh to do as others did, to surrender and let go. What though the joining of two bodies does not make two individuals less alone! No matter—there must be something in sexual pleasure to renew itself ever and again, something which brings you to desire it unendingly.

Whereupon I looked at all the women with the eyes of the seventeen-year-old I had once been. I started going from one to another, roaming down the Avenue du Maine and the rue de la Gaité continually passing the same cinemas and music-halls and theatres, amusement arcades, and lighted bars—on the point of responding to a call with each step I took. But at the last moment I turned away from this woman or that: she would probably have been disease-ridden and anyhow my deepest needs would not have been satisfied by her body alone.

Eventually, weary and sickened, caught between fear and desire, sadly wondering if it would always be like this, I went into a bar and leaned up against the gleaming counter where the whores were laughing and throwing me inviting glances. While I was being served, I saw opposite me, in a glass, a pale face from which the mask had been stripped, as it once had been with Mado. With dark circles beneath them, the eyes had that same hopeless and obsessed gleam which I had met on my first "night of love."

Without even finishing my drink, I left the bar and went out

152

into the soft night, back to my lonely room. For that evening too I was saved. But I wanted to delay the evil hour when I knew I should have to resist again, and it would be harder than ever.

So when I left my room, tired of working, I seldom went beyond the lawn. There were always little groups of students to be found loitering there, and one evening such a group welcomed me in their midst; since then I had often come to join them. On the whole they were not specially congenial, in fact I found them coarse and shallow.

They almost always talked of women, endless chatter about women they had accosted or broken with or slept with. Grosrichard was the most sex-obsessed of all. He was supposed to be reading law, but like the Burgundian Barrière, he thought of practically nothing else but sex. Like Barrière too, his enthusiasm in this pursuit was so cheerfully matter-of-fact, so completely unaffected, that his disgusting descriptions almost lost their obscenity. The rest of the group seemed anxious to outdo him in the lewdness of their conversation, as if they were thereby refuting some slur on their virility.

This Sunday in spring was like summer. I lay there with the rest of them, my face turned towards the sun. My eyes half closed, all I could see was a red blur. The lawn smelled of warm grass and pungent roots. Sprawled out against it, lulled and dizzied by the feel of the warm earth beneath me, I was half transmuted myself into grass and root. I fell gradually into a blissful state of self-obliteration. My companions continued to give marks in the beauty contest, and I dimly absorbed what they were saying, like the unimportant background of a dream. The coarseness of their comments was wasted. Even the vulgar and stupid women who passed us were still women, and as such, merely by passing through it, they added a certain grace and beauty to the boulevard. Through half-closed eyes I saw these women passing in a glorious red haze, like shadows in Paradise, or like bathing beauties at some glamorous resort. In essence they were all so beautiful my dream needed no distortion of the facts. Had not the older ones reached their full beauty, and were not the younger ones adorable for what they might later become! Naturally, in this marvellous universe of fantasy, there were no ugly ones whatever.

My companions had given up all pretense at detachment; their eyes were practically popping out of their heads. "B minus . . . A plus . . . B plus plus . . . brunette . . . blonde . . . redhead." I paid no attention to their more detailed comments, nor did I care to look at the objects of their enthusiasm. I felt a jumble of tenderness rising within me, a desperate wish to offer someone my undying devotion. Among the infinite numbers of women and girls on this earth, surely one at least would have been glad of this tenderness and devotion!

"The last few have all been flat in front and fat behind," said someone.

"Here comes the Sorbonne vamp," cried Grosrichard, and as she passed he went on mocking this student I knew to be aggressively plain. I included even her in my tenderness, and thought of the loving names I would invent for her, how passionately I would take her in my arms—this poor girl who must have waited spring after spring for the dream lover who would never come. Should I always be like her, looking longingly towards the beauty of girls who would always pass me by? I began to visualize the one special girl who would at last appear before me, coming from the ends of the world to find me. How I longed for this girl who would merit in my eyes an Alpha pure! And when she came I could rest my weary head, for one evening at least, against a loving breast.

"Beautiful, just my style, what a perfect specimen! A! A plus!" shrieked Grosrichard, gesticulating in his enthusiasm. "What a perfect idiot," thought I, echoing his shouts. "Why must he stop my dreaming?" I was very sorry for myself, and for a few moments I did not dare open my eyes to see the slut in her Sunday best he would certainly be leering at. But I knew my dream must end sooner or later, and this was as good or bad a moment as any. I opened my eyes.

A girl in her teens was coming up on the boulevard and had almost reached us. Sixteen or seventeen, I guessed, slim with

154

pretty legs, wearing high-heeled shoes and swinging her hips. She had a shy immature grace, and there was still a hint of girlish gawkiness. During the few seconds when she was passing us, my eyes never left her face. What would she do? Turn her head towards us with a sickly smile, like all the others? My pals fell silent, and even Grosrichard stifled the vulgar compliment he had ready on his lips.

I felt my anxiety must be reflected on my face. For I suddenly realized that it would be a terrible disappointment if I saw her look our way. But she did not. She passed us, walking very erectly, and her serene face and lovely clear eyes seemed to be saying: "Just you dare."

We watched her right till the moment when the corner of the hostel hid her from us. Then I rose slowly, and left the group with an air of casualness and calm. But as soon as I had gone past the corner of the hostel, I started running frantically down the boulevard.

"You don't talk like the others." These were the supremely wonderful, unhoped-for words she had said to me, shyly turning her head. Sometimes her voice was muffled by a procession of hooting cars, and I had to bend towards her in order to hear her. Sometimes too I even touched her for a moment, and through her light dress felt the movements and warmth of her body. Since then the whole world had changed for me.

I had followed her at first from a distance, watching the way she walked. Those high-heeled shoes seemed a poor base for her frail ankles, and I saw her stumble slightly on a stone. I felt infinitely tender towards her, and longed to take her in my arms to support her, or rush in front of her and sweep all the stones out of her way. Other men turned to stare at her, while I still walked behind her, scowling with jealousy, thinking of the phrases I would use to introduce myself—when I had walked twenty yards further. I found the phrases all wrong, they would not convey the meaning I wanted, so I started changing them, and gave myself twenty yards more. My courage failed me, and I began another twenty yards and another twenty phrases; and

155

then all at once I plunged forward like a drowning man reaching for his proverbial straw: "Excuse me. . . ."

Heaven knows what I stammered out to her as we walked side by side together in the crowds going up and down the Avenue d'Orléans. But whatever it was she seemed to be listening—I could hardly believe it. I saw her gradually turning her face towards me as if against her better judgment, her eyes traveling all over my face and coming to my eyes with a secret questioning, a troubled curiosity. She must surely have read in them the thrill of turbulent joy which gripped me. There was a sad little smile on her mouth, and I saw the corner of her lips quivering slightly with emotion. It made me want to go down on my knees in the dust before her.

And so there I was a few hours later, waiting for her to arrive at our first date. A clock I could see from the park told me that I was quite absurdly early. But I did not care, my heart was bounding with joy and I had a thousand thoughts to occupy my mind while I waited. I felt I had always known her, though in fact I knew very little about her. I knew her name was Josette, that she was sixteen years old and a dressmaker's apprentice. This last she had told me very modestly, and when I started talking about my medical studies, I could read in her eyes, shining with admiration, her idea of a woman's destiny: to love, honor and obey. With delicious pride I could already imagine myself helping her to rise to my own level. But then again, when I closed my eyes, and pictured her again, so much prettier than I could have dared hope or even wish for, I found it ludicrous to claim any superiority to her at all. The thought scared me at once. Probably she would not come, and then how dark and dreary the evening would be without her.

I was waiting for Josette at the bottom of the park, in a remote corner where my friends hardly ever came. But this evening I was waiting for something far more than a sixteen-year-old girl; I was waiting for pure unsullied love, for the old dream which the discipline of work had helped me to forget. Or perhaps it was something even simpler, just a warm presence at my side, which would bring me a renewal of my secret self.

Suddenly Josette was there in front of me. With a smile which made me feel we already shared a wonderful secret, she told me breathlessly she had had to run because she'd been detained by the aunt she was having supper with. I was bold enough to take her bare arm while we strolled gently down the paths, and our conversation mingled with the cries of children and the smell of flowerbeds and trees.

Evening was falling. Gradually the shadows chased away mothers and children. In the recess of a rockery, among clumps of laurels, there was an empty bench, and there we sat down. Round us the park became dark with a drowsy warmth. A few tall lamps lighted up the corners of lawns and sections of paths.

In our dark recess we were now alone. Together we were both taking our first steps towards the heart of a mystery, and only through each other could we learn its great secret. We were a little scared of the secret and of each other, so for a long while we stayed there without contact, more restrained even than old and satisfied lovers. I kept talking, for I dreaded facing too long a silence, and with a novice's nervousness I said everything that came into my head without trying to make it sound secret or intimate. Josette stayed silent, and I guessed that her face was turned towards me, probing my casual chatter, straining for the words I did not yet dare speak.

Gradually she too began to talk, diffidently at first, as if beside my student's life I would find her existence insignificant. At first I had to question her, and she saw that I was excited by my discoveries. Full of surprised relief that I could like so many things in her life, she began telling me about them now with the joy of a child showing a grown-up her treasures. It was strangely sweet to listen to this pretty little dressmaker's apprentice, remembering how proudly she had passed the group on the lawn, shaming them out of their ribaldry, how horribly nervous I had been in following her. And now, only a few hours later, a fresh and innocent soul was revealed to me, like the petals opening out to reveal the heart of a flower. More wonderful still, her shrill girlish voice carried a tender, shyly caressing note, which I knew was there for my benefit.

Sometimes we were silent, listening in the night without knowing what we hoped to hear; but the silence no longer scared us. A gentle wind sent long shivers through the leaves of the trees. The sweetness of this silence was something I had never known before, and it was almost unbearable, building a whole world of tenderness between us. I let it go on and on, this silence of smiles and high hopes and much else beyond our imagining. It was the same silence which I expect has always fallen between very young lovers, ever since the beginning of the world.

Though right on the edge of the convulsive city, the park was like a desert island, and the murmur of Paris, invisible at our feet, might have been the distant roar of the sea. From some distance off the noise of a bell broke into the night. Every evening since spring began I had heard its gradual approach, at the time for closing the gates, chasing couples from their shady corners; and every evening the bell went on resounding through the park, like a sad reminder of time flying past.

We rose, and remained standing close together without seeing each other. In the dark my hand met Josette's and I took it. The palm I brought to my lips was burning, and her pulse was beating with such strength that all her blood might have been right under my fingers. Before such emotion I myself felt strangely happy and calm. At this minute my senses were brimming over with the tenderness I had longed for, and I wanted nothing else of Josette but to have her near me. I could guess the stillness of her body before me, and as I drew nearer I only wanted to stroke her gently.

Now, thinking back to that love, I smile at my emotional immaturity. We were so happy then and so sure of ourselves, like two young blades of grass blown together by the breeze, swaying at the slightest breath of wind. Our hearts swelled with happiness amidst the deep serenity of the night. I had forgotten Mado. I held Josette in my arms, and pressed her gently to me, for this was indeed how I had pictured love in my boyhood's dreams, and this was how I would have wished to go on loving

her for ever. Contradicting cynicism, all my ingenuous hopes
had been justified.

I bent over towards Josette, and kissed her on the neck. She
did not try to escape. My lips gradually travelled up to her
mouth, and on her closed lips I planted a light kiss. I desired
something more, but felt her lips trembling under mine, and her
body shrinking away from me. Then abruptly she half opened
her mouth and returned my kiss with a clumsy violence which
startled me despite my own inexperience. I was thrilled to find
she was even more of a novice, even less adept than myself. She
seemed now to be almost breathing from my lips, as if she never
wished to let them go; so that when I stopped for a moment she
jerked her face towards me, with the unashamed candor of the
child who has suddenly become a woman.

In the darkness I heard her quick breathing, and I too felt my
heart throbbing violently. This innocent breath against my
mouth had set me aglow; awkward and ardent, her caress had
penetrated to the very depths of my flesh, destroyed my will-
power, and left me defenseless before the sudden onrush of desire. Almost reeling, I drew Josette closer to me, and though she
did not try to escape, I sought to press down on her with all my
weight, to nail her down, to cage her between my limbs. I had
taken her lips again, and they were now quivering and submissive. I began to caress her all over, in a sort of blind frenzy, and
through her dress my caresses confirmed the relaxation and surrender of all her muscles, as it confirmed the sweetness of her
breasts and hips and slim curving shoulders.

Then came an overpowering curiosity: I must know if she
was a virgin. For a moment I hesitated, but the temptation was
too strong. Still leaving one arm round her, I moved slightly
away from her body, and with hypocritical slowness my free
hand descended towards her stomach. She did not resist at first,
but when she realized where my hand was going, she drew back
sharply and pinned my wrist with her hands. When I insisted,
she tightened her grip on my wrist, digging her fingernails
slightly into my flesh. Against my side I again felt her stiff and

159

trembling, and heard her murmur "No! No!" with the imploring voice of a frightened little girl. Then all at once, as abruptly as she had offered me her mouth, she let my free hand finish its movement, indicating that she accepted all I wanted, without hesitation or choice. Through the darkness I heard her weeping softly, in anguish, surrender, and love.

My hand fell back, as I stayed against her, strangely shaken by these tears. I dared not move any more; there was nothing I could say. I was bitterly ashamed of this prying hand which had dared assault her frail trembling flesh. Yet she who was pure had accepted the unlimited power over her body I suddenly demanded. Her trustfulness was almost terrifying.

Her acceptance restored my calm. I still held her in my arms, but only as one might hold some over-trusting child. I felt the tumult in her breast slowly dying down too, and now there was one more invisible bond between us. All at once I felt an immense respect for this shy little girl, such candor and innocence shone through her devotion towards me.

Like a disapproving witness, the bell came nearer. We left our dark corner, and the park-keeper appeared round the bend of a path, dragging his wooden leg and walking very slowly. I took Josette's hand, and the shrill sound of the bell pursued us to the gates. We were like two good little children walking hand in hand. But before leaving the park, I stopped at the foot of a lamp-post, so that she could see my face clearly, could read, I hoped, the remorse I felt for the impulse of a few minutes earlier. I wanted to kiss Josette once in the light, outside the shadow of desire. While I took her lips in mine and held them there, my eyes were closed and I guessed that hers would be wide open. When I opened mine and saw her looking at me once more, my heart stood still. I felt as if I had solved one of the mysteries of the universe. In those big wide eyes I could read whole volumes of pure and selfless love.

Chapter 3

So SEVEN MONTHS of a sober studious existence came abruptly
to an end on that Sunday in May. Like a sorcerer's apprentice,
I was no longer master of my own spells. But I surrendered to
this sweet compulsion, and let Josette fill my heart, which had
too long been bare and now suddenly had no room for anyone
save her. At last I had discovered the joy of loving other than
in dreams, and in the wonderful serenity and innocent contentment it gave me, I began to forget my old sensual conception of
love and took no thought for the future. All I cared about was
that every triumph would now be doubled by the touch of a
delicate shoulder against mine, by the warm savor of a kiss.

I continued my daily life of solitary cramming. I was alone
in the streets, the hospital, the Latin Quarter, in the midst of
my fellow students, alone again in my room before my open
book. Outwardly I was always alone, but in my inner eye the
image of a slender figure was everywhere superimposed, it was
with me all through the day. Then in the park each evening,
when I saw Josette again in the flesh, I felt she had never ceased
to smile for my inner vision.

I began to know the tyranny of love. About half past eight in
the evening I began to lose all interest in my work, and at nine
o'clock, as if hypnotized, I would rise from my chair. I knew
that in a few minutes Josette would be arriving at our meeting
place as she did every evening, and already I was overcome with
impatience for the dusk and the night. But I accepted in advance

all handicaps and disciplines, and in return felt enormously ready for any sacrifices or devotion. I wanted to forget myself completely, to suffer for her sake. In my exaltation I had abandoned that critical sense which since my encounter with Krysia had led me to judge all women with the same stern ferocity.

As soon as I was with Josette, I basked in the sunshine of my own foolish tenderness. Even her physical imperfections, too large a mouth, a slightly bulging forehead, made me feel more tender, attached her to me still more. Often I looked at her admiringly for so long that she eventually blushed and told me: "I'm scared when you look at me like that. You'll only see my faults, I'm sure." But she had nothing to fear. When I took her hands and covered the open palms with kisses, I did not feel the rough skin and innumerable tiny needle-pricks left by her dressmaking. I saw only a caressing hand and the fond dreamy expression on her face.

She made her own clothes, from remnants or surplus material, and her hats were put together from a few ribbon ends. But they suited her so well that I did not even notice how worn her shoes were, how full of darns her silk stockings. Together we explored the contents of her old handbag with its broken clasp; it was stuffed with a thousand girlish trifles—old letters, photos and souvenirs, by the side of lipstick, mascara, and cheap powder. Not having had any sisters or known many girls of my own age, I was thrilled to examine this motley collection, which was my first real contact with feminine fripperies.

A girl does not turn into a woman all at once, and sometimes Josette still relapsed into childishness. I liked these moments, when she would be clumsily flirtatious, alternating fond glances and coy giggles; and at these times, as if she were slightly tipsy, she would lose her usual reserve. She would say anything then, calling me all sorts of affectionate and absurd little names, such as she might have picked up from the girls with whom she worked. It was the age old vocabulary of love, somewhat weakened and coarsened by previous use. "You're my sweetie-pie," she would whisper in my ear, and I felt I was listening to words in some delightful unknown language. It never even occurred to me that she could ever invent for me any more original or profound terms of endearment.

It was in these periods of childishness that we had occasional quarrels, but whereas with another girl I should have felt full of aggressive obstinacy, with Josette I would sue for peace straight away. Feeling her so young and weak and defenseless, so exposed to all manner of distress, I determined to love her more than ever.

During the first evenings we did not leave the park or even the quiet corner where our first rendezvous had taken place. When the watchman and his bell chased us out, I went back with Josette, by small, deserted, dimly lit streets, to quite near where she lived. However slowly we walked, the distance was all too soon covered, and in a flash we had come to the corner of the road where we always stopped to avoid meeting her neighbors. There we had to part, and a sadness came over us which showed the deep feelings in both our hearts. At this moment we desired neither sensual pleasure nor even a caress. All we wanted was never to be separated.

One evening Josette bent her mouth gently towards me, as if to tell me a difficult secret, and whispered to me: "I wish I could sleep by your side every night"; and that was when I suddenly became aware of something I had always obscurely desired. When I was back in my room again, I did not put on the light, but threw myself on the bed, so symbolically narrow, where I could never bring Josette—for the rules forbade it. With eyes open in the darkness, I thought of the happiness I should have felt to have her stretched out next to me. I should have stayed near her, warmed by her very presence, without even touching her, only to dream she was mine. In that dream I should attain a pleasure purer and more intense than any actual possession, as if not our bodies but our two hearts were sleeping together.

For a long while I lay still in the quiet of the night, full of wonder at how spiritual my love had become. But for all that it was saturated in the sexual pleasure which Josette's body had just given me, and this placed our love on a much finer and deeper level than did a passion rigidly separated from the flesh

163

and stripped of all sex. This was no longer desire, as I had known it with Mado, but the fusion of two beings in a world purified and innocent.

Josette would do anything I asked of her. She left me the sole judge, as she had done since the moment on our first evening when lust had taken hold of me, impelling that unhappy move towards her body. When I thought of that moment I was glad that some saner part of me had stood out in defense of scruples as deep rooted as the most brutal of primitive instincts. But what Josette now represented for me, the joys she gave me, were so precious that I could easily forget her body—though admittedly there had been nights when I imagined smuggling her secretly into my room or taking her to a hotel.

But by now I felt incapable of suggesting such a thing, or even using the appropriate words to do so. One evening at St. Luke's I had been told of a shining chastity, so different from a narrow, negative, prudish rule. When I thought of this, I believed I had found the secret for the first time. The love I now had was so perfect it could do without the act of love. Serene in this love, I could fall gently asleep without sinfulness or fear.

Sometimes, instead of staying in the park, we went for a walk, and when I suggested a place to go, Josette always said yes with a touching indifference: "I don't care where I'm going," she implied, "as long as I'm with you."

Often we went to Montparnasse. Sitting on the terrace outside a café, I savored for an hour or so the lighthearted atmosphere of frivolity. I saw with pride how our neighbors stared at Josette, and was childishly happy to be taken for her lover. When on leaving we had to cross the crowd of bohemian eccentrics and tourists, the hideous filthy beggars, I was thrilled to be young and feel the hand of a pretty girl on my arm.

Some evenings we went to the pictures. I chose some small local cinema where they ran old films, classics of the screen. To see *Tabou* or *Dr. Caligari* again, I had no hesitation in shutting myself up near the Porte d'Orléans in an old hall with wooden benches, smelling of dirt and dust and stale tobacco. We called it the flea market.

Completely docile, Josette followed me, and tried to like the films I admired. But she much preferred the opulent cinemas designed for the local *bourgeois*, with their blinding lights at the entrance, their plush seats, their films showing wonderfully impossible lives. When on the screen the rich young man full of noble sentiments married the pretty and unselfish little typist, I felt her lean tenderly on my shoulder. But when the millionaire's daughter offered her fortune and heart to some modest and handsome young man, she would start crying softly in the darkness. As if to beg my pardon for being so poor, she would take my hand and humbly press it. And then I would forget the silly things happening on the screen, and feel a delicious sense of wellbeing, without even wanting, like the other couples, to link arms, impeded by the arm rests, or join our lips.

Once, after a depressing morning at the hospital, when we had been let out earlier than usual, I conceived the idea of going to surprise her. When I got to the rue de Rivoli, I knew at once I was on time: a group of well-dressed men of all ages was already waiting under the arcades. I recognized immediately the main entrance of the building where she worked, which was just as she had described it. "You can't miss it, the shop on the right sells old English prints, the one on the left shows ladies' underwear in the window. If you ever come to wait for me, stand in front of the one in the middle, darling." When I looked at her in surprise, she explained to me that a popular pastime at work was to look out and see where admirers were waiting: the younger men tended to look at the English prints, while the older ones usually preferred the lingerie; and when anybody "changed sides," it gave rise to endless jokes and comments. So I remained discreetly within the shadow of the center door itself.

In the dark passage there was a sound of rushing feet, and out into the daylight poured such a stream of high-spirited girls that I was afraid I might not recognize Josette. All at once I saw her, coming out with two of her friends, and I felt relieved. In all that crush of pretty faces hers stood out. She saw me, left her companions, and ran towards me crying: "Jean!" so loudly and gladly that the other men looked at me with curiosity. Then she took my hand, but before dragging me off, she threw a proud glance at her friends. While we were crossing the road to go into the Tuileries gardens, she leaned towards me and said: "You saw how surprised the other girls were. Just think of it, sweetheart, you're the first young man who ever came to wait for me."

She led me to a statue which, with its surrounding shrubbery, made up a tiny square in the large gardens. "There's never anyone here at lunch time," she explained, "so in the summer I come and eat my lunch here, or else read when I want to have a little peace and quiet." I imagined her all alone among chattering sparrows and big pigeons, pink and gray in the sky. This was how she clung to her solitude right in the heart of Paris, dreaming of the prince charming who would perhaps one day escort her there. I was happy to be that prince.

I got into the habit of going to meet her every day at noon. Coming out of the hospital, where each morning I continued to spell out painfully the alphabet of disease and to watch humanity show me its innards, I still hesitated for a moment before going out into the turmoil of the Paris streets. But I wished to become an ordinary young man again, so I dashed off to Josette at once, the sooner to draw from her presence my own fair share of happiness.

Sandwiched between the austerities of hospital and the dissecting sessions, already beginning to be unpleasant in the first heat of summer, the hour from twelve to one ceased to be serious and gloomy; instead it was young and springlike, full of the lightness and effervescence I felt inside me. Often in fact I wondered if this hour did not take on value and reality from being placed between the two otherwise sombre halves of the day. For a little while I could forget my constant concern with pain and death, and join the ranks of normal youngsters whose only goal was happiness. Moreover, even while I was in love the hospital maintained its importance in my life, the stark realities of the morning were not contradicted. I loved Josette for her frail grace, which might always be threatened by the hazards of ordinary life; but here was I to cherish and protect her.

166

As with the patients like Armand, whose loneliness I had been trying to alleviate all morning, I was proud to feel that Josette depended on me. I hoped to understand her as I understood the patients lying in bed in my ward. Yes, it was good to be the ear she had long waited for on her path, the ear to which with complete confidence she could pour out all the wonderful freshness of her simple and appealing little heart.

Each time I came to wait for Josette, we walked for a little while under the arcades, but I did not want her to stop and look in the shop windows. I felt she must feel badly when she saw these tempting displays, since I could not offer to buy her anything. Our lunches and evenings together had taken considerable toll of my finances. I would quickly rush her off towards the Tuileries, and we would go to a small restaurant near there. When we ordered, her desire to agree with me in everything was such that she would slavishly take everything I took, and I had to be quite ingenious to discover on the menu, stained with greasy fingermarks, what she really liked best, as a true Parisian: always spiced dishes, burning hot sauces, and vinegar dressings. I detested them but now choked them down as if there were nothing I liked better. Afterwards I brought her back to the entrance of her shop, and before dashing off to school, I would wait to see her figure and the bright indeterminate blob that was her face, still turned towards me, disappearing in the half-darkness of the passage.

One day she came out with a box under her arm, and when after lunch I started going back towards the shop, she laughed triumphantly and told me: "Today I can go out with you. I've got a really chic dress to wear." So she walked with me all the way to the medical school. It was the time for a written test, and students were arriving from all sides. I gloried in being seen with Josette, and feeling her shrink a little closer to me beneath so many admiring stares. Suddenly she asked me: "Are they *all* medical students?" And when I answered: "Yes," she seemed a little surprised and even shocked. Love always makes of the chosen one something exclusive and unique. For Josette, in the teeth of all logic, I represented the only medical student there was; the others must be impostors.

I looked at her, hanging on my arm, with her expression of purity and happiness, and felt she had never looked so pretty as she did then under the envious gaze of my fellow-students—and that I had never been so fond of her. So much is male love stimulated by the sense of competition.

This was my first real love affair, unsullied by sensuality, and what joy it had brought me! Had anyone asked at that moment whether I was completely happy, I should have answered without hesitation, with a great surge in my heart: "Yes, this is happiness." Forgetting the day when I had approached her so humbly and marvelled to find her listening to me, I should have thought of Josette turning her face eagerly towards me when I came to meet her, with that submissive, slightly sad smile on her face, as if till the last minute she had feared I might not turn up. This would have given me confidence enough to add casually to my answer: "It's easy to find happiness."

It happened imperceptibly. Yet in these early summer days there must certainly have been one particular day, outwardly like any other, when everything began to change between Josette and me. What changed us? Some trifle, some subtle shade of difference, yet it was enough. If after that day someone had again asked whether I was happy, I should probably have turned my head away and hesitated to use the word happiness—an overstatement for an adventure which was moving inexorably towards its close.

The date of the final exams drew near. I had done enough work during the year to have a rough grasp of the vast syllabus of anatomy; but these university exams were somewhat overshadowed by the public, competitive examinations at which hospital dressers are recruited. Accordingly, like most of the other students of my year, I had only studied thoroughly the sections of anatomy which might figure in the latter, and in the same utilitarian spirit had completely abandoned the histology course with its paraphernalia about eggs and cells and tissues and such microscopic solemnities.

One fine morning I awoke from my idyll of leisure, began to face stern realities, and was horrified by the gaps in my knowledge. I saw myself flunking all the exams, and my whole year's work lost. Around me was the feverish atmosphere of the last few days of cramming. Away with time wasting and idleness—frantic work was the order of the day. The students everywhere were isolating themselves in their books with heroic if belated determination, or else they went off in pairs to test each other and sustain flagging energies. It had begun to get very hot. The last dissecting sessions were over, and I spent the afternoons in my room, head bent in study, with an occasional desperate glance at the big hand of the clock, which seemed to move on at a quite impossible speed. Afterwards, my head would feel completely empty and my nerves were strung to breaking point. But in the evenings, when it struck nine, I just could not go on working any longer. Realizing that I might be courting disaster, but incapable of resistance, I went to meet Josette, strained and irritable, torturing myself with the thought of all I had left undone.

Once near her I kept on thinking of my obvious lack of willpower, but instead of blaming myself for it I would suddenly feel angry and resentful against Josette, and took every opportunity, however unreasonable, to show it. Josette would listen to me sadly without saying anything, and then, full of remorse, I would make a tremendous effort to forget the coming exam for one evening more. Looking at her again then, I would be deeply touched by the expression on her face of gratitude and reassurance.

To gain time for study, I went less often to meet her in the lunch hour. One day when she was not expecting me, she came out of the shop with a friend I'd never seen, an adorable little blonde, typically Parisian, merry, and full of life. When she saw me, Josette left her friend at once, but I saw the latter turning round several times to look at us going off together. Casually during lunch Josette mentioned this girl, and I asked: "You mean the one with the beautiful blue eyes?" I saw her look at me in surprise, as if to say: "So you noticed that?"

Her surprise irritated me. Had I ever given her cause to be jealous? I had always glanced at her companions with complete indifference, but did that mean I must now go around with my eyes blindfolded? The next day I arrived unexpectedly, and when Josette emerged with her friend, I went up to them before they could separate, and all three of us had lunch together. I played the dashing young man, very witty and high spirited.

The friend's name was Marcelle. From close to, I found her eyes still prettier, her face extremely gay and vivacious, with a tip-tilted nose and saucy mouth. She laughed shrilly at all my jokes. Beside her Josette seemed very gentle and reserved, almost too dainty. Under the influence of two or three glasses of wine, and with the secret intention of making herself attractive to her friend's sweetheart, Marcelle started chattering, saying anything that came into her head, giggling happily and bestowing on me absurd knowing glances. Josette looked at me from time to time, and so as not to seem sulky tried to follow Marcelle's lead. Consequently I was regaled with a barrage of gossip about all the personalities in the workroom, the manager, the customers, the other girls, the forewoman: "Oh, she's an old bitch, honestly she is. She doesn't like us being waited for outside, the silly old fool. What's it to her who we go to the movies with?" Josette's love for me had also attracted the said forewoman's notice, apparently, and she heartily seconded Marcelle's indignation.

This futile endless gossip went on and on, and the moment came when I completely lost interest. I smiled vaguely, nodding approvingly and thinking of other things, like the work waiting for me back in my room, and the fact that only four days separated me from the first exam, yet here I was wasting my time with two stupid adolescent girls. Looked at in the cold light of reason, Marcelle suddenly became very vulgar, and I began to examine Josette too with a fiercely critical eye. I looked at her well-worn clothes and the darns in her stockings, I observed the flaws in her face. I had deliberately ignored the existence of such flaws before, but now they seemed to stand out and point to our coming separation.

"My dear, you should of seen what I saw this morning, when I went to deliver that new model to the American lady at the George V. Gosh, her undies and silks, and the jewels and flowers everywhere, all over the room, my dear, you've never seen anything like it."

Which of the two had spoken? It made little difference. For a moment I imagined the fine lady at the Hotel George V. Beside her cheeky little Marcelle, with her turned-up nose and round cheeks and mischievous Parisian eyes, was only a poor little errand-girl, though admittedly pretty. As for Josette, with her frail delicacy, her pinched little shoulders, that gentle charm suddenly seemed quite inadequate. I felt an abrupt desire for something else, for women of a different quality and different circumstances, where there would be no suggestion of petty economies and cheap finery. Perhaps, too, I subconsciously wanted a love which would be equally tender but less restrained.

When we were in the street, Josette seized my arm, a gesture of taking me over again as her property. I was in a hurry to be rid of her, and started walking very quickly. The constraint on my arm was intolerable, and I felt very silly with my two companions trotting along on either side of me. They both looked very disconcerted when I left them at the first Metro station we came to, with the air of one making a quick escape.

A thousand little incidents began coming between me and Josette at every turn. Before this they would have been unimportant, and I should have very easily overlooked them. But now they were continually provoking me to quite unfair attacks of temper and unkindness. Josette, without answering in words, would raise big startled eyes towards me, sad and reproachful, the eyes of a dog being beaten without cause. Sometimes, knowing my hostile silence hurt her more than any words I could speak, I would spend the entire evening with her without saying a word. She would timidly try to talk to me, but in face of my obstinate silence she would very soon apologize for having dared disturb my silence, seeing I had decided not to talk. How she must have loved me to humiliate herself like this—but at times this humility exasperated me even more, and I was seized by an impulse of sadistic cruelty which urged me to see how far I could go in tormenting her.

Afterward, when I was alone once more, and thought of her again, I would feel sorry for her. I pitied her for the uncertainty of her future, destined all her life to do menial tasks and to live with a husband who would certainly be inferior to her. Eventually she would grow used to living with him, and all the other stupid people who would fill her existence. Often she would feel like crying for no apparent reason. But what was happening now would be the reason, and she would try to believe herself happy, to forget the few weeks when she *had* been, to forget the dreams which could never come true.

At times my pity almost became love again; but I observed a terrible difference: perhaps I still loved her, but I no longer suffered because of her. She had no more power over me, whereas I could torture her whenever I wanted. So I had to admit to myself that really I did not love her any more, that I too was an ordinary selfish male, desiring all women, always ready to take everything without ever giving in return. From now on our relationship would be merely tedious for me, painful and hopeless for her.

The exams had begun. The letter drawn by lot to decide where the series should start was R, so I should be among the last. I profited by this postponement to try to review the syllabus as a whole. I no longer went to the hospital or to tutorial classes; the only time I went out was for a breather in the Latin Quarter, at the beginning of the afternoon, near the examination halls. At the entrances, in the big hall, in the corridors, wandered students showing pale worried faces or else a forced gaiety, the girls among them liable to hysterical giggles and nervous movements.

After having listened to the exam questions for a minute or two and checked on my own chances, I would go up to the library, where the atmosphere was stuffy and oppressive. The big curtains were half drawn, but the roar of trams, the hooting of cars and all sorts of other street noises slipped through from the

172

boulevard outside, masking the muffled whispers, the rustle of pages, and the clap of books being closed. A tremendous weariness reigned, very different from the cheerful hive of industry on winter afternoons. On all these taut and sweating faces you could read an overpowering desire to reach the end of the year, no matter whether it ended well or ill.

My turn came at last. I passed easily in anatomy, but in histology the chromosomes almost tripped me up—and I only just scraped through.

Already the Cité Universitaire was emptying. The hubbub in the restaurant had turned into a confidential murmur. The sun-baked lawns, showing bare strips where the students usually lay, were deserted. The hostels seemed almost out of use. I for my part planned to leave for a fortnight's holiday in Toulouse, before returning at the beginning of August and getting down to concentrated work for the dressers' exam.

I decided to leave on the twelfth of July. Three evenings in succession, drawn away by Grosrichard and his friends, I had not met Josette in the park. The evening before I left, I went to meet her, and found her sitting patiently on a bench waiting for me. I told her of my departure quite casually, as merely a little break of a few days which would give us the new joy of writing to each other. I had wondered nervously what her reaction would be, and I dreaded a flood of tears. But as soon as I had finished speaking, for the first time I saw her face set in hostility. With a fury almost amounting to hatred, she shouted at me: "Why do you lie to me? You know very well you never expect to see me again." It was, for her, such an uncontrollable outburst that she had to stop after that. I thought how terribly she must have suffered to abandon her usual slavish adoration and to dare to reproach me like this. I hesitated for a moment, but already I felt a selfish joy inside me. This aggressiveness on her part would make the break easier.

But it was evidently impossible for Josette to keep up a tone so contrary to her nature; she seemed almost stupefied by her own words, and promptly dissolved into tears, snuggling against me as she had done on our fondest evenings of love. Raising great tearful eyes towards me, she stammered in a voice strangled with sobs: "Oh yes, I knew all along you weren't for me, that you'd leave me some day for someone of your own class. But I never thought it would be so soon . . ." She began to cry even more violently and to press passionately against me as if to make me understand the full fervor of her grief. I heard her saying: "I was so happy because you loved me at all." And then she began to repeat in a childish voice all the affectionate names she had so delighted to bestow on me.

But suddenly she reached up to my ear and used the word she had never dared use before: "My lover." She repeated it several times with a violence of pain in which all her heart and flesh seemed to join. She raised her eyes towards me as if to possess my face again and delay the moment when all would be over between us. I could only sit there under her look, ashamed that she would see on my face only casual pity and tenderness, nothing at all comparable to her own emotion. Probably Josette had guessed the impossibility of our love some time ago, and every time I was unkind or unfair, a shaft of agony had pierced her and warned her that one day I would leave her. She had foreseen that she would be completely helpless to stop it, it would slip through her fingers like running water. This modest, sensible little girl had long been taught by instinct and experience to distrust all happiness, and perhaps she had bravely prepared for this ever since our first meeting. But no, she could not in any case have imagined it would hurt so terribly. Yet she accepted her suffering with a sort of proud hopelessness, and was too honest to think of begging me to stay, forcing me to mean lies, and a denial of what we both knew to be the truth.

And now I at last suffered with her, ashamed of making her adult life start in such bitterness and sorrow. Yet even at that moment I also felt a certain pride in being capable of such noble sentiments. It was really only a masculine kind of suffering, paltry, half-hearted and superficial, slyly blending an easy pity with the vanity aroused by this boundless love for my person.

174

She was the first woman who had suffered through me. How many others would there be?

There was a subtle pleasure to be holding in my arms this body, which was almost my property, which I had the power to destroy; and as she pressed violently against me, I dimly regretted being deprived of her physical presence. For a moment I had the idea of dragging her off straight away to some hotel room; I was sure that even now, when she knew all was over, she would not refuse me this, that she loved me too much ever to refuse me anything. Just then she looked at me, always ready and submissive since the first evening, but in the tearful eyes she raised towards me she seemed to be giving me her very heart to crush. Surely I could not do her even more harm? Pity wiped out my desire. I even tried desperately to redeem myself in my own eyes by reducing myself in hers, showing myself as I really was, full of evil thoughts and lusts. I tried to tell her she was all wrong about me, that I was just like all the others, like all those who tried to accost her any evening in the street.

She stopped me with a sharp cry, as if I had uttered a blasphemy: "No, no! You're *not* like the others. If you only knew how nice you can be. . . ." She paused a moment and smiled at the inner image of me she would obstinately guard, and then repeated softly: "You can be so nice, so very nice . . ." and then very slowly, as if it were a vital question for her, she added: "In fact I've sometimes wondered why you've been so nice to me. Were you just being kind, or were you really in love with me? Please tell me, did you ever really love me just a little?"

I was staggered by the anguish in her voice. I realized that the poor girl was trying to lay up a treasure of memory, my voice, my words, my face—before being once more alone; that she was trying to gather a few timeless grains from the harvest of her first great love. Bending towards her, exalted by the joy I was about to give her, I whispered in her ear with almost complete sincerity: "I swear to you, my darling, I shall never forget you." Her eyes literally shone through the tears with overwhelming happiness, and as I gazed into them I thought for a few seconds that we might have been able to live and be happy together. Perhaps we could have—but there were so many invisible forces setting up barriers between us.

In the distance the keeper's bell rang out, and as on the first evening, I took Josette's arm. We walked towards the gate, watching our two shadows, joined by our hands, growing smaller on the gravel of the path, then vanishing, and then growing long again at each lamp. It was our last evening, superficially so very like the first, so very like all our evenings in the park, where despite the beating of our hearts we achieved an illusion of time standing still, forgetting the old keeper until he came to chase us out. But there he would be each night in the distance already, and we must have felt some indefinable warning in the cool breath of the night wind, for we always knew he was coming before we actually heard him. He was over there now, coming towards us with dull clumps of his wooden leg, ringing his bell in the night, on and on, monotonous as an endless nursery rhyme.

While we walked away I felt Josette's hand taut in mine; she slackened her pace, with the instinctive, unreasoning hope that she might never emerge from the garden and from our love. I tried to pull her, to drag her on a little faster—so I could escape from her desperate tenderness, so much greater now than the remains of my feeling for her could sustain. I wanted to walk quickly so I could finish this stupid affair with the first little girl I had met in Paris, so I could reduce to its true level of a very small adventure what I had once believed to be a grand, profound, and passionate love.

The old keeper appeared. Josette had told me one evening how she had often come and played in the park when she was a little girl, and how the keeper's wooden leg had frightened her. I had imagined her singing, with her wild curls whirling:

> "Join in the dance, see how they dance,
> Sing, dance and kiss the one you choose."

It was an old nursery song, which leaves a sweet echo in little girls' hearts through all their lives.

"Kiss the one you choose . . ." The day I had come into her life, she had believed I was fulfilling for her the golden dream she had always dimly longed for; and for a moment I had thought myself able to do so. But to succeed in love is not so simple a matter. I had loved Josette tenderly in her purity and grace and even in her weakness. But I had loved her on a plane outside the physical, and this was why our love had not really counted. Not from lack of desire but through a remnant of prudence, a last touch of integrity, I had felt I should not take her body as well; I was certainly right not to involve her whole life with mine. And so our love had lacked this exclusive bond, this firm reality, which physical love must add to tender affection. So tonight it was I who stepped out of the nursery ring, and said goodbye to Josette: "Goodbye, little girl I thought I loved. In the great love I want, heart and soul and body will act in unison to make me love for ever."

When we reached the gate, at the exact spot where I had kissed her in the lamplight the first evening, she stopped me and said: "Kiss me." Her voice was imperious for the first time. She raised towards me her sad little mouth, her solemn eyes dark and trembling like water at the bottom of a well. I gave her a last kiss. I saw her almost swoon, hanging on my lips, the only ones for her in all the great city. Then she began to cry softly against my shoulder, and her stifled sobs brought a last murmur of remorse and regret to my heart. For a few seconds more I pitied her, because I could not love her as she loved me; it was impossible. Then, as she continued to weep, I felt my remorse growing smaller and paler and finally fading; faced by this hopeless grief I had nothing more left than my subtle and slightly cruel masculine pride that I had been the stronger. Since love cannot last for ever, I was glad to be the one who had been delivered from it first.

We took a few steps more, linked under the tall lamps, and at each of them our shadows against the ground came up, passed and departed. Each time it was like the image of a new love. Then our hands separated; she brought hers up to her face as it faded swiftly from my inner vision. Now there was only a great void between our two shadows. Near mine I no longer saw Josette's, but the shadow of the woman who on some new evening would walk there by my side. Already, straining into the night, I was trying to imagine her face.

Chapter 4

I ENJOYED my vacation in Toulouse. I did not, of course, tell my mother about Josette, but I think she guessed my need for relaxation, even apart from the exams just finished. To the background of unobtrusive but affectionate solicitude I was able to spend a lazy two weeks, which I needed, with clear conscience. I returned to Paris much refreshed, ready to work furiously for the dressers' examinations.

Dressers are paid a nominal salary, and their responsibilities, under an interne, extend to giving anaesthetics and many of the advanced treatments on the wards. Recruiting them, like the choice of other hospital personnel, is quite separate from the results of the ordinary university studies, and university students can qualify as doctors without ever taking a dresser's post in a hospital. Most of us, however, even some of the more indolent, were eager for the clinical experience to be gained as a dresser, and I for one meant to start my second year as a salaried member of some hospital's staff. The exams took place at the beginning of October, which gave me all August and September for concentrated studies. Unfortunately I soon discovered that these hot holiday months in Paris are not conducive to clearheaded concentration.

The atmosphere at the Cité had changed remarkably. The master of my hostel was on holiday, and in his absence an easygoing tolerance prevailed. The few students who were obliged to stay in Paris had been joined by a floating population of provincial or foreign students, for whom each summer the Cité constituted an agreeable and economical hotel; these birds of passage did not know or heed the sterner rules of the establishment. The torrid silence of the lawns, and the drowsy calm in the hostels were invaded by noisy laughter and dance music from scores of radios and gramophones. Girl students moved freely about the corridors, and you could hear a babel of different languages. This was far from unpleasant, and the occasional joyous laughter I would catch in the building had, too, a charmingly international flavor. While I was trying to force myself back into my room to study, I would see attractive girls from far away stretched out under the trees and pergolas, waited on by the "natives." These latter probably could not afford the expenses of a holiday on the coast, but a week's or month's flirtation doubtless provided the next best thing to the pleasures of the seaside.

Work became more and more painful for me. Fortunately the classes started again at the beginning of September, and with their aid and my own plodding review I at last began to reap the harvest of my virtuous life in my first two terms. At last the elusive facts and formulae stuck in my head. Nevertheless, I was far from confident when at 8.20 on a gray October morning I walked into the huge examination hall, already buzzing with the nervous murmur characteristic of the last few minutes of suspense. I looked at the endless chairs and tables, twelve hundred of them, numbered in advance for each candidate. I sat down in front of the ink and blotting paper and sheets of blank paper, set out on the table my fountain pen and watch, wrote my name and other necessary details on the paper, and then, having nothing else to do, gazed round at the other eleven hundred and ninety nine heads, all obsessed with the same hopes and anxieties, all mentally rehashing their last desperate hours of reviewing.

I was detached enough, during the tension of the last five minutes, to recognize some of the mannerisms which I had studied on psychoanalytical lines. Some students rubbed their eyes and blinked, not so much from sleepiness or because they could not see properly, as in an unconscious effort to clarify their ideas. Those who kept on sniffing were perhaps simply trying to unblock their nostrils, but more probably they found this the best way of struggling against their general sense of obstruction and constraint. Those who looked as if they were chasing flies off their faces were unconsciously pushing rivals out of their way, and others, as if blowing their noses, kept pinching them with their fingers—another way of liquidating rivals. Others again, who yawned or mechanically massaged their stomachs, were clearly hoping to rid themselves of the inner spasms which had us all tied in mental knots.

Some had completely vacant stares on their faces, fixing a point in space and revealing unwittingly their intimate habits, foraging feverishly in their noses, feeling inside their armpits, or else placidly investigating their teeth with toothpicks. A few in the nervewracked crowd kept a stern watch on their gestures, and in a violent effort to achieve comparative calm had buried their hands in trouser pockets or the armholes of their coats. Finally, a very small minority sat in their places waiting sensibly, looked lucidly around them, laid their hands on the table with the fingers still and relaxed, testifying to genuine confidence and self-mastery.

The examiners entered, went up on the rostrum, and took their places behind the long table; immediately a tense silence reigned. The presiding official, a well-known hospital consulting surgeon, began slowly dictating the fifteen questions which he drew by lot from the urn; after each the uncertainty dwindled, and after the fifteenth the entire hall, knowing their fate at last, drew a moment's noisy breath before concentrating on the blank sheets in front of them, searching for words as if the salvation of their souls were at stake.

Without trying, I caught a glimpse of the chap on my right bent over the first sheet, distracted and hesitant. His Adam's apple trembled with excitement and he held his pen poised in the air above the paper, like a conductor before the opening bars of a symphony. The place at his left was empty, but next to that a girl with glasses betrayed her taut nerves, her face flushed and contorted in a look of almost demoniac concentration. The fatal hour and a half had begun; six minutes for each question—there was no time to lose. Feverishly I too bent over the blank sheets before me.

From all the tables rose the noise of twelve hundred pens scratching away at a dizzy speed. Pausing for a moment I suddenly decided it was the unending squeak of twelve hundred little nibbling mice given ninety irrevocable minutes to gnaw through the whole contents of a vast library. From the pens in regular rhythm poured an endless spate of words, words, and more words, thousands and thousands of them. Twelve hundred heads bent more and more avidly over pages hungry to be filled; not a single second must be lost, not a single syllable of the little black signs which would transform three hundred of us into hospital dressers.

I had been lucky, or rather my tutors had done their work well. I could cope quite competently with almost all of the fifteen questions, for we had come across them, or something very like them, in our recent review. Indeed, directly I had heard the questions I decided that everything was going to be all right.

At ten o'clock, when we handed in our papers and left the hall, I felt exhausted and curiously deflated: so short a test after so much work put in. The pricked-balloon mood lasted all that day. Finally I planned to go home for a month until the beginning of the winter term; that would still be before the results of the exam were announced. But after a splendid night's sleep, my brain reeling with a wonderful sense of unaccustomed freedom, I felt a great deal better. Yes, I was confident of being one of the lucky three hundred, and that was certainly no small thing. I had come through my first year of medicine, if not with flying colors, at least with no particular cause for gloom or despondency.

Part 4

THE INTERNES' HOP

Chapter 1

UNEXPECTEDLY, my second year started in style. Just as I was packing to go home for a month, Bouvray, the only fifth year man in my hostel, came into my room with an unexpected suggestion. One of his friends was seriously ill and had to leave his post of dresser in the surgical wards of the Charité Hospital. The Chief Surgeon there was Hauberger, one of the most celebrated chiefs in Paris, and to work under him was a coveted honor for internes and dressers alike. Would I like, asked Bouvray, to replace his sick friend as dresser? It would mean I did not have to wait for the result of the exam. He wanted me to start tomorrow, drawing, of course, my eight francs a day. Would I like it indeed? I was highly flattered that Bouvray should have thought of me, and he had no need to offer extra inducements. Naturally I jumped at the chance.

In consequence, ten nights later, when I might well have been peacefully in bed at Toulouse, I found myself in Wagram Hall, with a pretty girl at my side, watching the proceeding at the "Internes' Hop," a glorious affair which occurred every year. It was in fancy-dress and was organized by the internes of the Paris hospitals, at the end of the year's public examination by which their new colleagues were recruited. This extremely stiff examination lasts three days and is highly competitive; for there is only one interne's post vacant in each hospital wing. The exam of ten days ago, which had caused me so much anxiety, was a mere trifle by comparison. Candidates for the interne's exam worked at fever pitch for many months, and the tension on the

185

fateful three days was terrific. It was no wonder that their relaxation at this party was on an equally terrific scale.

The floor was covered with a mass of exotic and unlikely characters, an incredible medley of costumes from all corners of the world, culled from history and legend, representing every age and race and color—a glorious crazy carnival, providing excellent opportunities, of course, for fairly complete nudity.

Native drumbeats and the blare of brass thundered forth from the loudspeakers. Most of the crowd were already more than half drunk. As they whirled and swayed and pranced to the music, they accompanied it with bawdy songs shouted at the tops of their voices, happy at any excuse for rowdy laughter. One moist body glued to another, there were some queer combinations on the dance floor—Egyptians with Chinese, Assyrians with Indians. Greasepaint was everywhere, and dyed muslin and gilded paper made ingenious substitutes for brocades and jewellery. Many had found it simpler to assume the disguise of savages, vaguely daubed all over, wearing nothing beyond a bit of rag round their loins. Others wore tight panther-skins, attracted no doubt by the chance of showing off their well developed muscles. Five authentic Negroes had painted themselves green. As for the women, their costumes were reduced to the minimum demanded by history or legend: according to the way it was worn, a scanty length of silk or muslin could be made to suggest a goddess or a ranee. The least sketchy costumes would not have been out of place on a beach, and a few seemed to be emulating Eve before the Fall. Pink flesh swaying gracefully in the dance, they all showed a pleasant freedom from self-consciousness; in more senses than one they seemed to find it natural.

All round the room, under the circular gallery, delicate constructions of canvas and cardboard had been set up as special boxes, even weirder and more anachronistic than the costumes. In a strange confusion of continents and centuries, the ochre entrance to an underground cave was next door to the gorgeous gilt of a Chinese pavilion; the whiteness of a Greek temple against a turquoise sky was overshadowed by the gray stone spandrels of a mediaeval portal. This was the setting for the Internes' Hop, for the medical world the year's night of nights for mirth and madness and magic, gaiety and licentiousness, bawdiness and burlesque.

At a beat of the big drum, sturdy internes painted black from head to foot, waving femurs instead of truncheons, began clearing the dance floor in highly constabular manner. They were the "Black Watch," responsible for good order at the ball.

Followed a regrouping of colors and costumes. Ruddy fellahin and blue-veiled Egyptian girls returned to their papier-mâché caverns; Greek shepherds and shepherdesses to their canvas colonnades; and the prehistoric men and women carried out a difficult migration, through all history's obstacles, back to their caves. When all the spectators were squatted round the sides of the floor, the pageant began. It was in ten tableaux (one for each hospital), depicting *Medicine through the Ages.*

The band began to play a medley from *La Belle Hélène,* and the first performers took the stage for a delightful fantasy set in ancient Greece. The King of Thessaly led a procession including his grown-up son, his bodyguard, his wives and courtiers; it moved slowly forward toward the white temple of Hygeia, daughter of Aesculpius and goddess of Health. Under the concentrated beam of the floodlights Hellas was alive again: a crowd in tunic and chlamys, women carrying amphorae, soldiers and slaves—all so realistic that you expected to see a blue sky above them and a blue sea, with cypress and myrtles on the horizon.

When the king arrived with his court in front of the temple, a spotlight abruptly picked out the goddess, standing naked on the altar in radiant beauty. Loud clapping from the entire audience. On the loudspeaker a master of ceremonies explained the sequence of events. The king, a choleric tyrant, having amused himself by beating a few slaves, starts shaking his son, who appears half-witted and is sprawled dejectedly in a small chariot. The king implores Hygeia to restore his languishing offspring to health, and as if summoned by the goddess the great Hippocrates appears instantly, with a long white beard and traveler's staff. Majestically he wanders thus from town to town, according to the fashion of doctors in those times. On receiving the king's appeal, he goes down on his knees before the altar, and then agrees to treat the young patient, on condition his orders be followed, whatever they may be.

The king is choking with rage, but bows to the need of doing anything to save his heir. Hippocrates comes up to the patient, still slumped in his chariot, takes his wrist and feels his pulse. Then he gives orders that the prettiest girls in the kingdom should file before the prince. A glorious procession of naked beauties passes by in single file, amidst vociferous applause from the audience; but the young prince remains apathetic. The beautiful girls continue to file past, while the king shows signs of high displeasure. He is about to have Hippocrates thrown out, when suddenly the Father of Medicine, who has continued to feel his patient's pulse, makes a sign that the procession shall be stopped at a lovely golden-haired shepherdess. Not daring confess it to his terrible father, the prince has been secretly enamored of her, and when he sees her in the procession his pulse beats betray him. But Hippocrates has the king's promise, and for the royal patient he orders—marriage.

The young prince revives at once, and moves towards the altar with his shepherdess, followed by Hippocrates, who knows that no healing takes place without the help of the gods. Behind come the king and all his court, dancing forward to incline before the all-powerful goddess and sing an epithalamium.

I should have enjoyed this pageant in any circumstances, but the circumstances tonight were exceptionally favorable for enjoyment. I was watching it from the gallery, which was almost in darkness, feeling a warm feminine body against mine, while my hand was on a bare shoulder, pressing hungrily against the soft flesh. The light-headedness I felt was not caused by the wine I had drunk at dinner in the internes' common room at the hospital before the ball.

Our interne had invited all the dressers on his ward to this dinner as well as to the ball. On reaching the common room I

188

had been given some rags to wear. I was supposed to be a medieval beggar from the Cour des Miracles. I was rather overawed by the occasion, and when we came to the table I felt extremely lucky to be there at all. Just as we were sitting down, with some of the diners still pushing for places, I found myself next to a girl in a very scanty gypsy costume. Women were rare at our end of the table, and the man on the other side of her, an art student who had come to help with the decor, had immediately captured the gypsy and was caressing her thighs as he taught her the words of the student songs. She had not even looked at me. I found her pretty enough, but childish and vulgar, so her indifference did not worry me. In any case my main concern was to see and hear as much as I could, and after the first few bottles of champagne, I was confident there would be plenty to see and hear in the course of the evening.

Then an orderly came to look for the interne on call, to deal with an accident case. The idea of a serious injury, of a bleeding body so near, of a death perhaps, seemed to excite my gypsy neighbor. The art student knowing nothing of medical matters, she turned to me. Did I think it was serious?

I had drunk a bit, and was beginning to feel more at ease. I reassured her in such a positive, authoritative tone that she asked me: "You're a surgeon?" Without thinking, driven by that reflex of male vanity before a female, I said that yes, I was. Well, after all, I was replacing a dresser on a surgical ward—it was as nearly true as it needed to be. She abandoned the artist at once; I had acquired an immediate and irresistible interest in her eyes. Rubbing herself against me, she murmured: "How strong you surgeons must have to be!" I felt myself swiftly transformed to the iron-nerved, ruthless surgeon admired by women, and all the signs of naïve admiration were certainly visible in the girl's blue eyes. She told me at once that her name was Nadia.

Till then, despite an enormous sign on the wall in Gothic letters: *DRINK OR GET OUT*, I had succeeded in not drinking too much. The glass in front of me was still full, and I swallowed it at one gulp. Immediately I was bursting with self-confidence, and a warm glow of good humor spread over me.

Nadia herself was drunk and by no means shy. She kept on looking at me, very eager to please, and I did not mind her being vulgar and stupid. She was young, sufficiently pretty, she admired me; that was all that mattered. She clung to me all through the end of dinner, and during the bus ride from the hospital to the ballroom she never left my side.

During most of the pageant she scarcely took her eyes off me. At first I tried to explain the medical allusions to her, but I soon saw she was not listening. She laughed vacantly, showing fine teeth, which shone in the darkness; then she drew me closer, hanging on my lips with a ready anticipation of all my desires. Her hands pressed my hands, my waist, seemed to enfold me. Her flesh was offered me freely, almost too much so, and yet I felt I could never have enough of it. Bending over her, I no longer saw the sea of faces in the hall, the hundreds of excited eyes and hands and mouths; I scarcely heard the clapping and shouts of applause.

Nadia, feeling me trembling and breathing heavily against her, redoubled her caresses. She turned her hips to clasp me closer, in a movement of sheer sensuous delight. I felt the call of my senses overcoming me again. Since Mado and Josette I had fought them repeatedly, I had built up all sorts of defenses. But desire was too cunning, and often took me unawares. The very directness of tonight's unexpected attack swept me off my feet in a sudden glorious access of dizzy enjoyment. Thwarted by months of sobriety and study, my instincts were now too strong, and drove me unresisting towards this new objective. Nadia's skin was soft and velvety to the touch, and as I held her in my arms I felt the warm life beating through her. My hands thrilled to hold her thus and my whole being became aflame with carnal love.

Was it love—or merely desire, appetite, pleasure? Who cared? I let myself be carried away. How powerfully our bodies respond to any contact with the nakedness of another. The excitement I felt in caressing Nadia's naked shoulder was enough

190

to set me alone on a desert island, utterly impervious to the uproar all around us.

The pageant drew to its close. The last tableau had a comic subject: *Artificial Insemination in the Year 3000*. To a breathless machinelike music, a battalion of stiff metal-clad figures, men and women hardly distinguishable, advanced in pairs with the perfect order of robots. The house lights and the floodlights went off, and the scene was illuminated by vibrant, slanting rays, crackling forth from a huge electric machine. Under these blinding arc lights, the human robots continued their well-oiled march, as if their steps were controlled all the time by some sterile, empty force, joyless and soulless. Man and machine alike glittered with a dead metallic brilliance. At one end of the dance floor, the doctor of 3000 A.D. in immaculate white waited before a façade which bore the legend on its front in luminous letters: *Universal Fertilizer*. Underneath, in a sort of loggia, the façade was adorned with a splendid sculpture, a man and woman stretching their arms towards each other. It was the Eternal Couple, that obsolete pair with their unhygienic kisses and bestial intercourse, preserved at the entry to this Temple of Science like a monument to primitive civilizations now extinct. This sculpture in pink stone was there to preside at the state-controlled fertilization of the new-type men and women.

The first couple came forward. The whitewashed doctor seized a large syringe—which for tradition's sake had been left in phallic form. He was just approaching the male robot, when the huge electric machine in the background abruptly blew up, demolishing the doctor and all the metal men and women in a fearful grinding of machinery. For a moment darkness and silence reigned. Then the orchestra took up a new melody of muted violins, while a single eerie beam of soft light seemed to break from the sky. It travelled round the stricken stage, strewn with robots. Then it rose again, searched the façade of the temple, and focussed on the loggia. The music swelled, becoming strong and joyous; the light grew warmer and rosy like the com-

ing of dawn. Then the statues quivered, the petrified couple of
the sculpture began to come to life. The man took a step towards
the woman, and placed his hand on her shoulder. She waited,
her lips parted, her head tilted upwards, offering herself to him
in magnificent nakedness. When the man bent over her, the
music reached a crescendo of joy, and the lights blazed out like
a new sun in this hymn to love, heralding the beginnings of a
new world.

Throughout the pageant the spectators' enthusiasm had been
growing; for this final tableau the whole house seemed to explode. As soon as the applause had calmed down a little, the
orchestra struck up a dance tune. At once the crowds squatting
on the floor leapt to their feet, dashed on to the floor, and began
whirling round once more. Nadia, tired of looking on, wanted
to go down below and join the mass of dancers clinging together in an atmosphere of sticky sweat and perfume. Far from
being sobered by the heat, they fell in with the frenzied mood
of the band, and the rhythm of the dance became even faster
and more furious than it had been before the pageant.

Nadia asked me to take her to the cloakroom, and I waited
for her just outside the hall, watching the girls who were dancing: the mistresses of internes, models from Montparnasse, casual
guests like Nadia, all seemed ecstatic to be there. I felt bold and
adventurous, capable of anything. Why, merely by lifting a
finger, I could have had any one of these girls as easily as Nadia.
I was planning more difficult conquests for the near future when
a familiar voice exclaimed in my ear:

"Well, well, well, if it isn't the official delegate from St.
Luke's, looking for a modern Magdalene. Or are you just a spy
from the Sin School, seeing the sights on the sly?"

"Shut up, Paul. Chav yourself off somewhere, can't you?" The
Great Chavasse had taken part in a tableau showing *Surgery in
the Napoleonic Era*, and under a huge black coat he was
wearing nothing but two drumsticks and a drum. He swung his
hand round with a magnificent gesture, like a guide demonstrating the beauties of the hall.

"Not a bad collection of tarts, eh? Up to scratch, and not exactly shy. You tell them to sit down and they lie down, they fall into your lap like ripe fruit. Trouble is, though, you can't get the real peaches. All on the house, of course, but when you come down to it, they seem to be marked 'For Internes Only.' "

Just then Nadia returned, and after I had made the introductions Paul slapped me on the back; his eye had a sly gleam, suggesting a bond of man-to-man understanding between us. "Ah, my ambitious friend, so you're already studying to be a specialist. A beauty specialist, what?"

He added gallantly to Nadia: "A pleasure to meet you, little girl. In case lucky old Jean should ever be stupid enough to leave you in the lurch this evening, just give me the high sign. Even if my hands are busy with the drumsticks, I'll always have a finger to offer you."

He then left us with a roll on his drum. Watching him go, Nadia said: "I like your friend. Is he a surgeon too?"

With a certain pleasure I explained that Paul was a mere student (the dressers' exam had in fact been too much for him, as we all expected), and Nadia's interest in him at once declined. I of course remained delighted with this encounter; with no one to witness them, such triumphs lose their savor.

Nadia then declared she was thirsty. I took her to our hospital's Box. Ample stocks of refreshments had been laid on, and the drinkers were crowding round the bar. I left Nadia at the entrance and plunged into the melee to get two glasses and fill them with champagne. I returned just in time to see an interne grabbing Nadia by the waist. Without even a pretense at consulting her, he dragged her off to the middle of the floor, clasping her tightly in his arms. Nadia shouted to me in the distance: "One dance—I'll be back . . ."

Rather put out, I remained where I was, still holding in my hand the two glasses and watching the little bubbles darting impatiently to the top, eager to escape, to burst and be happy. I felt a little like a champagne bubble myself, rising to the surface of life, which was pleasure.

I waited for Nadia. As soon as she came back, I would take

her off somewhere, it didn't really matter where, to the nearest hotel. I felt giddy with impatience at the idea of the sensual pleasure ahead of me. Everybody in the hall was now drunk. Alcohol carried all before it, flooding over inhibitions and anxieties like a huge tidal wave. We were all free to give full rein to animal instincts, forgetting all but the uproarious exhilaration of the moment. I recognized that right through the evening, even at the dinner, everything had been working up to this vast primitive outburst; I saw nothing in it to shock me. But then I could not see much of anything at the time. Nothing existed for me but my waiting—turning almost to panic the longer I waited—for the feel of a girl's body near to mine.

All through the next dance I went on waiting in the same place. Nadia did not come back. I thought she might have failed to recognize our Box, so I explored the neighboring ones and the crush of people round them, all in varying stages of intoxication. Next to a group singing little fuddled snatches of smutty songs, I saw a girl being laid out on the floor. One dancer had taken hold of one of his partner's breasts and was squeezing it like the bulb of a horn, shouting: "Titty-ho, titty-ho, out of my way." Someone else entered into the spirit of the occasion by shrieking out: "All hands to the pump—women and children first." Women screamed abuse and encouragement, and the Black Watch dashed up to keep the peace. Yelling gangs began to join in the fray, swiping at anyone they saw and stripping the women of what remained of their costumes.

I could not find Nadia, although I extended my search, visiting all the other boxes and looking everywhere I could think of. In a corridor I discovered a hospital, where about fifteen drunken "patients," wrapped in blankets, were snoring on the floor, dead to the world. Everywhere couples were kissing. Two or three times I thought I recognized Nadia. On reflection, it would have made little difference if it had been. The interne who had taken her away from me must have told her that *he* was a real surgeon; and I could imagine Nadia swooning against his chest at once, sniffing on his hands the exciting smell of blood, forgetting me completely before they had been a quarter round the floor together.

Then I began to think I might get my own back, console myself elsewhere. There were plenty of suitable consolations, of every variety: blondes, brunettes, and redheads, thin girls and fat, tall girls and short. I searched for a girl I liked. I watched the dancing for a moment. What a waggling of bottoms and shaking of stomachs, what ticklings and pinchings and peals of fatuous laughter. Suddenly I found them all positively ugly. Some were bloated, as well as lit up, with the alcohol they had drunk; others showed the sallow dissipated look, the rings under the eyes, characteristic of mornings after. I thought of Nadia's stupid, common little face, badly made up, and felt sure I would have found her as ugly as the rest, had I seen her again. An interne pranced by in front of me with a big whore straddled on his shoulders; I could not help remembering that a certain well-known doctor, having caught a chancre on the neck when still a houseman through doing the same thing on a similar occasion, had finally died of it, paralyzed and insane. This was not an old wives' tale, but a real-life drama, told us by the tutor when we were studying venereal diseases with him. Perhaps Nadia might have been equally infected!

I had no further interest in examining these bleary, vapid, fuddled faces. I had no wish to go on dodging round prone bodies, avoiding pools of vomit or being caught up in random brawls, where the Black Watch knocked out indiscriminately anyone who seemed at all excited. Looked at coldbloodedly, with the new scientific detachment I had found since Nadia disappeared, all this frantic pleasure seemed a mere mechanical debauch, an empty travesty of enjoyment, the meaningless capers of drunken animals. At dawn the light would be cut off to chase out the last obstinate couples, and the frenzied music would stop. While waiting for this all those staying on, as ritual demanded, would try desperately to look happy. The ball, starting off in magnificent light-hearted enjoyment, would end as a chilling spectacle indeed.

My head was beginning to ache, and I felt a painful nervous tension. I decided to leave. I had to edge round a group of weary lads and lasses who were sitting in a circle and singing with drink-sodden sentimentality. I stopped to watch them. Someone caught me by the arm and said: "Hullo, old chap. Disgusting, isn't it!"

It was Julot. I had seen quite a bit of him during the vacation, and he had even worked in my room for a while, forswearing obscene conversation at least during our hours of study. With his enthusiasm for death, he planned to specialize in forensic medicine, and during the day had worked with what for him seemed remarkable concentration. Strangely enough, for I still disliked his attitude a good deal, I found it a considerable help to have him as companion for my studies; in bringing him up-to-date with questions he had neglected during the year, I refreshed my own mind. And when he set his mind to a thing, Julot knew how to work hard, so I was sure he would be one of the three hundred gaining a post as hospital dresser. I felt sorry for his patients, but perhaps hospital discipline would eventually make Julot's approach to human beings slightly less abnormal.

At this particular moment, however, his appearance was even more disconcerting than in his customary undertaker's get-up. Apart from his head and goatee beard, he was completely denuded of all bodily hair, smooth, plucked and polished. I looked so startled that he explained to me at once:

"Didn't you see me as the Male Nude in the *Fifteenth Century Anatomy Lesson?* To think that only a fortnight ago we were sitting in your room working for the exam. What a change, isn't it!"

Then he came back to his first idea. "What do you think of this party, Jean? Personally I find it disgusting."

Had the licentious Julot suddenly turned puritanical, or what? Rather than find the orgy disgusting, I would have expected him to lap it up, leaping on naked girls like a satyr. Perhaps he had reached the phase of drunkenness where one suddenly grows serious and highly moral. Or perhaps like Samson his powers had been destroyed by the loss of his hair.

196

But Julot was neither drunk nor reduced in potency. He explained his views as he dragged me away: "As decadent a show as ever excited a choirboy who's just been to the Folies Bergère for the first time. If they're going to start singing bits of *Faust* at four o'clock in the morning at an Internes' Hop, they might just as well have a triumphal procession of nuns and orphans. I'm disgusted, let's get out of here."

In the men's room I took off one of my sandals to take out the ticket I'd slipped in it on arrival, for safety's sake, along with some money to get me home. I was handed the blue cloak lent me by my interne, and Julot slipped into a short old overcoat which left his bare knees sticking out—we both looked as if we were emerging from a bathroom; then he put on his inevitable undertaker's derby. On the pavement, despite the hour, the fog, and the cold, there were a few patrolling policemen and a crowd of gapers watching the guests coming out. When Julot appeared at the door, they all seemed nonplussed. He passed them with dignified indifference. When we had gone a few yards, he remarked to me:

"See them? The same crowd has been waiting there since eleven o'clock. Five hours waiting on the pavement to catch a glimpse every now and then of someone's thighs under a coat. What a thrill! And the cream of the joke is that they undoubtedly envy us and pity themselves, because we can go in and they can't. Whereas actually we're the ones to be pitied, not they."

After the hubbub of shouting and laughter we had just left, the Avenue de Wagram, sunk in thick fog, looked deserted. Fifty yards away, the entrance to the ballroom was nothing more than a red halo between two pink halos from neighboring cafés which were still open; further down, towards the end of the long avenue, the Place des Ternes was a steaming swamp of fog. A sharp little wind drove the fog towards us, swirling it round the sickly glimmer of each street lamp. Passing long dark blocks of houses, we went towards the Arc de Triomphe in complete silence. Julot was preoccupied with attempts to light his pipe, and I walked several paces ahead of him, nervous and exhausted, my head aching furiously, sick with disgust. Despite the interne's cloak, I felt chilled to the bone, and so miserably depressed that I could almost have burst into tears.

Nor would they have been tears of vexation—rather of regret for the pleasures that had escaped me. No more soft lips to kiss, soft flesh to caress; no more of those arms so swift to embrace—and so swift to disappear. The beginning of the night, the sparkling magical delight of the pageant, the canvas temples and flesh-and-blood statues and gilded pagodas, the band and the nudes and the whirling dancers—all that had scattered and shrunk, fading in the end to this cruel loneliness. My second year was starting badly.

Careless of the cold, Julot, who had succeeded in lighting his pipe, started up a conversation on the usual lines, in the calm voice he reserved for his more extravagant obscenities. He asked me if I had read Forberg's *De Figuris Veneris*, and when I shook my head, he reproved me for my omission, telling me that it was an excellent treatise on classical erotology, demonstrating what a party like the Internes' Hop might have been like in Roman times. I gathered it would really have been something.

"Nearer our own times," went on Julot inexorably, "we have Grimaud in the 17th century experimenting in his castle with love as a team game. Not bad that—but you might say it was an amusement for the upper ten, and rather beyond our means. So let's go on to the doctors of great-grandfather's time, a century or two later. When they had worked a whole month—really what you can call work, only four hours sleep a night without undressing, and the lice getting into their boots—at the end of it, for a bit of a change they had a real honest-to-God superbinge. Three days of women and wine, and they were real men then, *they* didn't fall down dead drunk the first evening. No, I'm afraid people don't know how to enjoy themselves these days."

We reached the Etoile, and one of the entrances to the Metro. From it rose a current of warm air, a temporary defense against the piercing wind. The gates were closed, but on the bottom steps tramps were sleeping on outspread newspapers, huddled one against the other. Julot stopped me, as if the Metro entrance had given him an idea.

"Did you see how superior the internes looked as they passed the crowds at the entrance to the ballroom? They think they've been tasting the utmost in dissolute debauchery, and tomorrow they'll pretend they're real devils. My God, they haven't a clue to what decent immorality is. What was there tonight but a lot of girls a bit more nude than at the Folies Bergère, a lot of drunken louts singing about John Thomas and his red plush breeches, and poking a pâpier-maché phallus on a stick at people. It's all much too undressed to be artistically indecent. Five minutes after you've come in, you can't even notice the nakedness of the prettiest girls there. One couldn't expect a real rape and flagellation scene or a little session of collective intercourse. Still, the evening would have had a bit more spice if we'd at least had some rather more suggestive strip-tease. Tonight left no room for imagination, anticipation—or guesswork."

He paused for a moment to puff at his pipe, and I marvelled again at his indifference to cold. Despite the warm air from the Metro I was shivering violently, and would have liked to leave the Etoile. But it was the best place for a taxi, and Julot had buttonholed me with his usual persistence. It was easier to hear him out.

"Tell you what I heard the day before yesterday. In the Metro there are some really special cases who choose a place opposite a pretty girl. With many apologies they put a big basket between her legs. A mirror is arranged at the bottom of the basket, at a suitable angle to let them see under her skirts. Good idea, what? Better than all the ranks of nudes in the pageant and the hordes of maudlin internes. They may be all right in medicine, but when it comes to vice, they're beaten hands down by the merest kid who peeks through convenient keyholes."

At first I had listened to Julot somewhat absently, thinking what a bore he was, especially on his pet subject. But despite myself I was interested in his disgust at the Internes' Hop, which

I found went too far and he not nearly far enough. Also, by ridiculing the whole collection of internes, he helped me to avenge by proxy my setback with Nadia and her interne. He stood there on the edge of the pavement, blowing jets of steam and smoke from his mouth and nostrils, and went on mulling over his disappointment at what he called "a most inept piece of sottishness, sexually quite unimaginative." Then he calmed down soon, and eventually concluded: "After all, if they enjoy it, that's their business. And if I've lost my hair for the Hop, that's my funeral. Nobody's forced to go to it."

While Julot returned to more moderate ideas, I began to feel more tolerant myself. I had not been forced to go to it either. Why should I be a priggish wet blanket just because Nadia had gone off with someone else? After the exam for dresser, supposing I had had the chance, like tonight, to sing and drink—well naturally, I should have sung and drunk with the rest. One gets drunk at birthdays, at reunions, at University dances, anywhere and on every occasion where young people are gathered together. To be dead drunk on leaving a good dinner or some anniversary celebration seems to be the only way the young can prove they are thoroughly enjoying themselves.

If I had danced with Nadia, and had been as tight as almost all the other dancers, why, the Hop would doubtless have seemed enjoyable. The internes themselves seemed to find it so, having taken all this trouble to organize it in honor of their young prospective colleagues who had taken the exam that morning. Present internes, of course, would see in it the fulfilment of an old tradition, and find in it, besides, a wealth of happy memories from past years. As for the candidates of the morning, who had just finished several months of study and the nerve-racking tension of a three days' competitive exam, they had merely fallen like wolves on their first liberty, on alcohol and female flesh.

Julot drew meditatively at his pipe. After spitting on the ground he informed me of his conclusions: "Well, before going back, I hope to find some satisfactory consolations round Les Halles. The market quarter, I can assure you, is quite different from the artistic tableaux, oriental visions and barrack-room nudes we've just seen."

He seemed quite revived at the thought of his back-street partners, very different from the girls at the Ball, so ingenuous in their pleasures for his exacting taste. As for my own night, I realized it was a complete failure.

Nadia had asked me at one point: "You love me a little, dear?" So as not to lie, I had kissed her and merely answered: "You're a darling!" I could hardly have explained to her just then that I was grateful to her because she was the first to return me to thoughts of love, but if she read more into my caresses she would be sadly deceiving herself. I could hardly make her see how happy I was just to have a woman near me, even without loving her, after such long loneliness. If I stayed by her side tonight, it was a purely provisional arrangement. The women I wanted, and meant to have, were of a good deal higher quality than she was, and I should abandon her for them if ever the opportunity offered.

Since then, of course, she had got in first, and abandoned me. I found I could easily forgive her. By a road studded with blazing lights she had brought me back from a distant land, a stifling purgatory of books and files and notes. Thanks to her I had tonight been reborn to the life of the senses, I had found the strength I had been seeking in the ten days since the exam, to relax and break the spell. Nadia had given me self-confidence enough to choose my path. From now on I would live from day to day, without inhibitions or scruples. Work, ambition, morality, even my vocation, with all the gravity of that word, seemed empty. They were concepts invented perhaps by old men, who, as La Rochefoucauld had said, enjoyed giving good advice now they could no longer give a bad example. I was sure now of having more desire for women, for the miraculous short-lived pleasure given by a woman's body, than I had self-interest or ambition or pride.

I shivered with impatience, thinking how I would make women suffer for having known me. "I'll have *them*," I swore to myself, "before they get the chance to have *me*."

At last a taxi rose out of the fog like a ghost, and stopped at the edge of the pavement. I had had more than enough of this icy, open, wind-swept place. Before telling the chauffeur to go to the Charité Hospital, I suggested to Julot that he should share this providential taxi. He refused, explaining that he did his best hunting on foot.

I did not press him. I had nothing more to say to him, nor any great desire for his presence. He had time to remind me of Spinoza's aphorism: "Everyone is bound to desire or avoid what he judges good or bad, according to the laws of his own nature." How blindly I had refused to admit the validity of this maxim all through the summer, when Julot had quoted it for my benefit. Fool that I was to be so long recognizing my true self! But I could endure a last night of solitude, feeling confident of future hunting of a better sort than Julot's.

The taxi started up. I felt almost sorry for him as I watched him vanish on his furtive fogbound prowl. The fumes of the night's debauch seemed to disperse with his going, as if they and that grotesque figure were inextricably bound up together.

Chapter 2

THE MAIN COURTYARD of the hospital was dark and deserted. A pungent smell of vomit still hung about the corridor in the residents' quarters where we had put on our costumes. I went to the bathroom, but there was no hope of using the bath, which was blocked up and overflowing with dirty water. Some of the worst sufferers from the night's amusement had been laid out in little crumpled bundles, in any rooms which had happened to have their doors open. There they snored and hiccoughed and grunted like the occupants of some particularly nauseous pigsties.

The only bath I could depend on was the one on my ward, and I might also find a bed in the consulting room, to snatch a few hours' sleep. I took my clothes and white coat out of my valise. I passed the dining room, its lights still on, revealing a table littered with the ravages of the meal. The tablecloth, soiled with wine marks, had been pulled to the floor, partly covering pools of spilt wine and a mass of dirty crockery and smashed bottles. It was a dismal scene without the songs and uproar of the dinner, and even more dismal, with the gloom of a graveyard, seemed the big deserted court, no longer resounding with cheerful voices or buffeted by gales of youthful laughter.

After an arch and a second courtyard, equally sombre, came endless corridors, with glass doors firmly closed on each ward. Through the doors you could see the nightlights silently flickering. None of the noises from the town outside seemed capable of filtering through the high walls of the big dark buildings, to redeem the oppressive silence of deserted courts and empty corridors. It was all as dismal as death, and no less dismal was the clang of my feet on the white tiles of the corridors.

I went into the ward bathroom and turned on the hot faucet. Glorious boiling water flowed immediately, and I began to feel better. This bath would make me a new man, and afterwards my only desire was for sleep.

Afterwards, to reach that bed in the consulting room, I had to go through all the other wards. I pushed the first door open, and was blinded at first after the relative light of the corridor. I could see nothing but a huge area of semi-darkness, broken here and there by blue nightlights which gleamed dimly towards the high ceiling, but left large tracts of the long ward in the deepest shadow.

It was in fact the first time I had seen a hospital ward at night, and for a moment I was staggered by the density of shadows and smells and cries. Though sights and sounds were muffled, I felt the darkness to be very much alive, a concentrated mass of struggle and suffering. Stertorous breathing mingled with sudden screams of agony, the strangled cries of feverish sleep, and the incessant dull moaning of those who lay awake in pain.

The windows were hermetically sealed, and the fetid heat of the ward could find no outlet. The air was worse than I had known it on my worst mornings at hospital; the muddy sewer-like stench suggested decaying bodies left there slowly decomposing.

Three rows of beds, right to the end of the ward, gradually became visible through the glimmer of the nightlights. But on the faces of the patients I could only distinguish the gaps in the darkness, the black hollows of the eyes, the thin line of mouths. I went down one row, and as I passed I looked at the motionless bodies arranged like harassed travellers for a long night channel crossing. Some were shaking and groaning, and I thought how their parched lips might be counting the hours, feeling the minutes dig into their flesh like nails. Others were sleeping fairly placidly, having reached, perhaps, a resting-place between two bad dreams. I observed some buried beneath the sheets, as if the sheets were shrouds; perhaps they half hoped death might be fooled into forgetting them a little longer, and leave them in their corner unmolested.

I increased my pace. My lungs had had more than enough of this noisome, airless atmosphere. Between these walls the night's joyous beginning, Nadia, the dinner, the Ball, receded.

Near the door, at the other end of the ward, the night nurse was changing a soiled drawsheet. Because of my blue interne's cloak, she took me for the doctor on call, and when I reached her she said in a low voice: "Number 16 won't get through the night, I'm afraid."

I stopped. I had just recognized the patient, a cancer. At the morning round she could still talk; and now she was dying. Her neighbors, awakened by the disturbance, were beginning to go back to sleep. I could see their faces better, and all of a sudden I felt a strong affection for all these women, so lonely and forsaken. "To love your neighbor . . ." These were all my neighbors, they were just like me, they were suffering for me and in my place. For a moment I wished to go to them all, trying to bring relief by word or deed. But I did not want them to make the same mistake the night nurse had made. They would have opened their eyes as I passed, drawn by the blue cloak over my shoulders, like iron filings to a magnet, to beg me to stop their suffering. I should have had to admit that I was not the interne on call, that affection and good-will cannot, alas, replace medical knowledge. I walked to the door as quietly as I could, so as not to reawaken them to disappointment and new pain.

Having pushed the door open, I reached a wide landing on the stone staircase. After the frowsty ward the air here seemed almost fresh, except for a rancid bronchial smell; I found that it came from a sort of flowerpot full of greenish spittle. I lit a cigarette and opened one of the windows; it looked on to some peeling walls and a courtyard. In the corner of this courtyard, next door to the kitchens, an undertaker could be seen almost every morning, waiting near a hearse. The fog had lifted, and the night was now clear and frosty.

Two dim lamps lit up the landing; they had been placed above the doors so that you could easily read, above each door, the names of the wards: *Guinard, 1856-1911*, and *Pozzi, 1846-1918*. I repeated them several times to myself: "Guinard and Pozzi."

It was one of Chavasse's habits, when we walked down the corridors of the St. Louis Hospital last year, to read above the doors the names of well-known doctors which had been given to the various wards. He seemed to derive some disrespectful enjoyment from the way the names sounded, and more especially from any scurrilous stories about the doctors in question. One day he had shouted in disgust: "I'm getting sick of all these dead men's names. They abuse their privileges. They've already established a monopoly in anatomy and pathology. Thing-ummy's Gland, Soandso's Disease. You'd think that might be enough for them, but no, they have to have their names over the doors as well. It's not a hospital any more, it's a cemetery with permanent concessions for doctors. All medicine is one vast cemetery with all the best people wanting to have their names written up. It's like learning an old telephone directory by heart."

Guinard and Pozzi—the two names had been unfamiliar to me. On consulting a volume of medical biographies, I learned that both were hospital surgeons and had had their moments of celebrity; but if they figured opposite each other on two iden-tical doors in the Charity Hospital, it was certainly because of the drama of their deaths. Each was wounded in the stomach by a madman he'd treated in the hospital. To the surgeon who was going to operate on him, Pozzi said: "I received four bullets. Undoubtedly two are in the abdomen and one in the kidneys. I am going to die, but you may as well operate. Surgeons ought always to try." He died just as they were sewing up his eleventh perforation. Guinard showed the same serenity after the fatal wound, telling the surgeon to make a deep incision and explore the whole of the intestine thoroughly, and to remember thát per-forations of the intestines go in pairs. Then he told his internes, "My poor boys, I shall be giving you a lot of trouble for three days—but I'll be out of your way on the fourth." Four days later he died, as Pozzi had done, clearheaded and without illusions or self-pity.

So much for the spirits of dead doctors. My cigarette was finished. Before going into the Pozzi Ward, I stubbed it out on the edge of the flowerpot, where it spluttered among the spittle.

This was the ward where I spent my mornings as a dresser. But without the name above the door I should scarcely have recognized it in the half-darkness: the same rows of beds as in all the other wards, the same smells and groans. This one smelt in addition of tobacco, being a male ward.

After eight days I knew almost all the patients, and I went straight down towards the last bed, knowing I should find an old man there with a friendly smile on his face. I needed to see that smile very badly.

From a distance I looked towards the last nightlight. Directly under it I could already see the white form I was looking for, half sitting up in bed, backed by numerous pillows. I came up to the bed. Old M. Thury had had a long series of illnesses, and he had once with a smile compared himself to an old car: "Separate parts break down in time and are replaced without apparent mishap. But one day the whole body and engine get tired, and the poor old machine collapses altogether, all at the same time." He was at present in the ward with a fracture of the femur, but in addition his heart was tired. This one could tell at a glance from his pasty bluish complexion. This was why, too, he had to sit up in bed. All his features bore the marks of resigned weariness but the mouth was relaxed and almost at peace, like a child's mouth smiling at some beautiful dream. I thought the old man was asleep and was about to tiptoe away, when a whispered voice detained me: "What's our young doctor up to so early in the day?"

"I've just left the Internes' Hop, M. Thury, and what's more, I've caught you out now. You told me that with digitalin you manage to sleep all through the night."

"Yes, I do sleep. Well, I sleep part of the time. You get so strange when you're old and sick. Time is really the only treasure old people have left. So I listen to the hours chiming, sitting up in my pillows like an anxious mother on the lookout for her children to come home."

I had to bend over him to listen, for at times he became breathless and his voice failed him. He stopped speaking, and at the same moment there were a few seconds' silence all through the ward, seconds of acute danger or anxious peace. "The angel passing," I thought to myself, until the pause was broken by another groan, and the ward returned to its slow rhythm of fever and pain. But something seemed to have been changed by the silence, and I felt as if a soul had suddenly passed on, its earthly span completed, having done with suffering forever. Almost by telepathy I knew that M. Thury had read the same message into the silence, for he murmured: "How shall I die?"

I started telling him he was silly to talk about dying like this; but he stopped me.

"Oh, I'm not asking *you*, my lad; you wouldn't tell me the truth. I'm asking myself. Of course, every single thing is a gamble all through one's life, but death seems the most incredible gamble of all. One man is snuffed out like a lamp without oil. There's no expression of joy or deliverance on his face; he just looks extinguished. Others go on shrieking for days and nights on end before they can die. You remember the Theban shepherd in the play of Sophocles? Didn't he say something like this? 'Learn to turn your eyes to the last days of life, and only call happy those who have come to the end of their allotted span without misfortune.' "

Then he asked me abruptly: "Do you sometimes think about death?"

"Well, yes. At least not usually. But tonight much more than I should have expected when the night began."

"Yes, I know," said the old man. "Outside hospital, or when one's young and healthy, death is a vague impersonal word like so many others. You either have the conventional ideas about it, or else you carefully dodge it. But at hospital, for a young student or an old patient, the word grips you, don't you find? A mysterious, all-absorbing business. For us two death is actual, now, tonight; and when you have one and a half feet in the grave like me, it has an even more personal interest. Sorry, my young Doctor Nérac, why am I always talking to you about such sad things? Please forgive me. You had a good time at your famous Hop?"

I said yes without much conviction, and M. Thury went on at once: "I believe you're half ashamed of admitting it to me. Why should you be? Because while you were enjoying yourself, there were patients in pain here, and I was one of them? I really can't grudge you that, I'm not such a hypocrite. The pleasure you'd deprive yourself of wouldn't make a single patient happier, and you must enjoy yourself sometimes, my boy. If you enjoyed your orgy, don't be ashamed. We've all got animal instincts and at your age it's only human to give free rein to them now and then."

I did not answer at once, and he continued: "Yes, I know, I can read you much better than you think, young man. While the rest are drinking bad champagne, dancing and shouting and singing, you do a spell of night duty. You come and have a chat with your old friend, and help him to wait for the dawn."

So M. Thury as well thought I was deputizing for the interne on duty. I wanted to undeceive him, but just then he had a sudden spasm of coughing, and I thought I might have tired him. I made a move to go away, but he put out his hand to keep me there.

"No, please don't go. If you only knew what a lot of good you were doing me! It's so terrible never having anyone to talk to. All round me in this whole forty-bed ward, I feel nothing but selfishness and indifference. A young doctor is the only person left to cling to, and the patient is very rarely deceived about the doctor with a real fellow-feeling for his patients, who tries to understand their minds as well as their bodies. Some of them may go on suffering the whole twenty-four hours, they can't always distinguish day and night so easily. So when I find a young medical student, bursting with life, who leaves his bed at the first call, forgetting about time and place, his own rest and his own pleasures, simply to help his patients get through the night more comfortably—I know that student will one day be a real doctor. He is already marked out, branded."

This speech had certainly exhausted him, but he took one of my hands in his own hands, big and flabby with oedema, and drew me gently to him in a sort of urgent appeal. Very softly, it was almost under his breath, he made the appeal articulate.

"You know, young man, you could be that doctor—if you wish."

It was like a stab in the back, that sentence. It was dangerously sweet to hear, catching me just now, at a climax of loneliness and self-pity. It gathered into a single stream all the separate currents I felt of doubt and uncertainty. It brought me sharply up against the alternative courses the stream might take; and either would lead me very far afield.

At first I was furious. I was chosen, was I? Where was the evidence, which branded me so irrevocably? What on earth could force me to become that sort of doctor, to become an interne at all? You could qualify and practice as a doctor without ever having taken a salaried post at a hospital, without ever being a dresser, let alone an interne. Till now I had taken it for granted that in two or three years' time I should take the interne's exam, and that having had such a post in a Paris hospital would in the long run greatly improve my future prospects as a doctor. But why should I not forget about long runs, how many French doctors had never been internes, and yet were doing quite all right, thank you? Why had I more obligations than the others?

Could I imagine Paul Chavasse, for instance, becoming an interne? He knew his own academic limitations, and had no intention of going in for such a stiff exam. But then Paul was not a very good example, for his natural skill with sick people, assuming he did sufficient work to qualify, would make him a very fair general practitioner. I could imagine Dr. Chavasse leading an extremely pleasant life, and for that matter an extremely useful one.

Once more I was jealous of Paul—because his outlook was so happily uncomplicated. On the wards he was far from indifferent, but his interest was that of the extrovert, and naturally his sensitiveness was limited: a priceless boon, it now seemed to me, for any budding doctor. I could imagine Paul there tonight in my place, bending over the soiled bed of the dying woman and listening to her death rattle with the calm of a veteran doctor. He would scarcely have felt on his own cheeks the cold sweat of her death agony, nor experienced in his own throat those last terrible pangs of suffocation. "Sympathy" in its literal sense of "suffering with" was not for the Chavs of this world, even if they were doctors; but was not his own brand of practical sympathy quite enough? I thought of him going from bed to bed, tossing off a comforting joke, giving an old woman some water, wiping a forehead streaming with sweat; and all that quite instinctively, without suffering himself, without thinking a single moment about pity, without wasting any opportunity to enjoy himself or have a good laugh immediately afterwards? Why couldn't I do the same, and why in any case need I do more? I felt full of coldly practical and reasonable arguments. I brought up all my old reserves, in defense of my plans for future happiness, which M. Thury and his words had suddenly threatened.

The old man's feeble hands softly pressed my wrist in the darkness to indicate: "Whatever you may say, you know quite well that you are chosen, marked out for it, the sign is on you."

I looked round me. The end of this night was typical of what countless others would be like, if I accepted; and I could already believe myself the only one watching over the great hospital and its inhuman darkness. My life in the future was dark and enclosed like the hospital's walls.

But the darkness around me began to grow less grim. It was still overpowering, and I should like to have escaped from it. The old hands did not release me, as if they were still trying to convince me of their message: "Do not go—but think of the time when you will become an interne. You will return to the ward for the evening round, when the long grim night is approaching, and all the patients will be in your hands, you alone will be their shield and their defense. You will know wakeful nights on call, where the responsibility is almost too much to bear, where you will be weighed down with hopes of victories or losing battles, with pain and death. You will watch all through the night, so that life may continue here, so that you can save it wherever and whenever it may be saved, so that the chain of healing may never be interrupted."

M. Thury let one of my hands go, and broke into my reverie. What he said to me in fact, raising his fingers towards the window, was: "Look. Morning already! My young doctor friend has helped me to wait for it, and certainly tonight I've had nothing to complain of. How quickly time can pass when a kind friend is near you."

The big windows gradually turned from pitch black to dark gray, and then to gray; the cold light of dawn was seeping through. Day sneaked furtively in, like a deserter. The gray light came to rest on the faces in the beds. Patients began to wake and stretch themselves, whimpering and yawning, some of them worn out by the long night.

M. Thury was silent. Like me, he was watching the light slowly becoming firmer, with a cold, steely brightness. The ball would be finishing now, amidst empty bottles and dancers strewn on the floor in drunken stupor like green-faced cadavers. The last couples, refusing to admit their weariness, would be shouting and singing and dancing more vigorously than ever, to make up for their reduced numbers. And if I had slept with Nadia in the stuffy heat of some squalid hotel room, smelling of sweat and sex, we should have lain side by side like two enemies exhausted in the same struggle. I should have wakened with heavy head and cracked lips, sickened by those soft and stupid eyes, that flesh too easily given. I should have been disgusted with her and with myself.

Whereas here, at the end of a sad night with a weary dawn breaking, I had never before felt so full of mental clarity, so cleansed and rested physically. This was the prelude to a doctor's sleepless nights, and I was light-hearted, stripped for action, delivered from myself. It was reassurance after doubt, a new feeling of power and self-confidence, a grave decision well taken, after which there should be no more turning back. The morning washes and temperatures and all the daily routine would soon begin, but as yet the light was almost for me alone, and the ward was scarcely awake. I looked round it like a conqueror on the morning of victory, who gazes on the lands of a new empire. I could almost have wished time to stand still at this dawn, to preserve the full power of my resolve and my new happiness.

M. Thury must have sensed through his hands the onrush of vitality and joy. He straightened a little to whisper: "At your age, my lad, dawn means also the song of the lark." Then he let himself relapse, but several times still I heard him murmuring: "Ah youth, youth," as if he had just seen again all the youth of the world. Perhaps it was then, without realizing it, that he dropped gently off to sleep, so that I could at last withdraw my hand and free myself from the ghost which held me.

Lying down to sleep in the consulting room two minutes later, my heart beneath my interne's cloak was filled with a proud warmth.

Part 5
SECOND YEAR SIGNS
AND SYMPTOMS

Chapter 1

"You want to change your room?" said the Secretary of the Cité Universitaire in indignant surprise. "And you wait for the beginning of term to ask me."

Ten minutes earlier I had suddenly decided that my sunless room, with its hideous wallpaper covered with red nasturtiums and the melancholy view of the one poor little cherry tree on its corner of deserted lawn, was at the bottom of all my discouragements. If I wanted to be happy in my work and stick at it with the steadiness desirable, I must leave these stagnant waters without delay.

The Secretary had begun to study the list of hostels, which was lengthy. But eventually he said: "You're lucky. Take No. 24 in the Jules Ferry building. You'll get plenty of sun there, only don't come back and complain if you find in July you're getting a bit too much."

As soon as I came in the door I liked my new room. It was large and very light, with two big windows. One looked onto the big central lawn where I could see all the activity of the Cité. The other opened onto the Slum, an area scheduled as the site for our future playing fields. At present the first houses of the suburb of Gentilly rose in the distance, tall and sheer, like a coastline, and the Cité might have been a huge grounded liner with an indescribable solid scum all round it, the filthy backwash of the town. Between Gentilly and the Cité was a stagnant desert of rotting wood, ordures, and small hovels, over which a dense silence reigned. The only sign of life was provided here

and there by some small bonfires, smoking away in holes protected from the wind. Sometimes a pungent smell from this
burning rubbish would be blown our way; but usually it was
diverted towards the distant suburb—as if the palings, by which
the Cité was bounded on this side, continued invisibly upwards,
and no part of the lives running parallel on either side of them
could ever be allowed to meet. Without any hesitation I pushed
my worktable in front of the window looking onto the lawn.

By the middle of the afternoon I had finished moving in. My
pictures were up on the walls, my books and papers were
arranged on the shelves, my blotter was in place on the table.
I was about to put the skull beside it, as I had done last year,
but then I hesitated. Only first-year men went in for this sort
of macabre exhibitionism, and eventually I put the skull away
at the bottom of the cupboard along with my other bones.

After this I decided to explore my new surroundings further.
In my old hostel I had been used to a monastic silence; the
proximity of the Master had acted as a damper on all loud
voices, singing, or other unnecessary noise. Here the whole
hostel seemed to be in a permanent hubbub. Doors banged,
gramophones blared out the latest dance tunes, people went
rushing or slithering by, laughing and humming and whistling;
up and down the staircase the handrail groaned continuously
beneath the grip of many robust hands.

When I came out of my room, the corridor was empty. I went
to the door opposite mine, remembering how a year earlier three
yards of exploration had brought me to Petitjean's door. The
name inscribed on the visiting card was unfamiliar to me, and
no one answered when I knocked; I was disappointed. A little
further down I knocked again, and again there was no answer.
At last, at the end of the corridor, I was told to come in. I had
read on the card outside this door: *Pierre Prichard, Medical
Student.*

Long introductions proved unnecessary, for we had seen each
other at the school, and this put us on a friendly footing at
once. Prichard offered me an armchair and then a cigarette; he
seemed pleased at my visit and very ready to chat. I learned that

218

he was just starting his fourth year in medicine, that he too had been able to come to the Cité Universitaire because his father had been killed in the War, and that his mother was now an assistant postmistress at a small post office in the Yonne area; after which I told him my own very similar background. Prichard was twenty-three, but his dark suit and rather peremptory voice, as well as the lines on his brow and round his mouth, made him seem a good deal older. He looked and sounded like a young doctor already in practice.

I looked at his room: everything in perfect order. But I was rather surprised that a man in his fourth year should have it furnished so self-consciously: a skull with a pipe between its teeth was much in evidence on the bookcase, where it was complemented by a wizened foetus in a jar of spirit. On the walls, encircling a piperack with an imposing array of pipes, a collection of beer mugs alternated with frivolous pictures illustrating well-known hospital ditties. On the table the skeleton of a hand served as a paperweight. I found all this rather lacking in taste, but it was redeemed by the heap of files and books in the bookcase, which gave a flattering idea of Prichard's capacity for work and methodical habits. I decided that he was a likeable enough neighbor, and I thought I might even have found the real friend I was looking for.

I took it for granted that he would be taking the interne's exam fairly soon, and scarcely even thought it worth asking him. But when I did ask him, he answered contemptuously, to my great astonishment, that he was not going in for it.

"I started working for it," he explained, "but luckily I found out the truth in time and gave it up. Start thinking in terms of competitive exams, old man, and you're through. They stultify and sterilize you. Fancy wasting all those years cramming. It isn't even as if the things you learn had any sense in them. No, you have to stuff your head full of out-of-date theories and idiotic official mumbo-jumbo. By gosh, I could tell you a thing or two about official medicine, and the high priests of our medical school. What a bunch of benighted morons you've got there!"

Prichard got up and began pacing up and down. The subject was obviously one on which he felt deeply. His tone became even more dogmatic, and he stuck out his jaw in a way which emphasized the contemptuous lines round his mouth.

"I was lucky," he went on. "I got out in time, when I happened to discover homeopathy this summer. You've probably noticed that they never mention it either at the hospital or the medical school, except to make fun of it. Well, actually, old man, it has all the answers. Which is extremely tiresome to the old dotards of the medical school. Just imagine—their clique haven't discovered homeopathy yet, and it works better than their own methods. Oh well, in two years I'll have my degree, since you need that priceless possession to practise at all, but the day after that they can stuff their damned allopathy, which kills more than it cures. I'll set up in practice, and I bet you I'll have more patients than any former interne *and* some of your self-important chiefs. They'll be green with envy, I can just picture it."

It was the first time I had heard official medicine criticized with such rancor—or homeopathy praised with such enthusiasm. Prichard was so dogmatic and seemed to base his convictions on such firm experience that for want of a better argument I merely remarked: "Isn't homeopathy extremely complicated, though?"

Prichard seemed disappointed by my lack of enthusiasm, and opening here and there the pages of a large treatise he was reading when I came in, he set out to convince me, with truly apostolic fervor, of the extreme simplicity of the homeopathic creed: "*Similia similibus.*"

Night was falling, and Prichard went on with his discourse. He had switched on his standard lamp some time ago, so as to be able to support his points with quotations from the big tome. Eventually he looked at his watch. "Nearly seven. Going to eat? If you like, we can drop in on Carleret on the way. His room's a sort of hostel mess. You'll get to know most of the chaps at one go."

On the lower floor Prichard took the righthand corridor and went towards a door from which a stream of noise was issuing. The key was in the lock, and Prichard opened the door without knocking, pushing me in ahead of him. My first impressions were like entering a barn where some damp straw was being burnt, with a few pigs having their throats cut in a corner. The room was filled with smoke and frenzied cries, and that was about all I could distinguish. Besides being a smoking saloon, there was a touch of the gambling-den, provided by four bridge-players round a table, with several spectators standing near them. Most of the room seemed to be listening to a tall, thin, dark chap, who was jumping about and gesticulating, yelling out a furious mixture of arguments and insults. Although mental sparks were flying from him in all directions, they did not, for me at least, provide much illumination.

"It's quite impossible to argue with you, Bouchet, you bastard. You just run away into a lot of pious pseudo-scientific junk which I just can't take. Most of Darwin's disciples didn't understand him half as well as Engels did, and that's what you find so bloody inconvenient."

"Aha, so you approve of Darwin, you poor sap, but you won't accept *The Struggle for Life*. All right, Gédéon, my fine moronic materialist, try and explain that one. I'm sure we'll find it extremely interesting." Bouchet, Gédéon's tubby fair-haired opponent, emphasized the contempt in his reply by waving his short arms excitedly.

The others shouted encouragement to both of them, more or less impartially: "Go on, you've got him there," "Stick to him, Bouchet, you're winning"—and so on. I could not grasp how the material transmission of hereditary characteristics and Bergson's work could contain such explosive possibilities. I looked round me, enjoying the fun; details of the whole confused scene, and some of the personalities involved, were beginning to take shape. Books and magazines and papers and hotel ashtrays were scattered everywhere, along with skates, boxing-gloves, a hunting horn, and the traditional collection of stolen signs, posters, and nameplates, of which certainly the most ironical, in this particular place, read as follows: *If you have nothing to do, don't do it here.*

At one point Gédéon must have exhausted himself or choked with indignation; at any rate he was silent, and this silence seemed almost incredible after the spate of tumultuous argument the minute before. Evidently feeling that the contest had gone on long enough, one of the bridge players suggested in a drawling voice:

> *"The subject's dead, said Mardoche; I opine*
> *Your brain is made quite different from mine."*

Gédéon at once recovered his breath for a protest: "No, Carleret, that's damned unfair. As soon as I am about to be proved right, I'm told to shut up." And he returned to the attack, bringing up Plekhanov as a reserve. Bouchet should read Plekhanov, that would show him the error of his ways.

Beside the lean, explosive Gédéon and the bloated, excitable Bouchet, Carleret suggested some inscrutable Buddha, the very essence of phlegmatic non-attachment. His flabby cheeks made his eyes seem smaller than they were, which gave him a look of being permanently half-asleep. All his movements were languid and lethargic except when his short, podgy fingers touched the cards. Playing them, dealing or shuffling, these fingers showed surprising energy and agility.

In any case Carleret's personality could evidently be forceful enough in its own lazy way. When Gédéon took up his Plekhanov theme with renewed fervor, Carleret merely remarked, without raising his voice: "Moreau, the horn!" Moreau unhooked the hunting horn, took up his stand and after carefully filling his lungs gave a tremendous toot on it. The result was instantaneous. Gédéon, outclassed, relapsed into silence. And almost immediately afterwards the whole room emptied abruptly, like a fire brigade being called out on an exercise.

We went off to the restaurant in a gang. The dishes seemed

222

to have a delightful freshness that evening; for the first time while eating them I had lusty singing to add spice to the meal.

When we came to the dessert, Gédéon started raising Cain about the cheese supplied. "It's a scandal. Down with the pseudo-philanthropists who get fat off our substance. Sharks and profiteers the lot of them. My god, a franc for one portion of cheese, that would be eight francs for a box of camembert. At that price we ought to get caviare."

He worked the whole table up to such an extent that the manageress was attracted from her office door, peering through her glasses like a down-at-heel dowager. "Look out, the poisoner's here!" cried Gédéon as she approached, and then struck up a common version of *"Oh dear what can the matter be . . ."* which we all joined in heartily. The manageress beat a hasty retreat, and Gédéon commented triumphantly: "It's a good thing the old hag has some sense of shame."

Chapter 2

EVERY MORNING, from nine-thirty till one, the Pozzi Ward dealt with its patients like a huge machine, turning at full blast, working to a strict timetable controlled almost to the last second. The rigid punctuality, so perfect as to be inhuman, was largely due to the character of the ward Sister under whom I was beginning my career as a dresser.

As is traditional in France, most of the Sisters I had come across were country-bred. They were short and sturdy, with robust health and ruddy complexions which seemed little affected by the Paris air and their labors in hospital. Having seen a good deal of suffering, they had acquired deep reserves of patience and philosophy; and though their moods and temperaments naturally varied, they were on the whole a friendly lot for whom hospital regulations and routine were not a fixed, unalterable dogma, to be observed in every jot and tittle. They were capable, in fact, of exercising their authority with a sense of proportion.

Not so Sister Limagnac, a lean, angular figure with a yellowish face and hard suspicious eyes, who spent her mornings snapping crossly at everyone, always on the lookout for mistakes or negligence. The nurses liked her even less than I did, for she insisted on having the beds in a perfectly straight line, and would inspect every nook and cranny for illicit dust or marks or stains. She would presumably have been happiest as a theatre Sister, and seemed to hope for the same impossible cleanliness here. She had a nasty way of looking at my feet when I came on duty, which made me feel that it was slightly sacrilegious to be walking about on her ward floor at all. This was meant merely to shine, not to be walked on.

Her fussiness extended to the patients, who liked her, if possible, still less than the nurses. In securing the meticulous observance of every detail of the ward's routine, she was as cantankerous and sadistic as a sergeant-major unleashed on a troop of raw recruits. To confiscate the blissful banned cigarette or comforting cup of coffee introduced on the sly, she would appear at the door of her office, a bunch of keys rattling from her belt. Hearing this noise, which always preceded her arrival, the patients would warn each other, as if in a barracks: "Stow it away! Sergeant-Major coming!" And M. Thury confided to me: "That woman will be the death of us yet. May the Lord have mercy upon us, and make her forget us once in a while."

The morning after my visit to Carleret's room, I arrived at the hospital late, out of breath from having run. When I knocked at the door of her office and went inside, Sister Limagnac pointed out to me tartly, looking down her nose, that it was exactly nine-thirty-eight; and her expression discouraged me from offering the excellent excuses I had ready. Without leaving me time to recover my breath, she went on:

"Today being the beginning of term, we have the new students here. Dr. Hauberger will therefore be making his round earlier this morning, and there's a lot to be done. Please start your work straight away, with Twelve's stomach washout. Everything is ready on the table. The probationer is busy, but take someone else to help you."

She looked through the glass window which enabled her to keep an eye on the whole ward from her office. "Take the girl waiting near the big table. That will start her off on her student career very nicely."

Naturally sour, her voice was now acidity itself. She had become a sister the hard way, after years of apprenticeship as probationer and staff nurse. She did not, I knew, approve of students on the ward at all, and girl students least of all. Some girls in their early days would look disgusted and insulted if their refined fingers were required even to touch a urinal or a spittoon; they would prefer to be ministering angels arranging with loving care the pillows of humbly grateful patients. This romantic conception of hospital life did not commend itself to our Sister.

With scarcely a trace of masculine curiosity I looked towards the girl selected, wondering what her face would be like. I saw a figure in white, with fair hair, holding in one hand a red notebook.

Since the days of Krysia, I still maintained my theory about all girl students. It was nothing to do with me that this girl should have to help me with a rather unpleasant treatment. It might well have been one of the nurses, who were obliged to keep their hands busy with bottles and bedpans and spittoons for eight hours a day, if they were to earn their meagre bread and butter. As I went towards the fair-haired student, I thought: "A catheter! If she's at all squeamish, she won't forget her first day at hospital in a hurry. But after all I didn't make her take up medicine."

The girl watched me coming up to her with the alarm of a startled deer. Our conversation was brief:

"You are to help me with the stomach pump."

"Yes, sir."

"You know what that is?"

"No, sir."

What a model little girl, with her "Yes sir" and "No sir"! It gave me a horrible desire to treat her as a clumsy beginner, or indeed as the frightened schoolgirl her words and expression suggested. All the same, I decided, she was rather pretty in her white coat. She had a soft round face, a child-like chin, and large brown eyes which looked out with faint bewilderment on a disturbing new world.

Sister would be observing us through her window, and I wasted no further time in such reflections.

"No. 12" watched us arrive with a look of terror on his face. He was a man of about sixty, thin and dark-skinned as an old gypsy. I made him sit up, and then spread a mackintosh over him as far as the chin, like a bib; he might have been a fantastic elderly baby we were about to feed. I said to the girl: "Hold this kidney dish in front of him, and then keep still." After which I explained to the patient: "You're going to open your mouth and swallow this rubber tube. Don't be scared. It goes down by itself."

As soon as the tube reached his throat the patient gave a hiccough and abruptly vomited a brown mass of disgusting liquid made up of rotting substances, undigested bits of food, and black blood. The smell was awful. I myself had prudently dodged to the side, but the girl was slightly splashed on the arm. She dared not let go of the dish, but appealed to me with a helpless look. I told her to clean it off with some water from the jug, and then added in a bantering tone: "You'll be looking out for that next time, won't you?" She flushed with fury, which I could easily interpret as: "You might have warned me."

I began to push the tube again. The patient's face at once took on a really frightening expression: the muscles of his neck stretched like whipcord, his eyes became wild, and he gave hoarse choking gasps. Beneath the mackintosh you could almost see the whole thorax contracting and the diaphragm jerking madly, as if every effort were practically killing him. I continued to encourage him: "Swallow, grandpa, swallow. Try to keep calm."

Gradually, inch by inch, the big tube made its way down to the stomach. I looked at the girl; she was motionless. Completely occupied in holding the receiver in place, she certainly at present had more courage than I had given her credit for. We should see what happened later. "Why on earth," I thought, "must she put on so much powder and no lipstick? And that powder's too pale, it doesn't suit her." I was delighted to notice these irritating little details which meant I need not consider her too seriously. I should have been most annoyed to find her perfect.

The other first-year students arrived in little groups, and gathered curiously round the unfortunate patient, who seemed to be in the grip of a tremendous bout of seasickness. I stopped for a moment to let him have a rest. His face relaxed slightly.

227

A thread of yellowish dribble flowed from his mouth all along the tube, and with this rubber coming out of his lips and his highly lugubrious face he looked like a character from Grimm who was condemned to vomit serpents all his life. I suddenly remembered an illustration in one of my children's books along these lines, and this made me ask the student teasingly:

"Isn't there a fairy tale where the villain is punished by having to vomit vipers? I expect you remember the one, your childhood memories must still be very fresh."

The rest of the students smiled. As they had been looking at her all the time and she had nowhere else to rest her eyes, she had previously kept them fixed on the patient. Now she raised them towards me flashing with contempt. "I don't happen to remember that story," she answered, "but I'm sure of one thing—Prince Charming wasn't in it."

All the other students laughed, and I decided it was high time to get on with the treatment. The catheter was now in place in the stomach, and I started pumping. A jet of liquid fell into the receiver immediately, looking and smelling even more dreadful than the first matter the patient had vomited. I pumped a second, then a third time; and each time the smell became a little more nauseating, as if I had stirred the bottom of a sewer.

I looked round me. The other students had withdrawn in disgust. The girl had not moved, she had only turned her head away slightly. I guessed that she was sickened but was staying still by a determined effort of will-power. I had to recognize her courage, and in fact found her really rather charming in this position. I began to pump again, and when I looked at her once more she was completely mistress of herself. She had straightened up and stood in an attitude of quiet composure. She held her haughty little head very erect, but her mouth trembled despite itself. Talk about being proud! I had a sudden fierce desire to bite that mouth, to humble her pride, to punish her.

I began the stomach lavage: I poured water from the jug down through a funnel into the rubber tube; then I siphoned it several times. The girl still stood near the patient, attentive and obedient, but there was now a glint of mocking schoolgirl humor

228

in her brown eyes. I did my best not to look at her, but felt her quizzical gaze fixed upon me. The whole circle of students was watching us, and a sense of dull irritation made me stupid and awkward. Eventually, when I was about to withdraw the tube, the first-year students were summoned for a roll call, and the circle scattered at once. I released my assistant immediately, and watched her walking away, while helping the patient to lie down again. I was annoyed with myself, with the world in general.

"Nice little number, isn't she?" remarked a familiar voice in my ear. I had not seen Paul Chavasse since the night of the Internes' Hop, but was pleased to find him on the same ward with me. I was not so pleased just at that moment, however, especially when he added: "Yes, a nice little piece, even if she doesn't think very much of you."

But then he remembered his general contempt for girl students, and he also felt that second-year solidarity must be reasserted; so he finished his comment with: "No respect for elders and betters, any of them. We'll have to watch that. They're a sight too fresh, this year's freshmen, eh?"

"Oh, that girl," I answered. "She's just a silly little goose."

Paul took my arm and dragged me off, telling me all about his vacation as we went. After this he asked me how I'd done in the dresser's exam. I told him I was fairly confident about the result, and hoped to start working for the interne's exam very shortly.

"My dear old Doctor Nérac," he commented, "I've always wanted to be pally with a Professor of the Faculty, Member of the Academy of Medicine, and all that. The way you can swot is nobody's business, so just you take all these exams, and I'll give you more time and energy to work for them by doing everything on the ward you don't feel like doing. I'll be able to try out my hand with the customers here, while you will eventually go up for your exams, fitter than most fiddles, ready to snap your fingers at the best consultants in the country. Good idea, don't you think?"

How could I refuse so amiable a proposition? Unless you said "no" firmly to Paul almost before he had finished speaking, you could never refuse him anything. In any case I had no time to answer, for the door opened and as if by magic a profound silence came over the ward instantly. In came a tall, erect, imposing figure, in a white coat and cap, with a lean face and pointed silvery beard. The hospital's chief surgeon, the celebrated Louis Hauberger, holder of the Grand Cross of the Légion d'Honneur, Member of the Institute, and President of the Academy of Medicine, was about to start his round. He was accompanied by his resident and interne, and, a few paces behind them, by a band of first-year students, mightily impressed.

It was a solemn entry. One of the greatest surgeons of the day, his name was always in the papers, signing bulletins on the health of distinguished invalids, addressing international congresses on behalf of French surgery, receiving honorary degrees from numerous foreign universities. Fifty years of brilliant surgery, thousands of desperate but victorious operations, a host of titles, functions and honors, had built him up into an almost legendary figure; and the appearance of Hauberger the man in the Pozzi Ward that morning did nothing to reduce the legend. He could be recognized immediately as an outstanding personality.

He had taken a few steps into the ward. Sister Limagnac ran up with the report book, a nurse brought a bottle of spirit, and my fellow dresser, who would be showing his patients before I showed mine, fumbled feverishly with his notes and observations. Everyone was watching the great man. The patients knew that only the most serious cases were shown to him, and a terror shone from the eyes of each one. If Dr. Hauberger stopped in front of a bed, it was almost a sign that the patient was "dangerously ill"; but it also meant there was hope, for anyone on whom Dr. Hauberger operated would be saved.

The Sisters and nurses attended him with obsequious zeal, the interne stood by deferentially, while the dresser tried to master his nervousness and the new students gazed in mute admiration. All this made up an awful silence, heavy with suspense, while the Chief began to question the interne in terse sentences. His voice was icily imperious. Paul tugged at my sleeve, and I expected that he had already found some mannerism in our new Chief, which he would confide to me irreverently.

"No fun and games here, Jean, my lad," he murmured: "but I do hand it to yon graybeard. He's certainly a grand old man." His whisper was pregnant with a note of exceptional enthusiasm.

Between Dr. Hauberger's round of the wards and his first lecture, the morning passed very quickly, and I had little time to think further about the girl who had turned the tables upon me so neatly.

It was one o'clock, and I was preparing to leave, when Dr. Robin, my interne, asked for me in the operating theatre. He wanted to do a hernia before lunch, and asked me to give the anaesthetic. The operation took longer than the usual quarter of an hour allotted to hernias, and when the last stitch was in, the theatre clock read twenty-five minutes past one. By way of apology Dr. Robin asked me to lunch with him in the internes' common room.

I had not been there since the dinner before the ball. In two or three years, of course, I hoped to return there as a right. Meanwhile I would go past the common room windows, and glance at the room's contents. On the huge table I would see the rough cloths that had once been sheets, the thick bowls for breakfast coffee and the coffee jugs which had probably seen hard service on the wards. The chairs were like benches, the aged piano had lost most of its teeth, and on the walls above the rows of lockers, old pictures and caricatures stretched right up to the vaulted ceiling. When I left the hospital at one o'clock, I would slow down again on passing under the arch near the common room, and would strain my ear to catch the hubbub of discussions, the rhythm of the songs, the clatter of crockery, the shrill laughter of young feminine guests, and all the rest of that exuberant, tumultuous life, light-headed and light-hearted, which I had savored there one October evening.

Internes' Common Room. Private. Keep out said an enamel plaque well in evidence on the door. The patients' relatives I used to meet just before visiting hours would look at that door in alarm, as if the force of the shouting and songs might burst it open in their faces. When an interne opened it to go in, they would crane their necks forward towards the opening, hoping perhaps for a glimpse of something sensational inside. Then the door would bang in their faces, and I felt like telling these curious laymen that I was quite familiar with what went on behind these forbidden portals.

All the same, despite my acquaintance with the common room from the Internes' Hop, I felt like an intruder when Robin pushed me in there ahead of him. The meal was just finishing, and on the disordered table, among crusts of bread and the stains from wine and sauce, coffee had been served in big glasses, broad and solid as beer mugs. The paintings on the walls disappeared in a haze of cigarette smoke. Laughter and conversation mingled with the clatter of cheap crockery. As Robin was walking to his place, followed by me, he was greeted by a volley of chaff from the rest of the table:

"Nearly two o'clock, Georges. Don't overdo it, old chap."

"Don't spoil his first fine careless rupture."

"A bit of home work with the theatre Sister, eh?"

Besides this good-natured banter, I was rather startled to hear scurrilous attacks on the chiefs themselves: "It's superb, the famous Hauberger op. for facial neuralgia. The woman I sent you is beginning to suffer again already."

They all joined in. "Your patient was lucky, Pierre. With Marescot, where I was last year, she might well have got a purulent strabismus into the bargain."

"Oh, well, you can't make omelettes without breaking eggs."

"Does Marescot do the same as Joubert with his one-eyed friends, look at them in profile?"

"And does he mark them in profile when working out statistics of his miraculous cures?"

"Course not. He just forgets them."

"He wouldn't do a thing like that. Unworthy of him. He merely marks them: 'Lost sight of.'"

"Hauberger's a glutton for statistics too. Did you read his last article in the *Medical Journal* on his follow-up results with surgical treatment of uterine cancer, the famous Hauberger operation? It's really wonderful, there are hardly any relapses. Only thing is, in three quarters of the cases, they aren't real cancers. That, of course, he doesn't mention."

"You're a bit hard on him. Perhaps he didn't do the diagnosing."

They went on ridiculing the methods of their superiors, bandying about failures and deaths, talking of patients and cases like so many guineapigs. I could very well understand their coarse humor at the Internes' Hop, even their insistence on smut for smut's sake. But I was staggered by this casual, almost complacent, disrespect for everybody and everything. Even those whose bedside manner was quiet and gentle, were as rowdy and loud-mouthed here as the rest.

Georges Robin had sat me down next to him at one end of the table. He seemed indifferent to the jeers and chaff. His back was bent, his elbows were sunk on the table. He looked as if his mind were elsewhere, as if the efforts of the morning had drained his energy. Round him his colleagues were laughing at their ease, tilted back on their chairs.

I was shocked by the stupid, spiteful welcome they had given Robin, and I even thought he kept silent because secretly hurt. He had quietly drawn towards us a dish of meat and a carafe of wine, and had filled our plates and glasses. He swallowed a few mouthfuls, drained his glass at one go, and then seemed to wake up. He stretched himself, and looked round for a moment as if testing the mood of the audience. I was waiting for an indignant outburst of protest; Robin took his time. Finally, tilting back his chair like the others, with powerful but good-humored violence, he shouted at them: "You goddamned bastards." After this, relaxed and back to normal once more, he began to laugh.

I was beginning to understand things better. In seven or eight years of medicine, these people had known too many days of bending over bed after bed, without horror or disgust, with a bitter taste in the mouth from stench and decay; too many days where the doctor must show no emotion; only examine, act and pass on, measuring his words and telling lies of pity, without him-

233

self keeping illusions or hope. Ordinary mortals cannot go on squandering indefinitely, without a break, their reserves of kindness and compassion, or the virtue will one day go out of these qualities. Of course the internes at certain hours had to return to "normal life" when they could utter any extravagant nonsense that came into their heads, and be as cutting and coarse and disloyal and unkind as they liked.

The weight of these reflections was strikingly reinforced at this moment by a burly interne in the armchair, who emitted a huge sonorous belch of indolent satisfaction. It was somehow a reassuring sound, and I found I could relax myself and laugh with the others. I was hungry, and Robin handed me good solid food; I was thirsty, and my glass was full. I was young, and I too needed to forget the difficult morning, charged with dead matter, with groans and blood and wounds. I felt happy. Round this table everything was alive, joyously alive. And outside the hospital too the world was brimming over with cheerfulness—just as the wine was brimming over in our glasses.

Chapter 3

EVERY DAY at about four o'clock a stream of students poured
out into the street from all the doors of the school. For a minute
or two they flooded over the pavements and roadway like a
musical comedy chorus making an entrance; then they disappeared at the end of the short street among the indifferent crowd
of two boulevards.

"Jesus," groaned Paul Chavasse, "boredom might have been
born at a university. Term's only been going a fortnight, and already I'm thinking about next vac. People imagine that medical
students get tired in their legs or their head. But with me, the
way our educational system works, it's the buttocks that can't
take any more. By the way, they've changed the records at
the Jukebox, come and listen to them. All on me, come on. If
you're afraid of being undermined by the pleasures of the city,
we'll play for your benefit the ocarina solo record of *The
Maiden's Prayer*."

I refused the invitation, and Paul did not press me further.
When he had left me, I did not, like last year, dally at the boxes
of books outside the bookshops, but made for the Cité straight
away.

Since I had been earning eight francs a day at the hospital, I
allowed myself to spend more on fares, including the luxury of
returning to the Cité by bus instead of Metro. Before crossing
the road to my bus stop, I noticed the little blonde student waiting, presumably for the same bus. Several times since the morning of the stomach pump I had recognized her in the distance on

235

the Boulevard Jourdain, from which I deduced that she too lived at the Cité. No more than on the ward, however, had I tried to make further acquaintance with her. I watched her from the other side of the road. She was wearing a dark coat and a simple toque, which allowed her curls to flow freely. Standing on the pavement like that, her head slightly tilted in an expression half happy, half timid, she had the grace of a young flower. Near her you looked instinctively for a youth of her own age —or else imagined him coming to join her with great boyish strides, and her waiting to smile at him when he caught her up. Already men were staring at this girl who was too pretty to be alone, hoping to sit near her in the bus.

With a squeal of brakes and hooting of horns the bus arrived; the girl had just time to get on the outside platform. When it started again and went by in front of me, she seemed to me even more sensitive and helpless amidst all these staring strangers than she had before my sarcasms on the ward. For a moment I suddenly felt like running towards her, to catch hold of this warm life, which was fast disappearing. Then the bus gathered speed, turning at the crossroads, and I thought of other things.

When the bus delivered me, twenty minutes later, at the end of the Parc Montsouris, the Cité clock read only just after a quarter to five. I was delighted, for according to my timetable I could afford a good few minutes of relaxation. So instead of going up to my room straight away, I stopped at the first floor and took the corridor to the right. The key to Carleret's room was in the door, as always.

Every evening, on returning to my hostel, I played the same hypocritical little comedy with myself. I stopped at Carleret's room, merely to look in for a minute and then come out again. But once I sat down I was lost. The smoke drifted round me, enveloping me like an enormous soft eiderdown, and I would stay in my armchair, knowing by heart all its frayed parts, each creaky spring, quite incapable of leaving it.

Sometimes, hearing the quarter-hours chiming on the Maison de France clock, I would feel a moment's remorse thinking of time passing and all the medical books awaiting me on my table. But after all the year was only just beginning and the interne's exam, my next big hurdle, was still a long way off—so I stayed in the chair a little longer, listening to some young prophet busy rebuilding the world, or following the thread of some heated controversy, flashing with friendly insults, as it flew off at a tangent with magnificent light-hearted inconsequence. Levity, I decided, quite reassured, carried no less weight than gravity in maintaining spiritual well-being.

That day, however, when I went into the room, it was unusually silent. In an armchair a heavy, massive, bony chap, with the long limbs of a farmer, was enjoying a doze. I had already seen him two or three times in the same place, always half asleep, with a book lying abandoned on his stomach between his huge red wrists. Moreover it always seemed to be the same book, the first volume of Proust's novel, and to be open at the same page. I had looked with some disdain at this lout who calmly went to sleep over Proust, and who when he woke up listened to the discussion of the moment with a puzzled frown on his brow. Very soon this excess of attention seemed to make him dizzy, and without saying anything he would get up and go.

Prichard, seated on the divan, was choosing gramophone records, and called me over; I went and sat beside him.

Prichard raised his voice and called: "Wake up, Clément! Is there a doctor in the house?"

While Lucien Clément, the medical student thus adjured, opened a vague and uncomprehending eye, Prichard, determined to have his say on all medical matters, went on. "Carleret says it's easy enough to neutralize. But official therapy's no good for stomach ulcers. Now homeopathic treatment can be really effective." Prichard continued to hold the floor for homeopathy, his chin stuck out, his face furrowed in a pontifical frown.

To look at him better, Clément straightened up, showing a big nose, somewhat heavy cheeks, an unassuming brow under a thick crop of hair. He listened to Prichard with an expression of sincere astonishment. Several times he opened his mouth without saying anything, as if still hesitating to become involved in this debate. Eventually he made up his mind, and offered his contribution in a calm, unhurried, countryman's voice:

"You did say homeopathy, Pierre? You want to do homeopathy now?"

Prichard seemed to regret his imprudent profession of faith, and answered rather lamely: "Yes. Why not?"

"That's wonderful," continued Clément, in the same placid voice, but you could detect a note of annoyance not far from the surface. "Ordinary medicine is complicated and difficult enough by itself, and you haven't managed to digest that properly. Now you want to launch out on something not one doctor in twenty understands anything about. I know you, Pierre. Homeopathy may be all very well, though I've heard a lot of people say it isn't, but in any case it's not right for you.

"Nor for me," he added a moment later, with a candor I later found to be characteristic.

"Taken by and large," remarked Carleret, turning from his bridge game, "with all the fallacies current in the world today, it would be surprising if homeopathy were the only one which hadn't a small particle of truth. But it's obvious that Pierre wasn't watching his step last vacation. He just couldn't help listening to Little Arthur again."

Everyone laughed. There were often things like that, which set them in a roar, where I failed to see anything funny. It was a sort of secret language, a friendly jargon drawn from a fund of common adventures and memories, with passwords which I was eager to learn as soon as possible so as to be really one of their set.

"I protest," retorted Prichard, evidently stung to the quick. "Homeopathy is a remarkable thing. It has all the answers. The allopaths are all wrong."

"In my home town," Carleret slipped in, "there are certain wise men. So wise they can only read in their own breviary. That's from Goethe."

Clément ignored this ambiguous aside, and in quite a good-natured voice—he seemed so much in control of himself that I could not imagine him ever losing his temper—summed up:

238

"Anyhow, if your roads separate, *you* won't be a very great loss to official medicine."

Prichard put on the superior expression of a man who scarcely hears such insults. He shrugged his shoulders, and suddenly found he must go outside for a moment. One of the bridge-players said to Clément:

"You were a bit hard on him, Lucien. He's not a bad chap really. I know he can be pretty boring, he takes himself so damn seriously. But he means well."

"Yes, I know," said Clément. "I just couldn't help saying that. I always like people and things to be in their right places. Why on earth does he want to get mixed up with little pink pills? It's always the least intelligent people who want to do the most difficult things. I don't suppose he'll ever be able to carve a cow properly, and last year he was already planning a surgical career."

"Well," said Carleret reproachfully, "you could have let him try his luck there. According to Bernard Shaw, the discovery of chloroform has given every lunatic the chance of becoming a surgeon."

I asked him: "Who's this Little Arthur you were talking about?"

"Little Arthur? Aha, you know him quite well. He's the mischievous invisible character responsible for most of life's disagreeable surprises. A nasty little gremlin. . . ."

"Who makes shutters bang at night," finished off Clément for him, "and when you leave a piece of pie on a seat, will always bring an old relative to sit down right in the middle of it."

"That's right," took up Carleret. "Well, Pierre has his own Little Arthur to whisper bad advice to him or leave pie on the chair where he's going to sit down. It's very sad. Poor old Prich is not in a state of grace, grace has been denied. And that, I fear, will not be forgiven him."

Just then a whistle was heard outside, and a handful of pebbles hit the window panes. Everyone called out: "That's for you, Lucien. Paging Doctor Lucien Clément . . ."

Clément went to the window looking onto the Slum, opened

it, and leaned out into the darkness. This swallowed up most of the subsequent conversation, and only a few indistinct remarks penetrated into the room. Clément concluded "I'll be with you," shut the window and crossed the room to go out. Prichard had just returned and said to him near the door: "So you're at it again. Rather showing off, aren't you?"

Clément shrugged his shoulders with sturdy serenity, and went out. Prichard, full of rancor, could not let it go at that. "Just because he started to treat a couple of dogs with lice and one of these brothel keepers he gets on with so well, they all come to him now and he already takes himself for a modern St. Vincent de Paul."

"Don't get worked up," said Carleret. "You might do yourself some damage. And anyhow we all know you'll get to heaven before he does."

"How do you know that?" Prichard rose beautifully. He just could not miss any chance of reassuring himself about his own superiority.

"Because, my dear Pierre, the theologians teach that after death the sin of jealousy will be less punished than all the others. Those who commit it have already been through their hell, here on earth. So you see, old chap, you can sleep in peace," concluded Carleret with a laugh, and then got up himself.

When he had gone, I found the room sad and empty. I went to the window. The whole of the Slum was shrouded in darkness, broken here and there by a few tiny reddish glimmers, which seemed half ashamed of their light. All round it tiers of lights were blazing like beacons, from the hostels all down the boulevard on the one side to the outskirts of Gentilly on the other; in the middle of this ring of fire there was only the loneliness of night. One of the Cité's tall lamps lit up the fence palings; I saw Lucien Clément leap neatly over it, and land in the darkness on the other side. Then he reappeared in the light. He must have been very sure where he was going, for he never hesitated. He walked with long regular strides, as if ploughing one of his native fields; and I could follow him with my eyes for a short while, passing through the allotments and shacks, thanks to the red gleam of his pipe. Then the Slum became a stagnant pool of darkness. I forgot about Prichard and tried to imagine Lucien, moving sturdily forward in that black mass, crossing and recrossing it, as he had probably done with flocks of sheep in his boyhood. From my window I had often looked at this darkling region, but felt that nothing could ever connect me with it. Now the shadows had suddenly ceased to be impersonal and uniform; they had come into my life. Down there, the medical student Lucien Clément seemed to be keeping watch for both of us like an advance guard in the night. I hoped very much that he would let me come with him one evening, to explore this dark domain at his side.

Chapter 4

ETHER ON WOUNDS, ether in anaesthetics, ether everywhere: this invisible deity impregnated all my mornings. Its fumes became the unique and inescapable smell symbolic of my new functions as dresser.

When I put on the short-sleeved coat and the apron supplied by the authorities for hospital dressers, I ceased to be a mere student looking on with no real right to touch anything. I was part of a team, with a definite part to play, anaesthetics to give, dressings to do, charts to keep. I had become a responsible person.

My mornings were well filled. They usually started with a series of anaesthetics. An orderly brought those for operation on a trolley to the corridor in front of the theatre, and left me alone there to put them to sleep.

As soon as they saw me preparing the mask, most of the patients would work themselves up into a panic, and I could guess in advance those who would scream: "No, no. I'll die. I'll never go under." Or else: "I'm scared. Do you think I'll ever come to again?" Others brazened it out, or else accepted it with a special courage concealing their fear.

I soon learned to know all the symptoms of sleep, from those who went off very abruptly, passing into unconsciousness at a single blink of the eye, to the cases where the ether worked very gradually, and you could almost watch the refusal of the conscious mind to surrender its powers till the very last moment.

Many who were quite calm at the beginning would become panicstricken when they felt the ether burning the back of their throat, as if they were sinking into a monstrous pit of blackness. I would try to reassure them, almost shouting; but to little purpose, for the words slipped over them, and in their terror they could no longer hear me. Some winked just before dropping off, as if to say "au revoir," while others began laughing or crying drunkenly, or would stiffen and shake and writhe, hurling abuse at me, which was stifled by the mask. Where the orderly had taken the precaution of binding their wrists, the parts of the trolley near their hands were clawed like the bars of a cage.

Then, consciousness departed, they would begin the continual clearing of mucous, the long animal snore, which is only a grotesque imitation of peaceful human slumbers.

The orderly came to collect the trolley, pushed it into the theatre, where with my help he slid the inert corpse-like body on the table; then I settled on a small stool at its head. Once seated there, I could no longer see anything but the patient's face, upside down and shrunken beneath the nickel-plated bowl of the mask. Sterile towels rose in front of me in a small arc, and beyond them, by raising my head a little, I could see the gloved hands of the surgeons, and follow their intricate work between the mass of swabs. Above them the spotlight formed a luminous dome whose crossing rays left the wound fully exposed in every corner.

Most of the time I was content to watch from below the attentive eyes of the surgeons between their headbands and white cambric masks. Without looking at their hands I would admire the movements of their shoulders, and the deep reserves of power behind actions which often looked so slow and deliberate.

Everything seemed to concentrate round these two men, big white forms under a piercing beam of light which splashed with bright gold each glint of steel, every bloodstain and the whiteness of all the theatre linen. Away from the table the room was in a dimmer, bluish light, in which nurses walked to and fro with padded steps, and in a corner the group of students in off-white coats, who were reputed to endanger the asepsis of the

243

theatre, craned their necks forward trying to see what was happening.

The patient snored peacefully beneath the mask; in the adjoining room the sterilizer gave off a thin monotonous jet of steam. In the solemn silence these indistinct noises seemed like a hallucination; the only real sounds were the abrupt clatter of an instrument on the enamel tray and the occasional terse orders for swabs or catgut which were immediately and silently offered and taken.

Time and time again the operation would proceed in perfect order. I was well aware that this apparent smoothness and ease depended at each moment on superb technical skill, a flawless chain of exact and calculated actions, a perpetual harmony of hand and brain. Like the shadowy figures in the rest of the room, I too, alone at my end of the table, let myself be led by these two dominating figures, who minute by minute were carrying us forward to a new miracle of healing.

The Chief knew that we student-anaesthetists soon grew weary of our painful and tedious task. We could not watch the operation as a continuous whole, the ether fumes might dull our wits, we might be overcome by the heat from the spotlight. To make us realize the importance of our function, he had quoted to us the phrase of Mikulicz: "A well administered anaesthetic is a work of art." He had also very specifically forbidden us to pass on this delicate work to any novice eager for experience.

Near me, on a little table, were a tongue-clip, a gag, and a tube to free the air passages. All through the operation they would remind me that even the most ordinary anaesthetic can turn brutally to drama. I lived in terror of syncope, the whiteness which means disaster, the blueness which still leaves some hope; and I made the utmost efforts to insure that no incident should through my fault disturb the operation's planned and majestic progress. In any case, to rob me of the slightest tendency to carelessness, I need only lift my eyes towards the Chief. In the way he looked at the wound, you could read an extreme sternness towards his own work, a rigorous conrtol of all his actions, an unshakable will-power and endless patience—which in even the longest operation would only stop when the work was done. He showed the same sternness to all his staff, from the humblest nurse to his closest assistants.

The first weeks I had been shocked by the arrogant and almost insulting tone by which he would coldly rebuke the least mistake of omission or commission. I read into it the domineering mood of a man who had always been accustomed to command, and to assert his own personality, without any regard for others' feelings. I knew now that his sternness was not directed against us, but towards helping all that should come to pass through us, towards the life which it was ours to serve, as he served it himself. We held lives in our hands, and he moulded us sternly so that no operation, through some unforeseen negligence, should become a new risk of death for the patient being operated on. At any time an operation may go wrong through some technical accident or some combination of unexpected mischances; through us his will-power was striking at all these hidden forces, which can only be obviated if each single will involved is directed towards this end. One morning he said to us: "Probability and good or bad luck are bad masters for a surgeon. I refuse to accept passively the need to include such calculations in surgical realities." By acting as if will-power alone could prevent deaths, he built up that will-power, and each one, like a soldier at his post, felt himself a responsible member of the team. *Responsible:* for a doctor, the most important word of all.

One morning, like almost all the other mornings for a month now, I had given an anaesthetic, and the patient had only just been taken away on the trolley, when an emergency case was brought into the theatre: a young woman with the pallor of a corpse. The diagnosis was obvious: ruptured uterus, through which the blood was draining off into the stomach. The woman was put on the table at once, and while the nurses were getting the instruments ready, Dr. Hauberger said to me: "Put her to sleep immediately!"

His voice seemed to me to vibrate as if he were giving a battle order. I looked at the dying woman in terror; despite the

245

bleeding she remained lucid, but her pulse was impossibly faint; I did not imagine she could ever support the double shock of anaesthetic and operation.

When I let the first drops fall onto the mask, the young woman offered no resistance; she wore a peaceful smile which recalled to me a picture I saw each day in an antiquary's window. It was called "Girl Drowned in the Seine," and as she went to sleep, the dying girl was smiling, like this patient. She too looked serene and undistressed as she let herself be sucked down by the black water. Almost before the patient was under, the Chief approached the table in silence, with a look of such deep concentration that I felt I had never seen him like this before. He gave an order, and immediately the table was tilted, head downwards, in the usual position for gynaecological operations. Then, with a closed inscrutable face, he pressed the scalpel onto the stomach and made a deep incision. At the bottom, when he had put the retractors in, you could see the blood seething amidst huge black clots. And in this nauseating spectacle of butchery, the only thing which seemed to survive, with an ironical stubbornness, was the warm perfumed mass of her hair; it all came abruptly down between my hands as the table was being tipped up.

The operation was being performed at the very last possible moment. I felt her pulse ceaselessly almost without hope, and watched the pupils between those soft lids, wondering if the eyes would ever hold more than this glassy corpse-like stare; I watched each respiration as if it might be the final faint murmur where the dying woman breathes out for the last time. Never before, on the face of the clock in front of me, had I counted the minutes so anxiously. I felt these minutes were ebbing away like blood, each carrying away a hope, each squeezing out a drop of life. The interne and some of the students had come, struck by the sight of youth condemned; they stood round the table, grave and still like people round a deathbed. There was a grim silence, and on that day neither the whistle from the sterilizer, nor the clatter of the instruments, nor the Chief's terse orders, could drown for me one tiny sound which seemed tremendous and all-important: the rustle of the bladder on the side of the mask, feebly swelling and contracting with the patient's breath.

Sometimes she gave a feeble sigh and then seemed to stop breathing altogether. I waited tensely for the breathing to start again. I felt the Chief might suddenly look up at me and say: "Stop. She's dead!" The table would be straightened, the assistant would jerk the sterile towels away, and sew up the huge red wound with great needle strokes right into the flesh—a brutal, hurried, end-of-post-mortem suture, in a kind of sombre fury before defeat in this long battle. The nurses would finish dropping on the floor the blood-soaked linen, free the wrists, remove the shoulder-straps, and detach from its cross this pale corpse not yet cold. The theatre would empty, everyone would depart, silent and depressed, with a taste of dust and ashes on their lips. These instruments and swabs, the transfusion apparatus being prepared, all this equipment would seem a mockery, left abandoned to a silent empty theatre. I too should have to go away with the others, and the order which the nurses would restore when we had gone would be the same as the order left in dead people's rooms after the funeral vigil is over.

To recover my confidence, I would sometimes raise my eyes towards the Chief. From time to time, quite impassively and without saying a word, he would lean his sweat-covered brow towards a nurse, who would wipe it at once. The blood no longer seethed in the patient's stomach, like water at the bottom of a well. You could not see the scarlet stream to which the instruments and swabs and bleeding towels still testified. The careful needle closed up the torn sheathes, one by one. Methodically the operation proceeded; it was almost completed now, and I watched the pulse with growing anxiety, the very short and feeble rise and fall of the membrane of the mask. Suppose it stopped now! Suppose the eyes should suddenly be mere congealed blood, a little water in a muddy pit—for on a corpse, they say, the eyes decay first.

Never before this moment had I felt such a tremendous weight of responsibility, and it was growing from second to second.

247

With all the stern concentration of their efforts, the rigorous discipline of each action, with all their limitless patience, the Chief and his assistant were fighting against the surgeon's most redoubtable enemy, haemorrhage; and in an obscure but important fashion I was engaged in this struggle with them, at their side. For the first time, like them and no less than they did, I really held a life in my hands. Suppose I were clumsy enough to give an overdose of ether! Even at the final second, when all seemed saved, something I did might turn the scales—in the wrong way.

I no longer felt the weariness of my fingers clenched on the mask, nor the heat of the dome of light above my head, nor the dizzying smell of the ether. We dressers were interchangeable for giving anaesthetics, and any one of us might have been selected; it could not be at random that I had been intrusted with this responsibility on such a serious case. The Chief must surely have noticed me and chosen me. When finally he gave me the sign to reduce the dose of ether, and then, a few minutes later, to remove the mask, my heart leaped with a tumultuous, overpowering joy, blending with a sense of immense power fermenting inside me. I was no longer an ordinary student, a mere spectator, whose dealings with the patients could only be amateurish trivialities, on which nothing really depends. It was partly thanks to me, Jean Nérac, that this woman's life had been saved.

On the Pozzi Ward Paul Chavasse had taken complete control, and was almost acting as dresser instead of me. If I was kept too long at what he called my "ethereal" activities, he would choose among my beds the work he liked best, delicate dressings and plasters and minor surgery; so that when I was finally released from giving anaesthetics, I usually had nothing left to do but remove a few stitches and hear the patients repeating his witticisms. I should have gained nothing by protesting!

Paul's most brilliant achievement was that he actually seemed to have won over Sister Limagnac. Our redoubtable Sister accepted the dressers with fairly good grace, as long as they did their work properly; but any other students she treated as fair game. Being unable to chase them out of her ward, she would stop them taking any part in the treatments. We all knew that she mellowed slightly when talking to the interne, who certainly used plenty of soft soap on her. For Robin had learned by experience that an interne can at a pinch be cool with his Chief or look down on the Resident, but that to be on bad terms with his ward Sister will expose him to a permanent guerrilla warfare —in which the Sister is always victorious. But even Robin was less sure of Sister Limagnac's favor than was "M. Chavasse," a student with no official position on the ward whatever. Whenever he wanted, it seemed, Paul could bring a brief smile to her yellow face; and he was quite willing to tell me his secret.

"So you'd like to know how I charmed the rattlesnake?" He called her this because of the rattling keys on her belt. "It's really not so difficult. When you see our good Sister, so dry and angular and cantankerous, and yellow as a quince, anyone can see she has liver trouble. Having made the diagnosis, I decided to take a close interest in hepatitis. I went into it quite thoroughly, and for several days read the advertising matter of Parmentier's Pink Pills and the extreme efficacy of So-and-so's Herbal Cure for all liver complaints. Anyhow, once I was well up on the whole subject, I went along one morning and asked the rattlesnake for some samples of drugs. I groaned and talked of my migraines and itching and the sour taste in my mouth— and then of my constipation. I was testing her out. The first day she gave me a sample box like a charitable lady giving a few coppers to a beggar with lice, from a great height and a great distance. Two days later I became very humble, imploring her; she gave me some advice as well as the drugs. Eight days later we were exchanging confidences, like how difficult we found it to eat head cheese. A climate of confidence was created. But the day of days, which made me feel I was in, as you might say, was the morning she informed me in confidence that she had haemorrhoids. I had already hinted that I myself had been having some trouble in that quarter. Since then, united by our ideals, we have become real bosom companions. I can't be floored on questions of using horse-chestnut, witch-hazel, or arnica. I'm working up my pharmacopoeia that way, and we exchange formulas for ointments and hip-baths. Now we spread the same salves on our bottoms, it's only natural we should be real soulmates."

When I had been round the beds and finished the work Chavasse had been kind enough to leave me, I would often go and have a chat with M. Thury. He was still in the ward, despite Sister Limagnac's negotiations to hasten his departure to an old folks' home. Fortunately the administrative machine took its time, and M. Thury was still with us.

One morning I noticed on top of his bedside table a little bunch of violets. I was quite surprised: "Well now, you've had a visitor!"

"Oh no, I never have visitors. I don't expect any, and really I'd just as soon not have any. Most relatives are so impressed and paralyzed by the atmosphere of this big white ward that after the first kisses and greetings they hardly dare say anything. The wives want to straighten their husbands' pillows, empty the cups, but they don't dare, for they aren't in their own homes."

"But we can look after people so much better here, M. Thury. They can have all the treatments and X-rays and examinations they may need, and we can see immediately if anything is going wrong."

"Yes, I admit it's all right for those who might be starving if they weren't in a hospital. But there are many others eating their hearts out here, missing the affection and care they would get in their own homes. Sometimes these things can perform as many miracles as all your advanced medical science."

He looked at the little bunch of flowers on the locker and went on: "You ask me who these violets are from? To get violets in November you usually have to be either rich or dead. And so far I'm neither one nor the other."

"Who *are* they from, M. Thury? Out with it."

"Well then, they're from the young blonde girl student, the one you don't like."

I had very often seen her lingering by M. Thury's bed, when I was busy elsewhere. Outside the hospital I had always avoided her. Several times my eyes had met hers as I passed near her in the ward, and I thought I saw in her eyes the same ironical glint. Or else sometimes their expression was completely indifferent, as if nothing whatever had passed between us. I could not forget how on the morning of the stomach lavage I had felt such a fool because of her. M. Thury had not spoken of her to me before. As soon as I knew she was the giver of the violets, I could not stop myself saying sarcastically:

"Another Florence Nightingale, I suppose. Such complete sympathy with the patients. She will probably bring her lamp next time."

I looked round the ward to find the girl, and saw her near the big center table with four or five first-year students round her. They were dark young men with sleek hair, and were obviously telling her something funny, for she was laughing. They were convulsed with laughter, too, and by the way they looked at her, I was sure she was holding court among a circle of selected admirers. I felt vicious.

"Your benefactress is rather a flirt, don't you think, M. Thury?"

"Why are you so unkind? She doesn't want to flirt, specially with young men like that. She merely enjoys herself because she's still little more than a schoolgirl. And I'm very glad she's like that, for I can imagine nothing worse than a woman who's never really been a girl. No, she's not a flirt, nor a silly foolish giggler like some of them. You mustn't run down my little Marianne, I won't allow it."

"I'm not running down your Marianne, if that's her name, I was just making an observation. It's quite true I don't care for her, and of course, on principle, I'd prefer that all girl medical students should become chemists or diet experts or something."

"But good heavens!" exclaimed the old man: "I don't as a rule like female students any better than you do. But Marianne isn't like the rest, she really suffers with the patients, and just because she's extremely sensitive she's been finding life pretty rough lately. But she has remained soft and kind—and feminine: a true woman."

"So tender and so full of care? Do you really think so?"

"You're very harsh and unfair, my irritable young friend. I tell you from my own knowledge that she is not conceited. She is as fine morally as she is physically. I've seen too many people in my long life not to recognize at a glance the few beings who have received many gifts from Nature and who return them abundantly. Marianne is still near childhood, but there's a bursting of vitality in her, a look of intense hopefulness before life, which leaves no doubt in my mind at all. I tell you, the man who has the chance of winning that girl for his own is either a madman or a monster if he doesn't take it."

"You alarm me, M. Thury. You talk this morning like a father with a string of daughters to marry off."

I was interrupted by a crash of broken glass. One of the students had clumsily upset a tray full of syringes. At the noise the Sister came out of her office abruptly. Most of the students dispersed immediately, but this Marianne, the object of M. Thury's extraordinary eulogy, bent down to pick up the debris. Our rattlesnake swooped on her, rattling her keys. For some days she had been pursuing the poor girl relentlessly, and the high pleasure now of finding a new victim had clearly gone to her head, for I had never before seen her in a mood of such concentrated malevolence. I remembered somewhat ruefully how the girl had earned this apparently implacable hatred.

The Chief had a few mornings earlier been asking the first-year students questions, a dreaded occurrence. Fear of making a mistake, which would be followed by an icily sarcastic rebuke, seemed to rob them of all sense, making them stammer stupidly. This annoyed the Chief a good deal, specially if the student was a girl and started snivelling. Before questioning her, he said to M. Thury's Marianne: "Now please keep calm, young lady. Take your time and don't be worried, and think carefully before you answer." The girl stood erect in front of him, looking at him with wide attentive eyes. She replied at once, in a voice which was not at all forward but just serenely composed: "I'll do my best, sir. If I know I'll answer." Dr. Hauberger gave a brief smile and asked the question, a difficult one for a new student. The girl looked at the patient, reflected, then lifted her head. I had to admit that in this attitude of self-assured modesty she looked both charming and incredibly young; in a steady voice she gave a more or less correct answer. During all the rest of his round Dr. Hauberger seemed less severe, and several times he looked at the fair-haired girl as if the sight of her made him forget the tiring morning and his age—the struggle he had to make daily against declining years.

For once the Chief's bedside commentaries and quotations were sprinkled with a few mild jokes; he seemed all of a sudden quite human. The Rattlesnake-Sister had clearly been far from pleased when, after looking vaguely round all the women in the ward, his eye had finally rested on Marianne, who smiled in homage. Paul had whispered to me: "At last, he's thawing. Sleeping fires in this Hauberger. The girl has a nice touch, hasn't she, and she looks pleased as Punch. Members of the Academy of Medicine aren't to be hooked every day of the week."

At the time Sister Limagnac had managed to force a jaundiced smile; but Marianne had been paying for it ever since.

Just as Sister was about to pounce on her, while she was picking up the pieces of broken syringe from the tray, a nurse came to warn me that Robin was waiting for me to help him with an appendicitis. It seemed a fine opportunity and I did not want to risk missing it by being late; so I could not stay to see the end of the incident in the ward.

Already the patient was on the table, held down by nickel-plated shoulder pads. His wrists were bound and his big stomach was exposed beneath the golden beam of the spotlight. A nurse had already begun to anaesthetize him.

Robin was energetically scrubbing his hands at a basin, his hairy forearms bare up to the shoulder. I imitated him. When he judged his hands sufficiently soaped and scrubbed, he rinsed them, and then while waiting for me he exercised his fingers under the jet of hot water. He bent one finger; the others, instead of following, did not move. He bent another, unbent it, waggled it, without the rest of the hand moving; each muscle seemed to have its own intelligence and independence, and to be exactly in key with the others. Seeing me watching him, Robin said to me laughing: "I'm practising scales. Of course I can't compete with the Chief's fingering so far, but it's beginning to come now."

The theatre Sister handed him a basin with some iodized alcohol. He plunged his hands in this before slipping on the rubber gloves, and meanwhile I tried to imitate his exercises, with the concentration of a pianist stretching his fingers in the hope of loosening them up. Despite my best efforts each finger and each joint seemed glued to each other. I gave it up.

Needless to say, my first appendicitis would not be anything like the silent marvels performed by the Chief at the same table, the incredibly swift hysterectomies, where in what seemed like a few seconds the mass of the uterus would fall with a thud into the tray; nothing like the delicate sutures of arteries, the grafting of nerves, the fastidious joinery of bone surgery.

In the enthusiasm of the first appendectomy at which I had assisted, I had made a vow I would become a surgeon. While waiting for the time when I should be a virtuoso, performing complicated operations, I had practised making ligature knots with string, sewing my name on a postage stamp, cropping a toothbrush with a single stroke of the scissors; and on several occasions I had been naïve enough to attempt the tour de force attributed by legend to Dr. Hauberger. It was said that he could pass a needle cleanly through the thinnest cigarette paper—as if therein were the true secret of surgery. Naturally, I never succeeded in doing this.

I stopped all these exercises from the day when the Chief told us: "Almost anyone can make, say, intestinal sutures successfully. What makes a true surgeon is self-control, calmness, readiness of decision, the intimate union at every moment and in all circumstances of what the English call the three H's, heart, head and hand."

If this were true, I would not choose surgery. I did not feel, alas, that I possessed the requisite amount of calm and skill, energy and powers of observation; nor the immense stamina which keeps a surgeon going all through his life, rescuing thousands of patients from the innumerable hostile forces that threaten them. Yet I continued practising a little in my room with bits of string, so that Robin might not have too much to complain of when he asked me every now and then to help him with an op.

Gowned and gloved myself, I watched the house surgeon take out of a sterile jar the few instruments he was going to need, and place them on a side table near the operating table. This alone would have been enough to remind me what a very minor operation we were performing. Whereas when the Chief was operating, the theatre Sister seemed to be bringing out the best silver for a gala dinner, Robin looked as if he were merely laying the table for us for a very ordinary everyday lunch.

The Sister slid the scalpel out of its sterile tube onto the table. Robin took it, seemed to rub it gently against the stomach, and the skin, all brown from the iodine, opened up in two pinkish lips. Beads of blood formed, and immediately, as if a disastrous hemorrhage might occur, I applied a swab over the place, feeling as happy at that moment as if instead of the minor opening of an appendectomy I was about to see the huge hole, edged with yellow grease, from some big abdominal incision, with a sticky mass of entrails lurking below like a cluster of motionless serpents.

Ten minutes later, my operation was over. I pulled the gloves from my moist fingers. The Sister undid my gown at the back, and released me, soaked with sweat, from this aseptic shell. I felt that in taking away my surgeon's gown, she had taken all my pleasure as well.

Chapter 5

IN COMING to the Charité Hospital I had been even luckier than
I guessed, for during November Jean Debel, whom I had met
during my St. Luke's classes, took up an appointment as interne
there. He seemed pleased to find me at the same hospital, and
talked to Georges Robin about me; after which I became quite
a frequent visitor to the internes' common room. Robin made
a habit of needing me to give anaesthetics for minor operations
just before lunch time. I did not object. The op. over, I would
accept an invitation to have lunch with him. I said very little on
these occasions, finding it a signal privilege to be there in the first
place. Just to watch and listen, besides getting a hearty meal,
was an agreeable experience in itself for a second-year student.

Impressions from my first lunch there were confirmed, and
Debel's presence was, of course, a distinctly reassuring factor.
I enjoyed particularly his frequent arguments with Jacques Ba-
bar, a burly fellow whose belching powers had so struck me at
Carleret's. They rarely agreed with each other, but the friendly
tolerance between them was one more warning to me to avoid
forming hasty judgments about people. I counted it a virtue
in Babar that he clearly liked "old Donna," as he called Debel
(Debel-ladonna, belladonna, donna for short, was apparently the
derivation of this absurd nickname), and I could also see that
Debel respected Babar, though why he did so was less obvious.
For Babar's personality took some getting used to.

He had a genius for creating, wherever he happened to find

256

himself, the maximum amount of disorder and noise in the minimum of time. His brushes with the administration of various hospitals were notorious, and many a hospital steward, whose flat was under the internes' common room, had lost not only the tranquillity of his working days but his nights' legitimate repose as well. Should he be unwise enough to protest, Babar would organize reprisals, such as a shooting contest in the corridor or a game of skittles with iron balls bowled at enormous logs. He had also invented a system whereby one or two internes could create the conditions of a minor earthquake. He would balance all the chairs in the common room down the sides of the long table. In the middle of the night the interne on call, with a colleague perhaps as accessory, could walk along the table, using his arms and legs simultaneously, and sweep all the chairs onto the floor in the course of a few seconds. The only steward, in fact, with whom Babar had reached an understanding was the one here at Charité Hospital, who was rather deaf. The morning after the most terrific uproars had taken place, he would say thoughtfully to his secretary: "The internes must have been making a fair amount of noise last night. I could *see* the chandelier and pictures shaking opposite my bed."

I remember one lunch when Babar seemed to be pulling out all the stops of vulgarity and macabre humor. "I don't care for this pie," he said, "it tastes like a stiff's big toe . . . The stew's horrible, still-born calf makes rather depressing eating. Pass me the sardines with a little corpse grease. The nuts are like the brains of a foetus. . . ."—and so on, punctuated by more than his usual number of belches. He told us about his last night duty at a maternity hospital, and the woman from Marseilles who had cried in between her labor pains: "Funny little kid. Anyhow the pain he's giving me tonight can't be nearly as bad as the pleasure his father gave me nine months ago." Babar then gave us a scintillating if licentious sketch, showing the similarities in the postures, gasps and groans, of a woman giving birth and a woman making love. Comparing thus the complementary figures of Venus and Lucina, the most blatant indecencies flowed from his mouth like honey. After this he chose the lewdest of all the hospital songs, yelling it at the top of his voice and making us all join in the chorus.

In the course of the lunch I began to grasp the point of this special exuberance, from ironical glances made towards a certain Richard Saint-Aubin and the guest he had brought to lunch, who looked very much a society girl. On arriving in the common room, she had patronizingly looked over the long table with its rough tablecloth and canteenlike crockery and cutlery. Zaza was there that day, a good-natured little blonde, neither very pretty nor well-dressed, but always ready to oblige by sleeping with anyone who might suddenly feel the urge for it. Accidentally enough, Zaza was sitting next to Saint-Aubin's guest, who looked at her neighbor as if Zaza might give her V.D. merely by passing the dishes. The lady then inspected her surroundings, the historic vaulted ceiling, the famous old frescoes and also the more modern artistic additions. Notable among these was a banner, souvenir of a recent Internes' Hop, where the subject chosen for the hospital tableau had been *Lady Chatterley's Lover*. Naturally the banner showed the gamekeeper erecting a monstrous penis, which her amorous Ladyship was festooning with flowers. Jeannine, as we heard Saint-Aubin calling his guest, had at first assumed a very understanding and broad-minded expression, and appeared to find Babar's first remarks rather amusing. But as the level of his conversation deliberately sank lower and lower, Jeannine's face became progressively primmer, until in the end she could hardly conceal her disgust. When coffee was served, Saint-Aubin made a sign to her, and both discreetly disappeared. Babar at once let out a whoop of joy.

"I think that's fixed her. She won't be coming back here in a hurry, I reckon."

"Well, I think you went a little too far today," said Debel. "Poor old Saint-Aubin looked pretty fed up when he went out, and even admitting his guest was such a prude, I think any layman would have been a bit shocked by your frankness, shall we call it? You take certain words and facts for granted because you're used to them, they seem quite natural. But you can't expect a girl like that to enjoy listening to such language."

"My dear old Donna," said Babar, "first of all, Saint-Aubin didn't introduce her to us as his fiancée or his sister, so why the taboos? And secondly, what do you call *such language?*"

"Well, you can guess, more or less. Any excessive or unnecessary exposure, whether moral or physical."

"All right then, what I said wasn't indecent, it was essentially and absolutely necessary. If Saint-Aubin wants to stage a circus to amuse his girl friends, I refuse to be one of the freaks. That girl is the sort who puts down in her diary 'Lunch at Internes' Common Room' between 'Perverts Party' and 'Visit to Opium Den.' Afterwards she hopes to boast about it to her girl friends. They imagine this room must be a sink of ghoulish iniquity, and they're disappointed when they find we don't drink out of skulls and are not served at table by naked women. Perhaps the girl was expecting that by the dessert stage we'd all be having a go at Zaza in turn. She looked very disgusted when she discovered old Lady Chatterley's banner over there, but you may be quite sure she read the book a long time ago. That kind of scandal-mongering little bitch can't get over the fact that instead of our being monsters of depravity, we're really quite ordinary fellows, who want to keep our spirits up, our brains and tools in good working order, and who don't mind saying four-letter words in front of the ladies—like some D. H. Lawrence character whose name I can't remember. Anyhow, I thought we needed to provide Mlle. Jeannine with a breath of the scandal she was really hoping for."

"Fair enough," answered Debel, "but don't forget that most people have more shame about words than deeds. In fact, that's just what gets doctors a bad reputation: they talk a good deal more than they actually do or even think. Most people are exactly the other way round, so they get quite worked up at others merely saying what they wouldn't at all mind doing. In hospital life people say a whole lot more indecent things than they think . . ."

"I suppose you're right, Donna," Babar broke in. "It's mostly words really. If it weren't, we'd soon get very tired of all that's said around here."

Just then a porter opened the door slightly and put his head round to say: "Emergency case. Interne on duty please."

Babar waxed indignant: "That's a good beginning. We don't even have time for lunch now. Last time I was on call, I was wakened up all night for sheer trivialities. Including a chap who woke me at four o'clock in the morning because he hadn't had his bowels opened for three days. From his attitude you'd think he hadn't been to the lavatory since the end of the war. Four o'clock in the morning, and for three days' constipation—well, I ask you! I tried to suggest it was a bit steep, but he didn't take it at all well. He told me he paid the taxes which paid my salary, and he had the right to receive treatment when he felt he needed it, just like everybody else. I wondered for a moment whether I should restore the tax-payer's rights by crowning him or kicking him in the backside. Then I decided it would cause a lot of unnecessary trouble, so on reflection I just went on, in case there should really be something wrong there after all. Afterwards I offered him a finger stall, and asked him whether for a monthly salary of five hundred francs he would get up at four o'clock every morning. I think that laddie may have seen the point. But if it's another bastard of the same breed, disturbing me for an unsuccessful fart, he'll get my foot somewhere, instead of my finger, to teach him to ruin my digestion," he told us. "Anyhow, he can wait till I've produced those three little belches in B sharp."

After the hubbub of dinner, most of the dialogue between Debel and Babar had been heard in replete silence by the rest of the table. But now an orderly was beginning to clear the table, strewn with plates and pieces of bread and cigarette ends and ash. After coffee a few had risen and gone into the next room, which served as library and changing-room, where they read papers and magazines. Most, however, remained at the common room table. The smoke from their cigarettes floated upward in a mellow gray haze.

When Babar had finished his imprecations against the abusive constipee, everyone began to talk at once:

"Hey, Robert! What happened to the old man I sent over to you the other day. Did you get a diagnosis?"

"No. He died, and there wasn't a P.M."

"Good God, that's tough. Fancy letting the poor old chap die without a P.M."

"I was at Pitié Hospital yesterday evening for Trollot's farewell dinner. He's getting married to the daughter of a big liquor distiller in Caen. He's planning to set up his practice in his father-in-law's house."

"He should do very well in a few years' time. Trollot the wine merchant, on one side of the door, and on the other, Doctor Trollot, for diseases of the liver and digestive system."

"Doting pa-in-law and antidoting son-in-law, what!"

"I read yesterday in the *Paris Echo* that Juillard was called into consultation for the Maharanee of Mysore's baby. That'll be a nice bit of publicity for him, won't it?"

"He's much too clever not to announce some complications—so he can save the situation miraculously at the eleventh hour by his obstetrical genius."

"He's got his eye on a professorship, I suppose?"

"I say, Miral, what are your mortality figures for urology?"

"About five per cent."

"Dear, dear. We don't do much better either, but that's not the Chief's fault."

"Your Chief is very religious, isn't he? Is it true he goes to Mass every morning and confesses every Sunday? I wonder what he finds to confess. He works all the time, he doesn't drink, he never goes on a spree, he doesn't deceive his wife."

"Far more serious, I'm afraid. He operates. When he thinks of it, he must lie awake all night suffering pangs of remorse."

"Have you already introduced yourself to your new Chief, Pierre?"

"Yes, I have. I asked the maid: 'Is Dr. Tannery there?' She replied that Dr. Tannery, Fellow of that, Member of the other, would be back shortly. Either one has distinctions or one hasn't, she implied. I suppose she took me for a customer. Meanwhile

Tannery arrived, and we had quite a long chat. I was most favorably impressed."

"I gather he lets his house surgeons do a good deal of operating."

"Mine wants to do everything himself. Luckily you can always learn something by watching a consultant operate. You get a bit of self-confidence by seeing the way not to do it."

"Tannery's really a grand chap, though. He even asks your advice when he's operating."

"Ah, these Chiefs! If one only had the courage to train them in the way they should go."

"You're right. This morning I saw mine bungling a ureterotomy. Still, one has to be fair. Since I've been with him, I find he's making some progress. Anyhow he's trying hard."

I should have liked to see the faces of the distinguished consultants thus pilloried, had a microphone been installed near them to record their interne's remarks. Presumably, though, it would have served to remind them of their own younger days, when they had criticized and observed their superiors no less ruthlessly. Ah well, I thought, it certainly keeps them up to the mark, having such stern witnesses, quite given to exaggeration, ready to pick on the slightest errors of diagnosis or technique. And in the end the patient gains, for it gives these doctors and surgeons very little chance of cheating or dodging difficulties or letting things slide; they know they're being continually watched. In spite of what might be thought, I said to myself, there's nowhere you'll get as keen a respect for human life as in hospital.

I looked at Babar. He had not taken part in these judgments, and had apparently been engaged in filling his pipe with extreme care and fastidiousness. Then he lit it, and lolled back in his armchair, looking as if there were easily time to smoke the whole pipe in the same relaxed posture. I remembered with a smile how I had trembled with indignation during my first few lunches in the common room, when there had been a call for the interne on duty, and I had seen him calmly carrying on with his meal, or his conversation, as if the completion of either of these were the first priority. Meanwhile I would envisage a disastrous, car accident with someone bleeding to death, or a woman being delivered of a baby without any help on the rack of an ambulance. I was soon reassured however, on observing that the interne being called out always put on the same act; it was practically a ritual. When the porter had withdrawn his head from the door, the interne would swear loudly: "Goddammit, never a moment's peace, and always for some damned stupid thing. If that's going to start now, my eyes will have to be prised open tomorrow morning." After a few minutes, when nobody much was looking, he would quickly swallow a mouthful and finish his glass. Then he would casually throw his blue cloak over his shoulders, speak to a few friends, and bang the door behind him. From my position by the window I could follow him with my eyes as he crossed the court. He walked fast and the expression on his face was different, concerned. Already he was thinking about his patient, and he would almost run.

The same thing happened now, and I decided that to see the true face of these internes, without their artificial mask of cynicism and insensitiveness, you would have to go round the dark hospital with them every night. You would then find the same seriousness of purpose which I now saw on Babar's face as he strode rapidly across the court.

When he had gone, they went on talking about some of the medical stars, including a certain Dr. Etiévant, of whom I had some knowledge. Last year, after my surgical term at Saint-Louis, I had done a term on his ward at Beaujon Hospital. At first he dazzled me. He had a splendid figure, a very elegant short beard, and gray hair with a steely glint. (According to rumor he had it dyed.) He would arrive late at the hospital, pass rapidly through the wards with an Olympian air, tap the stomach or back of two or three patients, say a few words to the students, and then disappear, leaving us to his assistants.

Although his arrival was usually late, it was certainly full of solemnity. When we heard the bell at the gate rung sharply three times, and then another three times, we would rush to the windows. It was obvious by the respectful way he took off his cap that the porter was much impressed by the appearance of the famous Dr. Etiévant, member of the Academy of Medicine, and his splendid limousine. The chauffeur would dash forward to open the door of the car, and the great specialist, as I then thought him, would descend majestically, having just returned from signing the bulletin on some Napoleon of finance or politics. Most of these distinguished invalids would hardly have dared die or recover without Etiévant being present to assist them in whichever it was.

At the same period, when I arrived at the hospital each morning I would see Dr. Mazel, resident in the next wing, modestly getting off a bus. He would bid the porter good morning as he went in the gate and walk off through the court with a self-effacing air. For him the porter would merely bring his hand casually to his cap. I too regarded with slight disdain this very ordinary doctor, who arrived by public transportation, with no pretense at prestige.

I had to wait nearly a year, and lunch often in the internes' common room of Charité, before I discovered that the imposing Dr. Etiévant was a charlatan, while the modest Dr. Mazel was a great neurologist. An interne had just told the company how two days earlier there had been an attempt to get Mazel put up for the Academy of Medicine, and he had answered his well-wishers gently: "No, I don't think you'd better. There are few people who say to themselves, why isn't he a member?—but there'd be far more who'd wonder why I *was* one." Abruptly a picture came into my mind of the shy, slightly bent figure whom I had despised for a whole term, and I felt a sudden burst of affection towards him.

The internes' discussion continued, turning to a more philosophical level, in which Debel was naturally a protagonist. But eventually he looked at his watch and announced that he was going back to his ward, having still two lumbar punctures to do. This seemed to be the signal for most of the others to leave, and after I had skimmed through a few magazines they had left lying about, I went out myself. I left the hospital with a curious reluctance. Somehow I should have liked to stay there till the evening, to prolong the interest of the morning, and perhaps even more, the pleasure of that lunch and the discussions afterwards. It is true that I had been merely a tolerated spectator, but even if I did not say a word I felt that invisible bonds were being forged between the internes and myself, giving me on each occasion a little more right to sit at their table. Their work was harder and more responsible than mine, but we were members of the same profession, and whether our present obligations were greater or smaller this made us all in a very real sense "one body."

Near the gate, just as I was going out, I passed Babar, huddled under his cloak. Between the white cap and the turned-up collar, his massive face showed its usual exuberance. He was making his way to Reception for a new call, and gave me a grin of satisfaction as he passed: "Well worth being disturbed that time. A perforated ulcer, and the chap was nearly pegging out. Gave me a fine chance for an emergency diagnosis. Some days one has all the luck. If only it holds right through my duty period."

The same callous Babar, who had spoken of this patient with such complete indifference, would readily have spent day and night by the man's bedside had it been necessary. Even then he would probably have pretended to be activated by mere technical curiosity and the impulse to win an impersonal battle with one particular disease. At all costs, it seemed, unselfish care and devotion must be disguised; it was part of an almost unconscious code observed by the Babars of this world. I watched him disappear into Reception, humming cheerfully.

Visiting hours were just over, and the relatives were pouring out into the court, going under the porch, and then scattering in the rue Jacob, among flower sellers and peddlers.

I stopped on the pavement to look at the scene. The departing crowd jostled me to and fro just like the touts and the beggars.

265

Without my white coat, how could all these people know that in the ranks of the doctors I was no mere private but already a junior officer?

I was just going off towards the school when I saw under the porch a patient from my ward. His wife was walking by his side, carrying his case. One leg had been amputated, and he walked diffidently and clumsily with his crutches, as if the brain in sending its messages to his limbs still remembered another way of walking. But he looked happy, he was smiling at the passers-by, at the gray sky, the noisy street, the life of freedom ahead of him. I watched him coming, and the crowd scattering to let him pass. When he was near me, he recognized me, and gave me a friendly salute. "Goodbye, Doctor," he said.

Doctor—in front of all these people. What a thrill! I did not even need a white coat here, "my" patients recognized me, and some of them did not differentiate between a second-year student and the genuine article, which I should surely be in three or four years' time. How wonderful to sit at the internes' table by right, to share their responsibilities and achievements—and pleasures. This patient had anticipated matters slightly, but after all it was a difference of degree, not of kind; and as I walked away from the hospital, I wished I could shout out to these poor ordinary mortals what a wonderful profession mine was. This was indeed the good life, to be a doctor, to be nearly, to be practically a doctor. The words formed part of a refrain, a hymn of happiness I hummed to myself as I boarded, almost unseeing, the next bus.

Chapter 6

ABOUT THIS TIME I abandoned Prichard to homeopathy and his evil genius, Little Arthur, for which I fear he never forgave me —and turned, full of curiosity, to the more athletic and esoteric François Surel.

His room was picturesque and at first glance disconcerting. He must surely have had a highly visual memory, for he had covered the walls with enormous anatomical diagrams, some of them drawn and some cut out of multi-colored cardboard. You could see there pictures of typology and gymnastic exercises. An articulated figure in zinc hung in a corner; a wall was decorated with skis and ski-sticks, small wall bars and a collection of light dumb-bells. Along the opposite wall on a bench was a series of chamberpots, each covered with a piece of glass, under which tiny drops of moisture were condensing—but you could still see a skull inside each, pickled in some preserving liquid. To lodge his books, François had built an additional bookcase in which the battle-green backs of classical medical treatises joined the serried ranks of books, notebooks, pamphlets, and files in all shapes and colors.

The books were of all kinds: old volumes of phrenology and chiromancy and astrology sat next to Le Corbusier's studies for the city of the future. You could find there an initiation into Hindu, Chinese, and Egyptian philosophy, study the Greek cosmogony, join up with medical thought by way of the homeopaths or read the latest work of American geneticists. From the underlining of important passages in red pencil, and the marginal notes in François' firm writing, you could tell that all these books had been attentively read by their possessor.

Faithful to his warm skiing clothes, he worked with his windows wide open. A placard fixed to a wall announced his timetable: *Morning, Hospital; Afternoon, Sport; Evening, General Reading.* A neighboring placard asserted: *Dum spiro, spero;* and another: *A human being is made up of nourishment, air, movement, and ideas.* A fourth text revealed that François placed medicine at the crossroads of Art and Science, Reason and Emotion.

The notices, the books, and the room in general, revealed clearly all aspects of the man: on the physical, moral and intellectual planes he was out of the ordinary. I attached myself to him. As soon as I was out of school, instead of going to the library, I would return to the Cité straight away. I could be sure of finding François in the central building, in the gymnasium, either training alone or coaching friends.

He had taken in hand some rather puny specimens, boys with drooping shoulders, narrow chests, and curved backs. Without thought for his own time or energy, he would try every day to straighten them up, to dilate their chests, to fill their lungs with air. He had almost failed one of his exams because he spent two months in the Pyrenees, in response to the appeal of some parish priests he had met in those high valleys. During this period he was trying to extend the use of skis among their backward and isolated populations. I had been told of this by Prichard, who had sneered at it as a silly thing to do; but even then I had liked this Surel for what seemed a very generous sacrifice of two months' valuable time with no personal advantage.

In his shorts, doing his exercises, François certainly looked a remarkable athlete. His skin was so bronzed that it never looked really bare. He had magnificently broad shoulders, and a lithe build which made each muscle seem to move for its own special pleasure. Outstanding physical beauty is a rare enough phenomenon in a man, but François was one of those who possessed it. This discouraged me at once.

"You must read the life of Kneipp," he told me. "Then you'll see how a sick man can become strong and fit. Look, Jean, just remember that a Hercules or Apollo who is born strong and handsome never has the strength of will of a man who makes himself strong."

I suppose I looked doubtful, so he told me his own life story, which certainly illustrated the point well.

"I was very delicate," he began, "never without a cold, which kept me cooped up in the house all winter. Every month I was taken to the doctor, a nice chap, whom I liked because he was gentle, but who had never realized the possibilities of physical education. He saved me from broncho-pneumonia, scarlet fever, and a good many other things. He was very worried about me, and came several times a day to see me, sometimes quite late in the evening coming home from his rounds. He was a good, faithful doctor, and that's the sort of thing you don't forget. But he had a great many patients, and plenty of serious cases to worry about. He soon found that all he could do about me was prescribe codliver oil for me or glycerophosphates, and send me away for some good country air. Unfortunately my nose was blocked and my lungs didn't open properly, so the good country air never got inside."

"And then?" I said.

"And then," said François, "when I was about fourteen, I became obsessed, seeing other, stronger boys, by the idea of becoming strong. I went to gymnasiums, I bought a bicycle, large dumb-bells, chest-expanders. In three years I nearly killed myself, and with what result? I was more bent and crooked and stiff in the joints than ever. My chest was still narrow, though I had gained large pectoral muscles which concealed it. When I breathed, I got so little air into my lungs that I could hardly run a few yards. That's when I was lucky: I met a doctor who was at once an athlete, a physio-therapist, and a man with a mission. He agreed to take me on as a pupil, and offered to unblock my chest in a year and finish my physical rehabilitation in five years. He kept his word. I admired him so much I decided to be a doctor too. He died two years ago of a stupid accident, mountain climbing. I continue what he taught me. What he did for me, Jean, I can do for you."

I accepted with enthusiasm, and he started the task of making me strong by making me more supple and teaching me to breathe properly. While still doing his own exercises, he never stopped watching me, with periodical exhortations to arch my back, or to think of my lungs filling up and then descending: "Relax, correct position, now breathe in slowly." I began to feel the deep satisfaction he had promised me, cutting through the inferiority complex I had always had about my weak body. My lungs were really filling with air, my chest was expanding, for the first time I was making the most of the physical machine I had been given.

Often François would replace our session in the gymnasium with a walk in the park. He would go off in shorts and sweater and heavy mountain shoes; and as I followed him, I felt all my joints loosening up, my muscles swelling with life and blood and power, ready to obey my will. After the hospital smells of the morning my lungs were almost drunk with the fresh air; and in that walk, all mixed up with children's shouts, the smell of wet leaves and fog, my brain cleared too, became free, swelling with energy and contentment.

About five o'clock we would find Carleret's gang having a snack in the restaurant. Then I would go back with François to work in his room. The hour for general reading had arrived, and with his brain revived he would fling himself voraciously at his books. Every quarter of an hour he would stop to do two or three of his breathing exercises, and every half hour he would get up and practise a little on the wall bars. Immediately afterwards he would return to his table and resume his studies with renewed concentration. This method must have been reasonably efficacious, since it had allowed him, while devoting all his afternoons to sport, to pass his university exams without too much trouble, besides enriching his mind with all sorts of knowledge foreign to the official lecture halls.

I hoped the same system would work with me, but I did not have the chance to continue for long under his guidance. In

December he left to replace a doctor in some mountain village lost among the snows. During the two days before he left, he was already in the clouds, and talked continually, with even more than his usual enthusiasm, of the educational value of skiing: pleasure and endurance, struggle and harmony of the whole body. On skis man rose to his full stature, to sing the song of muscle and youth and the joyful heart, he said. He did not even need to change his clothes, he could leave at once with his skis on his shoulder, ready to take him his thirty miles a day from hamlet to hamlet across the snowclad mountains.

I felt crippled without him, finding myself abruptly alone again among the city crowds, squelching in the winter mud, trudging their stupid stagnant vegetative way, instead of really living, like François Surel. How I wished I could have followed him.

Chapter 7

LUCIEN CLÉMENT, certainly, was no intellectual, and I remembered having put him down at first as a mere country bumpkin. I had soon altered this picture of him, but even now I often wondered what kept him in the ebullient atmosphere of Carleret's room, so alien, presumably, to his own tastes and background. Perhaps he felt that his own store of country common sense was somehow inadequate, or needed refinement; that he must at all costs pollinate himself with a few drops of city cleverness. He would listen to Gédéon and Bouchet, for instance, arguing or debating in a flood of words which would probably never make any practical difference to anything; I would see him straining forward with wrinkled brow trying to grasp something which would at least give him his bearings. But in the end the swirl of excited phrases would send him to sleep in the armchair; a sleep very like the man, suggesting a serene repose, powerful and organic.

Prichard and François having been eliminated as working companions, I thought of Lucien. One evening I went to borrow a book from him. The keynotes of his room were simplicity and order. In the bookcase nothing but medical books, on the bare walls not a picture or photograph which could distract the attention or cause the eye to stray. I felt sure that if Lucien would let me work with him I could add considerably to my resources of courage and will-power. He was agreeable, and I felt at once I had acquired something of a guardian angel. At an agreed time, punctual to the minute, he would tap me on the shoulder saying: "It's time, Jean, come on, let's work."

We would leave Carleret's room, full as usual of uproar and smoke. While I was settling down to my books and notes, Lucien would hang on the knob outside his door a piece of cardboard on which he had written: *Danger: Men at Work.* Then he would shut the door firmly behind him, confident of being left in reasonable peace.

One afternoon he was sitting at his work-table like a day laborer planted squarely in front of a huge pile of earth, when the voice of a small child was heard outside: "M. Clément! M. Clément!"

Lucien opened the window, but the wind was driving down heavy gray storm-clouds, and I could only catch a few mangled bits of the conversation:

"Daddy . . . can't breathe . . . please come. . . ."

Lucien shouted: "I'll be with you."

He returned to his table, filled his pipe carefully, lit it, took a solid-looking windbreaker off his coatrack, picked up an old leather bag in a corner of the room, and then said to me: "Like to come?"

Reaching the palings, he leaped over them without letting go his bag, and landed neatly the other side. I followed him with less ease, and dropped in a mass of slippery mud left there by the last shower. Lucien, with his heavy shoes, was already walking steadily down the footpath which wound in and out between the huts. I tried to follow him, but the mud soon became so soft that I was afraid of leaving behind in it the ordinary walking-shoes I had rashly come out in. Then the path became a long filthy sewer with only a few stones emerging here and there; and I was so busy jumping from one stone to the next that I had little time to observe the maze into which Lucien was leading me.

Finally he had pity and waited for me. He even allowed me a minute's pause to light a cigarette, and to take in at close quarters the desolate spectacle I had often seen from the window of my room. Till now indeed I had felt I was quite familiar with the

273

shanties made of rotting wood and the small gardens containing a few stunted drooping trees, surrounded by scrawny hedges and barricaded with scrap-iron. But the utter neglect and forlornness of the corner where we paused was something new in my experience. When we moved on, I found the silence of the whole region almost unbearably oppressive. Even the children, raggedly clothed, seemed to roam about and play without making any noise. Seeing us from afar, they ran to hide between great stacks of rubble; they did not poke their dirty faces out of their holes till they recognized Lucien. Then they became bolder and followed us for a while, still silently.

Eventually we reached the spot where the patient lived. It was a hut constructed from old crates and drums and squares of plaster and tarpaulin. The smell was frightful. A wholesale rag-and-bone man, Lucien explained, burned his old bones there, and certainly the stocks of these bones reeked of the charnel house.

When we came into the hut, the interior was so dark I was afraid of stumbling. As I carefully tested the ground, slimy rags, placed there to soak up the water, floated under the soles of my shoes. I nearly bolted because of the mere smell which was even more frightful than it had been outside. I felt it to be oozing from every single part of the hut—the ground, the walls, the furniture, and the occupants, whom I was now beginning to distinguish in the half-light. It really seemed to be dripping from the blackened ceiling, like water from a gutter. It was a nauseating compound of exhalations: the patient's sweat, the urine of the two half-naked little children kicking about near him on a worn-out old mattress, the oily reek of the old woman who was busying herself with our reception, the dirty clothes stacked in a corner, and the rancid fat in the frying-pan on the iron stove. Behind the rotting walls I could easily imagine great pot-bellied rats running about, and the silent swarming of bugs and cockroaches.

Lucien was already bending over the patient and questioning him; I understood now why he had brought his pipe and was

274

drawing on it regularly. Together on a corner of the mattress, the two little children watched him, fingers in their noses. Lucien was squatting near the mattress to auscultate the man. When he had finished, he told me to listen. I bent over. Just on the level of my eyes I saw the faces of the two children. One had a thin face with a blue-green complexion, and an almost rectangular skull between two protruding ears. With one of his eyes he watched me fixedly, while the other seemed to sheer away, producing a ghastly squint. His brother, equally thin and pale, stared at me too, with a resigned acceptance of suffering quite grotesque in such a child.

I stuck my ear against the man's back. The stench of the bedclothes and the smell of the fevered body nearly choked me; the skin was covered with the bites of vermin. I rose very quickly. "Pneumonia," said Lucien. "You heard it?" I had heard very little, but said yes at once; the last thing I wanted was to bend down over that bed again. From his bag Lucien brought out a sort of instrument-case, took out a syringe and chose an ampule; then he unscrewed a smaller case containing a needle soaking in alcohol. He made the injection with slow gestures, the precision and gentleness of which contrasted with the strength of his wrists. Then he folded up his equipment, gave some instructions to the woman, said a word to the man, patted the children on the cheek, and went off, promising to come back next day.

Once outside I tried to remember the most vigorous breathing exercises François had taught me, and used them now to clear my lungs. Lucien saw me looking rather pale, and said with a smile: "You couldn't take it, eh? You're not used to it yet."

I thought I had met in the hospital all conceivable horrors; I was beginning to realize that there were many sterner tests to face; that the depressing and unpleasant things I saw on the wards daily, where well-washed patients in white beds had their dressings changed regularly under hygienic conditions, were quite a different story from the intense misery to be seen here, so stark and unredeemed. It was a warning of what I should meet in my future career. From this man and his illness you could

275

divine the whole tragic picture and the various elements which made up its essential pattern: the wife and children, bad heredity, unemployment, poverty, and the slum itself.

Lucien went on talking: "I quite saw you weren't anxious to stay there too long, otherwise I'd have got you to palpate his liver. He has a remarkable alcoholic cirrhosis; you very rarely see such specimens at hospital—but here there's one in every hut. Pneumonia and alcoholism—I don't know if I'll be able to bring him out of that. And you saw what the children looked like. It's the hereditary effects of alcohol too, of course."

We walked on amidst a mushroom-bed of tumbledown old shanties. A little further on Lucien stopped me, saying: "I've a woman patient to see there."

The interior of this hut was as sordid as the one before. The woman had already had four children, and looked more or less tired out by the effort of producing them. The dull misery of her expression made her seem almost ageless, but I guessed she might be about thirty. Lucien was looking after her, he told me, in her fifth pregnancy. He examined and questioned her, and in spite of her weary faded face, I thought I saw in the expectant mother's lustreless eyes a kind of melancholy tenderness. Although near her time, she still went out ragpicking every night. Even in her weariness she found a smile to tell Lucien: "Oh, he never keeps quiet, Dr. Clément, and he's always such a weight."

I noticed she said "He"—a boy. And she moved slowly and carefully about the narrow shanty with her huge stomach, like any ordinary mother taking such precautions. Even this homely, wornout woman had a dim sense of the prodigious miracle she carried within her, the tiny bag of tissue born of a cell, the gelatinous little fishlike bundle which would later become a man. In this dark hovel, even she perhaps was building new dreams for her new baby.

Lucien wanted her to have more nourishment for her child, and on leaving, he took some iron and calcium and vitamin tablets out of his bag, and left them beside a bottle of white wine on a rickety table propped against a wall.

We went next into an old railroad car without wheels. In one

276

corner of it an old man was stretched out on a pallet. He had nothing near him but a stout stick, an old tin which must be serving him as a basin, and an old enamel jug. On the floor, in a semicircle all round the pallet, were rat-traps, and in one a huge black rat was lying on its back with paws contracted. When I was near the man, he seemed quite literally to be half-dead, or "only half-alive" might perhaps be a better description. For half of him was still moving, one of his eyes shone, one corner of his mouth spoke, one of his hands obeyed his brain; all the rest was inert.

Without delay Lucien had opened his bag, from which he drew forceps, alcohol, swabs and cotton wool. Then he asked me to help him turn the patient on one side and hold him there while he cleaned up and put on a new dressing. He then removed a bandage and uncovered a dressing stained with pus. Underneath the man's back was only a vast scabby sore. I thought I was going to be sick. Without giving me a minute's grace Lucien, still puffing on his pipe, put on a clean white dressing. Only then did he free me. After this he took the huge body of the dead rat out of the trap, kicked it out of the car, and reset the trap with a piece of cheese-rind he took from his pocket. Having checked the other traps, he looked at the basin, felt the jug of water and asked the old man: "Your daughter-in-law still brings you potatoes? You have enough oil?"

The man mumbled something which seemed to signify "Yes." Lucien went on: "You still don't want to go to the hospital?" The old man, in a passionate effort of will-power, distinctly pronounced the word "No."

We left. After a few yards Lucien remarked: "He's an obstinate old fellow. He can still use his arm and his club a little, but however many traps I put round him I'm afraid the rats will get him one night."

Did Lucien realize what his forecast actually meant? He spoke with such utter placidity, as if he had not visualized the monstrous red-eyed rats devouring the paralyzed old man alive.

"But why does he stay there?" I asked.

"Oh, it's all tied up with his daughter-in-law. She would like to live in the car at once, and put him into a workhouse. This car is a palace here. The old man knows she's waiting for his home, and he hates her with the special cold hatred old men can have for their relatives. So he clings to his car and literally, she'll take it only over his dead body. She does everything she can, I assure you, to hasten that day. For six months all she's brought him is a few boiled potatoes, which I supplement with some codliver oil. As you saw, I just about manage to keep him alive. I suppose his daughter-in-law puts her hopes now on the rats. I'm always afraid that before she leaves some evening, she'll unset the traps."

I thought at one stage that Lucien was trying to test me by picking out all his worst cases; but as we left the paralyzed old man's carriage, he showed me a newly painted caravan with curtains adorning its tiny windows. It was sheltered from the floods, resting on solid little beer-barrels; and the mere fact of putting it on wheels seemed to have enabled it to leave this "slough of despond" and return to a happier state. Washing was hanging on a line in the little garden enclosed with well-clipped hedges. Near the gate a homemade letter box said in huge clumsy letters: "Jacques Jouillat, Mason."

"No one here at this time of day," said Lucien. "Father's at the building site, mother's doing the shopping, and the kids are at school. Pity! You'd have seen that my practice does include a few folk who wash, have a white lace quilt on their beds, and framed photographs of their wedding on the walls. They're the sort charitable ladies like to visit when they go slumming."

Yet the Jouillats were slum-dwellers too.

Lucien's patients were prolific. He stopped in front of a hut where he had delivered a baby the day before. A virago with a bloated face, and a mouth full of black stumps, welcomed us with exclamations of gratitude, which blew in our faces the smell of alcohol and tobacco. Her daughter was sleeping, turned towards the wall. The old hag woke her, and the young mother sat up on a sort of long board which presumably served the whole family as a bed during the night. She rubbed her eyes with a yawn. She looked about seventeen and was almost pretty, but her unkempt short hair, her over-painted mouth and filthy face made her look like a hardened young prostitute. Lucien began to examine her.

I looked around the hut. On a table I saw the remains of a meal: traces of egg on a plate, the dregs of some red wine in a glass, between a half empty bottle and a chipped jug full of cloudy water. The mother's breath told clearly enough that the contents of the bottle were more to her taste than those of the jug. In a dark corner of the shanty a feeble cry suddenly rose, like the quaver of a ventriloquist's doll. I saw an old baby carriage stuffed with rags; and this contained a newborn babe swathed in dirty woollen clothes. I leaned over towards it.

It had a large soft white head, and this softness made its skin wrinkle up like an old man's skin. On the skull with its big blue veins you could see the hollow of the fontanelle beating; the child continued to utter its plaintive moan with the grimace of a bad-tempered old man. From closer up, instead of the smell of powder and milk which comes from well cared for babies, you could catch the tang of ammonia. The child was crying, and these first cries of a newborn baby, so like a deathbed cry, were painful to hear. In this wretched child, seed of workhouses and prison-cells, the old drama of poor heredity was being played out once more: syphilitic or alcoholic, perhaps both. No freshness or joy came out of this sordid cradle; this dawn of a new life brought with it no hopefulness. The very first utterance of this voice was a peevish complaint, and the blue-green eyes seemed closed to light and happiness. When the thin skeleton's fingers were unclenched, they opened on a void. There was none of that wonderful sense of blossoming, received in watching a new-born babe opening its tiny hand.

The grandmother came to take the sad little bundle of flesh, and undressed it on her knees with an expression devoid of tenderness. When she had undone the urine-soaked diapers she held the baby out to Lucien, with its body smoking in the cold air as if it had been wrapped in the diapers to cook. Naked, it continued to cry and struggle feebly; it looked like a spider with its thin limbs, big head and big body. At the ends of the legs it kicked weakly with two tiny club-feet. When Lucien had examined it and put on a new umbilical dressing, instead of returning the child to the old woman he placed it on the bed near the mother, helped her to put its clothes on, and then asked her: "Now you're not going to be naughty, are you? You're going to breast-feed him?"

The girl's face at once assumed a set expression, and she answered: "No." Lucien pressed her, and the grandmother came to her daughter's aid: "She'd like to, Dr. Clément, but she's so young, it'd make her too weak. Don't worry, the little angel will get fed all right."

I saw Lucien look at the jug full of cloudy water which would be used for feeding "the little angel." Then began a patient bargaining. Lucien pressed the young mother to feed the child herself for a month or two; she did not answer. He reduced it to a fortnight, ten days, a week. She kept the same set face, while her mother watched the proceedings with feigned fondness. Gradually Lucien appeared to get into a temper, and when it was quite clear that all further insistence would be in vain, that no appeals of sentiment would soften the two women, he rose, and walked towards the grandmother. Impressed by his angry face, she recoiled a yard or two. In a slow voice, in which each word stood out by itself, he said to her:

"All right. She won't feed it herself, but that child has got to live, you understand me, *has got to live*. You will have all its food boiled. No liquor in the milk to stop it crying, and see that it's never cold. And I'll come to check on it every day!"

The grandmother remained abashed at first. She stammered: "Poor little angel, sure we'll take care of him."

Then, with a gesture which she clearly meant to be pathetic and which in any other circumstances would have been grotesque, she took the child to her bosom and burst into drunken sobs. We went out.

Outside, after we had gone a little way, Lucien said to me: "I'd have been happier about the future if the girl had agreed to breast-feed him."

"Because of the water?" I asked.

"Not so much that," he answered. "There's a summer diar-

rhoea that often kills babies in a week. At this time of year
there's less risk from that. But if she had fed her baby for a few
days at her breast, she'd never have let it die after that." Almost
immediately he added: "Though with club-feet it may still survive. A crippled child is worth its weight in gold here. The
grandmother would never let it die."

I looked at Lucien in such bewilderment that he explained:
"She'll go and beg with the child bare-footed in her arms; or if
that's too tiring, she'll hire it out. Otherwise it wouldn't have a
chance. One frosty night they'd leave the child stark naked in
its cradle, then when it had caught a fatal dose of broncho-
pneumonia, they'd come and call me. Or else an accident, the
child choked under an eiderdown, and they wouldn't even need
to call me. Quite a few disappear that way."

"And you can't do anything about it, threaten to inform the
police? They must be frightened of the police?"

"No," said Lucien, "I can't. Those are professional secrets."
Seeing my continued astonishment, he added: "Yes, it puzzled
me too at first. I asked advice from my Chief at hospital. He explained to me that they had confided in me. In no case must they
ever have any hesitation in calling me. As for the child, obviously
I could save it by informing on the mother; but then I should
automatically be condemning others to death. Wherever there
was anything shady, no one would call me after that, through
fear of being betrayed. In this particular case, I have only one
way of trying to save its life—by going to see it every day. Perhaps they won't dare. I shall try because I am acting as a doctor
and it's our duty to save life when we can. Otherwise, consider-
ing what there is in store for it, the child would doubtless be
much better dead."

Since the start of this nightmarish journey Lucien had continued to speak in his usual conversational tones. He was used to
it, of course, and I could not really think him indifferent or insensitive or lacking in imagination, especially after seeing the
way he treated his patients. But I simply could not understand
his being so casual about all this misery. I felt absolutely devastated by it. He had shown me a whole new world of disease, of

physical and moral gangrene, of crime and terror and decay. I felt I had really touched rockbottom now, surely nothing could sink below the depths I had seen in these prison-like dens. I felt I had really grasped, for the first time, the true immensity of the human problem.

I walked in silence behind Lucien. Till now, in our course from shanty to shanty, we might have been going round an abandoned village, for we had met nobody. At the corner of one alley we saw several figures, their heads and shoulders protected by sacks; the rain was just ending. The boots they had on were a bizarre construction of old car-tires, which slip-slopped towards us in the quagmire of clinging mud. The last figure turned in passing us, and brought two fingers to his cap in a greeting to Lucien. I saw a beardless face, ageless too, the squat head of a degenerate, with a profile that might have been squashed in a vise. "They're coming from old La Frite's bar near the Porte de Gentilly," said Lucien.

I began to understand their drunkenness. They really needed to drink so as to have the courage, on coming out of the bar, to take up again their abominable life, immured in this great rotting silence which I already found so everwhelming after only an hour.

Indeed I should have been glad to return to the Cité at once; but Lucien stopped in front of a gate. All the dwellings I had seen so far had been rigidly enclosed, following no doubt the primitive instinct of self-protection in men who have reverted to savages. The enclosure here was even more impenetrable. The gate was solid, and tall enough to hide the whole hut; on both sides you could see nothing at all through the hedge. I thought the man who lived here must have more precise reasons than the instincts of a wild animal for hiding from the outside world. Lucien was surely leading me into some bandit's lair.

He warned me before we went in: "You can come, but look out! If you go in you'll have to shake hands with my patient. Otherwise you'd better wait for me here."

Intrigued, I hastened to reply: "Of course I'll come with you."

He opened the gate, and we crossed a narrow yard in which, beneath a shed, there were neatly arranged piles of old soles and shoe leather. Just as Lucien was knocking, I asked him: "What's the matter with this patient?"

In a very low voice he murmured: "Leprosy."

I would have run, but already the bolt, manipulated from inside, sounded against the door. To my ears it might have been the noise of the rattle which in medieval times these contagious walking corpses, like the one now opening the door to us, had been obliged to carry always with them.

The door was pushed cautiously ajar, and then, when Lucien was visible, it opened wider. We went in. I felt a shudder go through me, and my hands were suddenly moist. Evening was falling and the small room had narrow windows admitting little light; so at first I could not distinguish much of the figure, dark in skin and clothes, who was talking to Lucien. I thought it must be a Negro. Lucien had already put down his bag on the table and was taking out of it his syringe for injections, his needle, and an ampule. I remained standing, in a thick almost palpable smell of old leather. Unconsciously I avoided breathing too hard, as if behind that my instinct had scented another smell. The man had not held out his hand to me when we came in; I congratulated myself on this good luck, and not having gloves on, dug both my fists deep into my pockets, taking good care not to touch anything. Somewhat reassured by these precautions, I took a better look at the patient.

While Lucien was getting his syringe ready, the man was trying to light an old acetylene lamp, and I watched his clumsy gestures with burning curiosity. Everything had passed off very well for me so far, and I began to feel almost pleasurably excited, as a visitor to the circus might in entering a lion's cage with the tamer close at hand. I could boast afterwards how I had seen a real live leper near enough to touch him. Even now that my calm had returned, the very word, so near the fact, had an awesome sound: in its two syllables rolled all the terror and curses since the thundering anathema of the Bible, since the terrified

283

isolation of the Middle Ages, right up to the days of modern science, still at that time apparently impotent before this terrible illness.

This man had certainly chosen his hideout well. As in the lazar-houses where in other days he would have been shut up, he was lost in this slum full of other freaks and outcasts and outlaws, who would have fled before any civilized being daring to set foot in their lairs. Probably the leper would only go out at night to search the trash heaps, and his rags alone would turn the belated passer-by away from him, better than the rattle and yellow circle of other days. As to the dark hoods they were made to wear then, the darkness of this man's skin was a substitute.

I waited eagerly to see the classic mask of the leper on this swarthy face. But when the light spurted from the lamp with a long whistling noise, I was stupefied. This man was not a Negro, but something utterly unexpected: he seemed to belong to a new sort of race—the blue-skinned. It was the blue of night, sinking in parts to the blue of twilight, for there were slabs and patches of a slightly lighter color on this travesty of a face. The face was merely a mask, deformed by lepromas and knots of flesh, by swellings which enlarged the chin, puffed up the nose, and hid the eyes. Unconsciously leaning towards him, I stared with ruthless curiosity at the typical *facies leontina* described in the textbooks.

Luckily nobody was paying attention to me. Lucien was filling his syringe with methylene blue (the drug with which the patient was also dyed), and the man pulled back his sleeve, leaving the veins just recognizable because they rose above the rest of the colored skin. He held out his arm, and my gaze fell on his hand. This bore the mark too: three fingers were missing, the thumb, the index and the little finger; the two which remained were curled back towards the palm like a claw.

I understood better now the meaning of the very thick hedge and the solid gate. For this living corpse it was the vertical slab of his tomb. The blue of the drug would give him away, where mutilated hand and strange face might have passed unnoticed;

284

and even at this meeting place of all poverty and miseries he had renewed the ancient terror, and so was forced to hide. The curse of long-dead centuries had descended to a desolate hopelessness, keeping this man here in the isolation of a savage. At last, stronger than curiosity or fear, I felt compassion gaining sway over me. At the same time I felt a new surge of admiration for Lucien, who had evidently been struggling for so many months to repair this injustice, and bring back into the community of the living this half-dead creature from whom all others fled. The injection given, Lucien began collecting his equipment, while chatting placidly with the man. Without any precautions, the ends of his fingers resting firmly on the flesh, he felt the man's face to assess the results of his treatment; and he concluded in a calm voice: "The day after tomorrow we'll finish the series of twenty-four injections; after that we'll give you a bit of a rest for a month."

I was so overcome with admiration and pity that I almost said to him: "If you like, I'll come and give the next lot of injections." Already Lucien had taken his case in one hand and was holding out the other to the patient; the man took hold of the hand quite normally and shook it. Then, with Lucien watching me, I was horrified to see him stretch his hooked hand out to me.

I felt my hand clenching itself in my pocket with repulsion; I had to take it out, and push it forward. I felt the two-fingered claw beneath my own fingers, the tendons contracting beneath the stumps of the three fingers scaled off by leprosy. My grip must have seemed to the man very flabby and furtive, but anyhow he wished me good evening as he had Lucien, and then accompanied us to the gate. Outside it was completely dark. I had not put my right hand back in my pocket; I held it well apart from my coat and pushed back my cuff a little with the other hand, so as to be sure not to contaminate my clothes before I had washed.

Round us the Slum had become the pool of darkness I saw from my window each night, and the lights which invested it from all sides seemed really to bring its gloom into greater relief. It was indeed like some monstrous leper colony. I caught

285

up with Lucien, who was walking several yards ahead of me. I felt anxious and on edge; also ill at ease and dissatisfied with myself. I badly needed the reassurance of hearing Lucien talk. Not daring to ask straight out the question which was obsessing me, I merely said: "Why was it essential for me to shake your patient's hand?"

"Because that's the gesture by which a leper judges his fellow-men. He dislikes being someone whose hand is never shaken."

At the end of my arm, my hand froze in fear. As I could not spray it at once with alcohol, I could not restrain any longer my real question: "It's dangerous, of course? Leprosy starts with the fingers, I fancy; your patient has already lost three."

I heard Lucien laugh in the darkness his good hearty laugh at the daft things only city folk can think up. Then he said:

"My poor old Jean, you spent six months at the Saint-Louis last year. They're building a special leprosy block there, but till that's complete there are lepers on all the wards. You've met them by dozens in the corridors, and you've taken your breakfast next to them in all the cafés round the hospital. In France leprosy isn't contagious, that's been conclusively proved. The fear it arouses is plain stupid, purely imagination, a kind of superstition as absurd as sorcery or black magic. Lepers suffer far more from human selfishness, wickedness and folly than from their own injuries."

I took several steps in silence. I was relieved, relaxed, almost proud of myself. After all, when I had shaken the leper's fingers, even rather feebly, I did not know there was no risk in doing this, so there was a little merit in the action. I realized that in my excitement I had just put my hand snugly back in my pocket. I walked beside Lucien with a lighter step, feeling a thrill of courage, a thrill at being kind and devoted and compassionate— and ready to bring relief to the whole world. That terrible wretchedness, hardly a hundred yards from the comparative luxury of our radiators and bathrooms! There being nothing I could do at the moment, I was anxious at least to impress Lucien with my new enthusiasm:

"One should do something for that man, get someone to help

him. And surely there must be things to do for all those wretches we've seen this afternoon!"

"You talk like a reporter in search of a sensational headline," answered Lucien. "Leave that man alone, leave all those people alone. They don't want pity."

"What, you don't want me to pity them?"

"It's they who don't want it. Ask them and they'll tell you. Personally the word infuriates me, it's a word used by sentimental intellectuals. I feel no need of it whatever. I look after my patients there to the best of my ability. For them and for me I suppose you'd agree that's the main thing."

"All the same, if you built a few good roads instead of these trenches, and dug some drains and brought water to them, that wouldn't be mere sentimentality, would it? That would at least improve their circumstances a little."

"Now you're talking like a benevolent old lady, who insists on sending woolly vests to Negroes in the tropics, because winters are cold in France. These slum-dwellers you've just seen live in their shanties like wild boars in their lairs. As soon as you try to get near, they go somewhere else. They like their strange, savage life, and they accept me only because I don't act as if I found anything abnormal in it. Otherwise they'd soon stop sending for me. They've always lived like this, and it's *our* life they must think intolerable."

"Do you really believe that, Lucien? It doesn't seem plausible to me."

"Well, here's an example for you. There was a family with seven children which used to live here. Then some good soul got them out of their hut and placed them in a four-room flat on the sixth floor of a respectable residential block. There were special reductions in rent for deserving cases. A month afterwards the flat was as filthy and evil-smelling as their shanty in the Slum. Moreover, they all lived in the same room. Apart from wasting coal, why should underfed people like that go to the trouble of freezing in four rooms! They all missed their one-floor hut. Before concerning themselves with the poor, charitable folk would do well to take a look at their victims'

problems on the spot. Then they would stop reasoning so senti-
mentally from standards which are only essential for their own
way of life. To my mind the problem is first of all in men and
women; the water supply and eight-story concrete buildings are
definitely secondary. But then that problem is really too deep
for me. I don't pretend to be a politician or sociologist or philanthropist, I find medicine quite enough. General ideas aren't
my business. So much the worse for me. But anyhow, I know
it's a good deal easier to pity the lot of a thousand people, or ten
thousand, or a hundred thousand, than to do all you can for a
single man."

We crossed the railing again. Before going back into the
hostel, I had to wipe my feet very hard on the mat. On my shoes
was a thick, clinging mud, slimy with grit and poverty. I felt
as if my whole body had been caught in the same slime.

Back in Lucien's room, I looked at him. He was filling his
pipe and preparing to take up his book again, as though we had
just returned from an ordinary stroll. This deliberateness, this
thoughtful self-reliant face, above all this expression of perfect
steadiness and serenity, had never left him for a moment. Involved in all these dramas, he had done what he had to do without apparent excitement, emotion or haste, yet without wasting
a minute. Organic and effective as a surgical instrument, but
almost indifferent for the patient. I felt my curiosity would
annoy him, but even so, now he had started talking about himself and his purposes, I hoped he would tell me the whole story.

"Tell me, Lucien," I said: "why exactly do you look after
the health of these people in the Slum?"

He raised his head and looked at me in sincere surprise. "What
else should a doctor do, Jean, except look after people's health?
These particular people had nobody to look after them, and as
soon as I knew that I went to them." He shrugged his shoulders
slightly as if I had made him explain something obvious.

"How did you begin?"

"By accident. An urchin pushed by his pals. He fell from the
fence railing onto a piece of glass. He started crying, so I picked

288

him up, put on a bandage and took him back home. I saw his parents, then their neighbors, then their neighbors. That's the way you build up a practice, I suppose. And I'm not likely to have many rivals for this practice."

"And you think that will be useful to you?"

"Naturally. I've no intention of setting up in practice among the rich. This is getting me into the swing of things. Here, as you've seen, you have to do everything by yourself and improvise with very little. Do you think you could even examine a throat without a flashlight? At the hospital things are so simple, and no one teaches you to use a tablespoon as reflector behind the candle flame. It's an old trick, but I had to find it out all by myself through trial and error. Experience is something as personal as a toothbrush."

There was a few seconds' silence. I broke it to ask: "Are your patients grateful?"

Before I had said it, I realized I would have done better to keep quiet; and Lucien demonstrated this point fairly forcibly: "Really, Jean, you still talk like that benevolent old lady. Are my patients grateful? I don't know, and I care even less. Unless you consider it a sign of gratitude that the kids have stopped breaking our windows with catapults and that they go and toss their dead cats over the palings onto the other lawns instead of ours? Gratitude indeed."

I said I was sorry to be so stupid, and he softened, and went on after a moment's hesitation: "I do admit, anyhow, that there's one thing which pleases me more than any presents or payments would. For two years now I've treated a bit of everything in the Slum: very ordinary bronchitis and also some pretty shady illnesses and injuries, like the after-effects of abortions. Never once in that time has anyone said to me, please keep your mouth shut. They trusted me straight away. For people like them, living like savages and distrusting everyone and everything, it makes you feel there's really something in being a doctor. They treated me as a real doctor straight away, and that, you see, for a man only just starting means more than anything."

He had been speaking in his usual even voice. He started drawing on his pipe again now, took up a book, and returned to his studies. I went on looking at him for a long while. Each of his actions with the slum-dwellers had been natural and unforced; he had not apparently been driven by any need to outdo himself or preserve his self-confidence. I should never think of him again as anything of a yokel. For his face now revealed to me a human being utterly in harmony with himself. I was amazed and inspired by such simplicity and integrity.

Before going to bed that night, I went and leaned against the window. Against its panes the rain was streaming silkily. It is never a pure rain which falls on the town, and now it seemed to be beating down all its impurities onto the Slum. I could not even see the little red lights glimmering through the gloom like unquiet spirits. But my afternoon's walk had given a new meaning to this plain of darkness, which I had always taken for granted before; and now I no longer saw it with the same eyes. Thanks to Lucien I was no longer a stranger to the Slum—which I felt had more to teach me about medicine than thousands of textbooks; even now it seemed to be sending me messages through the night air.

In the midst of that catastrophic poverty Lucien had shared with me incalculable wealth. Still a student, he had faced all difficulties squarely, knowing that he must decide by himself the best way to deal with them. In so doing, he had shown me the true scope of the doctor's job.

What he had said, others had told me before; but their words had carried no real weight. Lucien had just shown me the true and definitive picture of the man I hoped to be, the man I one day must be: no longer posing artificially as a doctor, directed, supported, protected, but the genuine article, the doctor who has taken on himself the full weight of human relationships, the man responsible for other men's well-being, feeling the burden of a thousand hopes upon him. In one hour Lucien had showed me duty, not in the dry hackneyed academic sense, but the complete and voluntary giving of himself, beside which I could feel only shame at all I had failed to do through negligence or cowardice.

The door of each building in the Cité Universitaire is inscribed with the names of wealthy benefactors, some of whom have doubtless given millions so that people may know of their generosity. But here was the real philanthropist, who had gone to all these humble people in trouble without expecting or asking their gratitude. He fought for them for nothing, because he was the only one they had. They would not get better without his help, and in their primitive will-to-live they called him daily to help them. Each day, a true doctor, he silently went on with his job in the name of all the mighty unseen forces which fight for Life and against Death.

Chapter 8

THE FIRST TERM was almost over. How could such a brief flash of time make up a term? I felt it was almost last night that I had first set foot on the Pozzi Ward. But the time must have seemed much longer to M. Thury, immobilized with his fracture. About a fortnight before the Christmas holidays his heart had started to cause serious anxiety. My old friend had become huge, bloated with oedema. He could not get his breath, and as heart stimulants no longer worked, we had almost given up hope. He lay there unmoving, subject to terrible fits of choking, and in that swollen face only the eyes went on as before, living their tolerant smiling life.

I often saw the earnest Marianne near him, and when he was able to talk at all the old man sometimes talked about her to me; I humored him, for in his present state he obviously ought not to be excited. In a strange way I did not mind so much now hearing Marianne praised. When I came near her, however, she immediately seemed to find something urgent to do at another bed; and on the other hand, when she was chatting with M. Thury, I postponed seeing him and went elsewhere. On his table top there was always a little bunch of fresh violets.

Then, about a fortnight later, the old man's condition improved, and one morning he said to me in a less gasping voice: "I really thought that was the end, that the old wreck was slowly sinking. I was almost glad to go. There was a stage when I felt a sense of infinite freedom, as if all my earthly bonds had fallen away. In my last difficult steps I was being supported alternately by a fair girl and a dark young man, as the fortune-tellers might put it. It's humiliating to admit, but as soon as you get slightly better, you become a coward again. At the moment I just feel excited at my reprieve."

He held an orange in his hand, and tried to put it on the much-encumbered table top; it fell, and rolled under several beds. I went to fetch it, and when I returned, he said to me sardonically: "You see, another sign. Everything falls, everything leaves me. Even inanimate objects guess I'm only having a temporary reprieve."

I made room for the orange among the jumble on the table—the hospital patient's sole and always overpopulated domain. It contained in fact all M. Thury's worldly goods; and even then only the two old boxes of biscuits really have belonged to him. All the books with torn pages which straggled about the ward seemed to have collected here in unstable piles. It is true that at the head of the bed there was a shelf; and on other wards patients could use this too. But for her ward Sister Limagnac had decided otherwise: the only thing allowed to figure on the shelf was the specimen bottle of urine. The patients had continually to rebuild on their table tops small pyramids of extra provisions, clothes, and medicines, and these pyramids would always collapse at the slightest provocation.

On the other hand, when you entered the Pozzi Ward, you were greeted by a flawless alignment of beds and a streamlined perspective of shelves, displaying rows of small bottles in many shades of color. Our martinet of a Sister must often have regretted that she could not require the patients to produce a uniform tint or equal quantities of liquid; such urinary irregularity was their only way of protesting against the cruel waste of the shelves. From this point of view M. Thury got his own back quite satisfactorily by offering, at each morning's inspection, only a very small and cloudy mixture of reddish urine.

A little later I was making an examination at a bed quite near his. I saw him trying to pick up a book, but unfortunately he knocked over the whole pile. Marianne ran up immediately and began to repair the disaster. I had returned to my interview with the new patient, when the normal noise of the ward suddenly

293

stopped like a collective warning of danger: almost immediately, I heard the dictatorial step of Sister Limagnac and the bunch of keys jingling at her belt like a conscientious escort. She passed the bed where I was, and stopped short before M. Thury's bed, remaining there for a moment without speaking. Either she was out of breath or else it was the excitement of finding a victim within reach; she wanted to eke out her pleasure a little longer. When she spoke it was as if she had tried, but not very hard, to keep the sourness out of her voice:

"You know perfectly well, Mlle. Duriez, that I do not allow any personal property at the head of patients' beds."

Marianne had stayed motionless, still holding one of the books which she had begun to arrange on the forbidden shelf. Unsupported, the last book that had been put there toppled over with an ironical thud, and this seemed to make Sister lose her head. Meanwhile M. Thury, frantic and almost in tears, tried to say: "It's my fault, Sister, I drop everything, it's my fault."

"Keep quiet, you, it's no business of yours!"

Sister Limagnac's voice broke in, dry and cutting. Marianne's voice, which range out directly afterward, only sounded the warmer and more sensitive: "Whose business is it, Sister, if not the patients'? I thought we were supposed to attend to their comforts a little. That shelf . . ."

"Don't you think it might be more convenient, Sister?"

These words came from *me*. Acting on impulse, I had covered the four or five yards separating me from M. Thury's bed, and said the first thing which came into my head, so as to stop Marianne saying something irreparable. All this had happened so swiftly, so unintentionally, almost unconsciously, that I was still staggered by it myself. Sister turned sharply towards me, and I smiled at her as casually and noncommittally as I could manage. She turned back at once to Marianne, and so did I. Marianne was looking at me with astonishment, and I thought I could read a strong interest, almost an understanding, in her dark eyes.

Sister Limagnac had also observed this sudden collusion and she looked at me virulently. But I was even more frightened to see the look of positively black hatred she then turned on Mari-

294

anne. She seemed to have become very close to me. I felt wonderfully strong and noble, strong enough to protect us both, ready to face any scandal. I am sure my eyes must have betrayed some of these exalted emotions, and Sister evidently decided not to pursue the matter to these lengths. Her voice descended to its normal degree of acidity as she said to me icily: "So you are taking on the defense. Fortunately for me, M. Nérac, we are *not* in a court of law."

I was just about to make some sharp retort myself, when I saw Marianne looking at me with passionate distress and also gratitude in her eyes. I said nothing, and Sister, guessing she would be wasting her venom, left the scene.

M. Thury was still gasping, too deeply moved to speak. The patients all round us seemed to be holding a mute council, and for a few seconds there was a highly charged silence. Marianne and I remained facing each other, still stunned to have been brought together and reconciled so abruptly.

The whole incident was over so quickly that by the time Paul Chavasse dashed up from the other end of the ward and reached M. Thury's bed, Sister Limagnac had already returned to her office. But the gesture of friendship had been made, and Paul came ostensibly to show his solidarity with us. He looked at us with a smile, then hunched his back like an old woman, and stuck out his chin, sniffed some imaginary snuff, and in the quavering voice of an old granny telling a story, he raised a finger and began:

"Now, my dears, once upon a time, at the bottom of a very old hospital, there was a fair maiden in her first year of medical studies, and one day a wicked fairy, disguised as a rattlesnake . . ."

Our nervous tensions dissolved into fits of childish laughter. All my exaltation, all my unexpressed ardor, spilled over into a great outburst of hilarity, while Marianne's clear laugh tinkled merrily above Paul's jovial chuckles. M. Thury watched the three of us going off happily together, and as soon as he had recovered his breath a little, he imitated our reaction; little tears of laughter began forming under his eyes. From bed to bed friendly irreverent smiles spread through the ward. The conspirators were smiting the tyrant at last. I decided later with some relish that in the whole affair this laughter would be the one thing Sister Limagnac could never forgive us.

All the students gathered near the interne as he began his round, and the incident soon disappeared in the buzz of the morning's work. All that morning I felt bursting with life, extraordinarily happy, full of goodwill towards all these patients that I had defended in defending Marianne. Each time I raised my eyes and saw her in the ward, an unfamiliar joy came over me, a frenzy of delight and devotion.

Work finished fairly early that day. About half past twelve Marianne went to the first-year dressing room, and I had no wish to stay on the ward a moment longer. I myself changed hastily, and when I came out of the office where we had to sign on and off, I almost knocked her over.

We went through the gate together. There was already the beginnings of a crowd waiting for visiting hours; a sad little drizzle was falling, and on the edge of the pavements were the usual barrows of flowers, the same hawkers and beggars. I saw nothing of this familiar scene. The crush forced me to walk a little behind Marianne, and I watched the firm suppleness of her movements with a feeling of indescribable tenderness.

Since coming out of the hospital, we had been walking in silence. I thought only of the miraculous fact of her being there near me; but at the same time I was half conscious too of a dull anxiety nagging me. I should have liked to be absolutely sure that the new bond between us still held firm. Then she looked into my eyes with utter frankness, as if we had been friends or sweethearts for a very long time. She seemed to have weighed up carefully the situation between us. This look, uniting a child's candor and a woman's maturity, took my breath away, ended all my doubts. I read in it an understanding which by-passed our wills, which was like the secret harmony of our blood.

All at once I felt the passers-by must read on our faces, as on our bodies, how close we were to one another; bending slightly,

I pretended to come under Marianne's little umbrella to shelter from the shower.

We reached the bus shelter. It was full, but a little room was made for us. To avoid an abrupt silence, I told Marianne that I had a practical session rather early at medical school. I had only just finished saying this when she cried: "Here's my bus."

It was going towards the Porte d'Orléans and the Cité Universitaire. I had a thousand excellent reasons for taking it with her; but I did not dare. I let her go alone. She smiled at me from the platform, and I followed her with my eyes till the bus turned at the crossroads. Then I stayed a minute or two motionless on the steps of the shelter, with large drops of rain falling down my neck from the roof. I was disappointed and regretful—and wonderfully happy.

All afternoon I was still brimming over with vitality and enthusiasm. At the restaurant, in the street, at school, I kept on looking at the people near me. Could they read my happiness on my face? As for me, I had never before found them so ugly, specially the women, so dull and commonplace. Could they really love and be loved? For all of them today would probably flow stagnantly by, like any other day: a day which would have brought them nothing, which none of them would miss afterwards, which later would count as something for me alone. I caught myself smiling at these poor wretches with irrepressible benevolence, almost with pity.

I had dinner in the Latin Quarter, alone with my happiness. I returned to the Cité fairly late and as I passed Carleret's room I heard the noise of a great discussion. Without stopping I went to my room and straight to bed. I put out the light, not feeling at all sleepy, and lay awake in the darkness.

I began to remember that first day of term, when a slender fair-haired figure in white had glared at me in fury; already that morning she had penetrated decisively into my life. Later, much later, I said to myself, when I think again of that introduction, I shall always see an abashed child, leaning on the long marble table, answering "Yes, Sir" and "No, Sir." Everything which came afterwards started from there; and yet I had not dreamt of recognizing the girl at the table as the figure I had vainly waited for so long, ever since the beginning of my adolescence. But by my intervention of this morning, which was almost a reflex action, I realized that this figure had always been secretly present within me; so fully present that I might have known Marianne all my life. The things I guessed about her instinctively could have been drawn from an old album, crammed with snapshots of the two of us together.

I felt ready to sleep at last; but wanted to remember her thoroughly before I slept. Suddenly I was seized with such tenderness, so strong and sweet a desire to have her near me—that I could not stop myself thinking: how does she go to sleep? I pictured her asleep, frail and innocent, with her lovely fair hair; then I yielded to slumber, overwhelmed with delight and love. That night, in the impatience of my joy, I dreamt of Marianne, only of her.

Very early, the brightness of the day woke me up, and my joy was still so overflowing that I passed from dream to actuality without a moment's doubt, without the least fear of disappointment. I left well before my usual time, I was in such a hurry to be near Marianne again. On the Boulevard Jourdan I turned round several times in the hope of seeing her. The boulevard seemed less animated than usual and I saw very few students on their way to the Metro; at first I thought I must have started out much too early. But no, my watch registered the normal time, and in the Metro, reading the date on a neighbor's paper, I suddenly remembered that the Christmas vacation began this morning.

After this I only had one thought in my mind till I reached the hospital: would Marianne be there at all? As soon as I reached the gate doubts were resolved—the wrong way. Without students the courts and corridors and silent staircases seemed empty and the whole hospital had the drowsy restful air which it took on each Sunday. I ran up the staircase, but the ward looked gloomy, stripped of all interest and meaning, without the figure in white I was seeking. I put on my coat, then passed Sister's glass office without going in. While I was walking towards M. Thury's bed, as the only important place in the ward for me, I felt between my shoulder blades Sister Limagnac's stare knifing me. Some of the patients gave me a conspiratorial wink as I passed.

M. Thury watched me approach with a smile; he must have been waiting for me. "Here's my chivalrous young doctor. But you're alone this morning?" Behind his big spectacles the pale blue eyes seemed to be looking for Marianne's fair hair at my side. "It's vacation," I explained, and he looked rather sad, as if from now on he would only feel really cheerful when we were both there together. Before my rueful gaze he drew me near him with one hand and murmured: "Marianne—what a fine girl!"

Since the evening before I had repeated the name in my heart a thousand times: Marianne, Marianne! To hear it pronounced, even very low, to hear the quivering syllables, suddenly gave it a marvellous, almost physical reality. I would like to have thanked M. Thury who had slowly guided me towards her, for being the first to give me this happiness. But he left me no time to thank him; he went on.

"This is my nunc dimittis, Jean. After this last pleasure life has given me, I can really depart in peace. To survive—that's the haunting hope we all have. When I was twenty I believed I should live through my literary talents. Since then . . . but no matter. Now I am sure that something of me will survive. Though I die without family or children, part of me will never be quite dead. Two human beings will remember an old man who had a soft spot in his heart for them, even if he was a bit soft in the head at the end. And so the poor old codger will live on a little in your happiness.

He had talked himself into a considerable pitch of excitement, and had to stop to expectorate painfully. His hands were feverish and I wanted to auscultate him, but he would not let me.

Half relapsed on his pile of pillows, he began to laugh exultantly, as he had done the day before when Sister Limagnac retreated. And as on the day before, I felt I could hear at my side Marianne's clear laughter, and around us the smiles of Paul and all the patients. It was like an arch over our heads, like the arch of swords they form at a soldier's wedding.

Part 6

MARIANNE

Chapter 1

DURING the first term of my second year it had never occurred to me even as a possibility that a woman might decisively alter the crowded routine of my life. No nurse on the Pozzi Ward had succeeded in attracting me—living under the Limagnac terror, they would have had little chance to try—and the girls who frequented the internes' common room remained, in Paul's words, "for internes' use only." Nor were women likely to impinge much on the life of me and my friends in the Cité.

The ban on bringing women into our rooms, under penalty of expulsion from the hostel, was the major article in the regulations of the establishment; its rigorous enforcement, according to Georges Gédéon, was due to the headmaster's jealousy because he had never been capable of making love himself. "Elegant young plutocrats," our Marxist would declare, with considerable support from Prichard, "are provided with comfortable bachelor rooms, while we students, supposed to be the cream of the country's youth, must sow our wild oats in dark corners."

Some of the lads living in the hostel were too hot-blooded to tolerate abstinence indefinitely. They would go off to cheap dance-halls and dazzle some shopgirl with their sparkling wit and manners. Despite the risk of the headmaster's patrol and a consequent expulsion, they would bring her back to the Cité in the middle of the night. But if they were unwise enough to draw attention to their nightlife by amorous gasps or the creaking of mattresses, most of the hostel would line up outside their door, and organize a raucous medley of swooning, voluptuous moans

303

and cries, such as: "Really, I couldn't . . . I'll have to ask mother . . . don't touch me, you brute . . . I'm a good girl, I am . . . besides it always gives me a headache . . ." All this delivered in elaborate falsetto.

Few girls would be likely to appreciate such heavy-handed humor, and most of the hostel's Don Juans tried to find a suitable young lady who was in possession of a room of her own, so that they could transfer their scenes of dalliance to the big city. They would disappear for longer or shorter periods, and their beds in the hostel would not be slept in. Meanwhile we would continue the even tenor of our ways, and when they did return, looking pale and somewhat bleary-eyed, we would dismiss them, rather contemptuously, to their horizontal occupations.

I myself, since the night of the Internes' Hop, had suffered few temptations. I would sometimes find myself staring at a woman in the street, and then turning to look at her as she passed. If she turned too, I was pleased, but I never retraced my steps to develop this embryo conquest. Mornings at the hospital, afternoons at medical school, my work and diversions with François and then with Lucien, seemed to absorb all my energy, leaving few chinks by which temptation could enter, and in any case not enough privacy for the act of love.

And then all of a sudden there was Marianne, like a pebble hurled into a shallow pool, stirring up its stagnant depths so that the ripples on the surface grew ever wider and wider.

In the days following the discovery of my love, I lived in a state of lyrical happiness. Every morning, as soon as I arrived on Pozzi, I would go straight to M. Thury to hear him talk of Marianne. Because of the vacation, the tempo of the ward had slackened, and I found some time on my hands. I could not listen for long enough to my old friend singing Marianne's praises. I should like to have gone on talking about her later in the day, telling Lucien about my wonderful discovery. But he had departed, and the hostel emptied rapidly for the vacation.

Eventually I too had my vacation from the hospital. The morning I told M. Thury I was going to Toulouse for a few

304

days, he seemed to me feverish, exhausted, and very depressed. He could only speak with difficulty, but found the strength to smile at me and wish me a good journey. And then: "The new term does start on the fifth, doesn't it? Do you think *she* will be there?" I assured him she would.

I was resolved to tell my mother about Marianne as soon as I got home. She kissed me, felt me, inspected me, almost weighed me physically, and then announced straightaway that she had a surprise for me. She dragged me into the back room, and instead of the old table where I had done my homework, I saw a magnificent mahogany desk.

"I got it for a song," my mother declared triumphantly. "Four or five years' study goes awfully quickly, and I'm already beginning to think about your practice. A young doctor needs to inspire confidence, and a mahogany desk makes a very good impression, don't you think? And then, you know how selfish I am, Jean. I'll flick a duster over it before your surgery every day, and with that nice smooth surface, I shan't have any trouble bringing up the polish."

She looked at me, and smiled. It was a smile of loving possessiveness, insatiable, and exclusive. She already saw herself housekeeping for me a few years later, answering patients, to all of whom she would be "Doctor's mother." Her pride in my success would pay her for twenty years of unselfish work. With her building that happy picture, I had not the heart to mention Marianne; and as soon as I could, I made fatigue from the journey an excuse to go upstairs to my old room. Without looking round at any of my books or possessions, all in the same place as they had always been, I threw myself onto the bed.

When I first came back to Toulouse in July, I had leaped upon every object in the room, having remembered all of them minutely throughout the months at Paris. But though I remembered them so well, they seemed to have forgotten *me*; they said nothing to me. Everything had been transformed, had shrunk to tiny proportions. At first I did not guess what was happening to me. Had I changed so much in ten months? It took me some time to understand this new experience. Till then, having never

305

left home for long, I had no idea of the thousands of personal possessions one leaves behind on one's path through life, like a trail on the caravan route of unrecognizable whitening bones.

This time I did not look at anything in the house, nor in my room. Everything here had become completely indifferent to me; my life was no longer in it. Till this moment my love for Marianne had its place in an insubstantial world, outside time, almost outside life. Now I realized it had utterly changed me.

I went out in the afternoon, having still not had the courage to speak of her. I walked at random through the old streets, wondering how I could possibly make my mother understand. Towards evening I returned to the shop.

My mother was knitting near the window, bent over her work, to profit by the last light. It was inspiring to catch her thus in silence and solitude, bent from a whole life of humble tasks, of patience and unselfishness and kindness. Even in the golden amorous blur in which I had been living for five days, nothing could resist the true nobility and saintliness of this gentle face. She accepted her destiny with self-effacing humility, and I knew if I talked to her, entreated her, she would once more have compassion—on my happiness. But with a few selfish words I might take years off my mother's life, clouding her old age with a bitter loneliness. I had left it too long already to tell her about Marianne; and now I had not the heart to do it.

During the next four days I hardly went out of the shop. I told my mother hundreds of stories about my life in Paris, describing all my friends and acquaintances, all the hospital and hostel personalities. In the end I reduced myself to a state of numbness. I had managed to convince myself that I had now recovered; that with the help of reason and self-discipline I might completely pluck out the roots of my new life of this last week, however deep and swiftly they had spread. But at times the pain of this conflict must have shown itself on my face, for I felt my mother looking at me with loving solicitude. The tenderness of this look was like a knife in the wound; for some reason it reminded me unbearably of Marianne.

Term began on January 5th, just as M. Thury had reminded

me. The day before I announced that I would be going up by the evening train. I had a thousand very reasonable arguments for this departure, and my mother soon stopped pressing me to stay at least till the morning.

During these four days I had made a sincere effort at submission; but at the thought that Marianne would be on the ward next morning my impatience spilled over. For four days I had struggled vainly, and now I was like a man half-dead with thirst, far from a spring. Pale and distracted, with a dazed glassy look in my eye, I was already on my way towards a slender figure in white. If at that moment my mother had wished to restrain me, I should have brushed her aside without even hearing her.

At half past nine next morning, full of expectancy, I was on Pozzi Ward. The superintendent was beginning the rollcall of first-year students; and among them, smiling at me in the distance, I saw Marianne. I was surprised how little sense of shock it gave me; as soon as I saw her, my anxiety vanished, dissolving into a radiant serenity. Then I went to M. Thury's bed, only to find there a face I did not know; a patient in the next bed informed me that M. Thury had died of pulmonary congestion three days ago. I received the news almost without emotion: it seemed quite in the natural order of things, as if the kind old man had only stayed alive for three months in order to bring me and Marianne together. His mission was now accomplished, and he had departed.

As soon as rollcall was over, Marianne ran up to greet me. Then she begged me to take her to the mortuary. We went together to make inquiries of the attendant there; and as I had already guessed, the unclaimed cadaver of an old man with no family had already been taken off in the van with the zinc floor to the medical school's embalming room. But before disappearing completely in the destitution he himself had prophesied, M. Thury's generous shadow made us one final offering. Because of him, I saw Marianne weeping softly, and could say gentle consoling words to her like a brother, as we walked down the empty corridor.

With the new term Pozzi resumed its full surgical program. On returning to the ward we found the usual comings and goings of doctors and students, the jingling journey of the dressing trolley, the patients departing dumbly for the theatre, the nurses dashing madly about in obedience to Sister's imperious calls. Soon the Chief's round began. He stopped for a good while at the bed of M. Thury's successor, apparently an "interesting case." But I was thinking of other things, and in the crowd of first-year students bunched round the bed I kept on picking out Marianne's face, merely for the joy of looking at her again. Each time she smiled back at me, but a little sadly, probably thinking of M. Thury; it made her look adorably young and defenseless.

I remembered a morning a few weeks before when M. Thury was trying to tell me about Marianne, before I knew I should love her, or perhaps that I already loved her. "That girl is straight as a die," he said: "one of the rare people who can walk in the mud without being defiled; with others, the mud seems to cling to them naturally. You may smile now, but you will see what I mean later on, when you meet the real mud, and meanness and disloyalty and envy and all uncharitableness."

The memory was so vivid, so close to me, that when I raised my eyes towards the man in the bed, I almost expected to see M. Thury's friendly features once more. It was a real shock to see instead the gaping face of the new patient, who was listening uncomprehendingly, obviously much flattered by all the learned things the Chief was finding to retail upon his case. I turned my eyes quickly towards Marianne; she was looking at me already. This time I received her sad smile without hypocrisy. Never before had I understood so well our old friend's dream. What radiance I might have let slip through stupid blindness, but for his help! Full of wonder I smiled at Marianne. Without a moment's delay I must give her all my devotion, must cherish and protect her against all enemies, visible and invisible. Among the former Sister Limagnac, glowering at the world behind the Chief, was obviously one of the most immediate and most redoubtable.

The Chief finished his lecture on the patient, and passed on to the next bed. While the students were moving on with him, I managed to come next to Marianne. I stayed by her all through the round, full of an immense, unbroken, gentle surge of desire. Sometimes I felt through our coats the warmth of her body against mine, and, since we wore short sleeves, the warmth of her arm against my arm. I knew I must be at her side like that all my life.

Chapter 2

FROM THAT DAY indeed we began living side by side. Each morning we would meet on the Boulevard Jourdan and leave together for the hospital. On the ward Sister Limagnac now affected to ignore me: I learned the details of my daily work from a probationer: "Sister wants you to do this, Sister says you're to do that." When Marianne was not following the troop of first-year students, she would accompany me from bed to bed, although if I thought a dressing was liable to be specially painful, I would try to postpone it till a time when she would not be there. Some shocks were in any case inevitable, but I felt she must be broken in as gently as possible, and I kept reproaching myself for not having taken her under my wing two months earlier.

With unexpected discretion Paul did his best to refrain from disturbing us with his boisterous friendship. When he needed to talk to me and saw me isolated with "my pupil" in a corner of the ward, he would cough discreetly on approaching us, and leave again immediately, saying: "I return to the saltmines, my lambs. You two must have a chance to get to know one another."

To compensate for Sister's hostility, we felt the patients' sympathy surrounding us. Ordinary people usually like young lovers, and their knowing smiles concealed the same message: "You seem simple and defenseless, no different from us wretched patients. But you manage to be happy even here, despite that old bitch, so good luck to you." They took a vicarious pleasure, in fact, in our happiness.

The "old bitch" sternly forbade any first-year student's

touching the least instrument on her ward, but when her back was turned, I would hand "my pupil" a forceps and teach her to put in a drain. I prepared a syringe with which she practised giving intravenous injections. The patients let her do it, hid their grimaces, and even encouraged her.

It was a moving contrast for me to see her with her clear skin and look of absolute purity, strangely heightened by the white coat, bending over decaying flesh, soiling her lovely hands with blood and pus. Sometimes too she looked so frail and defenseless that a part of me could have dragged her off into some enchanted garden where her youth and grace should never again be affronted by dirt and destitution and decay. "Leave all this," I wanted to tell her; "You were meant for happier things." But Marianne had chosen medicine, and she was eager to learn from me all she could. Another part of me was singing with happiness whenever she raised her head to seek my approval or ask my advice; and when she was near me the most painful sights almost failed to move me.

Not that this could be entirely ascribed to lover's blindness. The fact was that after sixteen months in the hospital, completely unconsciously I was going through a bad attack of insensitivity, a malady old as the teaching of medicine itself. One morning Marianne herself opened my eyes to the danger.

A workman had been brought in from Accidents with a hand very badly mangled by a machine; and he was in my row of beds. A few days later when I had to change his dressing for the first time, it took me a long time to remove the dressing which had been put on when he came in. After bathing it continually in antiseptic, I eventually reached a complicated assembly of raw tendons, vessels, and muscles, exposed as clearly as in the hand of an anatomy model. You could even see the joints and bones underneath. Armed with my forceps I spent a long time in the delicate work of cleaning up; it was a sort of lesson in vivisection, and I tried very hard to understand and memorize how the various parts were connected, so as to be able to find my bearings exactly for the future.

When the dressing was done, I got up, delighted, and said to

311

the man as I was going away: "You see, my friend, it all went off very well. You didn't feel a thing, did you?" The man was very pale, and only looked at me oddly without answering. When we were a little way off Marianne said: "He must have thought you were joking, Jean."

"Why?" I asked in surprise; and she replied reproachfully: "But you have been hurting him terribly, he was screaming all the time." This time I looked at her in stupefaction. So passionately absorbed had I been in my swabs and tendons and muscles, that in all good faith I had heard absolutely nothing. It was a very well-known phenomenon: scientific curiosity and technical interest had anaesthetized my sensitivity.

As soon as the man devoured by a stomach cancer becomes for the student "a juxtapyloric tumor," or the woman choking horribly becomes "a cardiac failure"; as soon as you learn to recognize a tumor beneath the fingers, a murmur against the ear, as soon as you start thinking only of "a case," from then on the complaint obscures the patient or divides him up for you into his various organs. In the same way you become used to screams and blood and pus and smells, and above all you assume a sort of fatalism before pain, a phenomenon noted every day with every patient. You now think of pain only as a symptom at once precious and commonplace; always the same question: "Where does it hurt?" To guide yourself through the maze you even get used to causing suffering deliberately: "Tell me if I'm hurting you." And later: "Does it still hurt you?"

Under the weight of the finger the contour of the organ conveniently reveals its shape like a continent on a map of the world. In the end you are only stirred by certain specially expressive manifestations of suffering. Often while a patient told me some terrible story of his pathology, I caught myself thinking of something quite different, some film I had seen, or the color of a new tie.

From the time Marianne began going through Pozzi with me, I resumed the habit of lingering by each bed, as in my months at the St. Louis Hospital. I would get the patients to talk, and I would listen, with every appearance of thoughtful interest, to the recital of events very thinly connected with the reasons for their being in this ward. My round of the beds often seemed interminable of course, but I saw Marianne's face shine radiantly, and I felt she was admiring me unreservedly in my role of consoler and confidant.

In this happy unity the morning would pass like a dream. About half past twelve we would leave the ward together. I no longer accepted invitations to the internes' common room. When we passed in front of the door I would strain my ear for the excited roar of disputes and songs, and for a few steps I would feel a faint pang of regret. Before I had even crossed the court and gone under the entrance porch, I had dedicated this sacrifice to my companion. I only regretted one thing—that I could not tell her with what joy I did it.

Then we took the rue Jacob towards the Latin Quarter. I felt as happy as a king—and as proud—to be walking at Marianne's side with men looking at her admiringly and other women enviously. When we came up to the rue Buci, and the peddlers smiled at her and shouted out the names of flowers and fruits as we passed, like cheerful greetings, I wanted to pass her arm under mine to show she belonged exclusively to me.

We had to eat lunch very quickly, and I watched the time by my watch, so as to be at the Anatomy Wing by half past one. As soon as Marianne had vanished among the noisy streams of students I felt utterly miserable, partly because she was no longer near me, and partly because I felt she specially needed my protection in those anatomy sessions, so revolting to the sensitive novice. I pictured her feeling lost and alone, amidst cadavers, crude and rowdy neighbors, and the famous scraps: a girl with numbed and greasy fingers, silent amidst all that coarse hilarity, bent anxiously over a macabre mess. She had never said much about her reactions to anatomy, but these were the ones I guessed at, as I went off rather gloomily to my practical physics.

At four o'clock we would meet again in the main hall of the medical school, swarming with students. Marianne would walk up smiling, because this was almost her natural expression and probably she was thinking of our meeting. The smile irritated me because others might be deceived by it and follow her; I was jealous. But as soon as she saw me and the smile grew wider and more wonderful, the jealousy vanished in a flash, and then I could have forgiven her anything.

Often at four o'clock I did not find her in the hall. She would arrive five minutes later, out of breath, flushed from running, with contrition shining in her eyes like a naughty little girl. "Oh dear, you'll scold me now," she confessed. "I went to Olive's, I just couldn't help it."

Olive's was a shop selling exotic sweets in the street by the school, next to a dealer in skeletons and stuffed animals. Marianne still had her full share of schoolgirl gluttony, and I was astonished by the amount and variety of sweets she could swallow—Turkish delight, stuffed dates, and other Oriental sweetmeats—without feeling sick. Often I would take her to a Polish patisserie for the sheer joy of seeing her faced by a plate of cakes and a cup of tea. I could not help smiling, for the nearness of the pleasure ahead gave her a special, rather comical expression of bliss. Nothing else in the world existed for her just then. It was wonderful for me to watch this face, so clearly created for joy, so happy in being alive. Though her joy sometimes seemed excessively childish, I did not dream of saying anything. Her medical training would bring her to maturity quite soon enough.

Then we would go to the library. We had our two seats in a corner which was only crowded on rare occasions, when all the rest of the room was full. She would open her anatomy book at once, set out her colored pencils, and with her tongue out slightly, like a schoolgirl concentrating very hard, she would begin a diagram, while I got down to my own work. Every now and then she would turn towards me to ask me something. Leaning against my shoulder to avoid talking too loud, brushing my cheek with her hair, she would listen to my answer. Our neighbors, seeing us from a distance so near each other, must surely have imagined something more romantic than our scientific conversations, but they were wrong. I had placed our relationship on this level from the first day, and maintained an extreme

314

physical reserve. I would unhesitatingly have given my life for her, but did not even think of kissing her.

We were a very self-absorbed couple, and our zest for conversation never flagged. At seven o'clock the bell announcing the library's closing time surprised us as if we had only just come. We went back to the Cité for dinner, and we were so eager to be alone that after the restaurant we would go to the reading room in America House, where we were unlikely to meet anybody either of us knew.

About eleven o'clock I escorted her back to her hostel; and to say goodnight we stopped near the gate at the same spot where I should wait for her next morning. Then it was time for us to part. In the twilight I saw her features drawn by weariness; she would smile at me a little sadly, and I had to keep sharp control of myself not to take her in my arms. I dreaded, for both of us, the chilling emptiness which comes after an embrace.

I would look up at her window for a few moments after she had left me, and see the light go on in her room. Then I would go away, knowing that before going to sleep she would be spending a few minutes reading one of the books I had lent her. I had adopted the habit of putting pencilled notes in the margin of my books, and all down their pages she would be trying, by means of these notes, to conjure up my presence once more.

Reaching my hostel, I would go up to my room directly. Since Christmas I had hardly been to Carleret's at all. Most of the people in the hostel had become totally indifferent to me, and I felt incapable of hiding it from them. Moreover, if I entered without knocking as was customary, I should risk overhearing careless remarks on what they would doubtless already be calling my love affair.

The only contact I retained at the Cité was with Lucien; although in the circumstances I no longer had time or inclination to work in his room. But several times as I was just going to bed, or in the middle of the night, he was called out to the Slum by a voice over the railings or a pebble thrown at his window. A few minutes later I would hear him leaving his room, which was on the same corridor as mine. Instead of knocking at my door to take me along, as in other times, he would go off directly. I felt a pang of remorse, and would sometimes dress hastily to dash after him.

When he was called out at this time of night, it was usually to deliver a baby. He took his old leather bag in which he had placed, with all his array of syringes and ampules, an ancient delivery-forceps, which had lost its nickel finish in the course of a very long career.

Sometimes it was an abortion which had gone wrong. We would find a woman looking pale and blue. The cloths stuffed between her thighs were already soaked with blood, which was beginning to run over her bed. Often Lucien decided he could cope by himself, and set to work with great energy. But on other occasions he decided on an emergency transport to the hospital; I would have to return to the Cité to telephone for an ambulance. The ambulance would stop on the edge of the Slum, not daring to go forward into the mud and slush where the wheels skidded and dug themselves in. The paths there were so narrow that the stretcher could only just turn the corners, and the stretcher-bearers, momentary representatives of civilization in that jungle, would swear as they slipped in the mud.

Not all the women had abortions; some accepted their continual pregnancies with fatalistic indifference, as just one extra in the unending procession of misfortunes. Several times after leaving Marianne I saw Lucien going off with his little bag and went to follow him. Shut up in a black hut where the air was so fetid you could hardly breathe, I felt as if the woman, her husband, the midwife, Lucien and myself had all fallen into a dark dungeon from which there was no escape; we should have to go on now right to the end.

Lucien's patients were discreet in this respect: they only called him for difficult deliveries when the midwife began to worry. The women who served the Slum as midwives were two or three misshapen old Italians who had suffered repeated preg-

316

nancies themselves and now exploited their hard-earned knowledge, especially to show off their superiority to the men, cause of the present crisis. They stopped moaning and complaining about masculine egoism, however, as soon as they saw Lucien come in.

The woman continued her shrill labor cries from the bed: one and the same cry repeated scores of times between spasms. Lucien would very soon be bent over the huge stomach, listening to the baby's heart, studying the presentation, trying to see it should come into life cleanly, with its head well flexed like a graceful diver. Or else he would prepare his forceps, sterilizing them in a flame which for a moment set the hovel's shadows dancing. When the forceps were in place, he would begin to pull with a slow careful traction, so powerful that the first time it frightened me; I was only reassured when he had disengaged the forceps from the head. Then he would gather the head between the bleeding thighs to draw it gently with both hands; and the crumpled little pigmy would leave the mother's belly with a moist squelching sound.

The woman would lie silent and exhausted; but almost immediately the newborn babe, bare and bruised in the cruel light, would utter a long plaintive cry—bewildered to have left the warm haven which, according to some, a man remembers with wistful longing all his life. Lucien would give the midwife the little red body to wash, but before that he used to raise it in his hands gently and deliberately, holding the child out to life in a gesture of propitiation, as if in obedience to some solemn and secret law.

Obstetrics only comes fairly near the end of the medical course, and I knew nothing of it so far; I could not, therefore, be much use to Lucien. I had plenty of leisure to meditate on the mystery being performed in this miserable den. I saw Lucien bent over the woman, often for long hours at a time watching through the walls of the stomach the beating of that dark life, of that tiny mass of matter which would soon be suffering from hunger, cold, and passion, and would yet be raising its eyes to the stars.

317

Inevitably, under the spur of my love, my thoughts would turn to Marianne. I would picture her at the hospital, at the school, ardent as in the days of her childhood, yet thoughtful as a woman with much work soon to be done. I marvelled at my good luck. Our lives would always be side by side; already we seemed to share every moment. Later, like ivy creeping over a wall day after day, our profession would bind us still further; we should be working next to each other. Never would I be alone again; she would become my assistant, she would watch with me at the bedside of these mothers. Far more than any physical act, we could make our success and our difficulties, our weariness and our striving, into the symbol of our love.

Forgetting the dark hovel and its squalor, I saw a vista of an impossibly happy future stretching out in front of me.

Chapter 3

My love and my work seemed to merge so magnificently at every point that I was living in a world of my own, our own; my eyes were firmly closed on outside realities. But if Marianne and I were blinded by our happiness, Paul kept his eyes open for all three of us. One morning he took me aside to issue a warning.

"Take care, you Great Lover. While you two are billing and cooing in your Garden of Eden, don't forget our super-serpent. She's got all her apples out to tempt you, and just let one little pip go down the wrong way, you'll be out of Paradise before you can say Sister. Report to the Chief, report to the hospital authorities, and there you are; it'll be a very unpleasant business. I can't do much about it now, she doesn't love me any more—or about as much as an ingrowing toenail. Since you got on the wrong side of her, she won't let me do anything more on the ward. How about our all changing wards? If you're too busy to come down to earth, I'll arrange it. Good idea?"

I was astonished. In my ivory tower of happiness, I had thought myself invulnerable. But on thinking it over, to change wards seemed a very sound idea. "My pupil" agreed as long as she could come with me, so I told Paul to go ahead.

He went off at once to open negotiations, and on returning at noon seemed half satisfied. "It wasn't too easy," he reported. "I tried all the wards, but the Rattlesnake's reputation is known far and wide, and the only man I can get to change with you is the dresser on Bichat Annex. He's lonely all by himself there, way out at the end of the hospital with forty old witches for company, enjoying their Sabbath every day. And the building is an old temporary barracks at least thirty years old. The only advantage is the Sister: ugly as sin, but a good sport. We're sure to get on all right with her."

The next morning it was raining, and the sky was gray and lowering. We found the Annex surrounded by some sodden shrubs, back of the hospital, in the corner of a muddy yard. It seemed to be floating precariously in this yard, like an unseaworthy old ark, which might soon sink completely. Put up in a hurry to house the victims of some long-past epidemic, the poor old barracks would not have been out of place in the Slum, and doubtless in due course it would be pulled down or burned. Meanwhile the unsightly assemblage of rotting wood, the squares of plaster blackened by the rain, made the neighboring buildings, with their old walls of solid stone, seem reassuring and almost majestic by comparison. I began to feel a slight regret for the Pozzi Ward, and Paul looked at me sardonically.

"Come on, Jean. Don't you like our new harem? If you're worried about the outside, wait till you see what it's like inside. And when you smell it—you've been in the monkey house?"

We went inside. A double row of beds was concealed by a screen; but even before we had gone past the screen, a shrill garrulous racket of shrill gossipy voices met our ears. Clearly it was a women's ward.

As soon as she saw us, Sister Maurice (described by Paul as the ward's chief asset) waddled down between the beds to meet us. She looked like a majestic Roman amphora, with the sturdy linen of her apron nearly splitting at the seams. Her ankles were still slender, but her huge calves were encased, corset-wise, in curious high black boots laced most of the way up her leg. Paul had not exaggerated when he told us our new Sister was ugly. From close up she appeared to have a moustache and only one eye; but she was smiling, which was a notable change from our late unlamented Rattlesnake.

She at once showed us round the ward. The windows were small and let little daylight through. The walls and ceiling had

320

recently received a fresh coat of paint, but already new stains had filtered through almost everywhere from countless cracks and gutters. The equipment seemed lamentable: from old-fashioned stretcher-beds to instruments which had lost all their nickel, and enamel trays corroded by permanganate, it probably represented the discards from other wings of the hospital. As for the patients, they clearly included all those who had proved an encumbrance to the other wards: old chronics waiting to be placed in a home, women who had had abortions, uninteresting gynaecological cases—a depressing collection to find between these sinister four walls.

Paul, however, did not allow the sight to depress him. Five minutes later, his sleeves turned up and a forceps in his hand, he was already bending over a stomach and drawing gently on the swabs, which came away eventually to expose the bottom of a deep wound.

An orderly entered, bringing on a trolley a woman fresh from the operating room, who had not yet come round. He put her down on the bed, and Sister Maurice left us in order to look after the patient. She remained at the bedside, patting the blue cheek, wiping spittle from the corner of the lips, while the woman began the long process of awakening, groaning unconsciously from a pain which was still muffled and remote like steps in the fog. The long sighs gradually became stammering words, scraps of sentences, inconsequent shouts and entreaties. The ward just then was momentarily silent, and those who had been on the table already must have been disagreeably reminded of their own experiences. All of them had turned towards the moaning patient just coming round, and seemed to be waiting expectantly for something. She began to murmur again and again, as if part of a chorus: "Alfred, Jeannot, Dédé."

Her neighbor remarked in a disappointed voice: "That's her husband and children." The ward was evidently hoping for intimate revelations of a more picturesque nature, for another patient added: "I say, Eleven, do you remember the last Mme. 5 who never stopped crying 'I love you, my Loulou' when she was coming round? How we laughed when someone saw the data on her card, which showed her husband was called Gustave!"

"People always say far too much when they're coming round," said Eleven sententiously. "They ought to be more careful . . ."

"Well, do you want to know something? Her neighbor, Mme. 6, who went out two days later, copied the address from her card, and I wouldn't be at all surprised if her Gustave hadn't received a nice little anonymous letter since then."

As on the doorsteps of suburban houses on a summer evening, idle chatter and catty gossip started up all down the long line of beds. Meanwhile the patient gradually opened bewildered eyes on a queer, bursting, dizzy world, where everything assumed unfamiliar shapes and shades and dimensions: the walls, ceilings, windows, and also the big ungainly Sister watching patiently over this difficult moment of rebirth.

After that Marianne and I walked round the ward together, and the experience filled me with dismay. The tongues of these old women never seemed to stop wagging, and their spleen was equally inexhaustible. They were crafty, selfish, malicious and inquisitive, complaining about everything. They complained about the treatment they were given or not given, the quality and quantity of the food, the fact that there weren't enough nurses to come running at their beck and call, and the cheek of the younger women in the ward

I examined many cases of metritis, with horrible discharges issuing from the vulva; and I became very familiar with the disease known as Bartholinitis, after its discoverer—an inflammation of glands of the uterus. One corner of the ward seemed to be reserved for self-abortionists, who usually arrived in tears but quickly became arrogant again as soon as their "little tadpole" had been completely scoured away. Their average mental age must have been about ten, and quarrels, rivalries, and feuds seemed to occupy their whole horizon, as if their chief motive in wishing to regain a little strength was to have a better chance of cheating each other.

The atmosphere was certainly very different from a men's

ward, where things usually go much more smoothly, but this I would not have minded, had I not sensed among all these women a distinct hostility to Marianne. As soon as we came in they looked at her with baleful curiosity, and since then they had gone on whispering derisive comments every time we passed.

Our chief consolation for having left Pozzi was in Sister Maurice's friendly smile. She was a simple workingclass woman who had slowly reached her present position through years of conscientiousness and devotion. Whereas Pozzi Ward, with the administrative perfection secured there by Sister Limagnac, was evidently a credit to the hospital, it was not difficult to guess why the Medical Superintendent had entrusted this deplorable annex to Sister Maurice. So undecorative a Sister was to be stowed away with all the oldest equipment, in the remotest corner possible. It was certainly a shock when you first met the one-eyed Sister with the moustache and big shiny nose; yet the expression in the wide weather-beaten face carried a wealth of genuine kindness, rough and unsentimental. Her shoulders were squat but sturdy, bearing patiently the burden of responsibility and much suffering; and the big hands had a gentle touch which did not fail however painful the wound they were dressing. Altogether it was not long before you completely forgot about Sister Maurice's superficial ugliness.

Two days after our arrival on the Annex, Paul got flu, and told me he was going to stay in bed for the next few days. Reduced to my own resources, I was all morning changing the necessary dressings, and Sister Maurice, anxious to help me, asked Marianne to replace her at the bed of a woman who had just come back from the theatre. Marianne settled down by the bed, and I could see her from a distance holding the hiccoughing head over a receiver, and wiping away vomit from the woman's mouth and cheeks. The next day Marianne went to other beds to perform the same job with her usual imperturbable patience.

There could have been no surer way of winning these women's confidence and liking, and if she had planned her behavior, it would certainly have been a masterstroke. None of the patients whom she watched coming round from the theatre could forget the radiant face bent over them with its gentle and comforting smile. In the following days, when they were once more in pain, it was they who waited eagerly for the student's arrival. Marianne would stop and chat, listening to the patient's whispered confidences about how her husband drank and her elder daughter had gone wrong. They were not the sort of confidences which could be offered to the woman in the next bed.

Coming out of the hospital, full of animation and pink with emotion, Marianne told me all her discoveries of the morning. She took her role very seriously. "Oh, Jean," she exclaimed, "these women used to terrify me at first. But now I know them better, I really like them! You only need to look hard enough and you find something good in everyone. I do anyhow. I find something likable in all my patients. They only get difficult because they've suffered so much."

She said "my patients" in a very solemn voice, and I felt like laughing at this romantic lass, little more than a schoolgirl, talking to patients with the ardor she must have shown not so many years ago in playing with her dolls. Her faith in the goodness of human nature was very touching, but I thought it might breed all manner of disappointments for her future hospital career. My own observations were far less optimistic; on the contrary they revealed to me that insofar as the Annex patients were in pain and wrapped up in their complaint, their malice lost a little of its virulence; directly they were cured, it returned to its full strength.

The case of No. 18 was particularly depressing. She looked like a cantankerous old witch, and after twenty years both the suffering and the malice had become an acquired taste she could not do without. When cured she was no less aggressive; if anything more so. For several days before her operation the old woman had been screaming with pain almost without stopping; during any intervals she had abused the rest of the ward and the whole of the hospital staff with impartial fury. She had been operated on by Dr. Legendre, the Chief's assistant, and had come round, astonished to feel no more pain.

We expected her to relax, and begin to enjoy life again; we

also supposed she would be a more agreeable person. But Sister Maurice, coming up soon afterwards, received a volley of the grossest insults, and after that the woman turned on her neighbors once more. It was as if her pain had been with her so long, a shattering but familiar figure, that it became as necessary to her as oxygen to her lungs. For twenty years she had known spasms and storms of pain; finding health again, the greatest gift of which is silence, perhaps she was suddenly terrified by its monotonous calm. This at least was what I tried to suggest to Marianne, who found the woman's reaction very puzzling. But Marianne remained unconvinced by this explanation and I am afraid it rather upset her. She consoled herself by telling me in the lunch hour all the involved stories she had heard during the morning from the mouths of the patients, to which I should never have had the time to listen myself.

She told me about the diminutive Mme. Lolotte who for me was just a cranky old lady, bored away from her own fireside, her cat and her canary. She had come into the ward with senile gangrene, and it had seemed likely her leg would have to be amputated. Dr. Legendre had succeeded in saving it, however, and now that the leg was pink and fairly healthy once more, she was determined to leave the hospital before the leg was completely cured. I reasoned with her, but in vain; and I considered this an example of absurd senile obstinacy.

After chatting with her on several mornings, Marianne supplied me with quite a different story. Mme. Lolotte had protégés in different parts of Paris, helpless old men starving in garrets or rooms in sinister mews. She was about the only person aware of their existence. When the gangrene appeared on her big toe she had continued her errands on their behalf; never by bus, for that was too expensive, but always trotting along mouse-like on the pavements, for this cost nothing. At night too she had paced endlessly to and fro in her room until the dawn, because when she was lying down the pain of the spreading gangrene became unendurable. One morning her neighbors had found her unconscious on the floor, the leg a dark blue. When Dr. Legendre promised to cure her without amputating, I saw Mme.

Lolotte look at her lean legs and feel them greedily; then she began to weep great tears of joy—as I thought then, the joy of selfish relief. I was wrong. She was weeping for her aged protégés; now it was for them she wished to be discharged from the hospital, though not yet properly cured. Somehow she could draw on reserves of courage sufficient to make her forget what she had been through and be ready to start working for them again. Full of enthusiasm, Marianne added:

"Her neighbor, you know the one I mean, the great lump of a woman who's always complaining, said something magnificent this morning. Mme. Lolotte was trying to encourage her, and she answered: 'Oh, it's all so easy for you. You can call the angels by their Christian names.'"

For several days the patient in No. 23 bed had been medically a very ordinary case: a cancer, dying from a relapse localized in the vertebral column. A bone graft made eight months earlier had allowed her life to be prolonged till now. There was nothing further to be tried, and as she was in terrible pain everything was done to ease her last days with morphia. Marianne told me about this woman, and I knew now that she had not only accepted her death, but chosen it deliberately for the sake of her three small children.

Eight months earlier she had come here begging for an operation. When she was standing, her vertebral cancer gave her such agony that a strong dose of morphia could hardly assuage it any longer. When she was lying down she suffered less, and could hope to go on living several months longer. But the children needed her, so she wanted an operation which would let her stay on her feet right to the end. She would only lie down for good when it was time to die. Already she was very weak, and it seemed madness to operate. But the surgeon decided he had not the right to refuse her this wish, so he consolidated her back by grafting a bone taken from her leg. A week afterwards she got up and felt no more pain. Ten days later she had gone back home, knowing that in six months, or eight at most with luck, before the graft had even had time to take, the wonderful apparent miracle would inevitably be over.

326

It was over now, and she was back in the hospital to die. Thus enlightened by Marianne, I stopped more often at the bed of this dying woman, worn and shrunken, who had insisted on playing her role of mother to the uttermost limits of her strength, and had now completed her earthly task.

Marianne continued to conquer the ward in the same way, but she was still frightened by one patient, the coarsest and most repulsive of all. This was a big woman of forty-five, with drooping breasts, and a swollen face rendered more hideous by a trace of coquetry. The makeup on that flabby face was laid on in huge aggressive patches, and since her stay in the hospital her peroxide hair had been showing roots of a very uncertain color.

This patient's card carried a somewhat outlandish word for the diagnosis, and before this case I had never seen a kraurosis, and knew nothing whatever about the complaint. The first morning she came in, when the three of us went round the ward together we stopped to examine her. When I reached the lower part of her stomach Paul muttered aside: "Good God, it looks just like a dead mussel." This described it exactly: the pubis was without hair, and the skin over her genitals had taken on the white-gray, scaly look of an old seashell. It was like a scar, pale and leprous, between her pink fat thighs. As Marianne was looking on, I wanted to stop the examination there and go on to the next patient, but Paul, always curious, had already taken up a rubber finger-stall. As soon as he began to use this, the woman started crying out in such agony that he brought it out quickly. It was all red with blood.

When Jouvet, the interne, came round a little later on, Paul at once asked him for further details about this unusual illness. Jouvet told us that the sexual organs had become atrophied and withered in this way through an insufficiency in the ovaries connected with the menopause. A cure, he said, was more or less impossible. As for the bleeding sore, he explained that Paul, in using the finger-stall, had reopened a new scar formed over the pathway which the woman's partner had gradually cut right

327

into the flesh, to make up for the progressive disappearance of a genuine sexual opening.

"Queer sort of emergency entrance," remarked Paul, breaking an embarrassed silence. "What a gate-crasher!"

Marianne was silent and looked rather pale. I too felt disgusted, thinking of the number of rapings, filthy with blood, which it must have needed to open this passage, and of the brute who could have forced the wretched woman in this way.

In the next few days Paul was given the task of looking after the kraurosis, and I went by this patient's bed rather quickly; I noticed that Marianne too did not like stopping there long. But one morning while I was doing dressings, I saw her go up to the bed; the woman looked surprised and somewhat embarrassed, but the ice was obviously broken.

"It's unfair, Jean," she said as we were coming out of the hospital, "the way we've been leaving that woman alone. One has no right to pick and choose among patients. She needs sympathy as much as the rest, and perhaps even more."

"Your conversations with the patients are all very fine, my girl," said Paul, "but take care you don't overdo it. You hardly seem to do anything else these days. At this rate you're more likely to end up as a nun than a doctor."

"I can't help it," she answered, "it's something stronger than me. When I was little, and I saw another girl being punished and then crying in a corner, I always wanted to run up and console her."

The next morning and the mornings after that, she continued her good work, and gradually she came to spend longer and longer with her new "problem child."

A few days later we were just leaving the Annex as visiting hours were starting, when we saw coming in with the stream of relatives a huge and very debauched-looking man, already graying, his face purplish with alcohol. "The perfect pimp," exclaimed Paul under his breath, "the very prototype of all professional panders."

With superb condescension, the man walked up towards the bed of the patient with kraurosis. For the love of this man she had gone through agonies for months, and now he bent patronizingly over her while she gazed up at him adoringly. What incredible forms love can take! For all her wretchedness and unsightliness, this woman gave a striking impression of sheer happiness, merely by the way she looked up towards the sordid face of her god.

In the courtyard Marianne walked a few yards in silence and then, with an air of abrupt decision, put her hand on my arm like a guilty little girl, and said: "I wasn't wrong, Jean, was I? It was I who wrote to that man. She loves him but they aren't married. Since she was like that and had so much pain he had taken another mistress. To make him come I promised in my letter that she would soon be cured."

Cure a kraurosis? I started in amazement. This disease had been declared more or less incurable, not only by Jouvet but in a textbook on gynaecology I had read. Marianne's romanticism had really gone too far this time, and I began to feel my temper rising when she started pleading, "Please, Jean, please. Do ask Dr. Legendre to see her. Perhaps he'll find a way. She must be cured, we *must* cure all the patients. When the pain goes their characters improve too. I had proof of that only this morning. Today for the first time the old lady in No. 13 smiled at me instead of abusing me. You see what it is, she's getting the poison out of her system."

She smiled to coax a promise out of me, and this smile of extreme youth, making the corner of her lips quiver slightly, was accentuated by the burning sincerity of her expression. I could read there the wild obstinacy of youth, made up half of ignorance, half of defiance. I must have had much the same expression on my face a year ago when I looked at the poor wretch who was dying of Oslerian endocarditis.

She had said "*We* must try and cure" in such a passionate voice that I no longer thought of scolding her or laughing at her. The miracle she asked for was impossible, but her romantic zeal was far from being completely useless. Certainly she could not yet understand much about all these dramas, but thanks to her, a spectator full of goodwill and compassion, none of these

329

unhappy actors was without an audience. She would catch their appeals and complaints and blasphemies; and the pathetic little melodies of love as well. Bent over all these women, she made them a gift more precious than the relief of their pain. Merely by her willingness to listen to them with infinite patience, she gave these unfortunates the illusion of being no longer forgotten.

As I did not reply immediately, she put on a doleful expression. To restore her smile, I said very quickly: "I'll show the woman to Dr. Legendre tomorrow morning."

"After all, why not?" commented Paul. "It's extremely natural that on the request of a very respectable young lady, two very high-minded young men should make wholehearted efforts to support prostitution and encourage concubinage. So let us cure this distinguished member of our oldest profession as our number one priority. After that, my dear young nun, let us unite once more this handsome couple, whom the good Lord so carelessly forgot to bless."

Standing on the edge of the pavement with his hands joined together and an expression of solemnity on his face, Paul seemed ready to officiate at a wedding ceremony. For a moment Marianne wondered whether to be annoyed; then she gave in, and laughed a little, but still rather sadly.

Chapter 4

FOR TWO DAYS Marianne reminded me repeatedly of my promise about the kraurosis case. No better opportunity presenting itself, I was eventually obliged to call Dr. Legendre to the Annex—for a case which I believed to be both without clinical interest and unresponsive to any treatment.

Legendre came. I showed him the patient very bashfully, ready to apologize at the slightest remark. I was staggered to hear him say: "You did well to call me. It's a very interesting business and I'll tell you why. They're beginning to talk a lot now about synthetic folliculin, which is incomparably more powerful than the former ovary extracts. This will be a good opportunity for trying it out; it should provide some useful data. Please take great care to note down all that you observe. Very interesting the whole thing, very interesting. . . ."

Then he turned the collar of his blue cloak up again. Before leaving me he added: "I'll be away for ten days, I'm attending a medical congress in London. Remind me about this patient as soon as I get back."

Marianne was radiant, and as soon as he had disappeared Paul summed up: "Splendid. Everyone's happy in this affair. Legendre has had an idea; you, Jean, didn't make a fool of yourself. The patient may perhaps be cured, and Marianne's folly may very likely contribute to the advancement of medical science. . . ."

A few days later, going round the patients on my arrival, I saw that the woman with cancer of the vertebrae was dying,

331

and Sister Maurice told me that the chaplain had been with her this morning.

There were a few random and dusty notices posted in the corridors which declared the complete liberty of worship among the patients. But this apart, I should scarcely before now have guessed at the presence of a chaplain in the hospital at all. I wondered vaguely what he was like, and found it hard to imagine him. Was he a young priest with a missionary's burning ardor, bending anxiously over souls more inclined to blasphemy than prayer; or was he some gentle old man with the resignation of one who had seen so many people die? The grandeur of the serene benediction, *"Pax huc domi,"* would surely seem a mockery in this ward, of all places. The patients might think for a moment about how they would one day die, but very soon they were all back at their self-centered, scandal-mongering buzzing which the dying patient could no longer hear.

I stayed for a moment looking at the face of the woman with cancer, but when I saw her neighbors watching me, I pretended to be feeling her pulse, almost automatically trying to hide any stirrings of emotion before them. Having left me alone there, Sister returned a few minutes later with a syringe and ampule. The only thing to do for the patient now was to soften her agony, give her the charity of her last and perhaps also her first deep peace on earth. As I was going away Sister raised the sheet, and found under the yellow skin a piece of flesh in which to stick the needle.

She died that evening, and next morning I found a new patient in her place who had had one arm amputated. As soon as I reached her bed she asked me: "Will Dr. Legendre be making his round soon?"

I was taken aback by the really terrifying avidity with which she hung on my reply. When I told her that Dr. Legendre would be in England for another week, she looked utterly despairing. She told me she had come here in the hope that he would operate on her immediately, and she burst into a voluble and confused lament of which I could understand nothing. I had a great deal of trouble to get her to tell her story in an orderly fashion.

332

Ten months earlier she had had her hand and forearm amputated following a motor accident. Since coming round from the operation she had continued to suffer from the missing hand and forearm as intensely as at the actual second when they had been crushed by the wheel; she still felt the cracking and crushing of her bones and she told me she still had the sense of gravel penetrating beneath her nails.

I was extremely puzzled. I had already seen two cases of hallucinations of pain surviving a long time after the operation in the stump of an amputated limb. But this hallucination of reliving the moment of the accident was something far more extraordinary, quite passing my understanding. That the patient suffered was incontestable, it was obvious from the utter exhaustion of her face. But it was almost incredible that the past pain should persist as intensely as she described it in a limb no longer there. Was it really posible that she had not slept for months for more than a few seconds at a time? She told me that drugs were little help, she began to suffer again almost at once. I had the impression that to gain my sympathy she was "putting it on" a bit. Paul thought so too.

A little later Marianne made her own personal "round." Coming to the bed of the amputation case, she stopped and talked to the patient for a long time. When she rejoined us Paul said to her with a laugh: "Well, Marianne, I hope ministering angels get good overtime rates. If amputated people are going to start suffering in their missing limbs, we shall soon have to repair mechanical arms and wooden legs."

Marianne did not like this joking. "Oh Paul," she cried, "how can you possibly joke about it? Sister Maurice went through the woman's bag on her arrival, pretending to make an inventory. She found four tubes of veronal hidden there, more than enough for the woman to kill herself. If she commits suicide would it be for her own enjoyment? If she pleads for an operation, will that too be for her own pleasure? According to you she must have a very strong wish to suffer."

"Perhaps she's a masochist," suggested Paul tactlessly.

"No, really, that's going too far." I could see that Marianne was seriously angry. "You can be pretty aggravating sometimes, Paul, but I thought at least you had a heart. If you're going to be so hypocritical or cynical about any patient who happens to be difficult to cure, you'd be more honest to give up the idea of becoming a doctor right away. Otherwise I hope you're kept awake at night sometime seeing the reproachful faces of all the patients you've sneered at."

Under this storm Paul assumed a contrite attitude, and said in a humble voice: "Forgive me, O Sister of Mercy, for I have grievously sinned."

Marianne looked at her watch and dashed off, crying: "The Chief's lecture is beginning."

Immediately she had gone Paul exchanged his submissive expression for one of enthusiasm: "My God, did I get into hot water! No two ways about it, what a girl, our Marianne."

Calming down slightly, he remarked: "Well, that's enough work for one morning. I'm off for a game of billiards. I've just got to rest before old Pa Galleron's physiology this afternoon. The old blighter's got such a way with him you find you can't even stop listening. And working morning *and* evening is far too much for me in my delicate condition—at least judging how tired it makes me."

A little later on two neurologists, having been told about it by the interne, came to see the amputation case. They began the long examination again, discussed the case and summed up: "Interesting data there for anyone doing research on the memory. We must let Debel know about it."

The patient tried to ask them what they thought of her case. Carried away by the interest of their discussion, they hardly deigned to answer her, and left her with a vague: "Please don't worry, madame, you will be looked after."

I went with them to the door to get their opinion. Both of them confessed themselves unable to explain this phantom pain or say much about its treatment; they even seemed slightly skeptical about its reality. As they were specialists, I was secretly flattered to have formed the same impression on my own.

334

The physiology lecture-hall was a large amphitheatre with tiers of very rudimentary seats on three sides. The urine of mice and dogs and rabbits supplied the chief ingredient in its normal smell, as traditional as the uproar with which every session taken by M. Galleron was accustomed to end.

Galleron was the practical demonstrator whose effectiveness in gaining attention Paul had mentioned this morning. His nose was shiny, his moustache drooped, and his cheeks were blotched with scarlet. As he sat there near the experiment table, watching the seats emptying, the whole of his face seemed to wrinkle with a mischievous and paternal joy. His contemporaries had long been professors with various distinctions and chairs, treading the normal road as they cultivated their personal prestige. Galleron's prestige rested securely on the affection of his students, through which he succeeded in instilling into us a fair knowledge of physiology. His success in this respect, however, must have been less resounding in the Dean's ears than the singing and hilarity and general rowdiness of his physiology lectures; and he was accordingly passed by as far as promotion went in favor of others more versed in university intrigues, though their lectures might be very sparsely attended. So for twenty-five years he had remained senior demonstrator in practical physiology at a monthly salary of fifteen hundred francs. Luckily the old man, who was a bachelor, seemed to prefer our affection and scurrilous songs to advancement and money. He shared in fact the unanimous opinion held by the Dean, his own contemporaries, and countless generations of students, to the effect that all was very well as it was; doubtless he would be in this modest "permanent" position till he retired.

A particularly noisy session had just finished. On arriving we had noticed a stranger sitting near the door, a middle-aged lady with a long and rather horselike face, who eyed us with evident hostility. M. Galleron turned to look at her now and then, his eyes twinkling with an immense inner jubilation. When we were all in our places he introduced the unknown lady as a representative of the Anti-Vivisection League making an official inspection.

335

He proceeded to comment on this annual visit in a tone of ironical politeness.

"Last year you were short of cadavers to dissect because the so-called humanitarian societies reclaimed all bodies left in hospitals. This year the Laboratory is short of dogs because the anti-vivisectionists redeem them from the pounds. Sentimentalists are sometimes not very consistent, it seems to me. There's never enough money to build adequate numbers of day nurseries, but always enough to buy up stray bow-wows."

Our visitor listened to this preamble with the calm, almost unheeding expression of a martyr at the circus delivered up to wild beasts or populace. At the end of it she gave a short laugh to convey her contempt for such stupidity and disregard of logic. "Horse laugh as well as horse face," observed Paul, and began braying and neighing. This was the signal for general uproar, which Galleron allowed to subside in its own good time. He then told an attendant to fetch one of the laboratory dogs.

When the attendant returned with the animal, it ran up to Galleron as soon as it saw him, and nuzzled itself joyfully against his legs.

"Last year," continued the demonstrator, "you were so short of cadavers you had to dissect them right down to the bone. This year we're still shorter of dogs. Every time my attendant goes to the lost dogs' home, he comes back saying: 'I've only been able to get you one. Have to make it last.' Thanks to our anti-vivisectionist friends we can no longer kill the animals mercifully at the end of an experiment. Oh no—we now have to keep a really pitiful menagerie in our kennels. They creep along on their stomachs and lick their stitches, howling and whining between fits of epilepsy. Economy! Economy! We can economize on the animals, we can anaesthetize them during experiments, but how can we make economies in the pain they suffer between experiments?"

He stroked the dog's head with his hand, and the animal, thus caressed, gave little barks of pleasure.

"Here's Blackie," he said. "Blackie has been used for a whole

336

series of artery experiments. He has as many scars as an old soldier. Four or five times I've had him put on the table, and each time I've had to endure his look full of crushing and undeserved confidence. You know the way a dog can look at you with boundless trust in his eyes, and you have to turn your own eyes away to stop yourself feeling pity. One day, just as I was going to tie him down for a new experiment, he licked my hand. Experimenters are not all sadistic brutes, and I don't find it particularly amusing to sacrifice a dog which has just licked my hand. Blackie had his life saved then; but the attendant might have thought me a freak or a lunatic, so I gave the poor creature a fistula in the stomach. In due course we shall be studying Pavlov's experiments and conditioned reflexes. You will see Blackie earning his honorable retirement by secreting gastric juices each time a green flame is lighted in front of him."

M. Galleron had gradually lost his tone of flippant irony, and he continued in a voice charged with deep emotion:

"And that's the way of the world. Nobody has ever been able to stop useless massacres which destroy men's bodies without anaesthetic, yet sentimental souls would like to prevent experiments on anaesthetized animals, although the experiments are necessary and quite irreplaceable in the progress of science. All our values have been reversed in this age of false sentimentality and pseudo-humanitarianism. If you think I have used an unfair antithesis to demonstrate the point, please listen to this. A few years ago they had prepared an experimental explosion at the military camp of La Courtine. Some dogs had been tied up some distance away so that the effects of blast on their organisms could be studied. Journalists in search of a good scandal, and high-minded people with plenty of crocodile tears, started protesting, and the dogs were withdrawn. They didn't dare put men in the dogs' places. But do not let us despair. In the next war the guineapigs will be there all right, and you will be there too, my young friends. *You* will be used for all the experiments which the La Courtine animals were spared. This time there will be no journalists or other sensitive souls to come to your rescue."

Leaning on the table, M. Galleron breathed hard amidst a

337

tense silence. After a minute's pause, he seemed to have recovered his composure, and said in normal tones: "Today we shall be studying the conditioned reflex."

The session ended an hour later with a test of our knowledge. Barrière, one of the Burgundy boys, was called to the blackboard, and displayed abysmal ignorance. Galleron turned an apoplectic violet once more, and amidst applause from the audience treated the miscreant to a volley of abuse: "You moronic dunder-headed blithering idiot, whatever made you think you could ever become a doctor? If you ever manage to qualify, which I very much doubt, you'll kill your patients off en masse through sheer stupidity. You can't answer a single question, and you don't get a mark from me, you complete cretin, you. What are you?"

"A complete cretin, sir," said Barrière humbly. "Right," said Galleron, "a cretin gets no marks. Go back to your seat, and the whole class is dismissed." But hubbub broke out again as the hall began to plead for the culprit and debate the severity of the sentence, which was thereupon maintained, increased, and finally commuted. After this amnesty, in gratitude the company gave a spirited rendering of *The Song of Père Galleron*," to the tune of the well-known *Père Dupanloup*. Our hero listened with evident pleasure.

Barrière, reassured about his marks, rejoined the other four Burgundians complacently, and Jeannel proposed at once that exercise of a different type would be appreciated: "How about doing a little practical vinology on a bottle of Juliénas?"

Paul came up just then and started taking Barrière violently to task: "Aren't you ashamed of being so damn stupid and upsetting a nice old fellow like Galleron? Can't you show any interest in physiology? Is it too complicated for your wretched little Burgundian beetlebrain?"

Barrière found this indignation so extravagant coming from Paul that he stood there for a moment with his mouth open before saying: "Good God, Chav, that from you of all people. I was only having a quiet doze. You don't object to that, do you?"

338

"I strongly object to your being stupider than you can help. And when Galleron has been nearly killing himself trying to explain things to us, I consider it damn rude for you to expose your utter ignorance, so just look out. Either you give proper answers in the next test we get, or between us two there'll be no holds barred, Barrière, my boy. But *please* don't think I'm trying to influence you, of course you're perfectly free to do what you like."

"Keep calm," retorted the rebuked one, "and please observe how well I've grasped the point of today's demonstrations. The mere word Juliénas has brought saliva to my mouth. Short of a gastric fistula, I can't very well exteriorize the phenomenon for you as Blackie did. But I can quite clearly feel my stomach busy secreting, according to Pavlov's rules. I'm sure you'll find, Chav, that you're conditioned to Juliénas just as much as I am."

Paul clicked his tongue and seemed to be listening attentively to his own inside. Then he answered: "Definitely wine is the only thing, even in physiology, to give you a glimmer of intelligence, Barri. You're quite right, I *am* conditioned."

I did not hear the rest as we were nearing the door and quite near me I recognized Julot's voice, as suave as ever, his conscience completely clear as usual, not to say transparent. He joined me, and as he seemed to want to talk, I gave an anxious glance at my watch. Julot saw this look and said: "Oh, of course, you're a very busy young man. Your beautiful blonde. . . ."

My beautiful blonde! All my friends and acquaintances at the school, even those who did not know each other, now regularly referred to Marianne in this way. Julot added with a satyrlike wink: "Congratulations. You're on to a good thing. There's a piece I wouldn't at all mind sleeping with myself."

Julot and Marianne—the very idea was so disgusting that although I had no wish to discuss my affairs with Julot, I could not restrain an irritable: "She's not that sort of girl."

"Oh, I beg your pardon, I'm sure. Just good comrades? Ideal friendship, platonic love, or is it a mystic union with the banns put up in Heaven? And you've never felt like taking just one bite at the cherry? If you have, don't forget what Oscar Wilde

339

said: The best way of stopping temptation is to give in to it."

He gave a cynical chuckle. I felt like hitting him. Short of that, and without great hopes of success, I tried to annoy him.

"All women are not pros. I gladly yield you the high pleasure of running after them all like a dog, sniffing every bitch you come to."

"Well, you *are* in a state, poor chap. You should have announced right away that you were waiting for your wedding night. As to being like a dog, I'm afraid that's more your condition than mine."

"What do you mean?"

"Seems obvious to me. Remember what we were told just now about Pavlov's dogs? You're so conditioned it's painful to look at you. In five minutes you've glanced anxiously at your watch three times, and at the fourth stroke of four o'clock your secretions will be in full flood on seeing your blonde. Blackie only obeyed the green light. I suppose you're superior to him simply because you've multiplied your conditioned reflexes in a thousand absurd ways: the right eye bigger than the left, the mole under the chin, the color of the beloved's hair, the taste of her lipstick, and a lot more I don't know about. As for me, I'm not conditioned, I'm free."

"Free my foot. You can't make love except with whores."

"Correct. Only you are conditioned to a single predetermined woman, and I am conditioned to a type of woman drawn from several million examples the world contains. Believe me, Jean Nérac, if you don't want to have any regrets, sleep with your blonde straight away and then pass on quickly to a brunette. Try it out with all colors, otherwise you haven't a chance, you're done for. Psychology, sexology, anthropology, all go to prove unanimously that man is a natural polygamist. But you, poor sap, are busy falling into the reflex of monogamy. Beware of the consequences. It's now two minutes to four, so on your mark, get set, go. Sleep with her immediately, or else get rid of her. . . ."

We had come out onto the street. On the edge of the pavement, Julot tapped me on the shoulder to point out a car just starting up. Inside it I saw our classmate, Philippon, with a pretty redhead who was powdering her nose.

"Look at Philippon. He's seen the light. *He's* not conditioned in love. That makes his third girl friend since the beginning of term: a blonde, a brunette, and a redhead. With the aid of dyes he'll soon have all the colors of the rainbow, and infrared and ultraviolet too. Remember the Bohn law: monotony weakens vital activities, and leads human beings more or less rapidly to death. To stay young and really live, change is absolutely essential. Drop all your romantic literature, and learn something from your physiological lectures."

Julot departed, laughing maliciously, delighted at shocking me.

Marianne was waiting for me back in the hall, where students eyed her with considerable interest. Reaching the library, we found it full, and with some difficulty discovered two places a long way from our usual corner, opposite two students who stared at us and whispered their impressions to one another. I was already rather on edge from the discussion with Julot, and the knowing airs of our two neighbors irritated me greatly. Already conditioned to jealousy, Julot would certainly have taken malicious pleasure in pointing out.

It was very hot, and Marianne had taken off her coat. She was wearing a very light and close-fitting woolen jumper. Opposite us the two students looked at her breasts and then glanced at me, continuing their whispering. Like Julot, like all those who saw us walking familiarly near each other, they must have said to themselves when we arrived: *"He's* on to a good thing." Their eyes continued to express this sentiment very forcibly. My irritated jealousy turned to a dull discomfort. For weeks I had worked with Marianne every day; she had been always near me, and we had behaved like an affectionate brother and sister. Now I caught myself looking at her with other eyes.

Sometimes in the early mornings I had been with her to an indoor swimming pool, a pleasure I had been introduced to by François Surel, and which with Marianne became a sheer delight.

341

But even when I saw her in her bathing dress, with her breasts gently protruding, her hair gathered up tightly in the bathing cap, walking so like a child in her bare feet, her slender legs quivering on the diving board—even then I had looked beyond such details to the joy she took in these simple pleasures. But now in this library I followed for a moment the exact lines of her breasts, the curve of her neck, the round of her shoulder, all the seductive sensuous charm which her young body unwittingly expressed. I had to make an effort to look away and return my eyes to the book in front of me.

I had deliberately kept our relationship on a basis of affectionate friendship. The fiery sword should remain between us, eliminating anything sordid. If anyone had asked me why, I might well have pretended to subtle calculations of cynical pleasure. Yes, I could have posed as a refined hedonist, enjoying the slowness of my preparations, relishing the latent tension between us, my patient discoveries, and the gradual accretion of desire.

But inside I knew this was all false, that I was still the adolescent, naïvely hoping for a miracle with each amorous adventure, real or dreamed. My initiation with Mado had lacked mystery, and my desires had been unappeased in the affair with Josette, pale phantom without substance. But now the miracle had suddenly taken place, and I was numbed by the vistas of happiness opening up for me daily. What Marianne had given me already was so wonderful that I forgot about her body even more easily than I had done with Josette. I knew Marianne belonged to me, and no kisses or physical acts were needed to prove it.

Suddenly she raised her head and turned it towards me. So that despite the presence of others she could show our intimacy without speech, she smiled at me. It was a smile which made my heart thrill with ecstatic bliss, as if I had just been entrusted with the helpless body of a newborn babe and must defend it against attack from all sides. Temperamentally timid and pacific, I felt ready for a fight at the slightest provoking look from anyone.

342

But the two students' chairs were empty, and the library was about to close.

For some time I had been meaning to take Marianne to a Russian film which I had already seen, and this seemed a good night for it. We ate first at a little Russian restaurant, so as to create the appropriate atmosphere and prepare ourselves for the Slav mentality.

The program had begun when we reached the cinema. I took two seats in the orchestra, and was very surprised when the usherette pushed us into a box. "This way please, you'll be more comfortable there," she explained with a knowing wink, holding out her hand in obvious expectation of a tip. It was clearly a valuable service which she believed herself to be rendering us. I gave her a few francs.

When we were a little used to the darkness, the hall appeared almost empty, and judging by the noise and laughter I heard through the thin partitions of neighboring boxes, most couples were using the place as substitute for a small hotel. Marianne seemed to notice nothing, and was already looking at the screen. Every time one of the brighter shots threw a shaft of light into our cubbyhole, I watched her face. Feeling herself being appraised, she would turn towards me for a moment with a smile which made her lips and teeth shine in the darkness.

From one of the neighboring boxes flashed a woman's short muffled cry, descending immediately to a sigh of pleasure. The woman had been laughing when we arrived, and doubtless her partner had just been getting going, testing her resistance by little tickling kisses on the neck. His preliminary advances had been successful, and now his companion was uttering rapturous little moans which it was impossible to avoid overhearing. I became fascinated by the sound track of the couple's caresses, and would have liked to glue my ear to the partition, to eavesdrop on each creak, each gasp.

To escape from these desires, I leaned towards Marianne, who seemed to be only interested in the screen. By her even breathing

343

I noticed that I was almost panting myself; my heart was beating in great burning waves, bringing the blood feverishly to my face. In the collusive darkness of the box I sketched a movement towards her hand. After all why shouldn't I try too, why shouldn't I take the cool hand in mine and plant my lips in her palm between the half-folded fingers? Wasn't the obstacle of our clothes sufficient barrier to remove all seriousness from an embrace? I still resisted. I set my jaw and clenched my fists so as not to want more than a light kiss, not even on the lips, a brief artificial embrace, no harm done, nothing irreparable, merely something to calm my fever and give me some release . . .

But even then I realized I was lying to myself. It was not merely taking a hand that I wanted, but to draw the hand towards me, and the arm, the shoulder, the head, the whole body. Why pretend, why try to be a saint? I had known right from the first day that my love for Marianne was not only spiritual, that I loved her in the flesh, in her body, in her living reality; that I wanted her more completely and more naked than in the half-nakedness of the swimming bath, more profoundly than in the disappointing embrace of two clothed bodies, that I wanted her beyond all shame and regret and despair.

My back was stiff against the back of the seat to hide my trembling. With my teeth clenched, my chest constricted and my heart beating thunderously, I struggled with all my strength against the temptation to come closer to Marianne. All at once the screen threw a shaft of clear light towards us and she turned to me; she saw I had never stopped looking at her for an instant. Then she made a gesture of the utmost grace, meant, I am sure, to be merely coaxing, but which at that moment stung me like a whip: she placed her hand on my cheek to make me turn my eyes towards the screen. I could not resist further, I seized that hand and pressed it to my lips, sensing its cool freshness for a flash of a second longer before being carried away by a vast desire to press all her body against me, to gather in the dazzling purity of those lips and teeth shining through the darkness.

I seized her madly in my arms, took her mouth, and crushed it to mine; she delivered it into my power with a delicious consent. Crazed and blinded, I was no longer aware who it was. These were the lips of any woman, I cared not whose, and as I bent over them I was any young male gasping with selfish sensual enjoyment, the conqueror, the god. When I threw myself back to recover my breath and see better the blur of the feminine form I had under my sway, I was still half blind, and the blood was rushing in my ears so that I could not hear. With a fierce thrill of fulfilment I felt the warm body surrender in my arms, the heart throbbing so madly that it matched the huge hammer blows of my own heart. This virgin flesh must be given no time to recover from the brutality of my embrace; before it could do so, I would seize it again and plunge it into fresh ecstasies of violence. I was bending her neck roughly downwards, when she opened her eyes and looked at me with such unforgettable innocence and generosity that it brought a cry of wonder to my lips, and instead of an impersonal phantom I suddenly recognized—Marianne.

Brought abruptly to my senses, ashamed of my brutality and my triumph, I kept her in my arms, and let the tumult stirred in both our hearts die down gradually in a long exhausted silence. She was the first to speak; as if to see me better, she gently brought nearer her lovely soft face. She looked at my lips to watch their answer at its source, and whispered: "Happy, my darling?"

It was the first time she had ever called me that, and by the very words she might have been kissing me again. After the blind violence of my embrace she offered me hers in a trembling nakedness. Her tender question was at once a prayer offered to a god, a caress given to a naughty boy, satisfaction for my hunger, the appeasement of my fury. Once more my cup of happiness was overflowing. Now I was sure this love of ours had become far more than a thing of the senses; it was so miraculously beyond the flesh and the mind and all comprehension that I felt merged with Marianne in one single being, and knew I could henceforth take her in my arms in all purity of our single heart.

345

Bending over her I murmured: "I love you, my darling. Isn't that the best way to answer your question?"

From the well of darkness in which I could scarcely distinguish her face came the voice of a woman, no longer a mere girl, giving a magical reply: "No, Jean. Better still, by silence."

So silence it was, single and complete, expressing all the words our lips could never utter. Adoring, I listened to this silence deep in both our hearts. From behind the partition came the sound of chairs being moved, little giggles, and other trivial noises starting up once more. We hardly heard this vulgar intrusion on our godlike peace. For us joy and plenitude were everywhere. The symbolic darkness hid the universe from us, and we heard the silence as something more and more exclusive, more and more radiant, leaving us supremely alone while the panting world went on forgotten all round us.

As we left the theatre she took my arm, and we walked to the Metro thinking of all that had happened. We said little in the Metro, and when we came out onto the Boulevard Jourdan near the Cité, she took my arm again in a gesture of glorious intimacy and confidence. By the light of a street lamp I looked at her, and found her suddenly sad. "Tired?" I asked.

"No," she replied, "not specially. But I'm thinking of the patient in No. 23.

"The cancer case? But she's dead. It's all over for her."

"Yes, I know, it was a merciful release for her, and of course I realize no doctor could prevent her dying; they'd done all they could for her. It's not she I'm thinking about, but the new No. 23, the woman with the amputated arm who can't sleep. It's terrible, isn't it?"

"Is it?" I asked, somewhat irritated. Why should a mere case be allowed to spoil my pleasure in this very special evening, this memorable return to the Cité? "How should I know? When you're healthy and sleep well yourself, you can't go worrying over every patient who doesn't. Besides, I mistrust people on principle who claim not to sleep. An uncle of mine, who snores

346

every night, always says his sciatica's so bad he's not slept a wink for ten years."

Marianne looked at me in reproachful surprise: "You know that's not fair, Jean. You're talking like Paul at his worst."

All the way back right till now, there had been a note of special intimacy in her voice whenever she had spoken. This had abruptly vanished, and I felt the change was quite undeserved.

I answered huffily: "Oh well, I suppose I'm just as bad as he is. Etymologically speaking, sympathy with a patient is all very well: suffering with him and all that. But between a patient and a healthy person I've always found the barrier pretty thick and solid."

I saw she was on the edge of tears, and was ashamed of my ill humor. I hastily added to console her, "But you needn't be too unhappy about the amputation case. While you were at the Chief's lecture, two neurologists saw her and decided she was exaggerating. It's very common after accidents and often connected with claims for damages."

"Oh, Jean, you're all wrong, and so are the neurologists. That woman suffers as much as she says she does, I'm sure of it. I can't explain my certainty to you, it's irrational, indefinable. I expect you'll only laugh at me and call me a sentimental schoolgirl. But I know quite definitely that tonight, at this very minute, the woman in No. 23 is desperate. She came in to be operated on at once, but Dr. Legendre isn't there, and you treat her almost as a fraud. She's left to believe her case is hopeless, that nobody is going to do anything about her or even believe in her pain. These torments have been racking her now for six months, and the pain never stops, she says; it's so complete and so limitless that she can't distinguish day from night any longer. Try to imagine that, Jean, you who sleep peacefully every night."

"Well anyhow," I said, "she's waited six months without a new operation; I imagine she can wait ten more days for Legendre's return."

347

"I wonder if she can. I wonder how much longer she'll find her pain endurable when you've taken away all her hope. I talked to Sister who may not be a great neurologist but understands her patients, and I know she's very worried about this woman. She would like to have a nurse by the bed all night, but of course there isn't enough staff for that. To understand that patient and believe her, your distinguished neurologists should try going for a mere seventy-two hours without sleep."

She was angry and had been speaking with growing excitement. When we reached the door of her hostel, she stopped and said rather abruptly: "Goodnight, Jean. Till tomorrow morning."

She left me on the boulevard, much upset. Our first quarrel, and now of all times, after this evening of pure happiness. While I went along to my hostel, I felt ready to abuse the amputation case and all the other patients for deliberately setting Marianne and me against each other. It was their fault if I couldn't understand them; and I thought of all the inept and inexact words with which they tried to express themselves when I questioned them. My own organs remained in the physiological state which is called health, but I had tried to understand the mysterious alien world of pain existing all round me. Everything in that world was subjective, individual, unknowable, elusive: a world where nothing can be seen or measured, where you risk being taken in at every turn, where the intellect seems powerless. I was always stumbling on this mystery of flesh being tortured by suffering, and I was never able to grasp it properly. I had stayed outside it, troubled but uncomprehending, sometimes skimming with naïve fingers an area of pain as if I could feel what my mind could never conceive. But the fingers had usually to be quickly withdrawn, or they merely redoubled the pain itself.

Finding that patients expressed so inadequately what they felt, I had opened my textbooks. They informed me of the existence of fulgurant, lancinating, terebrating pains, etc., etc., distinguishing up to sixty-three varieties. But this was only putting more learned words on what my patients simply called "throbbing"

348

or "smarting" or "burning" or "boring into me" or the rest of them. So I concluded that between one's own healthy flesh and the nightmarish country of pain there was a rigid frontier, and no exact science existed which could penetrate through it. It was really not my fault, I felt, nor the fault of the two neurologists, if we had failed to understand what the woman with the amputated arm felt.

Entering the Jules Ferry hostel, I still thought with irritation of the patients in the Annex: they had brought my princess out of her enchanted garden of safety and happiness, and already with their dismal faces they were making her suffer. They stood between us now like cunning, treacherous, greedy dragons. Tonight, instead of thinking of me, she would go to sleep dreaming of curing them and bringing them relief one by one. In the end an ever-widening throng of patients would stand between us, blocking all our paths.

"Yes, she killed herself during the night," said Sister Maurice. "She got up about one o'clock and put on her coat as if she were going to the W.C. She went across the yard, walked up the big staircase which leads to the attic wards, and jumped out of the window on the second floor landing. She was killed at once."

We were putting on our coats in Sister's little office. I dared not look at Marianne. To keep myself in countenance, I looked out on the ward through the glass window. As in Sister Limagnac's office, on the morning of the first day of last term, I pictured again a fair childlike figure in white standing near the central table. That morning her eyes had never contemplated anything but life intact, knowing little about sickness and blood and death and pain. Even when I began to love her, or to know that I loved her, I had obstinately gone on thinking of her as the prettiest girl in the world, but childish, romantic, sentimental, ill-adapted to reality, hoping for the impossible, facing patients and their complaints with the absurd ingenuousness of a novice. I had forgotten my own cry when starting at the hospital: "All this terrible suffering!" And my presumptuous response: "True

349

goodness must be so easy!" When she had proved herself right about the kraurosis case, I thought of it as just a remarkable stroke of luck. My masculine pride would not let me admit that she had already penetrated further into the world of suffering than I could ever hope to do. But now I suddenly realized that in some mysterious way it was a world with which she had always been secretly familiar.

Sister was sitting in her office transcribing details about the dead woman on a special yellow form where the ink ran badly, making funereal smudges. Marianne put on her apron and then went out, walking down the ward between the worn stretcher-beds. I watched her through the office window, and found that the whole sordid Annex had taken on a new meaning, thanks to Marianne and the discoveries she made daily about all the unhappy women in it. I saw her go from bed to bed, and thought of her now as looking at each patient not from outside but from within. What sure instinct tells a mother bird how to protect her young or a homing pigeon how to find its direction unerringly, by signs which no human can grasp? Equally sure and mysterious was the intuition with which Marianne seemed to feel what was going on inside these patients, read their destinies, and know the paths they must travel. This was surely the supreme medical grace, the authentic doctor's gift—the capacity, at whatever cost to yourself, for imagining the suffering going on in the flesh of another.

Marianne bent over the bed of the woman with kraurosis. I saw her straighten up and return towards the office with the joyful expression of a child whom no bitter experiences can disillusion. At the door she told me, almost in a shout: "Come quickly, Jean. It's marvellous, the kraurosis patient says she's feeling better already."

I followed her in silence. I would not have dreamed now of smiling at her joy. I almost stopped her sharply to ask: "Who are you then? How do you know all this? How do you come to grasp the truth so often, outside all ordinary knowledge? I thought I knew you well already, my Marianne, but no, until

350

last night and this morning, I never knew at all the most wonderful part of you."

It was only a few yards to the bed of the woman with kraurosis, but as we walked towards it together, I felt this was one of the decisive and memorable moments of my life. Our intuitive intimacy, subtler and richer than desire, was something firm and enduring; no barrier could ever come between us again. "What achievements are not within my reach," I thought to myself, "if only she will go on loving me."

Chapter 5

IN THE EARLY DAYS of our period at Bichat Annex, exhausted by
four hours of anaesthetizing and treatments, I often wondered
whether I was not wasting my time in an atmosphere of such
squalor and stagnation. I could not really see how any of it
would be much use to me in the future, the fussy anaesthetics,
the long dressings all much the same, and the importunate gar-
rulousness of the women. After all, since I did not plan to be
a surgeon, I was not likely in my practice to have more than an
occasional abscess to open.

Paul, on the other hand, seemed perfectly happy. All morning
he would be busy with his forceps, exploring wounds, changing
drains, pressing abscesses, cleaning up purulent parts, massaging,
plugging, rummaging, full of self-assurance, delighted when
the pus came out thick and plentiful, always merry and vivacious and noisy, talkative as ever, with a pun usually ready on
his lips. The whole ward would at times relapse into silence so
as not to miss one of his puns, which never failed to find an ap-
preciative audience.

Moreover, it was quite clear that Paul was working very hard.
When I expressed surprise at the unusual consistency of his
efforts, he explained his reasons thus:

"According to reliable sources I learn that one's practice depends completely on women. If you want to succeed you
haven't got a chance unless your landlady, and the wives of
the butcher and baker and candlestick-maker are all on your
side. They are the ones who make and unmake a doctor's reputa-

tion, so naturally I'm trying to learn the tricks of the trade. In my feminine practice here, I've already made a few discoveries. The only way to get anything out of them is sometimes to put the fear of God in them; they all like a touch of the caveman in their treatment. Half brutality, half gentleness, that's the secret. You're always too gentle, Jean, it doesn't do you any good, you know."

He picked up a rubber finger-stall, and went over to a patient, a good old salpingitis, who had doubtless paraded her gonococci round quite a few other hospitals before landing here. As Paul was raising the sheet to uncover her, she began simpering coyly like a bashful girl: "Oh, M. Chavasse, not the finger, *please.*"

"Not the finger?" cried Paul. "How the hell do you think I'm getting up there? Come on with you, and no silly nonsense. Fists under your buttocks, and don't waste time."

The woman obeyed at once, and in submission to this lordly male the whole ward almost purred with pleasure like cats being stroked. Behind me a voice whispered to a neighboring ear: "Isn't that M. Chavasse a one! I didn't want to let myself be operated on, but he told me: 'There's not a fibrous tumor like yours in the whole hospital. If you let it be taken out, I bet they'll stick it in a big bottle in the Museum, labelled Champion Fibroma, extracted February 1933, with your name on.' After that I felt I just had to let them operate."

As far as the women went, the future Dr. Chavasse was certainly learning the tricks of the trade.

A few days after the suicide of the woman with the amputated arm, Dr. Legendre returned from his congress in London, which in the meantime I had learned was an International Conference for the Advancement of Surgery.

Two or three days later, Sister Maurice pointed me out a patient sent to Dr. Legendre by one of the local doctors. I went to see the new arrival. She was an old woman with a devastated face and almost white hair. When I read the details on her card filled up in Admissions, I observed with astonishment that she was only forty-five. In a low lifeless voice, little more than a

353

whisper, as if she were economizing on all movements of the face, she explained that she had facial neuralgia. For ten years, she told me quite moderately and resignedly, she had had to give up all activity. She never went out, she dared not wash her face, she lived in terror of the slightest incident which might provoke an attack. She had exhausted all her financial resources in treatments of every kind. She had been operated on fifteen times, one after the other; all her teeth had been pulled out; and she still went on suffering. When I wanted her to describe her attacks she was just like everybody else: unable to go beyond vague terms and inexact comparisons.

"First of all it burns my skin, makes it smart terribly, then it twists into me like a corkscrew coiling into the flesh and pulling it out. After a while it stops; if it didn't I know I'd go mad or kill myself. I can't really explain any better than that."

The terrifying gleam which appeared in her eyes as she thought of it was more eloquent than the mere words. I knew from textbooks that facial neuralgia is one of the most terribly painful complaints there are, and that formerly it almost always led to suicide.

Sister had Dr. Legendre notified, and during the morning he came to see the new patient, sat down at her bedside and got her to tell her story again. She began it once more with the same thin voice and the same expression of reasoned resignation. Dr. Legendre took a long time questioning her, and then made a minute examination. On leaving her he used the automatic, almost ritual phrases of encouragement, "We'll look after you here, and see that it's taken care of," but as he said them, I thought I could detect in his voice, normally firm and positive, an inexplicable slight hesitation. Nor did the patient appear to be taken in; with the same look of resigned sadness on her face, she brought out a whispered, "Thank you, doctor," as if his words and hers were equally a matter of form. She had had fifteen futile operations and all her teeth pulled out. Ten years of torture, ten years of false hopes raised, promises made and not kept; she had certainly good reason to be skeptical.

"You saw that patient," Dr. Legendre said to us as he went out

354

at the end of the ward. "Her ten years of suffering have aged her more than thirty years of normal life. At forty-five she is already an old woman. What an incredible waste of energy! She should be shown to the people who claim that pain is ennobling. What they say is false. Pain is not part of nature's plan, it is not an inescapable necessity of life, it is not in accord with the normal laws of physiology. It does not fade away or vanish or wear itself out, it only increases with time; it is something useless, evil, monstrous, causing blasphemies more often than prayers. Otherworldly poets may assert that it measures a man's greatness. Deeply convinced mystics may use it to fertilize the universe. I as a doctor must speak up in defense of the vulnerable flesh, and I vehemently deny the utility of pain."

During this "peroration" I happened to look at Marianne, and I could see she was preparing to say something; I wondered what it would be. Dr. Legendre had his hand on the handle of the door when the girl came out with her question: "Excuse me, Dr. Legendre, but in the case of *this* facial neuralgia, which is already several years old, could anything be done to relieve it?"

Dr. Legendre looked at Marianne. In the time he took to answer his face hardened, and when he replied there was a different note in his voice, cold and cutting, reminiscent of Dr. Hauberger. "Yes, Mlle. Duriez, something *could* be done."

He then left us abruptly.

We only understood the cause of his brusqueness a little later when Dr. Jouvet, the interne, made his round. I showed him the facial neuralgia, and told him about this incident. He explained that thirty years ago Dr. Hauberger had created a technique which had become the classical treatment for this complaint. It was a mild operation providing relief for two or three years. Since then other surgeons had discovered far more delicate operations with distinct improvement in the results, but Dr. Hauberger refused to have these operations mentioned in his wing.

"Why?" asked Marianne, "if the results are better?"

"Because, my dear girl," said Jouvet with a laugh, "it isn't

355

easy to give up *any* technique you're used to. When it's become the classical treatment which is found in all textbooks—well, it would be almost like someone asking you to kill your own son and adopt the child next door. You always see your own creation as something beautiful, perfect. Naturally, when a former patient returns to the hospital saying he's beginning to have the same old pain, every effort is made not to show him to the Chief and to stow him away somewhere at once. Which is why in all the latest surgical works you'll find that 95 per cent of the cases treated by the Hauberger technique have been definitely successful."

"But that's dishonest," said Marianne.

"That's a big word for a very human reaction. In the Orient, I seem to remember, those who brought tidings of disaster used to have their heads cut off. Well, I don't say the Chief would go quite that far if Legendre showed him one of these relapse cases —but anyhow it wouldn't be very good for Legendre to be the bearer of bad news. Whenever you do this, you always feel people are unconsciously holding you partly responsible. And then again, the more powerful people are, the less they know about what is really going on; they live in a world which is distorted to please them, and it's so easy to make statistics say just what you want them to."

"But I thought Dr. Hauberger was very strict about statistics," I said, remembering something I had heard in the internes' common room.

"He is that," admitted Jouvet. "I've seen him going through an annual report on the work of his block: for each death he would check the cause rigorously. If someone had loosely written pneumonia or kidney failure or some other diagnosis to cover a multitude of sins, or if he found the cause of death at all doubtful, he would correct it in the margin to 'Death by operatory infection.' You can see he has a good deal more scientific strictness than Dupuytren, who used to conceal the results of P.Ms. when they disproved his diagnosis. Besides, most of the time there's no question of deliberate falsification or lying. Try mentioning deaths through anaesthetic accidents among a

356

group of surgeons; nobody will ever have had one. Are they lying? No, they merely don't remember the occasions."

"All the same," persisted Marianne, "when he sees the results of other methods, Dr. Hauberger must see that they also give cures. In fact they can't be far off a hundred per cent, what with improvements in technique."

"Quite possibly. But as he knows that all statistics, except of course his own, are more or less false, why should he give up his technique to try others which are more complicated and more radical, and equally liable to accidents and failures? These new techniques depend on neuro-surgery, and the Chief is getting old, while neuro-surgery is still in its youth. He's been a great surgeon in his time, it's too late for him to become even an average neuro-surgeon; he's quite out of the race. Whereas Legendre is the coming man, and neuro-surgery is his life. He's come back from London full of enthusiasm, and he told me yesterday about an operation Dandy performed in his presence, using the latest American technique, a superb operation where you go right behind the brainpan, between the cerebellum and the bone. Two hundred and fifty cases operated and only four deaths; follow-up results perfect. Which makes the Hauberger operation look pretty small. But if Legendre risked mentioning it to Hauberger, what a storm there'd be!"

"In that case," said Marianne, getting things clear in her mind, "this patient will have her operation, and in two or three years the trouble will presumably start all over again. Whereas Dr. Legendre could give her a definite cure?"

"That's about it. Only to give her a definite cure, as you put it, there'd have to be a sort of mutiny of the Bounty. Unless Legendre operated without the Chief knowing, and risked one of his fits of temper. Woe betide anyone who provokes that. If Legendre wants to get himself thrown out of the hospital and risk his whole future, he only needs to try it."

"But it's his duty," said Marianne with such force that it made us all feel a little embarrassed.

"Well, really," said Jouvet, "you have a highly surgical way of cutting the Gordian knot in cases of conscience. Quite apart

357

from respect for superiors, what about gratitude? Legendre owes Hauberger all he knows about surgery. If he criticized the classical Hauberger operation the Chief would never understand. He would just think his former pupil was being ungrateful. There's also this to be said: after all, the Hauberger op. isn't so bad, it's without danger, it relieves the patient for quite a while. Ought Legendre to risk his whole career over a case where there's no question of saving a life? Perhaps his *duty* would be not to risk his career, in which he'll do far more than alleviate one patient's pain. He'll certainly do great things, save the lives of thousands of poor devils. You see it's not quite so simple . . ."

Marianne said: "Yes, I see," thoughtfully, but did not look really convinced. Jouvet laughed. "Doctors have cases of conscience," he added, "even where their own treatment is concerned. What would you do in the place of one of my friends who is House Surgeon under Rebillot at the Hôtel-Dieu hospital? He put his shoulder out and broke a leg skiing, and Rebillot makes him wear the famous Rebillot appliance which everybody knows is absolutely useless. My pal grouses but doesn't dare chuck away the appliance. He's scared of annoying Rebillot who is very touchy and also very influential. According to your ideas what ought he to do?"

This seemed to be addressed to Marianne, but Paul answered in her place: "Very simple: refrain from throwing away the appliance so as not to throw away career at the same time."

Next day Marianne was on the look-out for Dr. Legendre all morning, but he did not come. In his absence I was again questioning the woman with the facial neuralgia, and Marianne was standing near me. All of a sudden the patient stopped short in the middle of a sentence; an attack had begun. In a single second her face seemed completely convulsed, as if by an explosion of pain. It became tortured, inhuman, dreadful; the muscles contracted and slackened, and she started massaging her cheeks as if trying to relieve some agonizing burn. She went on rubbing

358

them violently, pressing her fingers against the bones. From her mouth came the broken beginnings of a moan, far more horrible to hear than outright screams. She might suddenly have been stripped of all her flesh so that we were seeing a skeleton. Never before on a human face had I seen evidence of such piercing pain, the prototype of all pains ever, a mad torture which went on and on. Dumb with horror I stood there not daring to move or speak.

I had completely forgotten Marianne's presence, and as I watched, it came over me with a sudden certainty that in some extraordinary way this poor woman was suffering for my sake. The mask of pure suffering, branded on a human face in its most unredeemed and unadulterated form, was there for me simply to *see*, outside all professional curiosity.

The attack went on for several minutes, no doubt for the patient an eternity of terror. Then the muscles of the face relaxed, she stopped her rubbing, opened her eyes and gradually resumed her expression of mournful resignation. Marianne had come close to me, and we stayed there in silence. What could we say to this woman, who as in some Greek tragedy had just mimed pure pain for us without a word or a cry or a drop of blood?

The attack was completely over. After the madness and the terror a sort of exhausted relief appeared on the woman's face. But there was something even more terrible in what we now witnessed: you could not read on her face the slightest ray of hope.

When we left the hospital at about one o'clock, Dr. Legendre had still not appeared in the Annex. In the street Marianne said to me: "If he doesn't come tomorrow, something will have to be done."

She looked resolute, even obstinate, and I decided it was wiser not to discuss the case further. I spent the afternoon and that night in a state of disagreeable uncertainty.

Next morning I saw Marianne go round the beds as usual, and a little later, as I was changing rather a lengthy dressing, she returned to the bed of the facial neuralgia case, and spoke

359

to her. I could see the woman gradually losing her expression of utter defeat, and lifting her head; wonder of wonders, she even tried to smile. I finished my bandage hastily, meaning to listen as casually as I could to what Marianne was saying. Just then Dr. Legendre entered the ward, and he reached the patient's bed a little before I did. I heard him telling her: "I shall operate on you tomorrow, late in the morning."

My heart rose. He had recovered the bracing, decisive voice which seemed to give the patients a transfusion of his own vitality. The patient answered, "Yes, Doctor, I knew that already. You're going to do a new American operation on me." For the first time her face showed signs of hope.

Her reply appeared to surprise Dr. Legendre, and he asked; "How did you know that?"

"The young lady here has just been telling me."

The surgeon looked at Marianne with astonishment, and she blushed like a schoolgirl caught misbehaving. He said nothing. Then he examined some other patients. As he was leaving, and we had gone with him to the door, he stopped abruptly and turned towards Marianne to ask sardonically:

"You arrange other people's lives very easily, young lady. Did you happen to know that this operation involved a serious decision for me? I only made it this morning, and supposing I hadn't?"

Marianne replied steadily: "I knew that it meant a very serious decision for the patient also. If you hadn't come this morning before I left the hospital I had made up my mind to go and look for you, and remind you that you were her only hope."

There was still a faintly mocking note in Dr. Legendre's voice as he went on: "All the same, you were very indiscreet to inform her I was going to operate without being sure I would do so."

Marianne's voice was clear and resonant as she gave her answer: "But I *was* sure."

There was a short silence. Near me I heard Paul give a little anxious cough. Dr. Legendre had bent forward, and was looking vaguely at the floor, mechanically kicking a stray piece of orange

360

peel. When he looked at Marianne again he could scarcely have answered her with more respect.

"Thank you, Mlle. Duriez, for not having doubted me."

The operation took place the next day at the end of the morning, when the Chief had had to leave the hospital for some official ceremony. Immediately afterwards the patient declared she felt some relief.

A few days later, on arriving in the Annex, I found another new patient. Her face was white and as hard as alabaster when you touched it. The eyelids were stretched so taut that they seemed almost upside down. The nostrils were flattened, and a perpetual thread of saliva dribbled from her mouth which she could neither open nor close completely. It looked as if some fiendish torturer had amused himself by squashing this face into a stone mask too narrow for it. I thought they must have sent us by mistake a case for the medical or skin disease wards. But Sister Maurice assured me the patient had come in to have an operation.

Next day a woman was admitted with terrible pains in her hands and feet. Her fingers first went quite white as if all the blood had suddenly left them; then it coursed back into the empty arteries with such violence that her skin became a blazing red and seemed ready to burst. The attacks in the feet were equally intense, and the swelling was so extreme that it made her stockings crackle, literally. Another patient arrived completely ankylosed by rheumatism from neck to feet; a nurse had to feed her like a baby.

Dr. Legendre had not visited the Annex regularly before; the cases there were mostly of little clinical interest. But the facial neuralgia operation seemed to confirm him in some secret resolve, and after that he came every day. He had other patients admitted to the ward to be operated on by him, and they all had equally grim and often equally bizarre complaints.

Pain, pain, pain! This word, with its onomatopoeic plaintiveness was all you could hear in Bichat Annex; the whole ward was full of it. Pain quivered in the air, and some days my young and

361

healthy flesh protested against it with every nerve. I longed to escape or find some refuge against it, to hear no more screams, to stop seeing these dozens of patients lying in their beds and swamping me each morning with the recital of their sufferings.

March had come, and between the showers there were some bright intervals showing us the sun and a blue sky once more. About noon the sun would dive down between the tall peeling walls, and then the grim prison lost a little of its gloom. There were a few birds singing among the small trees and shrubs outside, and from time to time the church bell of Saint-Germain-des-Près, ringing out in the distance, would remind us of a life of freedom and joy. The ward was still a dark hell, but these women, whose bodies were in torment, now had new hope; for every morning between these gloomy walls fresh miracles were being performed.

The patient with the dead fingers was cured, and when discharged had a simple scar on her arms and legs where her arteries had been.

The patient with the alabaster mask had been in agonies for months. She had felt her skin gradually shrinking, stifling her in a mould which grew ever harder and narrower; she was literally dying of slow petrifaction. Dr. Legendre removed two little glands in her neck, and the mask began to loosen and soften. He performed the same operation on the patient with rheumatism, and by six o'clock that night, Jouvet, making his evening round, found her beginning to move her hands. Next morning she was able to sit up in bed. A few days later she got up, repeating with incredulous joy: "I'm walking, I'm cured."

"It's like Lourdes," said Paul. "Would you mind leaving your crutches when you go? We ought to hang them up outside the door to attract new customers."

"Crutches!" she answered. "I never had crutches, young man. I've not been out of bed for eight years."

Often Dr. Legendre left the scalpel behind. At the patient's bedside he would stick a long needle into her neck, apparently quite at random; yet almost infallibly without breaking vessels or nerves, as if he had followed the point of the needle with his

362

eyes through two inches of flesh, he injected an anaesthetic into the tiny delicate ganglion cell. The patient, who had sometimes been suffering for years, felt cured instantly. Dr. Legendre listened carefully to them all, maintaining an inexhaustible kindness, and they felt themselves at last understood. It was a wonderful feeling for people to whom doctors had only half listened for years.

Dr. Legendre often returned to his theme for our benefit: "Pain is evil. It reduces man, makes a patient worse than he would be without it. Our sternest duty as doctors is to suppress it when we can. Tell fanatical stoics who talk to you of atonement and redemption—rarely sufferers themselves, by the way —that sacrifice is a gift, and therefore something completely voluntary. Nobody has the right to enforce it on his recalcitrant fellows and call it redemption. Tell them too that the doctor's duty is to bring a little illusion and hope to those who call for it. Just because some can bear suffering bravely, it does not mean that everybody can, and most people will reject their destiny rather than accept it. In any case I refuse to try and follow any fixed rules about how much pain a person can bear. That would mean weighing the strength of his soul, and only God can do that."

Paul's reactions to Dr. Legendre's new interest in the Annex changed with amusing rapidity in a short space of time. At first he groused a good deal about the long and uninteresting rounds which kept him from doing his "practical ward-work."

"Talk about interviews," he complained, "why, they never stop. He has to use a microscope on every atom of pain. 'Now tell me when it begins to hurt, Mme. Chose. And I want you to say whether it prickles you or tickles you or pickles you or just what.' He wastes a whole morning on cases I'd never meet twice in my local practice. If it always takes that long I'll have to take off for somewhere else."

One morning, however, there was an old woman brought in with gangrene of the leg. Dr. Legendre had operated on several of these cases recently and told us more about the new surgery for gangrene. I found Paul in a state of great excitement on this particular morning: "You've seen the new admission? Senile gangrene! She's been mad with pain from it for six months, and in two days more they'd have had to amputate her leg. Do these Paris doctors know *anything?* Are Leriche's famous sympathectomies to be reserved only for dogs in the lab?"

I remarked that it was quite a new method being used, and that it was fairly natural for old doctors and even young ones to know nothing about it so far. To this Paul replied with magnificent humility: "Why is it natural? Even *I* know about it."

"You underestimate yourself," said Marianne. "Personally, Paul, I think you've changed a good deal in the last two months. You're really becoming quite conscientious and scientific in your old age; before you know where you are, you'll have passed all your exams with distinction. You'll be an interne yet."

"I rather doubt that," said Paul. "Nice of you to say so, though."

"Well," said Marianne, "as a mere first-year student, I must say you're coming along very nicely. You certainly work hard these days."

"Hey, spare my blushes," said Paul. "I'll begin to think you want something out of me. I'm not used to these compliments. Anyhow, I'm afraid my industry has a rather more selfish basis. Since I've seen so many people in pain here, I've come to realize that what they want of their doctor is neither a diagnosis nor a lecture, they don't care a rap for all that. All they want is to stop suffering. And since I've seen Legendre, I've grasped that the doctor capable of relieving their pain better than other doctors is the real king of doctors. He has no need to put out his shingle. He can set up in the middle of the jungle, people will crawl there or cut new footpaths to get to him. When they go away they'll give him more than their purses, they'll give him their last shirt, should he happen to ask for it. Unless you're a complete nitwit, finding out something like this opens your eyes and ears and brain quite forcibly; and if I had only learned this one thing by coming here every morning, I assure you I wouldn't consider I'd wasted a year. Legendre is right: the real doctor is the one who first of all stops his patients' suffering."

Marianne was right, he had certainly changed. Even though he still claimed to be inspired by selfish motives, I suddenly realized that she, as well as Legendre, had been exerting a subtle influence on Paul which he himself hardly understood. Did people like Paul notice what was happening to them inside? I was still thinking about this when Paul continued, somewhat hesitantly:

"After all, I may as well tell you now, even if you accuse me of assault with violence. You remember the patient three weeks ago with angina pectoris? The one Legendre injected near the neck—an immediate cure. Well, my landlady had the same trouble, and this gave me an idea. I watched Legendre carefully, and questioned him when he made his injections. He explained the whole technique to me and why and how it works. You certainly can't accuse him of hiding any secrets under bushels."

"Go on," I said, beginning to guess what was coming.

"I gave the morgue attendant several drinks to get him to let me practise on cadavers, and yesterday I risked the deed. For three days the old girl had had so many attacks she could hardly collect the rent; twenty times a day she thought she was dying. I suggested a little injection to her; in her state she would have agreed to anything, even a little injection to finish her off. I locked the door of her room so as not to be disturbed by any of the other tenants. I had everything nicely prepared, needle, ampoule, syringe. It was like a carefully planned crime. I found the right spot and I can tell you my heart was beating as fast as my cardiac victim's. Then, bang, I plunged the needle in at one fell swoop. My landlady turned all red, and suddenly yelled: 'I can't feel the pain!' and dissolved into tears of joy. She couldn't believe her own senses. And as for me, Jean, it's funny. I was merely meaning to play the wonder-worker, the great magician, so that I could get at least six months' rent out of her free. But instead of that I felt as if I'd resurrected my grandmother. I was so excited and proud of myself I almost started blubbering like a baby."

If Paul had changed, so certainly had I. Anyone who saw me walking through the hospital grounds or even through the wards might have thought me no different from the new dresser of last term. But I had a strong feeling that the continual spectacle of concentrated suffering and its cure, thrilling and overwhelming at the same time, had made something burst into life inside me, had put there a new warmth, a mysterious fire. By myself I should have wearied very quickly, but for these exhausting plunges into the abyss I marvelled to find Marianne always at my side. I clung to her, pressed on her with all my weight, and felt myself receiving from this prop a positive and lasting strength.

I know now that never again in my life can I expect to experience a more dazzling mood of pure exaltation. At this unique climax of my whole adolescence, full of passionate and impulsive idealism, I believed, believed entirely in my work and my love. Perhaps nobody has more than one period in his life when he dedicates himself entirely, as I did then.

As evidence of the unselfish ardor of those days when I was trying to work out a code for my future life as a doctor, I kept for a long time among my papers an "Oath Against Pain," inspired by the famous "Oath of Hippocrates." I wrote it one evening on returning to my room. Here it is:

I swear by Apollo the healer, by Aesculapius, Hygeia and Panacea, calling to witness all gods and goddesses, that I will fulfil the oath of which this is the text, within the limits of my power and my intelligence.

I will try to care for all the patients whose hopes are summed up in the three words, Not to Suffer. *I will use the only true science of Medicine, which strives with all its willpower and all its imagination in the least of its actions, against Pain.*

I shall never see Pain as a commonplace symptom to be regarded in others with detachment, resignation, and fatalism, as part of the will of nature or the gods, where one can give up the struggle at once if it shows any resistance. I shall never forget that my Masters have taught me always to fight Pain and to hate it. I will never be the doctor to let a patient suffer because

I do not dare take responsibility for a difficult operation or an impartial piece of advice. I will be on my guard against routine and ignorance and negligence and scepticism; and each evening, as a good eternal student, I will keep a time in which to learn new ways of curing with drugs or the knife.

For the incurable I will try to preserve till the end the comfort of illusion. I will not yield to the temptation of fixing rigid rules, measuring out cruelly the dose of sedative to give my patients. I will not let them die unappeased in a last gasp of defiant suffering.

I leave it to poets, philosophers or mystics to exalt Pain if they can. As a doctor I shall never forget that Pain is not part of Nature's plan, is not an inescapable law of the species; that it knows no respite or rest or truce; that it comes from outside the living order and the world's laws; that it does not fade or wear itself out, but wears out its victims whom it tortures and crushes with teeth which are ever new. I shall never forget that it is always evil, futile, monstrous, something to be defeated and destroyed at all costs.

Next morning I found this oath too self-conscious and scholarly, too much a rehash of others' words, as if I were still half under the influence of Carleret and his "salon." Although we had no secrets from each other, I did not even feel like letting Marianne see it. It shows all the same the state of enthusiasm in which I lived then.

Chapter 6

ALL MY MORNINGS as anaesthetist were terribly long, and this one seemed endless. The Chief, assisted by Dr. Legendre, had been "doing a stomach," and he was just resewing the intestine to the gastric wall. With neat little movements he pressed the needle, pulled on the thread, and completed the hundreds of intricate seams on whose frail strength a human life was hanging. This is his famous "needlework surgery."

Under the dome of light the heat was almost tropical. I envied the group of first-year students parked in a corner of the theatre in an oasis of shade. Marianne was there—she always liked to be near me when she could—and I saw Paul beside her. He enjoyed watching sensational operations, just as some folk go to a circus —with a faint hope of seeing the lion-tamer eaten.

Three surgeons from Chile were watching Hauberger operate this morning. They paid him elaborate homage on arrival, while he greeted them briefly, implying, though the words were unsaid: "Too kind, gentlemen—but I've no time to waste, let's get to work." Since then the three Chileans stood near the table, craning their necks towards the incision with a look of extreme concentration, occasionally withdrawing to whisper enthusiastic comments to each other through gold teeth. The spotlight's ruthless beam made their morning shave appear inadequate; their chins were bluish. One of them had a sort of nervous twitch of the lips; he swallowed his saliva from time to time as if to keep himself from drooling.

Perhaps, though, he was only drooling with admiration; for

to watch the Chief operating was certainly to understand the full meaning of the term "operation." Here was a supreme example of "handicraft," the craft of the hands, and as such an end in itself. It is an art in which everything depends on the man himself, a duel of one man's will-power against evil, an act of authority over fate. Dr. Hauberger had begun the morning by removing an enormous tumor of the neck, and there was something challenging and dramatic in the mere site of the operation itself. The vessels here are so many and so thick, the nerve threads so complex, that the least deviation of the scalpel might easily provoke a disastrous haemorrhage and stop the heart abruptly; at any moment the blood might rush seething into the trachea, mingling with the death rattle caused by lightning asphyxia. When, in fact, the whole mass of the tumor fell with a single heavy thud into the enamel tray, none of the audience could restrain a gasp of admiration before so much steadiness and precision, power and control, so much continuity in every movement.

The Chief could remember surgery as it was practised fifty years ago by our great-grandfathers, when they operated with high formality in black gowns protected by aprons, sleeves turned up to the elbow amidst torrents of blood and screams of pain. Not so long before that Velpeau had declared it criminal for a surgeon to open up a stomach, and Nélaton had promised a statue of gold to anyone who could overcome postoperative infection.

The Chief remembered the miraculous advances which began with the discovery of anaesthetics and Pasteurian antiseptics. He himself had considerably extended these advances through his own work; he had helped to perfect this triumphant new surgery. He had written a host of books and articles and case-histories, created an arsenal of new instruments, elaborated an infinite number of operative techniques, and given his name to new diseases.

He had dedicated his whole life to his art in a kind of single-minded passionate pride. As proof of this pride the story went that an old lady on his ward, cured by one of his most daring operations, said: "Oh, Dr. Hauberger, with God's help you have saved my life." To which the surgeon replied: "Leave God out of it, madame, He can't perform operations like that." Another cry of pride and passion was his famous *A Surgeon Speaks*, published a few years ago, simultaneously a summing up of his generation and the testament of his own career. I learned whole pages of it by heart.

Addressing himself to all the surgeons of his age, to all his medical colleagues, whether living or dead, who had been with him in the great adventure, bringing their grain of sand or weighty stone to the majestic edifice, according to their strength or genius or good fortune, he wrote:

> *The only thing with grandeur and meaning is the Art which we pioneered; for behind us we shall leave nothing unknown. We have attempted everything within the range of anatomical possibility; we have removed everything that could be removed in a human body without endangering life. For fifty years Surgery has sustained us with the intoxication of its triumphs. Those who come after will have come too late; there will be nothing for them to do but repeat what we have done already. These glands, these brains, these entrails, which no one before us ever dared track down and violate in their lairs, have been forced to deliver up to us one by one their defenses and their mysteries. They cannot yield this glory more than once, and it is our generation which has first been able to snatch it from them.*

In the early days of my time in his hospital I read these pages with enthusiasm, and I looked at the great man with intense admiration, as the Chilean doctors gazed at him this morning. There was such virtuosity and audacity in every action, which surely few surgeons can ever have surpassed. But since I had come on to Bichat Annex and made a closer acquaintance with Dr. Legendre, I secretly allowed myself the luxury of feeling a little sorry for the mighty Hauberger, and on some occasions even indignant with him. Naturally I could not afford to show on the surface any trace of either of these emotions.

370

The Chief and Dr. Legendre had just removed a large piece of stomach from the woman I was keeping under the anaesthetic. The Chief operated as for an ulcer, though his assistant had suggested something different. Instead of the crippling operation now almost completed, Legendre had been for simply cutting one of the abdominal nerves which he believed to be the pain-conductor. This belief, he said, was based on observations he had made himself. The Chief interrupted him to comment drily: "I've opened up thousands of stomachs, and I've never yet seen that done."

"You can't see things without looking," Legendre might have rejoined, but he kept silent while Hauberger waxed sarcastic in front of the obsequious Chileans about the dangers for young surgeons of half-baked theories about what *ought* to be the case. "Trouble with you, Legendre," he said (and this was one of the times when I could have hit him), "is that you're still a romantic at heart. You let your imagination run away with you. It's all very fine, metaphysically, your talk about mysterious vital elements in the human body, but surgically it doesn't work out, you know. Actions are worth more to the surgeon than theories or discussions," he concluded, placing his scalpel on the patient's stomach, "so let's get down to work."

Now the operation was almost over, I took a look at the Chief's tall figure bent over the incision. The white cambric bib clung to the ascetic profile, and between the bib and the headband I saw the gray eyes peering sharp and cold and hard as surgical steel at the wound. Like steel, this brutal glint might be all they could ever reflect.

Opposite him stood the stockier figure of his assistant. A younger man, with more warmth in his expression, Legendre watched every movement of his Chief, ready to respond immediately with his own attentive counter-move, handing forceps, sutures, swabs. Above the bib his eyes sparkled with the brilliant clarity of a sensitive brain, as if a sixth sense were there to double the sharpness of his eyes. They were eyes eager to see beyond the simple brute fact, to understand the deep consequences of each action, to look further than the incision and find the vital principles behind it. While the Chief continued sewing his intricate seams, Legendre's eyes might have been saying:

"No, Chief, modern surgery is no longer quite the photogenic performance of your day. We younger surgeons are not so keen on making these huge incisions, removing organs by the dozen, establishing sporting records against the clock, or the scalpel's brilliant thrust and parry in so many duels to the death. That spectacular era is already a little old-fashioned. Your generation has invented perfect techniques and instruments for us, but aren't your scientific 'maneuvers' rather too empirical? You slash and remove and straighten out and clear passages, all with great confidence and vigor, but in these displays of virtuosity you scarcely consider the unfortunate results they sometimes provoke. After this necessary manual phase isn't it time to put surgery on a more firm intellectual basis?"

Dr. Legendre, secretly breaking his Chief's outworn rules, had achieved cures daily which till then would have seemed beyond our resources. I had seen him save Mme. Lolotte's gangrened leg, free the face of the woman with the alabaster mask, make a rheumatic cripple walk, cure the woman with dead fingers. To accomplish these miracles all he had to do was to abandon traditional ideas and attend with humility to the realities and limitations of life so that he might better understand and protect it.

Dr. Legendre's glance was always alive with the desire for greater knowledge and understanding. I could imagine him saying now, when he looked again at his Chief: "You know that I love you as a son loves his father. I owe you everything. And I admire you because none of the great work now beginning could ever have been undertaken if you had not made ready the material resources. But why must I hide myself like a heretic practising a new cult? You have announced the zenith of surgery, but where you say zenith, we younger surgeons call it a dead-end. If you will let us build on the solid foundations of your temple our own temple, a new stage in its construction can begin, and magnificent new heights will be within the reach of the art to which we are both dedicated.

"I know that my mental attitude is contrary to what yours has always been, and that in this new physiological surgery everything affronts and shocks you. The intellectual conflict between our two generations is the one between all novelty and all tradition. You have been brilliantly right for fifty years, and now, although you have the scientist's training in objectivity, you cannot abandon in a day the mental habits of a lifetime. You think you are just being rational, not going beyond certain definite limits; it does not occur to you that you are sterilizing the future of medicine. But I know the sincere passion with which you have sought after the truth all your life; and all hope between our two generations need not be lost. Only I can no longer obey you passively: you have always taught me since I began my medical career at your side, that the interest of the patient is the only thing which must count; this is the categorical imperative, our duty and our destiny. In a corner of this theatre one of the students, a young fair-haired girl, is watching us; it is she who showed me my duty one morning, even in opposition to you. But I am afraid of seeming ungrateful; and so I go in hiding to disobey you. Each time I do so this girl, who has judged me, judges you too and blames you—blames you for behaving like a human being when she admired you as a god. Each time I disobey you I have the terrible feeling of a son betraying his father."

"How did you tell me they calculate the retiring age for Chiefs?" Paul asked me, several weeks after this morning in the theatre.

I had heard this subject discussed too often in the internes' common room not to be able to give him the facts.

"The normal age is sixty-three, excluding any time spent in military service. For medical school professors there's an extra allowance of two years, and a few very outstanding people get an exceptional rebate, you might say, of three years beyond that. After that they've had it."

"Good," said Paul, "I like that. Completely senile or at the top

373

of their intellectual form, no difference at all. Time, gentlemen please, and out they go. There's a smell of real democracy there. No worse and no better than a porter or a postman."

This retiring age, in which Paul took only a casual interest, was causing considerable excitement among the hierarchy in Dr. Hauberger's part of the hospital. Our Chief himself was the object of the excitement.

In a few months he would be sixty-seven and would have reached the normal limits of his professorial career. Would he retain, we all wondered, the heavy dual burden of his university teaching and his hospital block, during the three supplementary years which his colleagues offered him as a final honor?

Destiny had been lavish with triumphs, but it had not spared him several crushing blows as well. One son was killed at twenty-five in an accident, and another had been lost in the war; then his wife, nearly two years ago, had died of a gradual illness which had remained mysterious right to the end. It was one of those illnesses which sometimes deliberately mock doctors inside their own homes. Since this last blow, said his pupils, the Chief had become colder and more arrogant; he had also aged abruptly. Several times I had seen him stop a minute for a rest during long operations; and when one of the nurses undid his bib at the end, his face would be sweaty and pale, a mask drawn by fatigue, which a few seconds later would flush unhealthily at the cheeks.

"The Chief's not very fit, you can see that," said his theatre Sister, who had been working with him for years. "When he operates these days, he's an ordinary man and gets tired very easily."

A good many plans would be upset if the Chief retired at once, and many were anxious to know his exact intentions. Those most directly interested in the matter watched him with the keenness of insurance brokers proposing a new policy. At times the whole block seemed like a sinking ship which the crew are preparing to abandon. Only Dr. Hauberger himself maintained a steadfast silence; nor would anyone have dared to ask him outright about his plans.

Marianne, left quite cold by this excitement over a professorial

374

chair, said one morning: "The Chief might as well clear out right away. The patients at least wouldn't lose anything. What pain that poor woman's enduring just because he insisted on taking a good part of her stomach out, instead of listening to Dr. Legendre."

In a spirit of fairness I felt bound to say: "What the Chief did was the regular thing. Dr. Legendre told me himself that he couldn't have guaranteed a hundred per cent success for the new operation he wanted to try."

"I don't care," answered Marianne dogmatically. "The Chief refused to try it, and he was wrong. The patient is still suffering; in fact she's suffering even worse than before he operated."

"Can't we drop the subject?" pleaded Paul. "I suggest we say as a compromise that the woman is still suffering, though she has been cured, officially."

In the next few days, however, her pain grew worse, and she begged to have another operation. When Dr. Legendre came through the Annex and Marianne pressed him, he told her it was out of the question: "The Chief has already operated on the patient, and I can't touch her again without his consent."

"Couldn't you ask him?" suggested Marianne stubbornly.

"I could, if I were absolutely sure of the result. But if my operation fails, the Chief will be even more sure that I'm wrong. There are times when a surgeon who tries out new methods must know when to hold back. I haven't the right to risk discrediting this method with the Chief in a case where there's any doubt of its success."

Marianne pressed him and pleaded with eloquence. Finally Dr. Legendre yielded: "The Chief is going out of town this afternoon for a consultation. He certainly can't be back before tomorrow morning. I will operate on your patient, and if he ever mentions it I'll say I had to open her up again because she'd had a relapse—as indeed she has. But I don't guarantee a cure."

Marianne threw him a grateful look and declared herself sure in advance of his success.

The next day, late in the morning, the patient was brought into the theatre. Marianne and Paul, obliged to attend a lecture,

375

could not come. I was alone at my end of the table giving the anaesthetic, while Dr. Legendre operated, assisted by Jouvet. The operation proceeded in silence apart from the familiar hiss of the sterilizer, and the atmosphere was calm and peaceful, very different from the terrific, tense silence when the Chief was at work. The operation was nearly over when the door of the theatre opened, pushed by a firm hand, a hand which clearly demanded obedience to its wishes. All three of us turned our heads. Dr. Hauberger had just come in. Stunned and motionless, we watched him come up to the table. In his iciest voice he said tersely: "Morning, Legendre," and nodded curtly at Jouvet and me. Then in the same imperious tone, he asked: "What are you doing?"

"It's one of the patients you operated," answered Legendre; "Gastrectomy for an ulcer. She was still having a great deal of pain. I have just severed her splanchnics."

There was no attempt at evasion. His voice contained neither arrogance nor servility; it was firm but respectful. The Chief stopped opposite me, at the other end of the table under the full light of the spot. I saw the skin of his face grow taut, become pale, transparent, clinging to the bone at the forehead, the cheeks, and the ridge of his nose. Below it his nostrils seemed to contract. All his flesh had suddenly shrunk, and his face was strikingly white. There was a moment's awful silence during which the sterilizer's familiar hiss sounded incongruous and absurd. I had lowered my eyes in terror; I looked only at the patient and the mask; with beating heart, as if I had been caught taking part in a murder, I waited for the first paroxysm of rage.

Doubtless because of the nurses present, the Chief decided not to make a scene. He merely gave the order to carry on in a tone even more cutting than usual. Then he swung on his heels and strode out. We remained there without speaking, listening to his step disappearing down the corridor. Jouvet's look crossed mine, and we both made grimaces of silent consternation. Legendre had not moved since his answer to the Chief. He was leaning on the table with his two gloved hands, his head bent. He might have been trying to recover his composure, pull himself together, withdraw himself so that he could forget for the moment anything but the completion of the operation. Finally he said to Jouvet: "Let's finish it."

A few moments later the nurses were clearing the table of its towels and blood-stained instruments and collecting all the scarlet swabs off the floor. Jouvet put on a dressing, watched absently by Legendre whose own task was now completed. Legendre took off his gloves mechanically, straightened up, breathed deeply as if to rid himself of a very heavy burden, and started dictating his report on the operation to a nurse. The patient, released from the mask, was still snoring. I wiped off the dribble at the corner of her lips, and the sticky sweat from her brow and cheeks, where the edge of the mask had left a dark blue furrow.

When Legendre had finished dictating, the whole theatre was silent. An orderly arrived with a trolley to remove the patient. I took the opportunity to leave at the same time, and returned to the Annex. Marianne and Paul were back from their lectures and were changing some dressings while they waited for me. Marianne, of course, wanted to know all about the operation. From prudence, and perhaps also from cowardice, I refrained from telling her of the Chief's unexpected and dramatic return. I was half afraid she would dash off on some quixotic impulse and try to take the blame on herself. Apart from the danger to her, it would of course have been quite futile. What could you expect from a tyrant like Hauberger? I felt sure now he would not refuse the three extra years so providentially offered him: three years in which he would be able to misuse what remained of his influence, and continue in the error of his ways with the proud obstinacy of the old.

About one o'clock all three of us left the Annex as usual. Just as we were passing under the grill connecting the second courtyard with the main court, a hearse abruptly blocked the exit; and at the same moment a stately old limousine, with which we were very familiar, came under the arch. The chauffeur brought it to a stop just level with the three of us.

Inside, on the back seat, sat Professor Hauberger. Every day we saw him drive by, his figure very erect, in an almost parade-ground stiffness. But today we suddenly saw through the glass an old man, slumped in a corner, his eyes staring straight in front of him. His face was so gray and drawn that you could almost see the skeleton looming behind it. The expression on that face was one we had never seen there before, dejected and disheartened, near to despair. It was as if death had at that very moment touched him with a rough and bony hand, serving him with a brutal summons.

Just opposite us, behind the door of the internes' common room, someone happened to start up a familiar song:

> *"Moldering in the workhouse, bored beyond all measure,*
> *A few miles out from Paris, yet such continents away,*
> *How often in the surfeit of my lamentable leisure*
> *I've thought about old age and destitution and decay."*

The last time I had heard them singing it in the common room, I remembered someone mentioning the tradition which ascribed the words of this song to Dr. Hauberger himself. I had found some difficulty in imagining the Chief as he must have been fifty years earlier, a young interne with perhaps a short fair beard and a black velvet cap such as students then wore, bursting into the chorus with his friends, like the internes of today:

> *"My friends, I bid you listen, the refrain is worth your hearing,*
> *This refrain from out the workhouse, from the ruin of a man:*
> *You cannot love for ever, youth is swiftly disappearing;*
> *You cannot love for ever, so enjoy love while you can."*

Dr. Hauberger heard the song too. An extreme lassitude seemed to have taken hold of him, and he closed his eyes, letting his head fall back on the gray velvet cushions of the limousine. After all his work and struggles and heartaches, all the sorrows and triumphs which had served as milestones in a long life, this poor old man, slumped in the shadows of his car, must have suddenly seen himself again as a young doctor, full of energy and optimism and vitality, facing a splendid future with a song

378

on his lips. To look at him at this moment was almost unbearably poignant.

"That's medical fame for you," Paul murmured to me, not stirring from our dark recess. "Seen from close quarters it's not very inviting, is it? Hardly worth growing old for the sake of that."

I did not answer, being afraid the Chief might hear me. But I knew that this drama, accidentally played out before our eyes, was not only that of fame and old age. The great wrench was near, and so certain it might have happened already; it really mattered very little now whether he went on for a few months longer or for three years. You could say anyhow that the great Professor Hauberger would shortly be retiring after fifty years of surgery. One morning he would arrive for his last working day at Charité Hospital, and the porter would salute his coming with a last stroke of the bell. He would make his final round of the wards, inspect his theatre for the last time—it would probably be empty for the day—and then depart, after thanking all those he had led so firmly forward in common struggles and common victories.

After this, for a little time yet, he would still operate occasionally at his clinic, to keep his hand in, to have the joy of healing, to postpone his old age as long as possible. But the day would come when he could no longer draw the finest silk through an intestinal needle; and then he would really have to stop. Before the intolerable necessity of complete retirement there would still be a few last papers to publish, the sessions of the Academy and the Institute, the presentation of the medal for fifty years of surgery, the reunion for the last time of his last friends and pupils, at least those who had not already forgotten him or predeceased him. The rest would be silence. He would be merely another human being whose destiny has long been accomplished, a mere ghost, in fact, unlucky enough to have remained on earth after his real life is done.

But behind this wrench was a still more terrible laceration. When all other hopes are dead, men's hearts still cling to the hope that somehow they themselves or a part of them will survive. But now even this was being taken away from him, and an hour earlier he had witnessed his life's work beginning to crumble, in his own theatre, before his very eyes. Soon nothing at all would remain of what he, like so many other pioneers, had believed to be an eternal edifice. Already, even in the eyes of his pupils, he was out of date as a surgeon, a mere manual virtuoso, stubbornly, incorrigibly manual in all his routine. He was only an old lion in a cage trying to roar so that he could survive the rest of his generation and his system. But the young no longer believed in the system, and as soon as he was dead they would hasten to bury it for ever with him. After so many struggles and triumphs and honors, this defeat would be far more cruel than outright death.

These things he must have thought as he lay back in his car, his eyes closed, weighing up the full sum of his sorrow.

All at once the hearse moved off, clearing the exit of the grill and leaving us in full daylight again. The car started up immediately, and the Chief opened his eyes. Noticing our little group against the wall, he swiftly reassumed his usual haughty expression. Then, recognizing Marianne, he smiled at the radiant image of youth she presented. But the pallor and hollowness of his features revealed unutterable weariness mingling with the smile.

"How old and tired he looks all of a sudden," murmured Marianne with unconscious cruelty as soon as he had passed.

A few days later the news spread through the block that the Chief had refused the extra three years. He had explained to his colleagues that he felt himself to be a surgeon of the past, and had not sufficient strength to carry so heavy a burden any longer; it needed someone who could face the future with courage and inspiration. The only thing he asked of his successor was to keep Dr. Legendre as his principal assistant. He was sad to depart but quoted a remark of his old Chief, Dr. Verneuil: "I want to step down from my chair, not fall from it."

It was only many years later that Marianne learned from me that she had administered the *coup-de-grâce*, that the operation performed at her pleading had shown him with fatal certainty that his medical life, for all practical purposes, was finished; not only his life, but his hopes of living on through his work. In one hour she had unseated a king of this world and made him into the most pitiable of ordinary men, travelling comfortless down a lonely road towards death.

Chapter 7

SPRING THAT YEAR was a long time coming, but seemed all at once to make up its mind. Travelling in our grunting, jolting bus from the school right to the top of the Parc Montsouris, for weeks and weeks we had seen only dull rainy skies. Then one afternoon the bus put us down at the entrance to a park transformed. It had become green and fresh like the countryside in spring. The lawns and trees sent up a powerful odor of damp grass and half-open lilacs, and dim clouds of pollen hovered in the light breeze. The driver of the bus jumped out and stopped to breathe this new air deep into his lungs before joining the conductor for a drink at the Châlet du Parc. Old man Coucourou, the proprietor, had already served three glasses of white wine as if on the spur of the moment, with a conjuror's dexterity; in fact he performed this trick each time they reached the terminus. All three of them near the big open door turned towards the light and raised their glasses together, drinking, so it seemed, to the health of this merry new sun.

The same evening, returning to my room about eleven o'clock, I opened both my windows wide. Night entered in a long sigh, bringing in all the fragrance of the park, and I heard very near me the sound of talk and laughter. I leaned out of the window looking onto the Slum; this unwonted noise came from the grassy hollow, never clipped or mown, between the hostel and the railings. Everywhere else the Slum inhabitants were constantly enriching the terrain with bottles, empty tin cans, old shoes and dead cats. When they came to the Jules

382

Ferry building, however, they left this piece of grass clean in gratitude, for most of them were Lucien's patients. In the spring, therefore, we of this hostel could "take to the Bush," as it was commonly called, without first having to clear a mass of rubbish away.

I could not distinguish the figures outside; they were sunk in the shadow of the hostel. But when they spoke I recognized with great pleasure the voice of Lucien. For a good many weeks now I had hardly seen or spoken to him; apart from one occasion about a fortnight ago, when I had met him in the Porter's lodge looking for mail. On leaving it we had walked a few yards together. I should have liked to say something, apologize, explain, but I did not know how to set about it. Lucien said suddenly without any preamble: "Well then, so this is the great love!"

He said it so gently that I was not at all ashamed to ask: "Is it as obvious as that?"

"More obvious than that," Lucien answered. "You're not the same person, you're calmer, steadier, more serene. This love is certainly doing you good, one might say it had filled up a gap in you. You're very lucky, Jean. There couldn't be many women capable of opening up the future for you like that."

I was very glad to hear him repeat an opinion which Paul had expressed with equal candor a few days earlier: "My God, Jean, love certainly agrees with you. Don't look now, but I think it's even improving your looks. Amazing!"

Paul and I had unconsciously begun walking round the central lawn as in the days when we used to return late to the Cité. He had never before spoken to me intimately of love. When he talked of women, it was always to express some peculiar theory, to maintain, for instance, that love will usually build best on a physical imperfection; this gives the beloved a special personality, and helps to maintain an interest which would otherwise be exclusively sexual. As soon as I tried to make him talk about himself he became evasive, however. But one evening, two weeks before, Paul opened a little of his heart to me.

"Yes, you're lucky," he said to me, and his voice was deeper, different; his look was dreamy. "You have come to port, while

I am still searching for it. Everywhere I go, I watch the women who come in, and at each door that opens my heart beats faster. I am always searching, hoping to find a haven. But all those I've met so far have been unsatisfactory. It must be my fault, evidently I am expecting too much of them. . . ."

I felt that till then I had known much about Paul from the outside, but never really seen the substance of his inner personality. He went on talking and talking while the lights went out one by one in all the hostels, so that the Cité was in complete darkness when at last we left each other and went to bed. While he was talking I felt very happy, sure of my own powers and equally full of pity for him because he was still wandering, in search of something I had found one day and for ever.

This first evening of the real spring his voice rose outside, easily recognizable among the others. For a long while I remained at my window, leaning out towards the group of blurred figures lying on the grass, as indistinct thoughts floated by me. How proud I was to be so certain of being loved! It made me indifferent to all other joys—and yet there were other minor joys, like the evenings spent in Carleret's room, which still had a glow about them in retrospect. Once in bed with the light out, I took a long time to go to sleep. I heard the voices and laughter of casual friendship flitting up to my ears like spirits of the night.

Next day I casually mentioned this to Marianne. Of course I had described to her, in our early days together, all the veterans of Carleret's room. She knew all about my former life, but since then I had not spoken to her again of those evenings of my past. Perhaps my voice now sounded regretful. She must obviously have thought so, for she commented: "I'm taking you away from your former friends, I'm monopolizing you."

I protested at once: she was the companion I always liked to be with. But she went on: "If I were a man, I'm quite sure I should want male company sometimes, however much I was in love."

"But *you* haven't any girl friends either, darling."

"It's not the same. I'm not really interested in women, and I

don't feel I understand my own sex. You know I'd like to have
been born a boy, and if I could I should prefer to stay with men
all the time. Only, of course, it isn't too easy when you happen
to be a girl. Outside good old Paul, things always get involved
at once. Anyhow, if you have the chance, go and see your old
friends whenever you feel like it. I want the man I love to be
free."

I protested vehemently once more. I felt in no way confined
or imprisoned. She seemed convinced and said no more. But the
same evening she complained of a headache and left me far
earlier than usual. I was surprised and a bit irritated; she had
not previously given signs of whims or moods.

Having said goodnight to Marianne, I went back to my
hostel. When I reached the door, I did not feel at all like sleep.
The night was soft and clear. I took a few paces down the side
of the building, and without thinking arrived at the Bush. My
friends were there, lying in the grass, talking away as if all
through the four months since I had left them life had gone
round in the same happy grooves like a well-loved gramophone
record.

"So you don't like the quantum theory, eh?" Dédé Bouchet
was crying. "It buggers your determinism and reintroduces
chance!"

"You're a stupid bastard," protested Georges Gédéon with
his usual fervor. "You're distorting my words, as always. 'Dis-
continuous' has never, that I'm aware of, meant 'indeterminate!' "

As infallibly as ever, Carleret's soft drawl sounded in the
darkness with a quotation, this time an echo from Mallarmé:
" 'One throw of the dice will never abolish chance . . .' "

Without a single question or allusion or reproach, the circle
opened to make room for me. I stretched out, and through the
warm dark night, my friends went on talking as I had heard
them talk a few months earlier, using the same abstruse arguments and cheerful insults and boisterous chaff. My back pressed
down on the grass with eyes half closed and I let the old magic
come back to me.

Next day I confessed to Marianne how I had spent the evening, and she surprised me by her joy: "Oh, I'm so glad, my dear." Then she explained: "It was just what I hoped would happen when I made you go home earlier."

This affectionate little stratagem must surely have cost her something. In gratitude, I told her the whole of the evening's conversation in detail, as far as I could remember it. She was radiant as she listened, but several times during the day I caught her looking at me rather sadly.

That evening again she tried to make me leave her early. This time I resisted. A little later I went up to my room without straying a single step in the direction of the Bush. The voices which reached me gave me a slight pang of sacrifice and regret; but to console myself I thought of Marianne, and once more was overwhelmed with wonder.

I began self-accusations. It was I who weighed heavily on her, held her down with all the burdens of my tastes and reading and moods and habits. Not for a moment had I paid any heed to her real nature, her own deep desires. Right from the beginning she had known how to fight for our love, and in return I had treated her for a long time as an ignorant, frivolous and greedy schoolgirl. I had built a void around her so that she could have no other existence outside of me.

After these searchings of conscience, I felt sure I had abominably exploited my generous Marianne. It was my turn now, I decided, to offer *her* freedom.

Four evenings later she was stretched out near me in the Bush, in the midst of my friends. First of all I had suggested to her, as if for a whim, that we abandon the restaurant in America House for the "Temporary Restaurant"; during the course of several meals there I resumed contact with my old pals, and one evening, quite casually, I left the restaurant at the same time as they did. On the Boulevard I made the introductions. They all looked at my "beautiful blonde" from close quarters with as much discretion as their very evident curiosity permitted. Our whole set, as if at full strength again, returned

386

afterwards to the hostel, with Marianne in their midst, and then strolled towards the Bush. As we went, I noticed, with some pride, that my pals had stopped swearing, and had toned down, to an almost drawingroom level, the crudity of their language and manners.

From that evening our life was altered. We abandoned the medical school library altogether. Despite the fact that the great bay windows were open, despite their white curtains, it had become extremely hot there. Sultry and stifling too were the streets of the Latin Quarter and the Boule Miche. As soon as our afternoon's practical session was finished, we rushed to the bus stop, and in twenty bumpy minutes the bus would deposit us at the doors of the Cité. On the central lawn a hose was turning, making its circle of water dance in the sun like a homemade rainbow. We went round our hostel with no fear of disappointment; in the warm shade under the railings we were unlikely to find the Bush empty. There were always a few students stretched out on the comfortable buoyant grass. Most of them were in holiday or seaside clothes.

François was usually in tennis shorts, and Lucien, who was working very hard for his finals, sometimes came along for a little mild relaxation in corduroys and sandals. Room was always made for Marianne and me; we sprawled out in the grass at once and savored the miraculous feeling of being city-dwellers no longer. Then, like all the others, we would begin a lazy sort of *alfresco* studying. By the Cité regulations anyone who failed in two successive exams was thrown out; and this ruling had spread a little zeal among even the least industrious of the hostel's inhabitants.

After dinner we would return to our books until the translucent June night, dawdling down the sky, finally fell, and made it impossible for us to read any more. Then we would stop work, and in this wonderful warm shade without a murmur, fragrant with the simple scents of grass and foliage, the coming hour would belong to Marianne, to her alone. It was all hers, the evening breeze, the whole moonstruck Cité, the fine noise of rain made by the turning sprinkler, the distant noise of the town like the distant murmur of the sea, and the softness of the night all round us. It was for her, sitting in their midst like a young queen, that these young men came together, and in the golden night formed around her an attentive circle of shining eyes, eager faces, and gay carefree hearts.

I had no fears. I was sure of myself, sure of her, without suspicions or jealousy. I loved this Marianne of the night, relaxed, light-hearted and ethereal. She was as full of purity in her second personality as the other Marianne who had loved me enough to accept being exploited; the Marianne who would return to me with the morning light.

Part 7

MARTHA

Chapter 1

THE BEGINNING of July was profoundly depressing. Abruptly depopulated, the Cité seemed to be enjoying a long siesta, basking in a sultry silence. It would soon be filling up again with the birds of passage assembled here for the summer session, but at present you only met in its pathways and corridors a few forlorn students from Indo-China or Martinique or other distant lands, who could not afford the long journey home.

Marianne and all my other friends had departed for reasons of economy, either to their homes or on vacation jobs, as soon as exams were over. On the whole this ordeal had passed off without too much mishap. Among my friends in the hostel Carleret had been the one most seriously endangered. Questioned on a point of Roman Law which he had neglected to read, he replied gloomily: " 'We always need the knowledge that we lack, and all we know has lost its usefulness.' That's Goethe, sir —Faust, you know," he added, seeing the examiner gazing at him in considerable astonishment; whereupon he was given another question. A pass mark expressed the average between his juridical weakness and his literary erudition. Paul, on the other hand, had failed in chemistry, and on seeing the results left me to write to his family: *Jury favorably impressed anxious see me again October.*

After the departure of my friends nothing broke the calm of the hostel and the Cité lawns. I was absolutely on my own. As a dresser, I did not get a holiday till September, and every morning I spent at the hospital; in the afternoons I planned to go ahead by easy stages with work for the interne's exam.

It was the first time since Christmas I had lived and worked alone. Immediately I felt stifled by loneliness without Marianne, with no Paul either on the ward, with no companionship in the hostel. I thought of the prospects for the next two months despondently, and remembering last summer, would even have been glad of the presence of Julot. Like me he had to stay in Paris because of his hospital post, and two or three times I noticed him walking virtuously out of the Parc Montsouris with a book under his arm. I ran into him one day just returning from the hospital to his room, and asked if he was working too for the interne's exam.

"You've seen me working in the park, eh? No, that's not for any public exam," he replied, "that's my private research work, old man. As you know, sex psychology is my special subject, and I was on the point of solving an extremely interesting problem, but I've had to abandon it. People have no scientific objectivity. I now take a nap in the afternoons instead."

He explained that he had been trying to determine the age when sexual modesty appeared in little girls. With a book in his hand to keep himself in countenance, he would settle down on a seat and watch the children playing. When a girl squatted and showed her thighs, he would stare hard at her, he told me, to see if she blushed and pulled down her skirt. The most authentic test apparently was a special gleam in the eyes. Unfortunately, all the mothers, as soon as they saw his black figure and faunlike ears, began calling their children to them, clucking like hens who smell a fox prowling near their chicks. The park-keepers, alerted, kept a strict watch on Julot, probably taking him for a kidnapper. "Now, I ask you," he groaned with the comical distress of a prophet dishonored in his own country, "Me, whose only thought is of Science!"

Since then, as he said, he had been sleeping in the afternoons, leaving the nights free for less inhibited orgies.

I returned to my hostel somewhat disappointed; Julot to work with would have been better than nothing. The same evening, coming out of my room to go to dinner, I met in the corridor a young student I did not know. He approached me with a shy "Excuse me," and asked me the way to the restaurant. I took him along, and he clung to me like a shipwrecked sailor to his raft; after dinner he would not leave me.

After losing both his parents at an early age, Louis Desselle had come direct to the Cité Universitaire from a religious college where he had been shut up for ten years. Returning to my room with me after dinner, he took a novel from the bookshelf and sat modestly in a chair. I realized with pity that he had never known the delights of reading for whole evenings at a time, sprawled out on a divan. I put on my bedside lamp, settled Louis on my bed, and propped him up with cushions; when he was stretched out like this, the tight-fitting suit of the overgrown adolescent was less conspicuous. He had very fair hair stuck down with great care and sleekness; I guessed that after dressing hastily in his shabby clothes each morning, he spent considerable time on this hair—his sole vanity. Disarranged by the cushions, the golden hair lost its sleekness, and stray curls began to fall over his brow.

Louis spent several days on my divan. When I went to bed, he continued to read in my room till the middle of the night. He would rise about noon, and dash to the showers, exhilarated as much by the sudden freedom from control as by the warm water. He had banished all the constraints of the college, and now could at last be happy and do what he liked.

As soon as I returned from the hospital he'd come to meet me, and would then begin to read again, his face tense and closed, with no confidences given, or for that matter asked. I avoided looking when he chose a book; I felt that would have been too much like spying on him. But I knew most of my books too well not to recognize even from a distance their covers. He was choosing all those which must have been forbidden him in college.

Adolescence is a battle in the dark between the beast and the angel, where the beast sometimes chases out the angel for ever. I could well imagine some of the troubled nights Louis had

393

spent, keeping his hands outside the sheets according to seminary rules, struggling with dimly felt desires and strange exciting dreams and fantasies. Thrust so abruptly into freedom, the forbidden fruit within reach at last, he meant to learn from books the well-trodden paths towards love, before venturing out himself on the direct and personal road. I suppose I should have said something to moderate his frenzy of sexual reading, but I was afraid my clumsy words might increase the fevers of adolescence instead of assuaging them. In the end I said nothing.

One afternoon about five o'clock I had gone to the porter's lodge with Louis, looking for mail, when I noticed a small sports car, which I thought I recognized, in front of the gate; the driver was waving his arms and calling out to me. It was Henri Philippon, the elegant and cynical Philippon with the scores of girl friends; in two years at the medical school we had hardly spoken to each other. He jumped out of the car, and came over to us, looking highly delighted. "Jean Nérac! What luck. I'm going to be here for the summer, and I don't know a soul, of course. You'll show me round a bit, won't you?"

He slapped me on the back, shook me firmly by the hand, and smiled at me with great cordiality and good humor. I realized that the impression intended, and successfully conveyed, was of a cheerful uncomplicated man of the world, of someone who knew how to enjoy life. In his car I observed several vellum suitcases, a couple of tennis racquets and a portable gramophone. It suggested some wealthy tourist's baggage, and seemed incongruous in our indigent student's environment. I could not restrain a sarcastic: "Forgotten the golf clubs?"

"Oh," said Philippon, "is there a course near here?"

"Of course," I said, pointing towards the fenced-in Slum.

Philippon refused to leave us. I had to take him to the Bursar's office. He asked for a room in my hostel, and as the one opposite mine was free, he insisted on having it. Meanwhile he explained why he had come to the Cité. I admit I was rather curious about this.

"I don't suppose you'll be very surprised to hear, Jean, old boy, that I flunked out in chemistry, physics and physiology:

394

three down doubled, you might say. You know—or perhaps you don't know—that my father has a hotel at Vichy. I was naturally getting ready to go down there during vacation, when three days ago I received an urgent telegram: *Stay in Paris live at Cité Universitaire do enough work to pass October writing.* I tried to discuss the matter by 'phone but the old man was adamant. It should perhaps be said that I've already had a little trouble in school and with the intermediate exams, and also with my first M.B. I had to take it twice. The old man was pretty tough, threatened to cut off my allowance and so on. I had to do something about that, of course. Whatever you get on the side, you need a basic income."

"But why the Cité Universitaire?" I asked.

"Yes, I know; that puzzled me too. You see, the old man started life as a café waiter and has worked himself up to being proprietor of a two-hundred-room hotel in the best part of Vichy; university matters are a little out of his field. He happened to see a report on the Cité in a newspaper: studious atmosphere, good companionship, no women allowed in men's hostels, no distractions, a healthy life for the cream of the country's youth. He told himself that would be a much better environment for me than Vichy or Juan-les-Pins—and here I am."

He seemed to find this idea of his father's bizarre but not without its amusing side. He liked the look of his room, and we left him to settle in. A minute later we heard him put a dance tune on the gramophone and accompany it humming.

Back in my room, I felt irritated. Damn Philippon's nerve in coming to live right opposite me. For two months I would have to put up with this lazy lout whom I could not stand. Released from his smiling good humor, I thought again of all I knew about him, of his commercial attitude toward medicine, his cynical ideas on the strategy for a successful medical career. I thought also of his many shady business deals, and the fake car accident which I had heard about from Paul. I had been shocked to think that people like him and Julot would eventually become doctors. In the days when he used to come and talk to Paul and the Boys from Burgundy, he must have sensed my coldness towards him. From the boisterous way he had burst into my present life, he was obviously exaggerating his cordiality to overcome my reserve. I was particularly irritated by his calling me Jean, as if we were already old pals, forcing me to call him Henri in return.

Louis, on the other hand, had let himself be won over at once. He insisted on carrying Philippon's valises up to his room, and I almost had to drag him away. This smart young man with his flow of words had completely dazzled him. Philippon, moreover, was extremely nice to Louis, calling him "my lad" or "young Louis" straight away; he evidently liked to create around him an atmosphere sympathetic to himself. When we were back in my room, Louis tried to make me talk about my friend, as he supposed Philippon to be. I found this embarrassing and told him I had to work; disappointed, he relapsed into silence.

A little later Philippon crossed the corridor, knocked at my door and came in. I pretended to be deeply absorbed in my work, and without looking up waved a hand to offer him an armchair. He dropped easily into it, and lay back with the poise and suppleness of an animal in repose. Looking up, I saw he had changed his tie, and my irritation increased at this childish vanity over a piece of colored silk. Who did such a silly fop hope to seduce tonight—one of the little waitresses at the Temporary Restaurant?

He remained in the armchair in silence. I deliberately said nothing myself, meaning to give him plenty of chance to feel bored; but I noticed that he irritated me less sitting near me than when he was not there. I attributed this to a queer sort of animal magnetism, for it was somehow agreeable and reassuring merely to look at him. He sat there so comfortably in his well-fitting tweed suit, with a neatness and cleanliness which indicated plenty of soap and water and careful attention to personal appearance. I noticed that Louis had stopped reading, and was gazing at Philippon with admiring eyes. I found myself becoming jealous, and this annoyed me intensely. It was so damned

396

silly being jealous of one who was certainly my intellectual inferior, just because of his superficial poise and easy manner.

We went to dinner. The way the restaurant worked amused Philippon greatly, and he was astonished by the meagre total of his bill. "Magnificent!" he cried. "For once I'm really going to save some money."

Leaving the restaurant, he invited us onto the terrace of the Roblin café, near the entrance to the park. We stayed there for a while watching the movement of the boulevard. The conversation began to languish. First of all Philippon watched with interest the girls who passed, as if he hoped to see some beautiful nymph emerge from the groves of the park. But the female students we saw were depressingly lacking in looks or charm, and Philippon expressed disappointment.

"Not very exciting, your local girls! I shan't find it too difficult to stay in my room. I can't think of anything worse than going for a walk with those females. Oh well, it's really turned out very well, I'm fed up with chasing the women. I've decided to turn over a new leaf, and lead a quiet, steady respectable life from now on." He yawned loudly, as if to demonstrate that he was settling down straight away to this virtuous existence.

Night had fallen when we returned to the hostel. It was still very hot, and I knew the atmosphere in my room would be intolerably close. We strolled over to the Bush, and threw ourselves down in the long grass, which was growing longer with each fall of dew. There was no moon, and the dust of a sultry July night obscured the stars; we began to lose sight of one another. Philippon was stretched out on his back and appeared to be sleeping. Louis was silent, and so was I—thinking of my evenings with Marianne. The grass was warm and soothing, reflecting the heat which had beaten down on it all day.

Suddenly Philippon murmured, out of the blue: "God, I needed this holiday badly. No women. Here at least the bitches will give me a bit of peace for once."

Louis had scarcely dared speak all evening. He must be feeling horribly "innocent" and unsophisticated, as I could guess from my own experience—and I at least had not been schooled in the strictness of a seminary. But as if emboldened by the darkness, he now came out with a question: "Why are all women bitches, M. Philippon?"

Philippon sat up to light a cigarette. The match cupped in his two hands momentarily lit up his face, revealing rancor and bitterness and contempt instead of the complacent smile I normally saw there. When he called them bitches, did he mean to insult the whole sex, or was he thinking of any particular women? "Why bitches?" he repeated to himself two or three times, as if giving the question careful thought. Then he relapsed into the grass, and eventually, after drawing nervously at his cigarette several times, he began to talk.

I cannot remember all he said, but its sense, and his tone of voice, did not belie the look I had seen on his face through the flame of the match. I had half hoped he would show himself up before Louis in all his vulgar licentiousness; but this Philippon, recounting the excesses of youth from the angle of hardened experience, was no longer the cheerful blasé rake I was familiar with. His phrases were often clumsy, and the veneer of self-assurance and cynicism only reappeared at intervals. He talked jerkily, following no logical sequence of thought, often stopping, breaking off into a digression, and then returning uneasily to his fragmentary narrative.

It was the depressing story of a spoilt adolescent reacting contemptuously to a father's extravagant hopes, running after a string of worthless women in a monotonously similar atmosphere of frustration, futility, and self-pity.

Although he had begun talking to answer Louis, he seemed later to be speaking merely for his own benefit. He stopped and lit another cigarette. The light of the match made him blink, and this grimace furrowed his face with wrinkles which suggested a long lassitude, untouched by real happiness. I had been listening in silence, though at times I felt like muttering: "How can you talk of love, when your experience is limited to the crudest kind of sexual pleasure? The heart doesn't enter into it with you—the thing you're talking about isn't love at all. You're misusing words."

In the darkness I could not distinguish Louis' face, but I could see that his head was raised, and I guessed how intently he had been listening, probably sweating with eagerness, his temples throbbing. What could a boy with his experience make of such a wholesale confession, when a man like Philippon ran through the women in his life, sparing no details? It reminded me what an innocent I remained myself in these matters, compared with Philippon.

But perhaps it mattered less than I thought to Louis, full of his own dreams and desires. How many men and women, cherishing the great dream of becoming one flesh, have found to their bitter disillusionment that the two sexes are irreducibly separate! All this would seem mere metaphysical theory to Louis; he must eventually part with his innocence and learn selfishly the taste of Woman; he would then have all his life to try and understand the miracle of love.

In any case his immediate concern was with something far more concrete, and now he suddenly found his voice, hoarse with eagerness, seeking reassurance, to bring out the only question which really interested him, the question he had been burning to ask all the time: "How did you actually start, M. Philippon?"

The tempter laughed softly and answered: "My first little guinea pig, eh, Louis? By the way, you needn't call me M. Philippon—Henri is my name. If it'll be any use to you, my lad, I'm very willing to tell you all about it—the story goes back some eight years. Only not tonight, I'm too sleepy; ask me again tomorrow."

We went back to the hostel. As he said goodnight to us, Philippon opened his door and turned on the light. What I saw from the door looked like any traveler's hotel room: cases opened in the corner, clothes thrown untidily over the backs of chairs, ties scattered at random, three or four books spread out on the table; but not a sheet of paper, not a notebook or folder, no sign of personal books or pictures or any other permanent possessions. It was the room and table of an indolent and luxury-loving young man, completely without roots and

399

without any interest in them. But thinking of my own table, crowded with files and papers, I did not feel like laughing. After listening to him tonight, I found myself understanding better Philippon's curious personal magnetism; it came from his having encountered so many women in something which he called love, and from living for years only through their emotions and his desire.

He went over to the window, and gazed sadly out into the night. In this picturesque pose he looked very handsome, a modern Don Juan. Then he returned, and noticed Louis diffidently feeling the silk of a tie. "English-type tie," said Philippon. "You've got good taste, Louis lad. It's yours if you like it." He laughed genially, and at once became a very ordinary young man once more, complacent and not in the least romantic.

We said goodnight, in Louis' case very reluctantly. He carried off his present proudly with him. Back in my room, I went to bed; but it was still very hot, the night was without a breath of wind, and I did not feel sleepy. I thought of my new neighbor, with his aura of midnight love-scenes, and a sort of sadness came over me. During the evening his words had revived old ghosts, carnal torments and desires, surprises and defeats, and all the vanished hopes whose distant echoes still rang mournfully for me like a sound of bells beneath the sea.

Suddenly I found it all too much. My task was too long and heavy, my duty was too grim and difficult, my heart was too starved and lonely. An obscure appetite was gnawing at my stomach, and perhaps I should appease it by kissing a woman's lips, caressing her body, flinging myself down beside her. Then I could fall asleep at last, dazed and drunk with flesh, incapable of feeling anything further, hope or disgust or pleasure or anger. Perhaps I should do this just once—but no, I couldn't, it was too squalid, too dishonorable. I could almost have wept to feel myself so reasonable.

Next day, returning from the hospital, I found Philippon and Louis in the restaurant, sitting facing each other. Or rather, Philippon was lolling back in his chair giving his young friend a lecture, and Louis was sitting bolt upright, almost too absorbed to bring the half-raised fork to his mouth.

"Above all, never make a fool of yourself with virgins. You never know with them where an affair is going to lead, and whenever it turns out badly, you'll be blamed by public opinion. Imagine the crime of daring to touch an innocent maiden! It's amusing, of course, when you know what really happens, usually. You take one of these lily-white lasses, pure as the driven snow, and give her a few little lessons. In a week or a month she's quite unrecognizable, a first-class nymphomaniac without any shame or even caution. The idea of the pleasure even makes her forget about the risk. Give her a single inch and she'll have your trousers off while you're still in the taxi. In a panic you try to reason with her, but too late, it's impossible to go into reverse. Her sexual possibilities have been revealed to her—that was your doing, and at all costs she wants to try them out; she clings to you, and that's where things start going wrong. The most serious thing of all is that these girls have only one idea in their heads: marriage. They're obsessed with it, and you can't stop them believing that you're only taking an interest in them because you're hoping later to found a family. However much you back out and explain that you're not the marrying kind of young man, you can never count on a girl's pride. The only hope is flight, which isn't always very easy. So, for greater safety, make up your mind that as a general rule every adventure of this kind is bound to come to a bad end: it's a heap of trouble or a wedding. Very moral conclusion: don't play about with virgins. There are plenty of women without that."

Louis was listening, his eyes shining with attention, brows knit beneath his thick cap of gold hair. The practical strategy revealed to him by Philippon must certainly seem to him a thousand times more exciting and agreeable than the romantic world found in my books. Anyhow, from this day on, he abandoned me completely and spent all his time questioning and listening to his new friend. Philippon allowed himself to be led on, and would answer in a tone that was half mocking and half protective. He spoke with a freedom not exactly cynical; it was, rather, the off-hand air of a man who has already seen a great deal of life—he would condense into three sentences the thousand delicate lessons of a science of women amassed in seven or eight years. Louis, bolder now, would stop him, make him explain himself, oblige him to go into exact and minute details. A conscientious pupil, he hoped to incorporate all his teacher's methods into his own work, so that he could plunge into his first sexual adventures with the *expertise* of one who has already conquered many women before. Philippon already predicted a fine future for him.

After this I only saw master and pupil at mealtimes and for a few minutes of post-prandial relaxation round the lawns. Although I distrusted him, I had to admit I derived a certain pleasure from listening to Philippon. For one thing he was often very amusing. He never reverted again, at least while I was there, to the bitter, savage, discontented mood of the first evening. But after I had heard the detailed recital of his amatory methods with women, of all his little secrets and ruses, he lost his prestige in my eyes, like a conjuror clumsy enough to show how his tricks are done.

I myself felt in no danger of corruption, I was surely separated from Philippon by the least of my thoughts. Meeting, flirting, planning, sleeping, parting—how could anyone be content with this sort of life? However much Louis gaped with admiration at each new lesson in amatory tactics, and for all the cheerful vitality you felt in Philippon's adventures, nothing could be more commonplace than this succession of naked women with willing bodies, whose faces and Christian names he often had difficulty in remembering. I excused him now for calling these monotonous sexual exercises "love," since only one word exists covering so many different things. Some sort of modesty prevented me from telling him that only something as pure as my passion for Marianne, slowly and tenderly maturing, could really be dignified by the name of love.

But alas, it was not only modesty which kept me from intervening; as always, I was unduly sensitive to "what other people think." Often enough Philippon would ask me to confirm one of his remarks from my personal experience: "Isn't that so, Jean?" he would say. I did not like to appear less sophisticated than he was in front of Louis, and I found myself assenting to the most cynical aphorisms; Louis was in any case dazzled in advance, and extremely easy to take in. So as not to look foolish in Philippon's eyes, I adopted the attitude of a young man who has to live a fairly sober life while working for exams. Like a sportsman in training, I was keeping myself in trim for the big match. This suggested, of course, that I would lose no time in making up for my temperance later on.

It was extraordinary that I should not only tolerate Philippon, but often found myself looking at my watch when it was nearly time for him to cross the corridor with Louis, so that the three of us could go off to the restaurant together. One evening I found him particularly outrageous, teaching Louis to despise innocent affection or Platonic love or any talk about common interests and ideals. Such things, he said, were a disgusting travesty of the real thing, which was honest-to-God physical love, and were only fit for impotent intellectuals who were scared to death of going to bed with a woman at all. There were not thirty-six ways of doing a woman good, but only one: to take her in your arms and make love to her. He did not ask me to approve this point of view, and I pretended not to be listening. Several times I was on the point of protesting, but I just did not have the courage. Although Philippon did not know it, he was pillorying my love for Marianne, and I should not have let him get away with that. All evening I felt bitterly ashamed of my silence.

I did not have to suffer much longer from this particular conflict. Louis' guardian suddenly remembered his ward, and instructed him to report without delay to a holiday camp which had been expecting him for two weeks already.

The farewells between master and pupil were very touching. Guessing that Louis after all this theory would pass very quickly to practical exercises, Philippon tried to equip him thoroughly for all love's contingencies. He gave Louis a brief lecture on the virtues of contraceptives, their utility against both V.D. and

403

having a baby. Satisfied that the instructions were now complete, he got the car out of the garage and drove the apprentice Casanova to the station.

Though Louis was gone, Philippon had learned the way to my room. As soon as he found himself too bored in his own room, he came to mine, bringing some physics or chemistry textbook. He would stretch himself out on my bed with a yawn, carefully refrain from opening the book, and then, like a tart at a café sitting patiently waiting in front of her coffee, he would watch me work till it was time for us to go off to the restaurant.

One afternoon he was on one of these protracted visits when we heard steps in the corridor which seemed to hesitate outside several doors, and finally there was a knock on his. He rose and opened my door; before he shut it, I saw the figure of a man in plus-fours. He showed his visitor in, and for a good while I heard lively discussion. Then Philippon's door opened abruptly, and he said "Don't let me keep you." The visitor departed, muttering angrily.

Philippon had already recovered his calm by the time he returned to my room, observing that it was a good thing the man went when he did or he (Philippon) might have lost his temper.

"He's a car-dealer with whom I sometimes do business. The day before I thought I'd be going home for vacation, I sold one of his cars for him, and as we'd previously arranged, he gave me my commission right away. Today, after 'phoning Vichy three or four times, he comes to badger me here. The customer didn't take the car after all, and now the man wants me to return the commission. Don't think I care a rap for a few thousand francs, but commission paid is commission paid. Bad luck for him, of course, but in business one must stick to principles. Besides, he annoys me. He claims I meant to swindle him by saying I was going home when I wasn't. Unfortunately he didn't press this point, I would have been only too pleased to teach him a lesson in manners."

Several times I tried to drag Philippon off to the hospital, but in vain. He preferred to sleep in the mornings, he told me.

"I rarely go to the hospital in term time," he explained, "I can't get up early enough. So why should I dash off there during vacation?"

"Are you going to spend the rest of your life in bed, sleeping or making love? Has it ever occurred to you that you may have some patients one day?"

Philippon's answer on this point suggested he might have been listening to Paul, though the angle with which he approached the matter was a good deal different.

"Patients, you say? Well, three quarters of one's practice is made up of women, so when I make love, you see, I'm really studying my future patients. I assure you I'm a very conscientious student. How can you hope to understand a woman, or treat her diseases, if you haven't previously learned the feel of the female body under your lips and your hands? If university exams were logically arranged instead of dealing with all sorts of absurdities, I should get first class honors merely on what I know about women. Fundamentally, even without gynaecology and all that, medicine is a profession concerned with women. You see what I'm getting at, don't you?"

"I don't think you need labor the point," I remarked, but the sarcasm was lost on him.

"I'm going to be a doctor," he went on, "so I shall have a lot to do with women, and I must study them at very close quarters to be able to understand them. And I shall get my women because I'm a doctor. In fact you've only to say you're a medical student, not even a doctor, and you can pick up any women you want. They throw themselves at you, they implore you, they *want* you. Well, you know what women want . . . and when a woman's pretty I don't find it easy to refuse."

"How do you explain the magic of the word 'doctor' in a woman's eyes?" I inquired; and Philippon again took the question with all due seriousness.

"Yes, I've wondered about that myself, in fact I've given some study to the question. I think it's partly a matter of class. The doctor is a gentleman. An erection on him is flattering to any woman. A doctor lover is after all much more respectable than a wholesale-grocer lover. Generally speaking, a doctor is regarded by the public as the right type; he guarantees honesty, morality, reliability; while as for surgeons some highly-sexed females consider the caress of a hand which cuts open stomachs as almost equivalent to the indescribable pleasure of being raped. But let's consider sentimental women who like to be treated gently: for them the doctor is a subtle psychologist, a sensitive lay-confessor, a man for the very closest confidences. They fall into your arms in confidence, they declare that you are the only person who really understands them. They take you exactly as they take the only brand of aspirin which doesn't give them a tummyache."

"Aren't you afraid of the unmarried ones?" I asked. "I seem to recall your warning young Louis the other day about the tendency of women to expect men to marry them."

"Yes," he agreed, "that is rather a snag, if you happen to be a bachelor. In fact, that's another reason why doctors are evidently superior in women's eyes to people like lawyers, who consider marriage a serious matter. Women know that only doctors are so stupid that they very often marry their mistresses. Well, to overcome that danger, as soon as I'm in practice, I'll have notices put up outside my consulting room: *Doctor Philippon is sorry, but he has no intention to marry*. A few of them will have their ardor dampened by that; but there'll still be plenty who refuse to believe it; at least they'll have to admit they were warned. Yes, old man, whatever the pessimists may say, it's by little signs like this that the medical profession retains its prestige with the public!"

"If that's medical prestige," I said, "I only hope you get caught, and find yourself married to a sour-faced shrew, who'll lead you a dog's life for the rest of your days."

"I can look after myself all right," he answered, not the least nettled. "And besides there are plenty of women who aren't interested in marriage at all. They merely want to have a lover, but they live between the terror of V.D. and the terror of having a baby. A doctor's erection is highly reassuring for this type. V.D.? No risk at all. A baby? A lovely little abortion, care-

406

fully performed, and naturally quite free. Of course that's out of the question for me; there are plenty of abortionists in town if that amuses them. And I've no wish to end up in jail, so I'll also put up little warning notices to say: *Dr. Philippon is sorry, but he does not do abortions.* He who touches pitch you know . . . Ah yes, by studying women I shall become a very high-class doctor—without going to the hospital every morning."

"That's all very well," I protested, "but even if your patients are impressed by your sexual possibilities, I don't see how you'll be able to ask them for a consultation fee. It would sound as if you were charging them for an orgasm. And the women you don't sleep with, what'll you be able to tell them if you don't know anything about medicine? It looks to me is if you're heading for bankruptcy or nervous exhaustion."

"Don't worry about me, old chap, I've already made my plans. Anyhow I don't really intend setting up in ordinary practice at all. It's my father who wanted me to become a doctor; personally I'd have preferred business."

"I quite agree with you," I murmured, "business would have suited you far better. I don't know what your father was thinking about."

"Well, I know just what he was thinking about," answered Philippon; "and I'll tell you. He was at the village school with Serre, the present Minister of Agriculture, who, as you know, is also a doctor. When you've started life as a waiter in a small hotel, even if you've later become proprietor of a luxury one, it impresses you to have a former schoolmate who becomes a doctor and a cabinet minister as well. Between Doctor Serre, even if he weren't a minister, and my old man, or if you prefer it, between two successful men, the old man feels there's still a difference. He thinks his wealthy customers, even though he's as rich as most of them are, will always consider him a superior tradesman, and anyhow not quite in their class."

"So he wanted you to become a doctor and not a hotel keeper?"

"On the contrary; he wanted me to be both. His idea is to build a huge medical luxury hotel, a sanitarium and thermal clinic for a rich international clientele, where people taking cures will find everything they need on the spot, doctors, treatments, X-rays, laboratories, diets, with every comfort besides and the pleasures of a palace. Inside I shall be retailing medicine, while the old man's career as a hotel man will have a brilliant conclusion, with a semi-scientific façade. His old pal the Minister will come down to stay as his guest, and will naturally see he gets a decoration. The old man dreams of that decoration, and to preserve his patience while waiting for me to qualify he draws plans, considers names for the hotel, the monograms for the plates and notepaper and so on. But as at twenty-three I'm only in my second year, and haven't shown much talent so far in passing the necessary exams, he finds the time a bit long. I try to show interest in his idea, so I send him all the names that come into my head, the more erudite and cultural the better: Hotel Therapeutic, Hotel Aesculapius, Hotel Therapeia, Hotel Hippocrates, Hotel Pasteur—oh I give him dozens. It keeps him busy looking up the names in encyclopaedias or dictionaries, and then he doesn't worry about how I'm getting on with my studies."

"How about Quackery Inn or Hotel Hypochondria?" I suggested.

"Don't be tiresome, my friend. Anyhow you see now, don't you, why I don't have to trouble too much about the scientific side? All I need is some well-polished instruments and an impressive setting. I wear a spotless white coat with a neat white cap on my head, and running to and fro are my nurses and lab. girls and assistants. Before I deign to see the patients my staff will have gone through the whole bag of tricks: examination of blood and urine, arterial tension, basal metabolism, radioscopy and radiography, electro-cardiograph, stomach tubes, analysis of stools and sundry other details. Meanwhile I shall be sitting peacefully on my bottom, acknowledged as the great specialist. The rest is a matter of psychology and intuition. You don't think I'm learning my job, do you?"

An obvious rhetorical question, but to break the flow, I had to put in: "I hadn't noticed you making any great efforts in that direction."

"Well, you're quite wrong. I already speak English, German, and Spanish pretty fluently, I play a good game of golf and tennis, and I'm generally acknowledged to be a real expert at bridge. When I've learned the two or three most fashionable maladies, I shall be all set. In cases of difficulty I'll call in some poor bugger of a consultant who's spent ten or fifteen years conscientiously learning all I don't know. He'll provide a good diagnosis, order the right treatment, and usually he won't be smart enough to pinch my patient afterwards."

"From the sound of it, the whole clinic will be one gigantic confidence game. I know what you ought to call the hotel—The Charlatania."

"Sometimes," he went on, "I must admit when I think of that future practice among plutocrats, they disgust me so much in advance that I prefer to forget as long as possible just what bastards they are. Perhaps it's because I already know all the filthy tricks they'll want me to do, that I don't feel like boring myself at hospital five years in advance for their future benefit. And if I find I really can't stand them and they want me to indulge in too many disgusting rackets, I'll chuck the whole thing, tell the old man to go to hell, and become an honest bookmaker."

That trace of bitterness again, showing the unhappy background he had been brought up in. But there was sincerity in this latest outburst, and I found I preferred it to his previous cynicism. But Philippon could not let it go at that; when he had calmed down a bit, he lit another cigarette, and went on tolerantly:

"My father thinks he can keep me hard at work by reducing my allowance, but I shouldn't be a true native of the Auvergne if I let myself be at his mercy. Since I knew how to walk, I've had time to find out how café waiters turn the uncertainties of the turf to their advantage, and I've learned all the best rackets from car-dealers and racetrack touts of every kind. As the old man's hotels have improved in quality, I've graduated from the common or garden cardsharpers to the great international rack-eteers. A luxury hotel is a good field for observation, if you take the trouble to keep your eyes open, and even if I get fed up with the new hotel or it goes bust, I'm not worried, I won't have to go on the dole or start up a suburban practice. I've already quite a substantial bank account, and I've done pretty well on the side this year, what with horses, poker, cars, and a little speculation. In fact, without tiring myself unduly, I should say I've made more on the side than a young doctor who's just become a hospital superintendant after fifteen years of frantic work. To finish up by earning more than he does, I shall have had fifteen years of leisure and enjoyment."

Having convincingly proved his original point, that he did not need to go to the hospital as I did, he yawned and sauntered back to his own room, to my great relief. I had long been familiar with his views on women, but this was the first time I had heard such a detailed *exposé* of his plans for the future and his preoccupation with "getting rich quick."

The great American depression had recently crossed the Atlantic, and we were just learning the meaning of the new word, crisis. Financial troubles were causing even more heartaches than usual all over the country, and students are notoriously among the poorest sections of French society. Most of us were more or less broke most of the time, on meagre scholarships or allowances, but students are resilient, and somehow we "managed" (a word in fairly frequent use), though poverty often led to unfortunate consequences. Petitjean was only one of many who ended up in a sanitarium with T.B. or pleurisy. On the whole, however, my friends treated their impecunious state as something of a joke—a bad joke, but one which was natural and inevitable and had to be accepted.

Internes too were poorly paid for an absorbing but very responsible job, made more attractive by the joys of exuberant male friendship and of work in a team. They also "managed," though many of them were married and in any other profession might by now have been independent in homes of their own. When I was in their common room, the interest of their

410

present work seemed to form a far more frequent topic than any lucrative posts they might hope to gain in the future; when they were ambitious, it was usually more for signs of medical prestige than for any financial profits to be made out of their profession.

Both as student, therefore, and as budding doctor, Henri Philippon seemed incongruous and unnatural, a dangerous animal to be let loose in our midst, with his cheque books, his trafficking in cars, his bank account, and his plans for a sanitarium. I had always been used to comparative poverty, and began to realize that I could not afford to regard myself as invulnerable. In my weaker moments, with Marianne not there, this was the sort of man, the sort of attitude, which might easily get a grip on me. I must pull myself together, and try to find some escape from an overdose of Philippon's company. But somehow I still could not shake myself clear of him, even when an alteration in the environment provided a strong diversion.

Chapter 2

TOWARDS THE END of July, one by one or in convoy, the provincial and foreign students began to arrive. The Cité came to life again, renewing its role of holiday hotel which I had seen it play the previous year. Pretty girls with a variety of accents could once more be seen walking along the pathways between the hostels, and in my hostel, thanks to the warden's absence, in the very corridors. After each meal Philippon would prolong our sessions on the Roblin café terrace to watch the girls pass, with an eye at once innocent and critical. When an Italian or Spanish girl passed, he would explain to me with a wealth of technical detail how certain races have an immediate bent for love, whereas it takes months, he said, to bring a French girl into the right state for sexual pleasure; nor was his opinion very favorable as to American girls. But all his commentaries maintained a perfectly disinterested objectivity, as if he would no more have thought of having amorous relations with these females than with animals he was studying at the zoo.

Afterwards we would soberly stroll back to the hostel. Philippon's sexual abstinence continued; he began to grow fat. Several times he stretched himself and repeated: "Oh yes, it certainly does one good." He did not make it clear, however, whether it was the freedom from female company on which he was lavishing this appreciation, or merely the extra pounds he was putting on.

When we were both back in my room, I returned to my work, and so, in a sense, did he. For he seemed little concerned

412

by the need to pass exams in October, as required by his father, and his real work consisted in reading *Motor* magazine from cover to cover, especially the advertisements, then looking at a financial paper, and finally at *Racing News*. This last gave him more trouble, for he made very careful notes in his diary on the names of horses and their odds. He had a system, which he took very seriously, and no one could have been more fluent on the subject of starters, odds, and form. He had a faultless memory for such matters, almost amounting to genius, and had he deigned to know a quarter as much about medicine as he did about jockeys, horses, and odds, he could have snapped his fingers at the stiffest exams.

When he had finished reading these magazines and making the necessary notes, he would go to my bookcase, choose a detective story and settle down to read it on my divan. He would begin one chapter, quickly become bored with it, get up to choose another book, glancing out of the window for a moment, and then begin reading again without much conviction, interrupting himself and me at every turn by comments and criticism. At other times he would sit motionless for hours on end, with a cigarette hanging on his lips, watching me with a pitying expression in those eyes half-closed like a cat's. I found his capacity for indolence and passivity almost pathological, more suited to a complete illiterate.

It was an extremely hot summer, broken only by short thunderstorms which did not bring new freshness to the air. Aided by the heat, Philippon usually relapsed eventually into a siesta, in which he would spend much of the afternoon; while I, left in comparative peace and solitude, would try to regain my serenity. This was not so easy, however, as soon as I looked at the somnolent Philippon, his head slightly thrown back, stressing the power and self-confidence of his body even in repose.

I could not stop looking uneasily at this confirmed hedonist sleeping on my divan, and tried to analyze my feelings towards him. I was revolted by the way his conversation was limited to two subjects: money and his sordid idea of "love." I detested his air of effortless superiority, the impenetrable thickness of his skin. But there was still that vague sense of magnetism in his personality, which made it impossible for me, in my heart of hearts, to condemn him completely. Perhaps I was merely impressed by the young man who had already been through so many experiences, and by the frankness of his taste for luxury and his primitive hunger for life. I found him unnatural, like a middle-aged roué posing as a student, but I could not help being impressed by the easy swagger, the outlaw's serenity, with which he carried off this extreme sophistication. In fact, when I got to the bottom of my contempt and my dislike, I was ashamed to detect distinct traces of jealousy.

Meanwhile the hostel soon became a place far from conducive to peaceful study. From all sides, from the lawn and the corridors, came the sounds of music and songs and laughter. At first Philippon's only reaction to these intrusive noises was to hum through his lips the refrain which disturbed our solitude. He resisted for a few days more, and then I noticed him taking a nervy interest in the slightest noise outside. There were too many temptations making their presence felt, too many possibilities in the air.

One afternoon, when he had finished going through the racing papers and noting the odds, he did not even make the gesture of taking a book. My best novels must suddenly have seemed excessively stale by the side of real-life adventures within such easy reach. For a short while he remained on my divan, with eyes following vaguely a scurry of dust dancing in a beam of sunlight. Very near us, almost against our door, could be heard the laughter of a young woman going past down the corridor. Stretched out on the divan, all Philippon's body remained still, except his eyes, which I saw grow hard and sharp. A fierce flame gleamed inside them, and it was not till a few seconds later that the rest of his body came to life. He rose and stretched himself, like a cat which has just woken and stretches itself ominously before seeking some new prey.

I saw him depart with relief. For half an hour I was happy in my solitude and silence, remaining wide awake despite the dizzying heat; but after that I found it almost impossible to keep my eyes open. All at once I felt sadly flat and forlorn—which I put down to the thundery weather.

The whole afternoon I did not see Philippon again. I dined alone at the Temporary Restaurant, and I had been back in my room for some time when I recognized his impatient step in the corridor. He was humming a gay tune, and when he pranced into the room after an offhand knock, he was almost unrecognizable in his enthusiasm and vitality. He dashed over, pulled me unceremoniously from my chair, explaining as he did so that it was absolutely essential I should do him a favor:

"I've just picked up an Austrian girl, and my God, Jean, she's terrific, just my style. The two of us will click marvellously, I saw it at a glance. The only thing is, she has another girl with her, and she doesn't want to leave her in the lurch. Tomorrow, you realize, it won't matter much; but this evening I can't drag both of them along with me. You've just got to take one off my hands. I've got out my car, and we're going to do a tour of Montparnasse, then see the moonlight over Notre Dame; not my idea, you can well imagine, but hers. Austrian girls are a bit like German ones, as I know from experience: the program always has to be slightly educational or cultural. There's always something tiresome they want to learn or visit. Do hurry up, go and put your clothes on. Come on now, they're waiting for us at Roblin's. I promise you we won't be back too late."

He patted me on the shoulder, and the happy gleam in his eye suggested a bond of man-to-man understanding between us. I started making excuses: I had to work tonight, and then there was hospital tomorrow morning. Philippon cut me short at once: "None of that please, Jean. One evening's fun isn't going to keep you out of the Academy of Medicine thirty years from now." He tried to push me towards the door, but I sat down again, saying: "I can't imagine anything less my idea of fun than going out with a Fräulein I've never seen and shan't be able to say a single word to. My German's confined to *Nicht Verstehen*."

415

"Aha, I see what's worrying you. You're scared my girl will be pretty and the other a horror—the old trick. You can put your mind at rest: yours isn't at all my type, but she's very sweet all the same. And then you know, all these foreign girls who make tracks for France, they've only got one idea in their head. With my little piece I don't anticipate any great difficulty, you can see at once that she's dead keen. A woman with the urge is something sacred for me, I count it a categorical duty to satisfy her. You can always try with yours, but if it bores you or you don't like her, don't feel yourself under an obligation. You can talk about literature to her, and perhaps she'll tell you lots of interesting things about Austria. She's bound to talk some French. Come on, Jean, make up your mind. The world comes towards us with a smiling face—at least try to make the most of it. Besides, as a member of the Cité Universitaire, it is surely your duty to work for a better understanding between students—especially when the duty is as agreeable as it is to-night."

His eyes flashed with excitement, and he had lost all his nonchalance of the preceding days. This period of abstinence seemed to have electrified him, and he sounded as if he was unable to live a moment longer without female company; he had just rediscovered his true element. His air of authority impressed me despite myself, and I felt embarrassed to give him an outright "No." I searched for other excuses. I was in shirt-sleeves and noticed my frayed cuffs.

"I can't possibly go out like this. It'd look as if you were taking out a poor relation."

"If that's all that's stopping you, it's easily fixed. Hey presto, I'll lend you a suit. It'll fit you near enough. Come on."

He was quite well aware of the ascendancy he had over me. He seized me by the hand, dragged me out of my room, pushed me into his, and picked out of his wardrobe a flannel suit, a shirt and a tie, saying: "If you don't put that on in a flash, our reputation will be mud. Remember, the honor of France is at stake."

Then he brought out his ace of trumps: "When you're a

416

famous specialist, probably half senile, you'll be sorry not for any of the things you've done but for all the things you've not done. I'm trying to save you from future pangs of remorse. Life only becomes pleasant directly you stop taking it too seriously."

I had never told him about Marianne, and I could think of nothing further to say which would fit my assumed character of a sensible but broadminded young man. All the time I was changing, he paced up and down the room, humming the same happy tune.

Down the road, in front of the café terrace, I recognized Philippon's sports car. As soon as they saw us, the two Austrian students, who were doubtless growing somewhat impatient, left their table and came towards us. Philippon said to me with a radiant expression on his face: "Damn fine build, isn't it! Lovely figure."

I could be in no doubt for which of the two girls he was claiming my admiration. It was the taller one. She had a rather obvious beauty, the sort nobody need waste time analyzing so compelling are its immediate attractions. Philippon stopped: "Lovely figure," he repeated.

I was a little disappointed by her companion, who was a slender girl, without any sparkle, with silvery hair and eyebrows, hunched little shoulders, and a pale unexciting face without any apparent makeup.

"Yes, that's the partner for me," I thought, sizing her up at a glance; but then adding as an afterthought: "Anyhow, for what I've got to do with her, it'll be less nuisance than having a big buxom creature who's always chattering." Already Philippon was making the introductions in German. If I had to waste an evening with this little Fräulein, I might as well pretend to show some keenness and leave myself with pleasant memories. I shook hands with the most charming smile I could manage. The bigger girl was called Rosi, and mine was Martha. We used Christian names at once, naturally, all four of us.

While Rosi got in next to Henri, I helped Martha to climb in the rumble seat with me. There was very little room, and

I took good care not to look as if I were taking advantage of this: I sat hunched in my corner. The car started, and after we had gone a few yards I tried to talk to my neighbor in French; I saw she did not understand a word I said, even if I talked very slowly. We tried English, but the result on my side was so lamentable that we gave up the struggle at once.

Henri in front was driving very fast and at the same time keeping up a conversation with Rosi. As he had told me, he seemed to talk German very fluently. His neighbor, to hear him better, turned her face towards him, sun-tanned and full of vitality beneath her beautiful golden hair. She was laughing as she listened to his male voice softening seductively. Perhaps it was only because I had to listen to the sound of words without knowing their sense; but it was certainly unfamiliar to me, this new voice which Henri used: reduced in pitch by the speed at which we were travelling, it reached me warm and musical and caressing. Sometimes he took a hand off the steering-wheel and rested it with a natural gesture on Rosi's thigh; she made no objections, and with her head turned towards him seemed only interested in the charmer's words. I saw, however, that she was not really listening: with submissive eyes she merely followed the movement of his lips, as if all round him she could pick up the scent of past love affairs, and guessed at all the mouths which had hung on his in the past. I understood better now why she had not wasted more than a fraction of a second looking at me when we were being introduced. She was already completely obsessed by the lordly Philippon.

We reached Montparnasse very quickly, and he pulled up outside a building fronted by flashing lights. While we pushed through the crowds on the pavement, he took the opportunity to remark happily: "See, Jean, it'll work out beautifully for all four of us!" Without waiting for any rejoinder he pushed all four of us towards a door with closed shutters, pierced by holes where ventilators whirred, letting through a mangled version of the music inside.

The hall was full, but Henri was not to be put off by small

418

obstacles like that. He used all his charm and diplomacy, and soon a waiter was conducting us down the side of the room to a table, where he joined up four folding chairs and squeezed them in between the larger chairs of the neighboring tables. The decorations around us represented an African village, with imitation mud-huts all round a central square, which was the dance floor. Between two enormous cardboard idols a Negro band beat its instruments with a roar loud enough to bring the house down. To this accompaniment the couples dancing, all wedged hard against each other, shuffled a few yards up and down in an atmosphere as stifling as the Metro in rush hour. Remarkably enough, they all seemed delighted; they shouted and laughed and jostled each other with every sign of intense jubilation.

Henri refused to waste a minute in sitting down; he dragged Rosi off at once. With bodies locked tightly together, they disappeared among bulky Czechs, hordes of Americans and Poles and Belgians, all wearing corduroy jackets or some similar "bohemian" garb, which might help them to be taken for genuine artists.

I remained standing for a moment to take the scene in better. Ventilators stirred the clouds of smoke round the ceiling. The dancers had sweat streaming from their faces; they puffed and panted, looking either ludicrous or repulsive or both. Georges Gédéon, had he seen them, might well have expatiated on the way snakes writhe and dart out their tongues in dances preparatory to mating. It was incredible to me that so many people could enjoy these frantic contortions in such tropical heat. Instead of fidgeting up and down, pinching and handling and fondling each other, they might just as well have simply gone to bed with each other; some indeed seemed to be trying to do this standing up. In the whole squalid mass of sweating humanity, only a very few couples kept some semblance of dignity and decency. Henri and Rosi were among them.

Dazed by the noise, the lights and the movement, I sat down; the back of an armchair separated me from Martha. I was tightly wedged between the two people next to me, the smoke made my

419

eyes smart, and my chair was extremely hard. I hoped Henri would soon have enough and would take me back to the peace and quiet of my own room.

Martha too was looking round her, with neither contempt nor guilty eagerness in her expression, but a bewilderment which I judged to be almost childlike. Gathering all my resources, I asked her in English whether she danced, and she answered: "Badly."

I was delighted; that released me from the duty of inviting her. Out of politeness I explained to her in very painful English that I too was a bad dancer. This was the truth; I had learned a few steps at Toulouse with the girls in the rowing club, but had made no progress since then. Marianne did not dance, and most of the "Carleret set" seemed to despise the modern French style of dancing as an absurd travesty of love-making. I had sometimes regretted my inadequacy as a dancer, but resigned myself to the fact very easily. I could not do something which the Philippons of this world found perfectly simple; it was not at all important. I made up for it very happily in other ways.

I smiled apologetically at Martha, and the smile she gave me in return seemed to excuse us both for not being dancers. While waiting patiently for the end of the ordeal, I took a straw and sucked some of the soapy-looking liquid which Henri had authoritatively ordered for the four of us; it tasted sweet and refreshingly cool. I sucked it through greedily, and by the time I had drunk half the glass, my head began turning and my stomach seemed to be on fire.

Several times Henri and Rosi returned to sit down. But as soon as the band struck up its frenzied rhythms once more, they leapt up and dashed back into the crush. My neighbors having also disappeared onto the floor, I found a little more space and was able to settle down more comfortably and nearer to Martha. She drew on her straw now and then, and the beverage began to make her cheeks flush and her eyes shine. Encouraged by the fairly heavy makeup of all her neighbors, she took a stick of rouge out of her bag and painted her lips with care. After that, when she looked at me with the smile

420

which had to serve us instead of conversation, I found her almost pretty.

At the same time everything else began to seem more natural, and my ear even became attuned to the frantic drumbeats of the hottest Negro jazz. I let myself gradually be carried away by the pulsing rhythm, ready to recognize, in old Prichard's sententious formula, that "Just the same, there's something in it." From time to time I would smile at Martha, finding it really quite tolerable for us to be waiting here together. Perhaps it was the glow of the alcohol, or else the domination, usurped by my brain for a whole year, had at last been restored to my body by the fierce primitive intoxicating music. Or perhaps it was Martha herself with her flushed cheeks and smile underlined by rouge, hinting at a touch of mild flirtatiousness between us.

My seat was very comfortable, and I was aware of being somewhat drunk. I could have stayed like this till morning, but Henri tapped me on the shoulder with the news that we were leaving: "Must go to another spot. We'll drink a bottle of champagne at Montmartre."

"Why?" I asked, more thickly than I intended. "I was just getting used to things. 'Sreally not at all bad here." The girls had gone to the ladies' room.

"Possibly. But there are certain traditions to be observed. Start off in Montparnasse, go on to a nightclub in Montmartre, create the right atmosphere, and finish up in bed—that's the regular round, the ritual. Can't do it any other way."

I had no desire at all to move. I tried another excuse: "Look here, Henri, I haven't much money on me, and I don't like always letting you pay."

"Don't worry about that, old chap. Two or three of my business deals have just come off successfully, and I'm glad to turn the banknotes into harmless pleasure. To be a success in love, you've got to spend money on it. So let's go."

When Martha was seated in the back, I let myself collapse heavily at her side, and as the car started up with a jerk, my knee touched hers. One evening when I was there, Henri had told young Louis: "If your knee should touch a woman's knee unintentionally, it's more polite not to apologize." Recalling this, I nearly burst into inane giggles, and refrained from saying anything. Martha would in any case not have understood; but I did not withdraw my knee. The car sped very fast through almost empty streets, sobering me up a bit; but having walked or used public conveyances all my life, I found everything delightful. I was fascinated by the speed, the caress of the night wind on my face, and the undeniably exciting warmth of an unfamiliar female body against mine.

Henri stopped on a hill near Montmartre. Expensive cars were parked on both sides of the road. A doorman with gold buttons rushed forward to open the gate, and then escorted us to an awning of red and blue velvet twisted with silk, above an entrance hall illuminated with Venetian glass and mirrors. Here an immaculate headwaiter took us in his charge. As I went into the hall, I caught sight of myself in one of the mirrors, and found myself almost unrecognizable in the borrowed suit. I looked almost as elegant as Henri, I told myself complacently. I followed the headwaiter feeling much less intimidated.

My self-consciousness returned when we lifted heavy brocade curtains and came right into a hall with gilded walls, where couples were dancing quietly to soft music. The headwaiter moved a table back to settle us ceremoniously on a deep banquette. We sank into it luxuriously, and then he brought a bottle of champagne. Henri looked at the label with a frown, asked to see the winelist, skimmed an expert eye over it, and asked for a different vintage. I had time to see the price opposite it on the list, and was appalled. Henri caught my look.

"Always keep to the rules," he said with a laugh towards the two girls, who could understand so little French: "When you go out with a woman, even most respectable, the essential thing is to flatter her by spending a lot of money. That's why, in affairs of the heart, money makes things go a lot more smoothly, and why I go to so much trouble to acquire some. Nice atmosphere here, don't you find? When you're used to silk, cotton scratches the skin."

Then he stood up and drew Rosi onto the floor. I stayed by

Martha, who was doubtless as naïve as I was, and as much impressed by the luxurious decor. We looked in silence at the sumptuous room, the slow procession of couples dancing gracefully by, half their bodies standing out above the white line of the tables. You saw evening dresses, tails and dinner jackets, and a few ordinary suits worn by foreign tourists. Waiters passed with muffled steps, speaking in whispers.

Suddenly I felt happy to be there, without moving, with Martha sitting virtuously at my side like any good-looking girl you meet by chance on a train or bus. I decided then that I could stay near her indefinitely like this, without any desire for her body, merely wanting to make myself pleasant to her, sometimes murmuring sweet nothings, born of my own wellbeing and her gentleness.

When Henri came back, he shook me: "Make some effort, Jean; you must try one dance, I'm sure the little girl's dying for it. Try the next tango, you needn't be afraid of looking foolish, it's all in the dark anyhow. Here's one now." He took my hand and Martha's, and dragged us both towards the floor. Somewhat panicstricken, I found myself among the dancers with Martha in my arms.

Henri was right, the half-darkness was comforting. At the end of a few turns without too many blunders, I felt less tense and anxious. Till then I had been too busy guiding Martha to think of anything else; only then did I really notice the slender figure I was holding. I saw very close to me the delicate white skin of her face and neck, the long lashes hiding the gray eyes, and her soft silvery hair. I heard too her soft breathing, as she followed my steps with submissive modesty. It was like being seventeen again and learning to dance—holding your partner chastely in your arms, all very exciting and agreeable. When the dance finished and Martha detached herself from me, I was quite sorry to release her.

We returned to our table, and Henri celebrated our exploit by ordering a second bottle to be opened. I sank down on the seat near Martha, feeling stiffer than after taking violent exercise without training; all my muscles ached. I drank two gulps of champagne, as I would have taken a strong tonic, and immediately felt easier. The wine, following the cocktails at Montparnasse, filled its role. My head, like my muscles, became light as air, and I felt bursting with complacency and self-confidence. Altogether, dancing was no harder than playing billiards. I stretched out my legs, relaxed against the back of the sofa, and looked at the room: the reflection of the lights on the glasses and silver, the graceful procession of dancers, lovely women in evening dresses which allowed you to guess at their soft thighs, their bodies secretly ready for a man. I sniffed the perfumed air, absorbing it to the full. Good old Henri was right: life becomes something quite delightful as soon as you stop taking it too seriously. To complete my self-conversion, I drank some more champagne.

Martha was wearing a light silk dress, and I followed with my eyes the contours of her firm little breasts, the curve of her hips; now I had held her in my arms, it was her body I saw beneath her dress. Just then Henri broke in on my thoughts, and I tried to adopt a casual tone when answering. The champagne acted as a drug, cozening me of half my will-power. My hand approached Martha's, rested upon it lightly enough, oh very lightly, just with the ends of the fingers, and stopped there.

I was a split personality. One me was watching the actions of the other me, who was an utterly different character. How pleasant it was here, said the other me, how sweet was this life of pleasure, soft and light, soft as Martha's flesh beneath her dress. My fingers remained motionless, and Martha was silent. It was nothing at all, this purely accidental, inadvertent caress, but strangely tempting to prolong it. The gilded walls, the delicate and exciting perfumes, the lilt of the music, swept over me in a surge of sensuality. I did not like this feeling, and made a great effort to shake it off.

"Falling asleep with ladies present, you cad," breezed Henri, shaking me. "Rosi's had enough, so we're going now. I'll bring you back to your beloved studies or perhaps to beddybye."

I found it hard to rise. I bumped against the side of the table, and upset a glass. "Walk straight at least as far as the door,"

424

said Henri, taking me under the arm. "Fortunately, you don't have to drive."

The gold-buttoned doorman helped me into the rumble seat again, and once there I passed an arm behind Martha as if to make our seat less uncomfortable. The night was close and warm. The car again travelled fast, and I sat there with my eyes closed, feeling the warm wind against my face. I could have stayed for ever with this light burden against my arm. I wanted to escape, forgetting everything; the morning was infinitely remote.

Henri took a corner very sharply, throwing Martha hard against me. She stayed there, nestling into me. Very near my ear I could hear her soft breathing mingling with mine. She raised her head slightly to look at me, and the smile on her half-open lips said all that was needed between us. It was a challenge to go further, and I realized that she was entirely willing, agreeable to my desires. She liked me—what a burst of pride this look of consent released inside me! Instead of the finger tips, I opened my hand wide and placed it on her thigh, only meaning to show gratitude by this gesture of possession. But to touch her like this swept away the remains of my resistance. Weariness had somehow added new charm to the delicate face, and when I saw it near mine, I was overwhelmed by a flood of dizzying emotions. Well before the evening had begun, probably right from the time Henri arrived on the scene, these feelings had been working to a climax, which had now been reached; and now I was succumbing at last. The sensual powers inside the male body, sleeping during the months of study, held enchained by my love for Marianne, had suddenly rebelled and shaken free.

At the time, of course, such an analysis could not have been further from my thoughts. In a confused surge of desire I bent over Martha, squeezed her in my arms and seized her mouth. In the rapid whirl of the lights above us, I saw her eyes grow wider and wider between the long lashes.

Henri was still driving very fast, and the few remaining peo-

425

ple in the streets, as they saw the car flash past, may possibly have noticed a self-absorbed couple three quarters buried in the rumble seat. My fingers searched the bare flesh for a more intimate caress. Martha relaxed, and I knew at once that she must have had previous experience of lovemaking. For a moment I had a feeling of resentment. Pretending to be so innocent, and she had already let men play about with her before, just like this, a good deal more than this, in fact! What Henri said was true: these girls who played the virgin were the worst of the lot. As for Martha, I wanted to hurt her, punish her forcibly; at least my caresses should make her bleed. I lost control.

Beneath my fingers she started moaning softly—not too loud, or Henri and Rosi would hear. Suddenly I saw her gray eyes darkening with pleasure, and I felt I was in command again. This little personal success helped to appease me.

The garage where Henri kept his car was in an alley by the corner of the park, very near the Cité. The garage doors were closed, and we all climbed out of the car, while Henri tried to pull the night-watchman out of a heavy slumber. As soon as my feet touched the ground, I felt not exactly drunk but distinctly dizzy. I had to prop myself against a wall, and Martha came over and leaned heavily on my arm, apparently wilting with weariness. The face she rested on my shoulder was now very pale, though somehow beautiful in a shy, almost frightened way. Her mouth wore an uncertain smile, mingling pain and pleasure, and was still red where I had bitten it.

To support her I passed both my arms round her shoulders, and drew her nearer me as if to cradle her. I felt her relaxing, she was still, she seemed to have dropped off to sleep. Looking down at the long silvery eyelashes turned down on the charming little face, I felt myself the proud protective male—a role old as the hills—standing with a girl in my arms, half-child, half-woman, guarding her warm and confident slumber. At last the watchman came out and crashed back the door of the garage. Henri drove the car in, and disappeared with Rosi into the back of the garage. Martha and I stayed by ourselves in the dark alley.

426

Then she seemed to wake up. Emboldened by the darkness, she raised her head, and found my lips with such force that our teeth clashed momentarily. With a slow but furious strength, her hands pressed on my chest, clenched against my neck, and seemed to be trying to entreat me. When our mouths came apart, I found myself breathless, trembling, tipsy once more; and Martha, with her head falling against my chest, began murmuring unfamiliar words, a sort of soft senseless lullaby. Bending over her, I listened to it blissfully, all my former aggressiveness forgotten, my only thought to be her tender protector.

Henri and Rosi returned, and pulled us apart. When Martha was no longer in my arms, I had a queer feeling of physical emptiness and cold. She leaned on me to keep herself from staggering. I should have liked to carry her instead of merely supporting her.

The two girls were staying at America House, but I realized at once that Henri was leading them towards our hostel. I followed him without saying anything. The railings were easily surmounted, and there was no chance of an unfortunate meeting with the warden, who was still on holiday. Quite openly, we followed the front path straight into the building.

Going in first, Henri felt for the staircase light without finding it. Taking Rosi's hand, he began groping up the stairs. I stayed with Martha at the entrance to the hall, halted by a peculiar uneasiness. I felt as if I were waking from a dream at the exact moment when I was about to succumb irretrievably to some terrible danger. Who was this girl hanging on my arm, and what did I want of her? Oh yes, she would obey my wishes all right, but I hardly knew her, and certainly could not have any real love for her. Perhaps it was the slightly acid, dusty smell of the corridors which once more sobered me up.

Suddenly I thought: I have never taken Marianne into the hostel. Yet I felt she could have gone to the staircase with her eyes closed, just as well as I could, and put her finger at once on the knob Henri Philippon could not find. The room where I was bringing this stranger was not mine: like everything that belonged to me, it was Marianne's, it was the room of both of us; inwardly I called Marianne to my rescue.

Probably I made some instinctive gesture of withdrawal, which Martha sensed equally instinctively. Raising herself on her toes and pressing hard against me, without leaving me time to react, she took my head in her hands, and kissed me with a fervor which promised me her complete surrender—if indeed I had ever doubted it. In the feverish panic of her breathing, I had not the strength to escape from her, and I dug my fingers in the pale hair. A sudden wave came over me and I sank with it unresisting. I had ceased to be anything but a machine for pleasure, palpitating, irresponsible, drained of all will-power.

On the landing we came up with Henri and Rosi, who were silent and breathing hard; they had evidently been kissing while they waited for us. In the corridor leading to our rooms Henri walked behind her. I caught a glimpse of his face in the faint light from outside; it had a sort of tortured gravity, as if he were about to bite deep into Rosi's neck. He brought out his bunch of keys, and while he picked out the one to his room, Rosi watched him, her healthy greedy lips slightly parted; she was as frantic with impatience as he was. There was no attempt on either face to disguise the crudity of their impulse. Their impatience was as irresistible as it was contagious.

The idea of sending Martha away and remaining with empty hands no longer even crossed my mind. For weeks now I had been hungry for any flesh, and Martha's was soft and cool. As Henri, having opened his door, was about to disappear, I asked him for no very clear motive: "How long are they staying?" To which he replied: "Exactly six days."

Six days! It was an adventure sentenced to death almost before it had begun. It therefore proclaimed itself to be without danger, it did not lead anywhere, it was limited, null. This idea banished from my mind any last remaining scruples. With dry throat and nerves tingling, I opened the door of my room, and pushed my partner inside without a word. The silence was already tense with the expectation of sexual pleasure.

Chapter 3

FOUR MINUTES MORE. Martha was just leaving. Till then we had stayed together in silence on the platform. The conductor had just gone by, closing the doors of compartments, and Martha and Rosi had to get onto the train. A breathless family and a porter loaded with luggage filled the corridor immediately and pushed the two girls back into their compartment.

Martha lowered the window and smiled out at me, her face already puckered up with sadness. We had practically no words in common anyhow, but this smile, which was so near to tears, gave me her real goodbye far better than any words could have done.

I was jostled to and fro by the crowds swarming on the platform, waves of people dashing for the train, seeing off friends and relations, constantly eddying backwards and forwards to escape being run down by baggage trucks. Once they had got their cases onto the rack, the passengers themselves came up to the window and leaned out their indifferent heads by the side of Martha's small strained face.

In the night, just as we were going to sleep, I had painfully translated on her lips the words: "I wish tomorrow would never come." But this tomorrow we had tried to reject had become today, this very minute, full of unknown faces, panting people, whistles blowing, smoke; and we looked at each other in dumb hopelessness, having nothing more to say to each other. We were torn between the refusal to believe, and the sad necessity of believing that in a few moments between the two of us there would be no more than a mere memory remaining.

Leaning at the window by Martha's side, Rosi strained her alluring face to see over the crowds on the platform; she was searching eagerly for Henri's return. He had noticed at the last minute that the girls had nothing to read on their long journey, and had gone off to look for some German and English papers. He eventually reappeared with a collection of illustrated magazines under his arm; we saw him making his way through the clusters of people with some difficulty, increased by the fact that he was eagerly scanning the racing news in an evening paper. This he politely closed and folded up on rejoining me in front of the compartment. He handed the magazines to Rosi, giving her a careless good-natured smile, which treated her tearful one as no more than an expression of friendly thanks. For him everything was already finished, in the past; he was only waiting for the moment when the train moved off, and would leave quite calmly. At this moment when I was almost choking with emotion, his calm seemed to me unnatural, monstrous.

These last minutes, all identical, seemed to be frozen in an intensity of sadness; but then all at once the frozen minutes exploded and dissolved in the strident blowing of a whistle. The train moved heavily out, then gathered speed and finally curved away round a bend. Already the platform began emptying; but I stayed on, watching till the last possible moment a confusion of smoke and waving hands, and two tearful faces vanishing in the distance. "What lovely silver lashes she *had*, what a darling she *was!*" From now on I must talk in the past of this wonderful affair which had only lasted for six days.

When we finally left, the platform was deserted. Henri was prepared to wait for me as long as he still had racing results to read in his paper. Then he became impatient, and taking me by the arm said:

"Come along, you poor old Romeo. There's not much chance of the train coming back, you know. So don't think any more about it. Besides, everything's gone off beautifully as far as I can see. They were very good, they didn't cry till they'd gone, when it couldn't matter. Rosi's really very nice—no exchanging addresses or promises to write, no emotional complications or tiresome lies to tell. For once a nice neat affair, with no after effects; just the job."

He gave the relieved sigh of a soldier swinging his pack down from his shoulder; the air was heavy with coal and dust, but he savored it greedily as if it contained for him some special taste of freedom. I was staggered to see him show such complete and cold-blooded detachment concerning a girl he had known so intensely for a week. "Rosi," I remarked, "didn't seem quite so cheerful."

"Naturally," he replied. "It's very naughty for a girl to sleep with a young man, so it's only fair that in the end she's the one to get punished. Besides, women always go wrong and try to mix love up with the boring idea of something permanent. Rosi and I had a good time together, I must say it wasn't at all bad, you could call it a distinct success sexually. But even successes shouldn't be repeated indefinitely, the sublime always becomes ridiculous far too soon."

Seeing me looking miserable, he added: "Don't look so down in the mouth. Probably in a year or even in a month you'll be the first to laugh at it. Which is just as it should be. All that really worries me, you see, is the idea that an affair might turn into being saddled with a mistress for life. I can't help it, the beginnings are the only thing I'm really interested in. The big moment for me is when I'm making my first advances to a girl I like, a girl I've never yet spoken to of love. It's then my throat goes dry, my heart races, and I get as nervous as a schoolboy. It's wonderful. Nothing afterwards can give me that first fine careless rapture over again, and inevitably the moment comes when I've just got to get away. If I ever stayed too long with the same girl, my nerves would go to pieces, I'd be ill. It'd really be the end," he concluded, recoiling from the thought in horror.

We left the station. Going out towards the car, we stood for a minute or two looking down at the boulevard below us. The street lamps were just lighting up, and the terraces of the cafés were already brightly lit and crowded with drinkers. Henri opened the door of the car, and I glanced dejectedly at the rumble which was no longer needed. While I settled in the place

431

Rosi had occupied for the last six days, he started up the engine. Before moving off, he looked again at the sky, the town, the people, the lights; he patted me joyfully on the shoulder and filled his chest full of the evening air, with the relief of a prisoner making good his escape.

When he had returned the car to the garage, we strolled back towards the Cité, and by tacit consent went to lie on the lawn a moment. It was already completely dark, and with the night rose a gentle breeze rustling through the leaves in the park. Its soft murmur blended with the sound of gramophones and laughter, and I found that my intense sadness of an hour earlier had already turned into a tender and pervasive melancholy.

As he threw himself down on the grass, Henri declared: "Basically, you know, it's a good enough formula. Just like a seashore romance, eight days or two weeks at most. Love 'em and leave 'em. You say goodbye, and it's over. One good night to make up arrears for six short ones, and tomorrow—back on the job."

I did not answer, and he murmured: "All right, I see you've not got over it yet. But just wait till tomorrow morning, you'll find you're feeling better already."

He lit a cigarette and smoked in silence. I caught myself envying his convenient faculty for forgetting everything not strictly relevant to the present or the immediate future. I alas could not see our brief affair as something purely sensual, strictly limited to our two bodies and to the time of our pleasure. I hated to let myself succumb to this emotional aftermath, both dangerous and futile. There was much to pull me out of it—the summer, the fresh air, the rhythm of the gramophones, the warm night, the whole atmosphere of indolence. They did their best, but it was not enough: for this evening I just could not emulate the cheerful polygamist at my side, concerned only with his own pleasure and a very rapid disappearance when that was over.

I left Henri yawning at his door, and went straight to bed. But as soon as I was in the darkness once more, my whole body felt miserable and forlorn. The act of putting out the light re-

432

minded me abruptly of the burning excitement of the six previous nights. I was seized with melancholy and a deep sense of loss: all my flesh was awakened and hungry, only to be suddenly frustrated of its pleasure.

I almost looked for Martha near me. The bed had been too narrow for our needs, and the blanket used to fall off. I would wake in the cool of the early morning and pull it over us again. Relaxed and refreshed by a few hours of sleep, I would smile tenderly to feel the thin young body against my skin, to caress her shoulder and small round breasts and narrow childish hip. When we first lay down' together, the embrace was almost wasted, it was too hot and hasty and distracted; but now, nearer the dawn, I would find a calmer, profounder embrace. I used to wait deliberately till Martha, still half in her dreams, seemed somehow to feel my need and obey it. She would hollow her body and let me come over her again, so that when she woke with a soft moan she found herself in my arms.

Remembering her body more vividly than ever, I could almost weep for desire and loneliness. Where would the memory of this new face lead me? Would it mean the beginning of an irresistible temptation, or was it merely to be one evening's fleeting melancholy? Deep down inside me, beneath the layers of conscience superimposed, I felt that something was changed. I went to sleep without being able to define it.

Next morning it needed a violent effort to get me up. I was still dazed, my head was empty, my limbs were moist; but after my shower I certainly felt much lighter. When she left, Martha had not done anything to tidy the room, and it was still in disorder. I smiled tenderly at the thousand signs scattered all over the room that a woman had been there. On a corner of the table I found a crumpled little handkerchief, stained with lipstick, between two medical books; I slipped it into a drawer.

Going downstairs a few minutes later, I saw that there was a letter in my pigeon hole. I was certain it was from Marianne. For several seconds I stood motionless in front of the box, in the grip of a strange inertia, my hand halted in the air. It was only

433

by a severe effort of will that I was able to take the envelope. I took it out into the street, and walked several yards down the boulevard before I could summon up courage to tear the envelope open.

Before Marianne and I had parted, she had insisted that our correspondence during the vacation should not become a duty for me, that I should always write light-heartedly and only when I enjoyed writing. From the beginning she had left me the initiative and usually waited to write till she heard from me.

I had received her last letter on the evening I first met Martha. The letter remained on my table; and the next day I pushed it under my blotter without answering it. I knew Marianne would not break our rules; she would not mind being forgotten for a week.

For six days I tried breathlessly to keep up with Henri. He cut short the only time in the day when I might have been able to pull myself together. I would reluctantly leave Martha still asleep in my room, and go off to the hospital, arriving a little later each day. Before twelve o'clock sounded, Henri would be outside the main gate in the rue Jacob. Five minutes later, already tired of waiting, he would come to the Annex and drag me away at once. The first morning, arriving on a ward where every detail reminded me of Marianne, I felt a sharp pang of guilt, and in the crowded day which followed my remorse was not completely set at rest. I had at once begun rationalizing my behavior.

First of all I pretended to be in the blissful position of a man loved by two women, flattered and touched to have so much love coming to me so easily. Without Martha my life would have been incomplete, I should have lost something superb. But I soon had to admit that I could never feel for her or for any other woman what I did for Marianne. Taking pleasure with an unknown girl could really not be dignified by the name of love, so I tried to make out instead that the pleasure was quite unimportant, merely intended to gratify a physical need which everybody felt. As for Marianne, what the eye did not see, the heart could not grieve over.

These sophisms did not prove very effective, and infuriated I

434

tried other means of self-justification. No, love was not a virtuous and innocent friendship, it was the feel of a woman's mouth and body against yours. I had asked too much of Marianne, and at the same time too little.

Against all reason and logic, I began to be annoyed with Marianne herself, because I loved her, and because in return she loved me so freely and so trustingly that I could not possibly love anyone else besides her. Henri was right after all: this sort of love was too pure and exalted and exclusive to be tenable. Meanly enough, I began blaming Marianne for her very beauty and perfection. Her superiority to me was crushing, was intolerable. I must find fault with her somehow, turning even her generous actions into a cause for reproach. In the spring, I pretended to believe, she had only sent me back to my friends in the Bush because she wanted to follow me there and flirt with them.

This piece of unfairness did the trick. I felt much less guilty, and after that, knowing the end was so fatally near, I wore myself out "loving" Martha. This was my only concern, besides sometimes sleeping for a little, so that I could soon begin loving her again. The rest of the time I let myself be driven round Paris by Henri, gliding down the primrose path in blissful powerlessness. Reflection then was far outside my reach.

But when, standing in the street, I at last decided to open Marianne's letter, I knew in advance what the letter would be like; and so it was. Her evident anxiety at my silence was veiled in a gentle tone of careful casualness. She was only writing out of turn, she said, because she thought I had probably written and my letter might have gone astray. But in each line of her letter blazed the fires of a faithful love, an utter acceptance of the enduring bond between us, the bond in which I had tried to disbelieve. Trembling with shame, I had to stop reading for a few seconds to get my breath. I looked once more at the familiar writing, the clearly formed letters and neatly spaced lines; somehow they brought me comfort, as if I were really yielding to the power of her handwriting. Even that, coming from her, could save me from my baser self.

435

In the sunshine of the early autumn, Charité Hospital dozed all morning between the melting asphalt of the Boulevard Saint-Germain and the cool little provincial streets around it. The wards were half empty, and the activity in them much reduced; but so was the staff, and those who remained found it anything but a holiday period. As soon as I arrived in Bichat Annex, I was caught up in a series of dressings and injections and plasters, and had little leisure for extraneous reflections till noon. But all morning the pangs of my remorse were like a vague throbbing ache, and I was glad to have so much work to do.

About noon Jouvet, the interne, came down to the Annex and asked me to give an anaesthetic for him. He was on call that afternoon and evening, and after the operation he asked if I could possibly stand in for him till seven o'clock. I agreed readily; I would have agreed to anything which meant I need not return at once to my room in the Cité and to my thoughts.

I had lunch with him in the common room, but it was rather a dismal occasion. Most of the internes were on holiday by now, and the few of them who were present got up and left immediately after drinking their coffee. Jouvet himself was obviously in a hurry to get away. He gave me a few instructions and told me his phone number in case anything happened I could not cope with; then he installed me in the room reserved for the interne on call, and left me to it.

I looked at the room: a table and chair, a hospital bed in one corner, a rickety cupboard against one of the walls, a cracked basin with water dripping monotonously from a leaky tap, and beige wall-paper over chocolate-colored woodwork. The general effect was a cross between a disreputable hotel and a barracks. I listened to Jouvet's steps disappearing down the corridor, and decided I was in for an extremely depressing afternoon in this prison cell.

I plunged at once into furious recriminations of myself. I was determined to be honest with myself at last, not to try to run away, to see clearly how low I had sunk, so that I could perhaps rise again, building on firmer foundations. I pleaded guilty to hopeless weakness and vanity and sordid lust. I had given in to the most pernicious of influences, knowing the danger yet scarcely even trying to resist. I had been dominated by selfishness, acting as if I did not know the meaning of sincere love or loyalty.

My solitary self-examination was interrupted by the noise of steps in the corridor. It was the admissions clerk, and I followed him across the court. An ambulance was waiting at the main gate, and inside it a policeman was mopping his brow by the side of a stretcher, on which lay a woman apparently in a coma. The policeman handed me two tubes of self-explanatory veronal. I climbed into the ambulance, and it crossed the court to the ward, where the patient was being taken direct. On the way I asked the policeman what he knew about the case.

"Nothing much at present, Doctor," he answered. "I'll be making my report when I've left here. She arrived yesterday at a little hotel on the rue Dauphine, with a young man. This morning a neighbor heard them quarrelling. She was crying, apparently. The young man left, slamming the door, and this afternoon when the proprietor went in with his passkey, he found the woman nearly dying on the bed."

A suicide for love! I looked at the woman again: she had a heavily lined brow, and the skin of her neck was soft and knobbly; her face had swelled like that of a drowned woman taken from the water. She was outrageously made up, with powder and too bright paint; there was too much blue round her eyes and too much rouge on her faded cheeks.

When we had got her into the ward, I made a comment to the nurse about this impulse to make herself attractive. "Quite common," replied the nurse. "Men shave and change their shirts —women paint themselves. It's presumably in the hope that their lovers will come to see their dead bodies. But they seldom do come, I must say."

While she was talking, she was busy tying the tourniquet and handing me the syringe. I pushed a first massive injection of strychnine into the vein, and looked at my watch. I would have to give the same treatment every hour.

Returning across the drowsy hospital to my room, I sat down

437

in front of the table. This activity had done me good, and I felt relieved to have a definite task till the end of my duty period. All through the afternoon, giving the injections would provide me with a few short intervals when I would have to think of something else. And it would serve little if any other purpose, for without doubt even if I saved this drunken old wreck, who had lost her last love and preferred to die, she would merely start all over again. Not that this consideration could count for a doctor—while there was a chance, we must try to save her life —but it offered little incentive for any special medical zeal.

Going past the internes' library, I took some stationery on which to write to Marianne. Before beginning my letter, I hesitated for a long time, fearing to hurt her, then abruptly I made up my mind. I suddenly found it intolerable she should remain tender and trusting for a moment longer, in ignorance of all I had done against her. I confessed, I accused myself, I did my best to explain. It was so simple to expose my heart freely and frankly that my enthusiasm grew the further I went with the letter, and the whole business with Martha seemed less and less important. I was quite sure Marianne would forgive me.

No, I had taken nothing essential from Marianne, she alone had filled my heart with a great love. Outside her, no attachment could ever be lasting, she held in permanence the secret keys to my heart. She was security, gentleness, the haven where no storms came. She was the substance of my life, all the rest was unreality. When she had forgiven me, we could begin again "from scratch." I would put away from us all disturbing forces, and go on loving her as I felt I loved her now, from deep inside me; and she would love me too, all of me, even the weaker, lower part of me, which needed her so badly, which she could forgive because she was Marianne and unique. My heart swelled with the fullness of this love, which seemed so simple after all my distress. Everything could become as it had been before, and I wished no longer for my freedom, seeing I had used it so ill.

Returning to the ward all through the afternoon to give the injections, I felt compassion now for the patient, perhaps because every hour I came to her I was feeling more hopeful of my own pardon; and also because the nurses or one of the other patients might call me doctor. This made me feel happy again, and my happiness sprang from two vital sources, my profession and my love. The miracle was that, throughout my life henceforth, these sources would be joined together, they would continually be overlapping. What splendid promise my whole life held once more!

In the early evening when I dug the needle into the vein for the fifth injection, I stayed by the woman a minute longer, seeing the arm give slightly. It had been lying on the sheet, with the hand flopped half open, in utter resignation and renunciation of life; but now the fingers seemed slowly to contract, the tendons of the wrist projected. The poor old hand, still sunk in unhealthy slumber, began clenching itself, as if to seize hold of life once more. The woman was now saved, she would slowly come out of her coma in due course. I had no difficulty in imagining her awakening. She would look about her in bewilderment, her eyes filling with terror when she did not find at her side the body of her young lover. No chance of his coming back, the nurse had said. I went away, full of pity.

All of a sudden, in the corridor outside the duty room, I stopped in panic. I had disposed already of Marianne's decision, but suppose she refused to forgive me, suppose she rejected me in disgust, leaving me on my own as the old wreck had been left by her lover? I had finished my letter and it lay waiting for me on the table in the duty room. I had already stamped an envelope and put the letter inside; now I started writing the address on the envelope: *Mlle. Marianne Duriez.* Then I stopped. I knew by heart, of course, her home address, but just at that moment I felt I must read the letter again, the second time already. I did so. Was it humble enough, did I show how deeply I was ashamed? I read it through a third time, wondering if I ought not to rewrite the whole letter. I could not face it.

Then suddenly, as sudden as the previous moment of panic, it came to me that this letter would serve, and I was ashamed of ever having doubted my Marianne's forgiveness. The girl I loved had such depth of understanding, she was far too good for me. But this goodness was the sort which knew how to forgive. She would turn the other cheek, she would not reject the prodigal son, she would forgive me up to seventy times seven. No, I would not rewrite the letter, I would simply add a single line beneath my signature: *I need you, Marianne darling, I need you so badly.*

I wrote my postcript and refolded the letter. I put it in the envelope, sealed it, and put it safely in my pocket. I felt absolutely sure that this last appeal, half demand and half prayer, was one she would respond to, all through my life, whenever and wherever it reached her. *I need you:* the fervent appeal burst from deep inside me, and the hope of forgiveness leapt in my heart.

Jouvet returned about seven o'clock, and we dined alone at one end of the long table in the deserted common room. I left him shortly afterwards. Outside the hospital, a sultry day had turned into a stifling evening. There was a postoffice fairly near, and I went straight there to post my letter. I did not look at it again, but tossed it through the slot, feeling an almost ludicrous sense of relief and light-heartedness. Then I walked all the way back to the Cité, humming softly all I could remember of Dvořák's *New World* symphony. It was Marianne's favorite.

On reaching the hostel, I went straight up to my room. I paused a moment before opening the door, thinking with disgust of the disorder in which I had left it this morning. But the maid had tidied it during my absence, and on entering, I saw at once that all trace of Martha's presence had vanished. My room was as it had been before she came, and now it was like returning to a safe and friendly harbor. The worktable was back in the middle of the room, where I had had it since the beginning of the summer so as to be more out of the sun. The curtains were drawn as usual; I always drew them in the morning before going to the hospital, so as to stop the sun's glare in both windows all day. I opened the curtains, and for a long time stood looking at the evening sky above the parched grass and the shanties in the Slum. High in the heavens there was still a pink afterglow, but the rest of the sky was luminous with the blue of twilight. Deep and peaceful silence outside; silence too in the hostel. I let the beauty and peace of the atmosphere take hold of me and calm my fevers and anxieties.

I went and sat down in front of the table, still gazing sky-wards, rejoicing to be able to relax at last. All that had disturbed me during the day, all the disorders of this last week, all the passions and temptations and lusts, fell away one by one, and for the first time since that morning I really felt I had left them behind. I was a new man, exhilarated by the return of happiness, tranquil and innocent.

Night had fallen completely when a cheerful humming, rising from the lawn, brought me sharply out of my dream. Almost at once the door of the hostel banged, and a swift impatient step shook the staircase. The tune which preceded Henri Philippon was the one he always hummed when he came to find me to go out with him.

Hearing it, my heart began to beat faster, my hands became moist and I was seized with a sudden panic. Could I hope that the steps would never reach my door? Could I hope that my will was proof against his blandishments? The answer came quickly, and when it came, the panic left. In that one moment, memory of time past and time to come flooded in upon me and in my heart I knew where my future lay. It lay with my work in the world of the doctors—my work and Marianne. And I knew, as his steps approached my room and his song grew louder, that tonight Philippon would go out alone.

When he knocked I had already opened my notebook and started to work.